IN THE EYE OF THE BEHOLDER

Maggie Mooha

PRAISE FOR MAGGIE MOOHA'S BOOKS

Elizabeth in the New World

"JANE AUSTEN FANS! THIS IS FOR YOU!!!!! This is an extremely well written "sequel" to Jane Austen's Pride and Prejudice. A tale of romance, intrigue, passion, exotic locations, heroism, and one of the greatest love stories for the ages!" ~dandelackland

"A breathtakingly original twist and continuation on a cherished Austen classic, Elizabeth in the New World *opens doors to "what-ifs" and imaginative, well thought out scenarios that will leave fans of the original book enthralled and satisfied. A well written, exciting novel that is both daring and unique. I look forward to more from this author!"* ~Sebastian Moran

"This book is a fantastic continuation of the Elizabeth and Darcy story. I'd read before bed and tell myself, "just finish this chapter, then go to sleep." But it was hard, because I couldn't wait to read what would happen next! The characters were very well-developed, and the story compelling. Great ending, too. I can't wait for a sequel so I can continue on their journey." ~Amy Pippins

"I consider this among the outstanding Austen variations that I have read and give it my highest recommendation. This book has it all, an enduring love story amidst historical references to slavery, other social and class changes, and characters who grew in character while loving each other. The depth of emotion is wonderful. This is quite a masterpiece for a first book." ~Donna D. Krug

"This is a romance, all right, but it is also so much more. It's an exposé on the whole class system. I was immediately drawn into the adventure story, and the further I read, the more engrossing the story got. Mooha writes the characters in such a way that you really care about them. At the conclusion I was literally in tears." ~Madelyn

The Darcys of New Orleans

"This *is an excellent sequel to the equally excellent P&P variation,* Elizabeth in the New World. *This novel has so much to admire! The historical elements really come alive. The characters feel true-to-life, providing little details such as Darcy's discomfort with the local custom of men kissing men on both cheeks in greeting and farewell. The forbidden fruit romance is both educational and angsty, and Darcy and Elizabeth's marriage is stronger than ever. You'll probably have trouble putting this one down. It's a spellbinder." ~* Debbie B.

"As good as the first book. I was not able to stop reading because the story kept my attention. Mooha is a fantastic new author who does her homework on the period and events in history that she writes about. Her characters are three dimensional and the situations feel real. It is a powerful insight into the life and events of the 19th century. For a few hours I was experiencing what it must have been like to be caught in a time when one's personal cultural perspective was fundamentally challenged." ~Lynn

"This book has an exciting, fast-moving plot and it is full of wonderful characters. I loved how the book put me in New Orleans high society of the early 1800s, the balls and dinners and opulence but also the wildness, which was especially fascinating because I got to view it through the Darcys' eyes. It's a book full of love--romantic, maternal, paternal, and most movingly, the strong friendship between Elizabeth and Poppy, the former slave now married to a French American aristocrat and plantation owner. I love the way Maggie Mooha writes!" ~braingirl

"In her two novels, Maggie has given us what we Jane Austen fans longed for....an imaginative pair of sequels. She knows how to capture our interest and emotions in this latest ongoing saga of the Darcy family as they traverse the very real perils of the time period. She does her research and develops her characters thoroughly so their behaviors and reactions are no surprise. The book is a page-turner with some sexy scenes thrown in that Austen may have

thought about but wouldn't have dared to write! I do love books with happy endings and this one does not disappoint. Keep on writing, Maggie!" ~Rita Ransom

"*Once again the author takes us into the realm of Lizzy and Darcy's tale of epic love. Based on the incredible journey Lizzy and Darcy made in* Elizabeth in the New World, *the Darcys travel from England to visit their dear friends who have moved from Grenada to New Orleans. Together with their children Emma and Bennett Fitzwilliam, they enter the strange and unfamiliar world of New Orleans society. The wealthy planters of New Orleans, however, turn the Darcys' English sensibilities virtually upside down! The temptations of the Creole world are strange, yet almost irresistible to young Emma. And Darcy's nemesis Wickham returns once again! A tale of forbidden love, conflict, heroism and sacrifice well worth reading!!"* ~Eileen

www.BOROUGHSPUBLISHINGGROUP.com

PUBLISHER'S NOTE: This is a work of fiction. Names, characters, places and incidents either are the product of the author's imagination or are used fictitiously. Any resemblance to actual events, locales, business establishments or persons, living or dead, is coincidental. Boroughs Publishing Group does not have any control over and does not assume responsibility for author or third-party websites, blogs or critiques or their content.

ISBN: 978-1-953810-61-8

To my mom and dad who both served during WWII

AUTHOR'S NOTE

Before you start, please forgive any glitches in the chronology of events or the veracity of same. There were more conflicting accounts of this war and its timeline that I have ever dealt with before. Having said that, if this little tome piques your interest in the Crimean War, I can wholeheartedly recommend a book I used as a reference. It is *No Place for Ladies: The Untold Story of Women in the Crimean War* by Helen Rappaport.

Another book I used as a reference, written by one of my "characters" the real-life Mary Seacole, is her biography, *Wonderful Adventures of Mrs. Seacole in Many Lands.*

Other books I used as a reference were – *Charge! Hurrah! Hurrah! A Life of Cardigan of Balaclava* by Donald Thomas, *The Crimean War: The History and Legacy of the Conflict that Modernized Warfare and Weakened Tsarist Russia* by Charles River Editors, *The Invasion of the Crimea, Vol. I* by Charles W. Kinglake, *Notes on Nursing: What It Is and What It Is Not* by Florence Nightingale and especially interesting, since he was there – *Eyewitness Accounts Battles of the Crimean War* by William Russell.

Speaking of William Russell… He reported on the war via the newly invented telegraph. I quote some of the reporting he did for *The Times*. Other "real life" people who appear or are mentioned in the book are the war photographer Roger Fenton; Major Easton who lost his foot; Captain William Morris who led the Light Brigade; William Brittain, the bugler who blew the charge (there is some dispute about who blew the charge, but I give him credit); Elizabeth Blackwell, the first female physician; Mary Seacole who ran her British Hotel or Iron House; Lord Cardigan, Lord Lucan and Lord Raglan who were the commanders; Captain Nolan who did not make it past the first few volleys at Balaclava; Mrs. Davis at the Balaclava Hospital; Fanny Duberly who lived in the harbor and rode her horse behind the lines; and Florence Nightingale, who changed nursing forever. I tried to stay true to the accounts of these people and their accomplishments. Lieutenant Wentworth was originally Captain

Wentworth, but I had to give the real-life William Morris his due as the captain of the 17th Lancers.

Some websites that were also valuable to me in writing this book are:

The Map Archive, avictorian.com, valmcbeath.com, victorian-era.org, wikimedia.org (for maps), sciencemuseum.org/uk, what-when-how.com, britishbattles.com

I hope you enjoy reading the story as much as I enjoyed writing it.

IN THE EYE OF THE BEHOLDER

Chapter 1

"I do believe she heard you, Mr Shaw." Rousing himself from his languid posture, Joshua eased away from the doorway that led to the garden and tilted his head in the direction of the fleeing figure who had disappeared through the French doors open to the lawn.

"Oh, I doubt that, and even if she did, what does it matter?" George Shaw said with a smirk. He shook his tousled mane of red hair and scratched absentmindedly at the mutton chops that met on his chin.

"It is not very gentlemanly behaviour to speak aloud such thoughts within earshot of young ladies." Joshua's comment provoked laughter from George, and as he swivelled his head to seek the approval of his peers, there were a few sniggers. Joshua, however, did not smile.

"Oh, hang it all. All I said was that she was an excellent dancer despite her lack of comeliness. What is the harm in that? I don't see why…" George cleared his throat and swallowed as Joshua's eyes narrowed. He then took a different tack. "If you are so concerned, go ask for an introduction and dance with her yourself."

Joshua Wentworth hesitated for a moment. The eyes of the entire group of languorous young men were upon him. He straightened the coat of his uniform. "A capital idea," he said. "After all, from what I observed, she is a very good dancer." He stepped away from his companions and went in search of the daughter of the house, Cordelia. Surely, she would introduce him to the small bird who had taken flight.

***

When Eleanor reached the garden, she took a deep breath among the fragrant flowers. An unusually warm April evening and the crowded, stifling ballroom must have broken down her usual defences. She had heard all the insults before. The comments that began as a compliment but ended as an affront were perhaps the hardest to bear. "A good dancer…but no beauty." Oh, what did she care for the opinion of George Shaw? Who was he to her? Her eyes filled with tears again as she recalled the slight and berated herself for caring so much. For caring at all, really. Surely, the heat and the anxiety of not having her sister, Julia, by her side had brought on her absurd reaction. She recalled their conversation of only a few hours before.

"The problem you have, Eleanor, is that you are so… so…. Oh, you know what I mean." Julia rifled through her extensive wardrobe of bodices, skirts, and gowns, choosing and rejecting as their maid, Annie, filled her travelling trunk.

"Please, Julia. Speak plainly. I don't know what you mean." Eleanor didn't really want to hear what her sister had to say. Julia was so circumspect with those outside the family, especially men, but uncompromisingly blunt with her, her only sister.

"You know very well what I mean. I know you say you don't care what people think of you, but I can tell you that gentlemen find you…" Julia stopped as if to study one of her prospective costumes, but Eleanor knew better. Perhaps her sister was endeavouring not to be as blunt as usual.

Eleanor didn't let her finish. "Deformed? Is that what you are attempting to say? Go on, say it."

Julia stopped fussing with her clothing and turned to her sister. "Oh, for goodness' sake, Eleanor, stop being so theatrical. I was going to say prickly. You are prickly. It is not what a gentleman expects."

Julia avoided saying what she really meant to say. That Eleanor's face was what men did not expect, not her "prickly" personality. Why were beauty and acquiescence the only things valued in a woman? Eleanor gazed at her sister in silence, admiring her free and easy manner, her perfect figure, and a face so like her own, yet elevated to a perfection so few enjoyed. Julia was beautiful and didn't seem to feel the constraints of her lot as Eleanor did.

"I really don't want to attend the Mosleys' ball," Eleanor said, returning to the original subject. "It's more like a market than a social gathering."

Julia had returned to her packing and then turned again upon her sister. "Eleanor, how can you say such things? I just adore balls. The dancing, the conversation, the attention of the young men."

"Yes, indeed. Your experience of balls is distinctly different from mine. Distinctly."

Julia left off with sorting her clothing and took Eleanor by the hand as they sat on the edge of the bed. "You must attend the ball. Cordelia is your dearest friend and invited you especially. It is one of the first balls of the season; you simply cannot miss it. I can't help that I must go off to Wales to Papa's relations. It has all been arranged. Cordelia will look after you."

Eleanor leapt up and dropped her sister's hand. "I don't need your pity, Julia, nor our mother's cajoling. All right, I'll attend for Cordelia's sake, but I don't expect to enjoy myself."

"Suit yourself," Julia sighed as she and Annie continued preparations for her journey.

As Eleanor dressed for the ball, she twirled before the full-length mirror in her room in their London town house. Turning to the right, she looked at herself in profile. She thought she looked quite splendid. The green of the gown set off the grey-green of her eyes. At least that was what Annie said. The full skirt gave the impression of a full figure, not the spare frame that was hers. With her hair artfully arranged with ringlets on the side and a modest chignon at the back, she hoped that the lack of vibrance in its light brown colour would not be noticed. Then, turning again, she faced herself in the mirror. There it was—the bane of her existence. What began as a "strawberry mark" above her right eye as an infant had blossomed into an angry red birthmark that spread around her left eye and down her cheek. Annie motioned her back to the dressing table, powder puff in hand. A dusting would lighten her complexion but would not obliterate that mark. Nothing ever did. A few moments later, her mother's maid entered to hurry her along.

***

"You did apply that powder to your cheeks as I asked, did you not, Eleanor?" her mother said from across the carriage.

"Oh, Mother, do stop fussing. Of course, I did, but in half an hour it will melt away. I will never be as beautiful and perfect as

Julia, so your efforts are not only unwelcome, but also futile." The powder her mother gave her did little to disguise the mark. That mark elicited sympathy at one time and revulsion at another. She preferred the revulsion. Pity always seemed barely disguised contempt.

"You have other fine qualities," her father, the colonel, snuffled through his moustache. "Any man would be proud to have you as a wife." Other fine qualities, but not beauty. She knew her father's remark was meant as a compliment, but it stung, nonetheless.

"There is no higher aspiration than to be a wife to a good man and mother to his children. Look at our dear Queen Victoria as an example." How often had her mother repeated those words? Eleanor hoped they were not true. She believed that neither of those things would ever be in her future. She turned to look at her mother and saw her reach over and pat her father's hand as it rested on his knee. They were two of the fortunate few who had affection for one another as well as an advantageous marriage. Her mother, who came to the marriage with money of her own, had endured much with her father in the army, but the two of them seemed content enough. Eleanor, however, was not content.

"I do not see how flower arranging and hosting dinner parties does anything significant for the world." As soon as Eleanor said these words, she regretted them. Her mother would be hurt, and her father would begin a lecture on how it was the lot of men to do the work of the world. She turned her head again to gaze out the window as the onslaught began. Her face was reflected in the glass. It was so similar to Julia's, yet somehow the features were sharper and less symmetrical. Her nose and cheekbones were a bit too long, giving her a severe look even when she was not feeling particularly severe. And then, of course, there was the obvious flaw. Julia, on the other hand, had a perfectly *petit* nose, rosy cheeks, sparkling dark eyes, and an alabaster complexion. Her figure was also pleasantly rounded, as was preferred by so many men, while Eleanor's own was so slim it bordered on gauntness.

"Are you even listening, Eleanor?" Her mother's voice finally penetrated the fog of her reflections. She turned wordlessly toward her mother. "Well, I really don't know what to do about you. Please try to have a good time. You are a good dancer, and Cordelia will find you partners. She always does."

Before Eleanor could respond, the carriage came to an abrupt halt. Her father smiled.

"Come along, dear ladies." He proffered his gloved hand first to her mother and then to her. "Your mother only wants the best for you, my dear."

She looked up at him. The years of serving abroad had tanned and lined his face. Some would still call him handsome. He had a profuse crop of white hair beneath his top hat and a great brush of a moustache. His eyes shone with kindness.

"I know, Papa. I will try to enjoy myself," she said as the footman showed them in. She was convinced that she would merely endure yet another social occasion in which she would be tolerated at best.

Eleanor entered the already stifling ballroom. They had arrived late again. She dreaded balls in general, but this one in particular? Her sister would not be there. She so relied on Julia, who always saw to it that they both had their dance cards filled early in the evening. For Julia, it was a matter of whom she honoured with her condescension. Usually, her sister was surrounded by flocks of admirers, being the "pretty one," and some of the young men would deign to dance with the "other" sister in hopes of an introduction to Julia. Eleanor had grown used to this arrangement. At least it kept her away from the wall. Tonight, however, would be different. Before she could ruminate further, her friend Cordelia, the daughter of the house, swept forward from the bustling crowd.

"Oh, Eleanor, I am so glad you could come," she said, smiling. Her long tresses of auburn hair with a sheen of red were done up in such a way as to set off her dancing green eyes. She seemed rather breathless, and her milky, nearly translucent skin was set off in a rosy blush. Her fan was fluttering. "It is difficult to believe it is only April," she said. "I am so warm." She acknowledged Eleanor's parents and promptly whisked her off and left them to their own devices. Cordelia leaned close. "Come along, Eleanor, I have something for you."

Cordelia's mother was from an old aristocratic family, and her father a captain of industry. His status was raised by his wife and her family enriched by the alliance. Cordelia was reared in the lap of luxury and at the pinnacle of society, but somehow retained a certain levelheadedness that Eleanor was drawn to the moment they met as children.

"For heaven's sake, where are we going?" Eleanor asked as Cordelia navigated their progress between chatting groups and then skirted the dance floor.

"Somewhere cooler so we can talk," Cordelia said slyly and led her out onto the veranda overlooking the gardens at the back of the house. "There, look." She produced a dance card and handed it to Eleanor.

"Oh, dear. Now what have you done?"

"I have arranged a few dances for you. I know Julia is usually here and you like to rely on her, but I took it upon myself to 'make arrangements.'"

Eleanor shook her head. Was she so hideous that everyone had to cajole young men on her behalf to dance? Why was physical beauty so important to young men? Women went quietly to the altar with some of the most gruesome physical specimens imaginable without complaint. Men and women, obviously, wanted different things. Men wanted a comely and passive wife and women a sense of security. Eleanor found the entire arrangement distasteful. She could hear her sister's voice—*You are so prickly, Eleanor*. Perhaps she did shun the idea of attracting a man with the purpose of matrimony because she was so incompetent at it. If she looked like Julia, had her easy grace, perhaps these social occasions would be more palatable. So, the first three dances were arranged by Cordelia, and Eleanor would accept graciously.

"Thank you, Cordelia, you are very kind."

"Kindness has nothing to do with it. I need your help in getting those malingerers dressed as gentlemen away from the doorway." She indicated with her head a knot of boisterous young men hanging about together. "I do not know why my brother invites them. I believe they only come for the supper."

"I will do my duty, as a favor to you." Eleanor smiled in spite of herself.

"I would expect no less," Cordelia said in mock seriousness. "Onward!" They left arm in arm to take their seats at the edge of the ballroom, in preparation for the arrival of their swains. Unfortunately, the first of those swains was George Shaw.

***

Eleanor dabbed the budding tears from her eyes with her handkerchief, took a deep breath, and internally chastised herself for being so vain. Why did she always react with tears instead of anger? She should be angry with George Shaw, not hurt by him. For good or ill, though, the only person who really roused her ire was herself. It was infuriating that she allowed herself not only to be vulnerable to thoughtless comments like that of Mr Shaw's, but to allow herself to hope for anything better.

Her father, the colonel, was probably right. There will be a young man, not too handsome, not too gifted at conversation, but bookish, like her, with a good living, who would one day ask for her hand. After all, she would come into some money from her mother's family once she married, and that would be the nectar that would attract the bee. Whatever that bee was, she would have to accept him. They did not buzz about her as they did Julia.

As she was contemplating these rather melancholy thoughts, Cordelia found her again. "Oh, there you are, Eleanor. Come, I would like to introduce you to a friend of my brother William."

Eleanor's throat tightened. Was this another who would torment her tonight? She bit her lips to give them some colour as she was sure her cheeks were already flushed. She readied herself for the onslaught. Pinning a smile on her face, she turned to greet the new gentleman. She was not prepared for the sight that greeted her.

"Eleanor, I would like you to meet Lieutenant Joshua Griffiths Wentworth of the 17th Lancers. Lieutenant Wentworth, this is my dearest friend, Eleanor Sherbrooke."

Eleanor inclined her head to the most perfect specimen of manhood that she had ever seen. He was dressed in the uniform of the Lancers, a blue coat with two rows of gold buttons running down the front, an immeasurably high gold lace collar, and gold and white cuffs. On his shoulders were large, gold epaulettes. His trousers were also navy blue with two gold stripes running up the sides. Although his chapka, that bullet-shaped helmet with the leather mortarboard attached to the top, was missing, it did nothing to detract from his stunning appearance. His hair was copious, raven black waves from which one curl escaped its careful arrangement and hung rakishly down his forehead. Above his lip was a full black moustache so often seen on military men. The only human being Eleanor had ever seen so flawlessly constructed by the Creator was her sister, Julia. Cordelia looked from one to the other. For a moment, Eleanor was speechless.

"You do have that effect on women, Lieutenant," Cordelia burbled as Joshua made a curt bow.

"I am sure I have no idea what you mean, Miss Mosley." He turned to Eleanor once again. "I would be so honoured if you would consent to a dance, Miss Sherbrooke, that is, if you have room on your card."

She continued staring at him for a moment. What did he ask for? Oh, yes, the dance card. *The card, Eleanor, think.* She had stuffed it unceremoniously in her small velvet bag after her last unpleasant encounter and had no intention of withdrawing it and engaging in another adventure upon the dance floor. This gentleman, however, made her forget what had just ensued and, in fact, made her forget nearly everything. Finally, she withdrew it, and pencilled his name in for the next dance.

The elegant Lieutenant Wentworth offered his arm to Eleanor, and she ever so gently took it, thinking that he might disappear at any moment. Even wearing such a festooned uniform coat, she could feel the taut muscles beneath. He was only a few inches taller than she, so when he looked at her, their eyes met. A rush of warmth radiated from the centre of her breast, into the rest of her body. The evening that had ground to an ignominious halt just moments before had now bloomed into something quite extraordinary.

***

He had asked her to dance Les Lanciers. She felt honoured. It was the dance of his regiment. Cordelia, no doubt, was the architect of the invitation. This officer was being exceedingly kind, and she had to admit to herself that it was a thrill walking onto the dance floor with him. There was a great deal of changing of partners in this dance, but also quite a lot of time standing and holding hands. That was the part she enjoyed most.

When the Lanciers dance finished, Lieutenant Wentworth led Eleanor off the dance floor and inclined his head in a slight bow.

"You are a marvellous dancer, Miss Sherbrooke, I do believe you saved me more than once."

"You do not give yourself enough credit, sir. It was my pleasure." Eleanor's voice faltered at the last word. She really felt in awe of him. It was a distinct pleasure dancing with such a man. A bevy of young women lingered near the edge of the dance floor. All their eyes were fixed on Lieutenant Wentworth, and for once, on her, envy in their aspect. This must be how her sister felt most of the time, as she commanded the attention of all young men and chose only the handsomest as her partners. It was rather an ebullient feeling, and she was determined to enjoy it while she could. No doubt his name was scribbled on cards belonging to the evening's beauties for the rest of the ball.

He was still lightly holding her hand as he spoke again. "I was wondering…."

"Yes?"

"I know you are likely to have all your partners arranged for the evening, but if I might inquire, are you engaged for the waltz just before supper?"

For a moment she hesitated. Did Cordelia really engage this poor man to take her into supper? Perhaps she should refuse him and free him for the rest of the evening. When she studied his expression, however, he really did look quite expectant, and not as if he were fulfilling some unpleasant duty. She made up her mind at once.

"As it happens, Lieutenant, I am free for that particular dance."

"And might I inquire if I may then escort you to supper?" His eyes were nearly as blue as his jacket.

"I would be honoured, sir."

He made a slight bow and only then released her hand.

"Until later, then." He turned on his heel and disappeared into the crowd.

***

Only a few moments had passed when Eleanor, intercepted by her friend, finally came to rest near the French doors that opened to the garden.

“Well, well, well, hidden depths, I see.” Cordelia waggled her eyebrows at Eleanor. “He is, by far, the handsomest man here, the most dashing, and only has eyes for you, Eleanor.”

Cordelia teased her. “You asked him to come and dance with me, do not deny it, Cordelia. The entire arrangement, up to and including taking me into supper, smacks of your designs.”

“He’s asked to take you into supper? Oh, Eleanor, you are fine.” Cordelia nearly squealed with delight. Eleanor levelled the most sceptical gaze she could muster at her friend.

“Do not pretend that you did not arrange all of it.” Eleanor sighed.

“I assure you I did not. He came to me and asked to be introduced to you. That is all. I swear it.” Cordelia laid her hand across her heart.

“Please, do not tease me, Cordelia. Why ever would he do that? Look around you. There are young women of every sort here. And none with—” She stopped short, then began again. “Why would he choose me?”

“It is simple, my dear.” Cordelia took Eleanor by the arm. “You are the best dancer here, and everyone knows it.” Cordelia steered her to the side of the staircase, where, unseen, she pointed to a knot of young bachelors. “He must have been loitering with those gadflies about the door, watching you.”

Eleanor’s gaze fell upon the spot where that George Shaw fellow was still standing. So that was it. The lieutenant had heard Mr Shaw’s rude comment and sought to rescue her, brave soldier that he was. Or perhaps they had made a wager of sorts. That would be intolerable. No matter. Introductions at a ball were just that: introductions at a ball. They meant nearly nothing. She was determined to enjoy his attentions for as long as they lasted, but not give too much away. Still, he had kind eyes. Piercing, dancing, unbearably blue, kind eyes.

***

Joshua Griffiths Wentworth did not return to his compatriots once he entered the festivities. Many attractive and well-brought-up young ladies sat expectantly with their parents, and by the way they fluttered their fans at him, he was receiving many “come hither” messages. He arranged for dances with many of them, biding his time to dance again with Eleanor.

He had to admit to himself that he was a bit taken aback by that mark on her face and thought her figure thin and her aspect rather defensive. Her face was not round and rosy like most girls that he found himself attracted to, nor was it perfectly proportioned. Somehow, when she first smiled at him, he felt a warmth exude from her that he had not felt in a long time. Most of them looked upon him, he felt, as they would upon a prize pig, evaluating his suitability to be trussed up in matrimony. Marriage to a military man, however, was difficult at best, even for officers. It was a fact not well known to proper young ladies. Of course, many of them would be well aware that he was heir to a cotton mill fortune and think it was possible to discourage him from his military pursuits and engage him in commerce. If his father could not accomplish such a task, he doubted that a wife could.

He carried the lion's share of their conversation while dancing, which was easy for him. Never without a partner at these occasions, he had many chances to practice being charming. Eleanor did not chatter on or flatter him as most girls did. She had the most piercing way of looking at him. They would have a chance to really converse at supper. Perhaps she would be more forthcoming then. He had to admit that he was intrigued by her.

***

Cordelia had arranged another two dances for Eleanor: a quadrille and a Polka Redowa with two gentlemen who acquitted themselves well on the dance floor. When Mr Towler ran off to fetch refreshment for her, Cordelia again appeared looking quite out of breath.

"That is all the dancing you should do until you meet Lieutenant Wentworth again, Eleanor." She was panting the words out. "You do not want to be perspired when he takes you in his arms."

Eleanor raised her eyebrows. "You are quite shameless, Cordelia, really."

Cordelia merely giggled. "You do find him appealing, don't you?"

Eleanor thought for a moment before answering. Of course, she thought him appealing. Breathtaking, really, but what did it matter? A man like him could have his pick of women, and she would not be one of them. Cordelia was still looking at her expectantly.

"Honestly, Cordelia, you can be quite silly sometimes. The man is obviously just being kind, or worse, is having both of us on for the benefit of his friends' amusement. And here you are constructing a romance."

"I would be ever so happy to construct a romance with him." Her eyes took on that sly look that Eleanor found alternately endearing and maddening. "But I can see you already have designs on him, so I will step aside." And step aside she did, as the two gentlemen with whom they had been dancing returned with some refreshment.

Eleanor let Cordelia lead the way in the conversation and did her best to contribute, but Cordelia was right. She only had eyes for Lieutenant Wentworth.

***

It was an odd arrangement of dances to have the waltz before supper. Eleanor knew that was Cordelia's doing. She told Eleanor that she had invited a Mr Stevens with the express purpose of waltzing with him and then having him take her in to supper. Although Cordelia spent a great deal of time helping her mother arrange dances for wallflowers such as herself with oafish bachelors such as Mr Shaw, Cordelia always reserved a few dances for herself with her favourite young man. This month, that was Mr Stevens. Eleanor envied Cordelia her effortless way with the opposite sex. She herself felt awkward with men, feeling that they were judging her, always staring. Immersed in such thoughts, she did not see Lieutenant Wentworth approach until he was directly upon her.

"Oh, Miss Sherbrooke, I did not mean to startle you," he said jovially as she jumped at the touch of his gloved hand upon her arm.

"I am afraid that I become lost in thought and drift away from my surroundings." She looked up at him and smiled.

He cocked his head to one side. "A woman who spends her time thinking. So, what were you thinking of?" he asked just as the orchestra struck up the waltz. She said nothing but gave him her hand. She felt the warmth of his right hand on her back, and he swept her onto the floor with the rest of the whirling dancers.

The waltz was obviously his dance. He led masterfully, and Eleanor felt as if she were caught in a whirlwind, her feet barely touching the ground. She practiced enough at home with her dancing master so as to follow any sort of cloddish lead, but this man was anything but clumsy. He did not hold her too close, nor did he push her away. Everything about his technique was perfect. She was looking over his shoulder and then turned slightly to look at him. His expression was sublime. He must have felt her eyes upon him, for he levelled his gaze and smiled at her. She wanted to lean into him with her body and touch her cheek to his. She tossed away such thoughts at once, trying to remain on her guard.

When the dancing finished, Lieutenant Wentworth led Eleanor across the ballroom towards the supper room. There were many gathered about already, and her companion screwed up his face. He stopped short of the crowd at the entrance room and said, "Would you mind greatly, Miss Sherbrooke, if I were to gather some victuals for us and bring them out to the terrace. I do so hate standing and eating."

Eleanor looked about. People stood or sat at small tables on the terrace taking in the cool air, so they would not be alone and create a scandal. "If you wish, sir. I have no objection."

He took her by the arm and led her to a small table with two chairs. Pulling the chair out sufficiently to accommodate her copious skirt, he leaned over near her ear and whispered, "I am setting you here as sentry until I return. Guard that other chair with your life."

What an odd thing to say. She looked up at him and his eyes creased into his mischievous smile. He was teasing her. She would play along. She raised her hand to her forehead and in mock salute said, "Aye, aye, sir."

He guffawed. "That is the Navy, Miss Sherbrooke, not the cavalry, but I will accept it nonetheless." With that he turned and joined the crowd.

***

"Wherever did you disappear to, Eleanor? Papa and I did not see you the entire evening." Her mother fanned herself in the carriage as it pulled away from the Mosleys' curb.

Eleanor sighed. "I was dancing, Mama. Dancing and dancing," she said as she gazed absently out of the carriage window. In the reflection, she caught her parents give each other a quizzical glance.

"Did Cordelia arrange some dances for you, then?" Her mother tried to adopt a careless tone, but Eleanor could see through it.

"You encouraged me to enjoy myself and I did. Is there need for further comment?" she asked, again turning her head toward the window, hopefully ending the conversation. She knew that she was being deliberately obtuse with her mother, but she did not want to talk at that moment. Instead, Eleanor closed her eyes and savoured the memory of her time with Joshua Griffiths Wentworth.

***

By the time Lieutenant Wentworth returned with their repast, Eleanor was armed with a battery of devastating verbiage she had rehearsed in her mind during his absence. What was his motive in seeking her out as he did? What did it have to do with that loitering bunch at the door who had to be constantly cajoled into dancing with the ladies? Was he poking fun at her? Did he pity her? She would tell him in no uncertain terms that she was not to be toyed with.

As he set the plates down on the small table, amidst other groups of small tables, her resolve began to weaken. He did have a most beguiling smile. He was, by far, the best-looking man in the entire gathering, perhaps the best-looking man she had ever met. A thought suddenly occurred to her just as he took his seat. She was reacting to him as men reacted to Julia. She despised them for looking only skin deep at a woman, and here she was doing the same thing. Oh, dear. He had spoken to her, and she didn't hear, she was so lost in her own thoughts.

"I do beg your pardon, sir," she said. "I did not hear what you said."

"Thinking again, Miss Sherbrooke?" he asked, showing his dazzling smile. "I do hope you will share your thoughts with me. Now, please, let us partake of this repast. To tell you the truth, I am absolutely famished."

With that he commenced upon his dinner. Eleanor made an attempt upon her meal, but her agitation was so great, she felt her stomach would rebel against too much sustenance. He looked up at her. “Did I not choose well?” he asked. “I can bring you something else if you like. There is a hot soup.”

No, hot soup was not what she needed. Reassurance as to his intentions was the only thing on her menu at the moment. “No, thank you. I do not believe hot soup is what I require.” She hesitated, and then, summoning her courage, said exactly what was on her mind. “Why did you ask Cordelia for an introduction to me?”

He looked up at her, his eyebrows raised, and stared at her for a long moment. She knew she had asked the wrong thing. Women were not to be so frank. They were to talk of the weather, or the latest fashion, or about each other, anything that was frivolous and small and of no consequence. She could not bear it. Of course, now that she asked him, she regretted it. She was afraid of the answer.

“Shall I be honest, or shall I flatter you?” He reached for a glass of beer that he had brought with him to dinner. While he drank a draught, she answered him.

“No one ever flatters me, sir, so the truth is what I need to hear.”

“Very well, then. I heard Mr Shaw’s remark and saw your reaction. I thought him rude and ungentlemanly, and not being able to illicit an apology from him to you, I decided to try, in some small way, to make up for his lack of etiquette.”

Eleanor didn’t know what to think. The man was being frank with her, so she would be frank with him. “You do not have to continue sitting with me, sir. I release you from your duty.”

With that he smiled and began eating again. “I do not want to be released. I find you quite interesting, Miss Sherbrooke. You have not once talked of the weather or anything dreary. You also cut to the quick, and I admire that. Do you know how weary I am of blathering conversation? I would much rather talk to you. Tell me about your interests… I mean, besides dancing. Oh, and please eat and keep me company.”

Eleanor again was speechless. The knot in her stomach began to relax. Perhaps she had found a friend at this ball. She suddenly felt quite hungry and tucked into a piece of roast chicken. He looked at her, chewing and smiling. Once she had swallowed, she said, “I would like to study at college… medicine.”

He put down his fork and looked quite astonished. “Really? You would like to become a doctor, then?”

“Yes, exactly.”

He shook his head, but then did something quite extraordinary. Usually when she announced her plans to study, everyone laughed at her. He did not. “How do your parents feel about such a plan?”

She sighed. “They find it most absurd and try to discourage me at every turn.”

He nodded sagely. “I know the feeling well. My father was adamant that I go into business with him and my brother and not join the army. Yet here I am.”

She did not hesitate. “Men have more choices than women.”

“Ah, you do have a point there. Still, he threatens to cut me off.”

“Has he?”

“Not yet.” He began eating again and took another drink from his glass.

“Why the army, and the cavalry and the Lancers? How did that ever come about?”

“You do not beat about the bush, do you, Miss Sherbrooke?” He looked at her so intensely that her heart leapt. She felt as though she was about to be party to a great and terrible secret. Instead, he asked her, “Do you know what they call us, the 17th Lancers?”

She had only heard one thing about them, and it was a disparagement of the ornateness of their uniforms. Since they were being honest with each other, she told him. “Brigham’s Dandies?”

He nearly choked, and bringing his cloth to his mouth, surrendered to a fit of coughing. Eleanor was sure he would be angry, but when his coughing subsided, he laughed. “You are the most surprising young woman, Miss Sherbrooke, and the most astounding things come out of your mouth. Yes, that is true, some call us that, but it is more important what we call ourselves: The Death or Glory Boys.”

“That seems rather ominous, do you not think so?”

“Not at all. We are the first in battle. We bear down on the enemy and send fear and panic into their hearts. I intend, Miss Sherbrooke, before I am through, to cover myself in glory.”

With that, he returned to his supper. Eleanor gazed at him a while before commencing again on her repast. He was already glorious. The most glorious man she had ever met.

***

Joshua's entrance into the stable at his father's house in Piccadilly woke the young stable hand. The boy sleepily and wordlessly took the reins from Lieutenant Wentworth and began to remove the horse's saddle. Even though he had attended a formal gathering, Wentworth rode on horseback, eschewing the more comfortable carriage. He had been in the cavalry so long, he never felt right sitting inside a coach.

Lieutenant Wentworth was on leave from the regimental headquarters in Sussex and returned home for a visit with his parents. He primarily came to visit his mother, who was in failing health. His father, however, was another matter. There was little warmth in the man, and he expected to be obeyed. Joshua and his father often quarrelled.

Thinking that everyone was asleep, he ventured through the kitchen door, which was the closest to the outbuildings. As he reached the main staircase, light escaped from the half-closed door of his father's study. It was nearly three o'clock in the morning. Whatever would his father be doing up? He nearly took the coward's way out, avoiding another confrontation with his father, but squaring his shoulders, he walked toward the puddle of yellow light.

As he entered the study, the dim light reflected off his father's bald pate. Joshua often thought his father maintained such bushy and formidable whiskers on his face to offset the lack of hair on his head.

His father filled his pipe and then struck a match on the mantel. "So, you finally return home now that it is nearly morning. We see very little of you since your return to London."

"William Mosley invited me to a ball this evening, Father. You will remember that we discussed it."

The older man merely grunted.

"You have been encouraging me to marry, sir. I cannot marry if I never meet any *suitable* young women." Joshua emphasised the word "suitable" for his father's sake. When he joined the 17th Lancers at twenty-two years of age, he was posted to Ireland. There he fell in love with a local Irish girl, and they planned to elope, despite the objections of both families. It was not to be, however. Mary was sent off to the south of the country, and although he tried searching for her, it all came to naught. His father was relieved not to have a "papist" in the family. Although he no longer pined for her, there were times, when he was alone with his thoughts, that her face would return to him.

His father turned on him with a glare. "So, you go off dancing and drinking for my sake, is that it?"

How was it, that he, Joshua Griffiths Wentworth, could send the fear of God into an entire troop of men, and here, at home, he was reduced to a chastised schoolboy? As a youth, his father's voice always sent shudders through him. Now, a lieutenant in the cavalry, a veteran of duty in Ireland, that voice no longer held sway. The question that his father asked, in the past, would have him stammering for an answer. Now, he just said nothing and returned his father's glare.

The elder Wentworth cleared his throat. "Well, did you meet any suitable young women? Come now, speak up."

It irked him to be spoken to in such a tone, but to not answer now would confirm to his father that he behaved like a pouting juvenile. "One young lady I found particularly interesting."

His father's head arched back in surprise. "Oh, really?" He smiled now for the first time. "A real beauty, eh?" The old man's face crinkled up in a smile.

Joshua did not answer immediately. Finally, he said, "Beautiful in many ways, Father. Many ways." He held his father's gaze for a moment and then, turning on his heel, said, "I bid you good night. I want to wake early tomorrow and take Mother for a drive. The weather should be fine." As he walked toward the staircase, he smiled to himself. It was the first time he talked of the weather all evening.

Chapter 2

The early afternoon sun illuminated the sitting room as Eleanor sat silently with her mother. She was trying to concentrate on a book, but her thoughts drifted back to the previous evening. She resolved to cherish all those moments with Lieutenant Wentworth as she was convinced she would never see him again.

"Whatever are you smiling at, dear?" her mother asked, looking up from her needlework. Without waiting for an answer, she added, "It is good to see you smile. You look so much more attractive when you smile."

Why did people say such things? Smiling or not smiling, the mark on her face remained constant. She did not answer. There was no need to explain. Her mother would never meet the dashing Lieutenant Wentworth, in any case.

The front bell rang a moment later, followed by the firm step of Baxter, their butler, walking towards the door. She sighed. Some lady friend or other of her mother's had undoubtedly come to call. Eleanor rose quickly to make a judicious escape, but her mother chastised her.

"Do sit down, Eleanor, we have a guest."

Eleanor tried mightily not to roll her eyes. Baxter soon returned with the silver tray they kept by the door for calling cards. He bowed and offered the card to Mrs Sherbrooke.

"Whatever is this?" Mrs Sherbrooke's voice rose in pitch as she took the card from the tray. She held it by the bent corner as if holding a dead mouse by the tail. Eleanor's breath caught in her throat. The unmistakable insignia—a human skull with crossed bones in its teeth with the words "or glory" on a banner beneath—Death or Glory—Death or Glory Boys—just as Lieutenant Wentworth explained the night before. To the side of the emblem—Lieutenant Joshua Griffiths Wentworth. The corner was turned down. He was here. He did not merely leave the card. He was outside the door.

Eleanor clasped and unclasped her hands, unable to keep still. Her mother's face held a quizzical expression. Eleanor now regretted not mentioning her dances with the lieutenant, and the supper, and the frank conversation. Oh, dear. What to do now?

"Show the man in, Baxter," she said, taking command of the situation. Her mother raised an eyebrow. "A gentleman I danced with at the ball, Mama. A lieutenant in the Lancers." Eleanor nearly laughed out loud at the look of utter shock on her mother's face. It was just at that moment that Eleanor remembered: she had no powder to mitigate the red mark and she knew that it reddened further still when she was in a high state of excitement or embarrassment. The thoughts of herself were soon banished as Lieutenant Wentworth strode into the sitting room.

Again, he was hatless. Baxter must have relieved him of it. His tousled hair gave him a look of breezy nonchalance. Dressed in full uniform, and in the light of day, he looked all the more robust and handsome. He looked straight into Eleanor's eyes and smiled. She finally found her voice.

"Mama, this is Lieutenant Wentworth of the 17th Lancers," she said. The words nearly did not come forth. He bowed, and it was then she glanced at her mother. She was as much mesmerised by the lieutenant's good looks as any other woman.

He turned to Eleanor and again bowed. Eleanor quite forgot her mother was in the room until she heard her clear her throat. Finally, he spoke. "I do hope I am not intruding."

"Oh, you are not, Lieutenant." Eleanor could not help herself. She was smiling so much that her cheeks began to hurt.

"Eleanor did not mention you, Lieutenant… Wentworth is it? Did you first meet last night at the ball? Do take a seat, sir."

The lieutenant sat in the chair next to Eleanor, facing her mother on the settee. "We had supper together last night… on the terrace."

Why did he put it in such a way as to make it sound so scandalous? Perhaps it was her imagination. Perhaps he was trying to be charming. The look of shock on her mother's face had returned. At first, Eleanor was irritated with him, but then he turned to her with the most mischievous smile. He was so confident in his charm that she had to laugh.

"Cordelia introduced us, Mama. The lieutenant is a friend of Cordelia's brother, William, is that not so?"

He nodded but would not take his eyes off Eleanor nor drop that roguish smile. She continued, "We danced the last dance before supper. The lieutenant offered to escort me. That is all."

Her mother's expression softened. "Ah, I see. Odd that you should not have mentioned anything to me or your father, Eleanor."

How could she say, in front of Lieutenant Wentworth, that she no more expected him to call than for the Thames to freeze over in August? She did not have to say anything, however, as he threw himself into the conversation once more.

"Miss Sherbrooke probably did not expect me to call. She had so many dances last night, I believe she quite forgot me."

My goodness, he was a scamp. No woman in her right mind could forget one such as him, and he knew it. She was about to contradict him, but instead agreed.

"I believe the lieutenant is right. I do apologise, sir. But I am quite happy you came to see us today."

She was overjoyed to see him. Bursting with happiness to see him. She stole a glance at her mother, who looked confused, or surprised, or perhaps both.

"I did want to continue our fascinating conversation. I have never met a woman who was so frank."

"Oh, Eleanor, you weren't *frank* with the gentleman."

"I am frank with everyone, Mama. It saves time."

The lieutenant gave a hearty guffaw. "That it does, Miss Sherbrooke, and I find it refreshing. Do you not agree, Mrs Sherbrooke?"

Her mother wrinkled her nose. "No, sir, I do not. It is unladylike and unbecoming."

"There I beg to differ," he said quietly and then turned his attention back to Eleanor. "The Polka Radowa interrupted our conversation last night. I believe you were about to tell me about studying medicine, was it? Then you would be the first… woman doctor, that is."

Mrs Sherbrooke shook her head vigorously and then turned her attention back to her embroidery. Eleanor knew that her mother was listening, but at least she wouldn't spend her time contradicting.

"Oh, no. That is just the point. There is already a female doctor, Miss Elizabeth Blackwell. Although she was born in Britain, she went to medical school in the United States and practices there. I would like to study medicine as she did."

Lieutenant Wentworth went silent for a few moments as if chewing and digesting the extraordinary idea that Eleanor had just proposed. Eleanor watched him and then turned her attention back to her mother, who was scowling at her and working her face as if she were trying to say something or endeavouring not to say anything. Perhaps she had gone too far expressing such radical ideas to a man she just met. Women were expected to be vacuous and servile, concerned only with their husband's and children's welfare, calling upon other women, and entertaining. Eleanor could not imagine anything more deadening to the soul. Still, in the seconds after she spoke, as she looked at her handsome companion, she could almost see herself giving up her dreams of education and medical practice for one such as him. She had probably shocked him already, and this call would be his last. Nothing was more unattractive than an intelligent woman. Her mother often said so.

"I do not see why women could not practice medicine. After all, half of the patients are women, and many are children. Perhaps it would be more comfortable for women to have a female physician waiting upon them. Of course, it would be awkward for men to see a woman doctor." He was no longer smiling but had a thoughtful expression on his face. Eleanor did not agree with him on the last point. She considered keeping still for a moment, but it wasn't in her nature.

"What do you mean, 'awkward for men'? Is it not equally as awkward for women to be attended by male physicians?"

Eleanor looked at Lieutenant Wentworth, who seemed nonplussed, and then at her mother, who looked almost apoplectic, but fortunately, she did not again enter the conversation. Eleanor was highly amused seeing her mother restraining her opinion in such a manner.

Lieutenant Wentworth, after a thoughtful pause, sighed. "I have no idea, not being a woman myself, but your point is well taken, Miss Sherbrooke." At that he slapped his thighs and stood abruptly. "I believe I have taken up much of your time. If you'll excuse me." With that, he stood and bowed to Eleanor's mother, and then to

Eleanor. “I did enjoy our talk,” he said, smiling. Eleanor didn’t know if she believed him or not, so abrupt was his departure. “Mrs Sherbrooke, so nice to meet you.” Her mother responded, but Eleanor could not attend to what she was saying. All she saw was her handsome young man depart in a rush.

***

“Now you’ve done it,” Mrs Sherbrooke said as soon as the click of the front door was audible. “You had to be ‘frank’ with him. Most unbecoming. Most unsuitable. And now you have scared him off. A brilliant young officer. Oh, Eleanor, I do despair of you sometimes.”

“All right, Mama. What’s done is done. There is no need to belabour the point.” Her mother resumed to her embroidery, but from the manner in which she was stabbing the fabric, she was quite cross. She believed her mother was right. There was no reason to begin a dispute with Lieutenant Wentworth. He believed as all men believed. Women were not to breach a man’s world, and the idea of a woman physician attending to men was indecent to say the least. She did not find it indecent, but certainly he did.

“I am sorry, Mama.” She sat on the edge of the settee and tried to catch her mother’s eye. “You know that he would tire of me soon enough no matter what I said and seek one more beautiful… and—” She wanted to say “vacuous” but chose her words more carefully. “—*charming* than I. Someone more like Julia.”

Her mother looked up at her then. The look on her face cut Eleanor to the quick. She thought she would see anger there, but what shone from her mother’s eyes was much harder to bear—pity. Of all the things Eleanor had to endure in her life, pity was the most dreadful. “I will be in my room,” she said before her mother could open her mouth to speak.

***

“Where have you been, old boy? It is nearly two o’clock.” William Mosley was already mounted on his chestnut mare.

“I do apologise, Mosley, I had a call to make.” Wentworth patted the neck of his bay, Merlin.

“A flirtatious female, no doubt. You are a rogue, Wentworth. You should do as your father asks and marry at once.”

Lieutenant Wentworth laughed. “I will marry the day after you do.” And with that, he chucked the reins, turned the stallion’s head, and trotted ahead of Mosley. He thought about Eleanor again and it surprised him. She did not flirt with him. In fact, quite the opposite. She was, in fact, the opposite of what he usually found attractive in a woman, yet…. He shook the thoughts from his head and set his horse at a gallop.

Wentworth enjoyed these riding jaunts with William Mosley and his bachelor friends. Their group was steadily shrinking as the young men dropped the reins of their bachelor lives and settled into marriage and family. Still, there was a small group of them left, and these civilians relied upon him to teach them cavalry manoeuvres he learned in the Lancers. Most of them were hopeless at controlling any but the most basic movements of their horses, and it gave Wentworth a sense of satisfaction that he was so masterful. Of course, he had been practicing for years.

When they returned to the barn and dismounted, Mosley invited them all to the house for a drink. George Shaw fell into step next to Wentworth.

“I saw that Miss Mosley arranged for you to take that girl with the ‘mark of Cain’ on her face into supper yesterday. Bad luck, eh?”

Wentworth turned to see a smirk on Shaw’s face. He stopped walking abruptly.

“You take back those words, Mr Shaw, or I will thrash you on the spot.”

Shaw’s smirk disappeared immediately. “Good God, man, you cannot be serious.” Those in closest proximity to the two stopped in their tracks.

“I am quite serious. You, sir, are not a gentleman.” Wentworth squared his shoulders, and his gaze did not waver from Shaw’s face. Mr Shaw instinctively took a step backwards and Wentworth closed the distance. “What is it to be, sir?”

William Mosley, who had been walking ahead of the group, stopped and turned back. He shouted as he ran. “See, here, Wentworth, Shaw, certainly there is no reason for a quarrel.”

Lieutenant Wentworth did not waver and ignored his friend’s entreaties. “I am waiting.”

Shaw's eyes shifted to the rest of the group. He must not have found what he sought there for he blurted, "I apologise. It was rude of me to speak in such a manner."

"In such a manner of whom?"

"In such a manner of Miss Sherbrooke."

Wentworth's shoulders relaxed. "Apology accepted, but watch your tone in regard to the young lady. I will not hear anything against her. Do you understand, sir?"

George Shaw swallowed. He did not speak at first, but then found his tongue again. "I will not mention her again." He offered his hand to Lieutenant Wentworth, but Joshua did not take it and walked away. The small knot of men saw the slight, and it quietened them for the time it took to reach the house. As Wentworth walked, he turned over in his mind what had just occurred. Was it his hatred of bullies that prompted him to act in so aggressive a manner, or was it that Miss Sherbrooke had succeeded where so many others had failed? And that was to get under his skin.

***

Eleanor sat at the desk she had commandeered from her father in the library and pored over the most recent publication of *Bulletin de l'Académie Nationale de Médecine*, to which her father graciously allowed her to subscribe. Her French, which she studied half-heartedly at first, thinking it only designed to enhance scintillating dinner conversation, now stood her in good stead in her efforts to learn of the latest advances in medicine. Her fondest wish was to attend a dissection class at the Royal College of Surgeons. She never spoke of it, thinking her mother would faint at the idea.

She was thusly engrossed when Baxter entered with a silver tray. As he approached, she could see a card resting upon it, the corner turned up. Her heart began to pound wildly, and she took a deep breath to calm it down. It could not be. Had Lieutenant Wentworth arrived again to call upon her? It was too good to be true. After another breath, she came upon the realisation that it was probably Cordelia come to call. She was a good and loyal friend, and Eleanor would greet her cordially. She shook her head at her own foolishness.

Baxter arrived at the desk. “A Lieutenant Wentworth is here to see you, miss.” Why did her body react so with the mere mention of his name? She closed her eyes for a moment and tried to steady her palpitating heart.

Her mother was out making calls, and no one was at home to chaperone but her rather deaf Aunt Sophronia. She was Eleanor’s great-aunt on her mother’s side. Aunt Sophronia never married and served as chaperone countless times to two generations of her mother’s family.

“Your aunt is in the drawing room, miss. I have shown the gentleman in there.”

***

Lieutenant Wentworth entered the drawing room and was surprised to find an elderly woman sitting upon the chaise lounge knitting. Apparently, she didn’t hear him approach, for she did not look up when the door opened. The butler approached her, and she started at seeing him.

“Oh, what is it now, Baxter?” She squinted at the butler, who indicated, with a wave of the hand, Wentworth’s presence.

“A Lieutenant Joshua Wentworth to see Miss Sherbrooke.”

The old woman looked up at him over the spectacles perched on the end of her nose. “Do I know you?” Her voice was rather loud and gruff, and as Wentworth replied, she raised her ear trumpet to her ear, confirming his suspicions.

“I am Lieutenant Joshua Wentworth of the 17th Lancers come to see Miss Sherbrooke.”

“Yes, I heard that. No need to shout, young man. You have come at the wrong time. Julia is off visiting in Wales. She should have told you.” She waved him off dismissively and turned her attention back to her knitting. He spoke again, slowly and loudly.

“I am not here to see Miss Julia, but Miss Eleanor Sherbrooke.”

She stopped knitting and looked up at him quizzically. “Here to see Eleanor?” She looked him up and down, her face screwed up in a grimace. With that, the door opened, and Eleanor entered.

“Oh, Lieutenant Wentworth, how nice of you to come calling.” She crossed to the chaise lounge and planted a kiss on her aunt’s head. Looking back up at Wentworth, she said, “This is Miss Sophronia Chesterton, my mother’s aunt.”

Wentworth bowed slightly. Aunt Sophronia nodded with a slight smile. “Pleased to meet you. Now, Eleanor, go take your young man and sit by the fire.”

Two chairs faced each other near the fireplace. Eleanor took the lady’s chair, without arms. He took the other. The fire warmed the damp April day.

Eleanor wore no powder today and dressed in a modest navy bodice and skirt. It was she who spoke first. “I am surprised to see you again, Lieutenant Wentworth.” She looked directly at him, almost accusingly to his mind. She did not flutter her fan provocatively, or even carry one, for that matter. Her tone took him by surprise.

“Are you, Miss Sherbrooke? Why? Perhaps my visit is unwelcome.” He regretted saying that the minute it was out of his mouth. Why did she put him on edge? He was always perfectly at ease with other women.

“That is not the case at all, sir, but you left so abruptly last time. I thought that I may have offended you in some way.”

“I believe I told you I had an appointment.”

“I do not believe you did.” She raised her eyebrows in a most challenging fashion. Should she not be happy he has returned and not contradict him?

“Are you deliberately treating me with disdain, Miss Sherbrooke? I do not think I have done anything to give offence… at least that was not my intention.”

Her shoulders seemed to relax at this last declaration, and she looked at him curiously with a half-smile. Despite her plain appearance, her smile illuminated her face. “You have not given me offence, Lieutenant. I suppose I am not used to gentlemen returning for a visit once they have ascertained that I am neither a flatterer nor a simpleton.”

She was most assuredly not accommodating. Never in his life had he met anyone like her. He should be offended by her tone; after all, women were to be subservient to men and not threaten them in any way. This one seemed ready to do battle at any time. For a moment, he was stymied as to what to say next.

"Since you will not flatter me, I shall flatter you, Miss Sherbrooke. I find you quite intelligent and honest, and that is like a breath of fresh air to me."

"It was my understanding, sir, that men are not partial to intelligent women."

"Some of my acquaintance need to puff up themselves at the expense of others, mostly women. I find that sort of behaviour most… ungentlemanly. I think you would agree with me?"

She was silent for a moment and regarded him with some curiosity. "If you are playing some sort of game with me, Lieutenant, I must ask you to cease and desist. You come here and flatter me and make me drop my guard, and then what? If your attentions are some grand joke…." She stood abruptly as if to leave. He could not let that happen. Why was she so distrustful of his intentions? On impulse, he took her hand. She stopped and looked first at his face and then at his hand upon hers. He took advantage of her silence.

"Please, Miss Sherbrooke, I am sincere in my desire to see you. I am so tired of—"

A hoarse shout came from the direction of the chaise lounge. "See here, young man, we will have none of that." Aunt Sophronia shook a gnarled finger in the direction of the couple's clasped hands. Wentworth let go his grasp, and to his relief, Eleanor took her seat once more. "What are you two talking about?" Wentworth cast his eye on the old aunt, who was now holding her ear trumpet.

"We were just discussing whether or not it might rain," Eleanor said calmly. The old woman nodded and mumbled something to herself as she put the ear trumpet beside her again and resumed her knitting.

There was silence between them for a moment, and then Eleanor leaned forward toward him and whispered, "I will tell you what I am tired of. I am tired of playing games that I cannot win." She looked at him with such sadness that his heart went out to her.

"I do not play games, Miss Sherbrooke. Of that you can be sure."

***

Lieutenant Wentworth, still on horseback, stopped before his family home and stared at it for a time. He dreaded coming home but would do so as frequently as possible while his mother still lived. Every time he returned, she looked weaker and frailer than when he left, yet his father and brother did not seem to notice. In fact, neither of them noticed much of anything but the state of their commercial concerns. Both could, however, find fault with him.

Neither of the men were at home, so Joshua climbed the stairs two at a time and knocked softly on his mother's door. If she was asleep, he did not want to wake her. Her nurse, Celia, answered the door. She was a plump woman of middle age and sunny disposition.

"Is my mother awake?" he asked softly.

"Aye, that she is," Celia said, smiling. "She be sittin' by the window, takin' the air. Go now. It always cheers her to see ye."

As he stepped into the bedroom, his mother turned towards him. The afternoon light cast shadows over her sunken eyes and sallow skin, but her face brightened when she saw him. "Oh, Joshua, come in. I did not expect to see you before this evening. Celia, bring us some tea, there's a dear."

When the door closed and they were alone, Joshua sat facing his mother near the window. He looked up into her eyes and then cast his gaze downward again. It was so disconcerting to be back home with his family. Whereas his father elicited the pouting and defiant adolescent in him, his mother reduced him to a little boy. He wanted to run to her side and have her stroke his head and tell him everything was going to be all right.

"You have come to tell me something, son."

Joshua cleared his throat. "No, no, not really."

She clasped his hand with both of hers. "You were opening and closing your fist like you did when you were little. That always means something is bothering you. Come, tell me."

He knew he would tell her of Eleanor because there was no one else in this world in whom he could confide. His father and brother would receive any confidence he would offer as a sign of weakness. His comrades in arms were just that, comrades. He had friends, but not close friends. William Mosley might be one, but he could not risk looking unmanly to him either.

"You know me so well, Mother," he said, attempting a smile.

"Come, tell me. What is it?" Her breath was audible, a wheezing sound really. He hesitated.

"Perhaps I should let you rest."

"Perhaps you should tell me what is on your mind, for I will not rest until I know." She patted his hand again. He stood and faced out the window. It was easier to speak if he did not have to look at her directly.

"I met a most unusual young woman."

"Oh, Joshua, that is wonderful." Her words came out strongly this time, and he turned to her.

"Please, Mother. It is very early days, very early, but she is like no other woman I have ever known." He looked out of the window once more. "I am afraid, though, that Father would not approve."

There was silence from his mother, which forced him to meet her gaze once again. Her eyes crinkled up and she smiled a knowing smile at him. "I notice that you did not say that *I* would not approve."

He shook his head. "That I do not know."

"Is she from a good family? Not a camp follower, I trust."

Joshua had to smile at that. Eleanor was surely no camp follower. He sat down again and took his mother's hands in his. "She is from an excellent family. Her father was a colonel in the army."

His mother looked confused. "And why would your father not approve?"

Joshua sighed and then chose his words carefully. "She is quite outspoken and frank…and intelligent."

His mother did not speak for a moment, but she turned her eyes from his and looked out into the distance. "Marriage and her duties will quell that soon enough."

This was not what he expected to hear. He thought she would commiserate with him, tell him that those qualities would be advantageous in a wife. He changed the subject.

"We are not at the point of discussing marriage yet. We only just met… at the Mosleys' ball."

"But you have already thought of it, have you not, my son?"

He sighed. "You know me better than anyone, Mother. Yes, it has crossed my mind. These large gatherings and balls are marriage markets, are they not? That is why young men and women attend. We are all looking to make a good match."

"With you it has to be a love match, Joshua." He could hide nothing from her. It made him feel uneasy in his own skin that his mother could see into the corners of him that he hid even from himself. "Come along, now. That is the truth, is it not?"

"I suppose it is, Mother. Yes, all right. Yes, it is."

"You are a romantic, Joshua. So unlike your pragmatic brother. I think that is why you chose the army. You are looking for something larger than yourself, something to which you can dedicate your life."

How could he confess that the army was a place for him to prove his manhood to his father? He would not say that, even to her. "I suppose you think you know me better than I know myself."

"I suppose I do. I am your mother, you know."

A thought occurred to him and his smile disappeared. "There is something else."

"About this girl?"

"Yes. About her. Her name is Eleanor Sherbrooke."

She looked back and forth for a moment as if searching the air for something. At last she shook her head. "I don't think I know the name, but then it has been some time since I have been out calling upon people." Of course, her illness confined her. He patted her hand. "I am not complaining, mind you," his mother added. "Celia takes good care of me and your father and Geoffrey come in at least once a day to see me, but I digress. You were about to tell me something."

"I am afraid that Father would not think her bloodline suitable."

His mother drew her head back and a look of disbelief crossed her face. "Her bloodline? She is not one of your horses, my darling. I thought you said she comes from a respectable family."

"She does. That is not what I mean." He hesitated again. "She has a mark upon her face. It looks like a great rosy patch that almost encircles her left eye and covers most of her cheek." He motioned with his hands as he explained. His mother regarded him impassively. When he finished speaking, she cocked her head to one side and was silent, as if waiting for him to continue.

"Is that all?" she asked.

He sighed. "That is something. That is something Father would latch on to and say it was a defect. One that must not be passed on." His jaw clenched.

"That mark is nothing. Many have such marks and their children do not. It is not a family defect. You are assuming a reaction from your father that he may not have."

With that he sighed, looked heavenward, and shook his head. "Oh, Mother. Why should he change his spots now?"

"If he disapproved, would that discourage you from marrying her?"

"No, not in the slightest. It is just…. I would not want to subject her to Father's or even Geoffrey's scorn."

She took a long, deep, rattling breath. "You have only met her a few times—"

"Three…."

"*Three* times and I am thinking that you are not ready to propose marriage quite yet."

He laughed. "No, Mother, not quite yet."

"Then you are worrying for nothing. We will broach the subject with your father if needs be. Until then, see if this girl suits you. If she does, you have my blessing."

***

A letter arrived for Eleanor two days later. Sealed informally with a blue wafer, Eleanor knew immediately that it was from Lieutenant Wentworth. She broke the seal and inside was a short note.

12 April, 1854
My dear Miss Sherbrooke,

I hope this letter finds you well. I have not much time to write as I have been called back to Sussex for a week or perhaps a fortnight. I leave in two days and there is much to arrange. I hope this does not inconvenience you too dreadfully, but when duty calls, I must answer.

I have enjoyed our talks and look forward to more when I return. My best wishes to your parents and your Aunt Sophronia, who was so talented a chaperone.

Most Cordially Yours,
Lieutenant Joshua Griffiths Wentworth

Eleanor clasped the letter to her bosom and then spoke sternly to herself. "No reason for such gross sentimentality, Eleanor. He doesn't declare his undying love, only informs you of his departure." Still, she could not help smiling through the day and all the time she dressed for dinner. Eleanor now had something substantial to hold that belonged to Joshua Wentworth. Despite her eschewing of sentimentality, it gave her a sense of well-being every time she touched it in the pocket of her gown.

They were halfway through the soup when Mrs Sherbrooke gave her husband a knowing look, and he nodded. She knew her parents well enough that she braced herself for something unexpected. “Oh, I cannot contain the news any longer. My dear…” She looked over at Eleanor. “I think you will be so pleased. Shall I tell her, Samuel?”

Her father looked up lazily from his soup. He obviously did not share in her mother’s enthusiasm. “I think you must now, my dear, having begun.” He then turned his attention back to his meal.

Eleanor wracked her brain trying to imagine what delightful tidings her mother was about to bestow. She hoped it would be that they had found a place for her at a medical school. No, it could never be that. It was impossible, and besides, her mother would not be so excited.

“Eleanor, you are to accompany Aunt Sophronia on her trip to the continent. You will visit the Italian and German States. Are you not thrilled?”

Eleanor was not thrilled. Weeks of boat trips and carriage rides with her dear, but deaf Aunt Sophronia was not a thrilling prospect. She loved her aunt as she would a grandmother, but… but… her Lieutenant Wentworth. He would return in a fortnight at the latest, and she would be gone.

“Oh, I see,” was the best she could muster. “And when would we be departing?”

“In a week, my dear.” Her aunt had her trumpet to her ear and joined the conversation. “We will have Annie help you pack. Our ship sails from Dover.”

Mrs Sherbrooke must have read Eleanor’s expression for her smile faded. “What is it, Eleanor?”

“Perhaps Julia could go.” Eleanor stirred her soup disconsolately. “She is ever so much livelier than I.” She stole a look at her mother.

Her mother’s expression soured. “Julia will not be returning for a week or more and the ship sails before that. You have been given a great gift from our aunt, now you should thank her for it.”

So, that was that. She looked at her father in appeal, but he would not meet her eye. She turned to Aunt Sophronia. "Thank you very much, Auntie. I would love to go."

***

By the next morning, Eleanor was beside herself. She must tell Lieutenant Wentworth of her impending departure before he left for Sussex. Eleanor thought to write him a letter, but her mother decided on another plan.

After taking a few, deep breaths and looking at her freshly powdered face and dark blue bodice and skirt, she heard Annie sigh. "You looks positively marvellous, miss." Eleanor did not turn to let her maid see how pleased she was, but in her heart of hearts, she thought so too.

A few hours later when the bell rang, Eleanor was nearly beside herself with excitement. She had asked Lieutenant Wentworth to dinner on short notice, and he accepted. Now, he was at the door and about to meet her father. When they sat down to dinner, however, her father monopolised the conversation. They were all seated at the far end of their formal dining table. Eleanor insisted. She did not want them shouting down long, empty spaces. Lieutenant Wentworth sat across from her with the colonel on his right and would smile or raise an eyebrow at her during various parts of the conversation. Her father appeared to like him enormously.

"So, my boy, you are a cavalry man. Stout fellow. I, myself, was infantry. Once you boys clear the way, we follow and finish them off."

"Samuel, please. What a topic for dinner conversation," Eleanor's mother said in a mildly chastising tone.

The colonel did not seem to hear her and continued. "Yes, yes. I was too young for the dustup with Napoleon. Spent most of my days in India." He pronounced it "Inja," as many who served there did. "Left when the girls were still infants."

"Julia says she remembers India. She said she remembers mostly colours. Lots and lots of colours."

Again, it was as if her father heard a train passing or a carriage roll by. His attention did not shift from his storytelling. "Didn't want the little ones absorbing the heathen ways, don't you know? Returned to finish my career garrisoned here at home."

"They say we might be off to stop the Russians soon, sir." The second course had just arrived, and Lieutenant Wentworth had barely said a word to her. The colonel commanded all his attention. "The French are pretty nervous about the vulnerability of the Ottomans."

"The Ottoman Empire. The sick man of Europe," Eleanor said. They all turned at once to look at her. "Did I say something wrong?"

Wentworth smiled broadly. "Miss Sherbrooke can never be counted on to remark about the weather, can she?"

"I really don't know where you get your ideas from, Eleanor." Her mother used her exasperated tone again.

"From the newspaper, Mother, as you well know."

The lieutenant gave a hearty laugh at that remark, but her parents were not smiling.

"Why should a woman fill her head with politics?" her mother asked pointedly.

Eleanor did not hesitate. "Because, Mother, someday women will have the vote." They all looked at her as if she had three heads. She pressed on. "Someday, perhaps a woman will be Prime Minister."

"Come along now, Eleanor. Surely, you do not believe such a thing is possible. A woman… the head of government." Her father snuffled dismissively into his moustache.

Lieutenant Wentworth spoke up. "We already have a woman as head of this country." He stood and raised his glass. "Ladies and gentlemen, the Queen."

The colonel could do nothing else but stand and raise his glass. Eleanor and her mother remained seated. She stole a glance at Lieutenant Wentworth and his eyes danced in that mischievous way of his. They all raised their glasses and held them aloft. "The Queen."

Eleanor had barely put her wineglass back on the table when there was a great kerfuffle in the outer room.

"Whatever could that be?" Her mother's words were barely out of her mouth when the French doors swung open and a draft of cool air blew into the dining room. And with that breeze came Julia.

***

"Oh, Mama, Papa, I am sorry. I did not know you were entertaining." Julia took in the room in a glance. Eleanor watched her sister's expression as her eyes fell upon Lieutenant Wentworth. It reminded Eleanor of a cat who had just been served a saucer of cream.

"Won't you introduce me?" She spoke to her mother, or her father, or even Eleanor, but would not drop her gaze from the ruggedly flawless face before her.

Eleanor said, "This is Lieutenant Joshua Griffiths Wentworth of the 17th Lancers. Lieutenant Wentworth, my sister, Julia Sherbrooke."

Wentworth inclined his head in a slight bow. "So pleased to meet you."

"Lieutenant Joshua Griffiths Wentworth," Julia rolled the name over her tongue. "Of the Wentworth Cotton, am I correct?"

"My father's business," Wentworth said curtly. He did not smile.

"And also the Griffiths of Griffiths Manor in Wiltshire?"

"My mother's family."

"Well, well," she said. "Please, do sit down. It was so rude of me to burst in on you this way. I thought my family would be at home alone tonight." She looked over at Eleanor and raised her eyebrows. Eleanor glared, but said nothing.

"Baxter, tell Marie to bring another setting and tell cook that Julia is here."

The butler left with a "very good, Madam" and Julia took her place next to Eleanor. It was so easy to keep the attention of a man when one was sitting and gazing directly into his eyes. From time to time during the rest of the meal, Julia stole a look at Eleanor. Now it was Eleanor's turn to try to communicate with her eyes. The messages she sent to encourage Julia to turn off her charming ways were not being received.

Eleanor knew exactly why her sister was ignoring her. Ordinarily, Julia had so many suitors that one or two could be sacrificed to Eleanor. But a man of Lieutenant Wentworth's family connections, a perfect combination of fame and fortune, and his astonishing good looks were too much of a temptation.

By the time dinner had devolved into a sherry in the drawing room, Julia took her leave. She stood very close to the lieutenant before her departure but deigned to let Eleanor walk him to the door. It was obvious to Eleanor that Lieutenant Wentworth was captivated. His gaze followed Julia up the staircase before he took his leave.

Eleanor could not decide if she was angry or hurt. Either way, she was irritated at herself for feeling anything. She knew this dalliance with Lieutenant Wentworth would not last, but to watch it shatter right before her eyes, and with her sister Julia, was beyond the pale. She handed Lieutenant Wentworth his chapka at the door. She would not look directly at him.

"What have I done?" he whispered softly. Baxter was standing nearby.

Eleanor leaned in, her voice barely audible. "I should say, 'You know what you have done', but I truly believe you do not. I saw the way you looked at her." Out of the corner of her eye, Eleanor watched Baxter shift from one foot to the other. The servants carried tales and Baxter, undoubtedly, would carry this one to the servants' quarters.

"I had to look at her. She joined us for dinner. Really, Miss Sherbrooke. This jealousy does not become you."

He could have said anything, but he said that. She pushed his hat into his hands. "Good night, Lieutenant Wentworth." She finally looked up at him, narrowing her eyes to convey her displeasure. Did he look exasperated? Penitent? She did not know.

"Will I see you upon my return?" he asked. She said nothing but turned aside. Out of the corner of her eye she watched him stare at her for a few moments, and then setting his jaw, he spun on his heel. Baxter nearly tripped over the two of them to open it. As Eleanor watched him depart through the small front garden and mount his horse, she whispered, "I will not be here when you return." In all the excitement, she had forgotten to tell him so.

***

The morning light filtered through the curtains into Eleanor's bedroom, and after she rose, filling the basin with cold water left from the previous night, she splashed her face. Parting the curtains, she could see the sun dissipating the dew on the garden below. The roses were not yet in bloom.

She had not slept well, turning over that brief conversation with Lieutenant Wentworth again and again in her head. Aunt Sophronia would be up soon, and she and her mother would be getting all last-minute details for their journey arranged. Soon they would be departing. It was now or never.

After sitting down at the small writing desk in her room, she put pen to paper. Eleanor was in the habit of writing her true feelings on the first letter, and then what was expected on the second. Sometimes these initial letters were filled with sarcasm or bile, and sometimes rank sentimentality. This one belonged to the latter category. Since no one would ever see this missive, she poured out her heart. Poured it out to no one save herself.

My Dearest Joshua,

I am so sorry I am such a fool as to betray the envy that seethes in me for my sister in such a public manner. The truth is, once Julia is in the room, there is no place for any other woman, especially me. Every man she meets forgets his own name in her presence. Alas, I have never had that effect on anyone.

You are the kindest and handsomest man of my acquaintance. I believe I fell in love with you from the moment you took my hand to dance. Normally, I am not prone to romanticism or flights of fancy, but you make me want to throw myself into your arms. That is why I hold you at arm's length, as it were. To let my feelings be known would be my ruin.

So, when you come back, I will, of course, see you again. There is nothing on this earth that would prevent me from seeing you again. I will take you on any terms. Just ask me. Please ask me.

All My Love,
Eleanor

She reread this confession and crumpled it into a loose wad. There was no fire in the grate, so a match did its work. In an instant, the paper flared, and her thoughts went up the chimney. She then sat down to write the letter that would be delivered to her lieutenant.

15 April, 1854
Dear Lieutenant Wentworth,

I regret that we quarrelled last night on the eve of your departure. It was bad manners on my part. When you return, I shall be abroad with my great-aunt on an extended journey. With Julia's surprising entrance during our dinner, the announcement I intended to make in that regard was forgotten in the excitement.

I have enjoyed our chats, and I hope to see you sometime again. I appreciate your friendship and I hope it may be renewed upon my return. If you, perchance, would like to write to me, you can entrust the letters to my family. They know my itinerary well and can forward the post on to me.

Yours Sincerely,
Eleanor Wentworth

Eleanor reread the letter and sealed it in an envelope as Annie knocked at the door, asking if she would like a bath before her journey. Yes, she would like a bath. Perhaps it would cleanse her thoughts of Lieutenant Wentworth. Before leaving, she deposited the letter on the silver salver on the cabinet before the front door. Baxter would post it, or Lieutenant Wentworth would claim it himself. No doubt, he would return to see one of them.

Chapter 3

Lieutenant Wentworth talked to his stallion, Merlin, as he readied him for the long trot to Sussex. He had been in attendance when this colt was born five years ago. He was a handsome bay, a reddish brown with a black mane, tail, and fetlocks. Besides his mother, Merlin was his closest confidante.

"Do you understand women, Merlin? Because I must confess that I don't." The horse shook his head and mane in such a timely manner that Wentworth almost believed he understood.

"Why do they start a quarrel just as we were getting on so well? Women. They're inscrutable, are they not, my friend?" Looking back on last evening, he had to admit that perhaps his gaze did linger on Julia just a little too long. His laughter at her every clever and not-so-clever remark a little too hearty. But what was a man supposed to do? Shaking his head, he put his foot in the stirrup and mounted the stallion. Men did not spend their time thinking of such things. He resolved to think of it no more. He patted the horse's neck, and they trotted down the cobblestone streets. When they reached the unpaved road that led into the countryside, Wentworth softly kicked Merlin's flanks, and he broke into a gallop. A good, hard ride would drive thoughts of Eleanor Sherbrooke and her sister out of his head.

***

The next morning, all the officers gathered to meet at Lieutenant Colonel Rafferty's request. They took their seats before a great map, centred on the Black Sea. Wentworth's heart beat a little faster. Perhaps the time was coming in which he could cover himself in glory for Queen and country. There were murmurings among the officers, and then the colonel arrived.

"Gentlemen." He took his place to the right of the map and took up the pointer. "As you may have been reading in the papers, the blasted Russians are on the move. Her Majesty's government has been keeping a close eye on the blighters from Constantinople to Varna and here…." He slapped the pointer onto a large peninsula, almost an island, really, jutting from the mainland of Eastern Europe into the sea. "Here, gentlemen, the Crimea."

The murmurings began again, and with another slap of the pointer on the map, they ceased. "Her Majesty's government is allied with the Ottoman Turks, and the Russians have turned their imperialistic tendencies in that direction. I know many of you have left the training of your men to the lesser ranks…" His gaze slowly took in every man in the group but alighted on no one. "But now it is time to take charge, men. Combat training. Discipline. We have not been at war since Napoleon, but we'll show those Russians the might of the British army." The silence was palpable. What each man was thinking was anybody's guess, but Wentworth was pleased. This is what he had been waiting for, training for all these years. "Are you with me, men?" came the colonel's shout.

They all rose to their feet and shouted assent in one voice. Now, finally, they would prepare for war.

***

When Joshua Wentworth arrived back in London, he returned to his parents' house. He did not know if it was wishful thinking on his part, but his mother looked better to him, and even took a turn around the garden on his arm. Having satisfied himself as to her well-being, he set off immediately to call upon Eleanor. He resolved to make right all that had gone wrong between them. When he was shown into the drawing room, he was greeted not by Eleanor, but by her sister, Julia. Her mother followed behind.

"So good to see you again, Mrs Sherbrooke, Miss Sherbrooke…." He looked past them toward the door, expecting Eleanor to arrive momentarily. Perhaps she was still angry and would not see him. "Is Eleanor not at home?"

A look passed between the two women. "Eleanor is on an extended trip to the continent," Mrs Sherbrooke said offhandedly. "Did she not tell you?"

He swallowed hard. “No, she did not.”

“How odd,” said Mrs Sherbrooke as she took her seat on the settee.

Yes, it was odd. She left without telling him and did not even write a letter. He had made her angry and this was the result. There was not much time to ruminate, for tea was served and Julia did much to distract him from his thoughts of Eleanor. They discovered that they were both invited to a dinner at the Mosleys’ that evening. With the London Season just beginning, there would be one gathering after another. How many he could attend was in question. The dogs of war were already howling.

Upon leaving the Sherbrookes’, he took a long ride on Merlin before luncheon and, afterwards, read for a time to his mother. He had just enough time to dress for dinner at the Mosleys’. The better families were always looking for extra men to make up a balanced table, and he was a frequent dinner guest at gatherings when he was in town. His thoughts, however, were not on which fork to use or which young ladies would flutter their fans at him. His mind was on war in the distant Black Sea. He longed to prove himself on the field of battle for all the world to see, especially his father.

***

As she readied herself for a dinner at the Mosleys’, Julia felt a slight twinge of guilt for her act of subtle subterfuge. She had to admit to herself that upon laying eyes on Lieutenant Wentworth for the first time, she felt drawn to his exceedingly good looks. Of course, her sister did bring him into the house and may have had some designs upon him, but truthfully, even she could see that he was head and shoulders above what she could expect. So, when she saw Eleanor’s letter for him at the door, she ever so gently flicked it off the silver salver, where it slipped into oblivion between the cabinet and the wall. Should it ever be found, she could claim ignorance. Yes, that was unkind in one sense, but on reflection, an act of kindness in another. After all, someone would take Lieutenant Wentworth from Eleanor. Why should it not be her?

When Wentworth entered the Mosleys’ house, Julia espied him immediately despite a quite brilliant assembly that had gathered. William Mosley stood at the door and pressed his hand most heartily. Many of the prominent families of London were represented, and Julia was in the centre of a knot of male guests. She found herself often in this position, surrounded by the most eligible bachelors in London, holding court. How many of them had fallen in love with her? How could she blame them? She was well aware of her appeal: her silvery laugh, her exquisite figure, her tresses of blue-black hair, her alabaster skin and features so perfectly made that only the angels would try to surpass them if they dared. Lieutenant Wentworth would succumb. Why should he be different?

"Oh, Lieutenant Wentworth, how perfectly wonderful to see you," she said, reaching his side after sailing through the swarm of admirers to cross the room. The Mosleys had them all gather in the first-floor drawing room before dinner. Since it faced the street, Julia glanced out from time to time, watching for Wentworth's approach. He gave a slight bow. She offered her gloved hand up and put him in an awkward position by doing so. As a gentleman, he could not leave a lady thus exposed, so he took it gingerly and let it drop forthwith. She knew that in the constraints of polite society, a man never touched a lady's hand unless strictly necessary. Perhaps he would offer it to prevent her from stumbling over uneven ground or some such situation. As a gentleman, she left him with a conundrum. Could he refuse to take her offered hand and embarrass her, or would he take it and compromise himself? She knew what he would do.

Cordelia was then upon them. She surely meant to make mischief, taking Eleanor's part even in her sister's absence. "Lieutenant Wentworth, how good of you to come. May I introduce you to my friend, Miss Nora Watson? Perhaps you would be so kind as to take her in to dinner."

That Cordelia. She could plainly see Julia was engaged in conversation with the lieutenant. Cordelia was a loyal friend of Eleanor, that was plain. No doubt the two had discussed the fine lieutenant. Did Eleanor really have designs on him? Impossible. Graciously, Julia entered dinner upon William Mosley's arm. She was seated too far away from Lieutenant Wentworth to make intimate conversation, another contrivance of Cordelia's, no doubt. Julia endeavoured, however, when he looked in her direction, to meet his eyes. She was flirting with him. The signs were subtle, but they were there. He met her gaze from time to time, and, with hers steadily upon him, he lingered there. She was resolved.

She would have Lieutenant Wentworth.

***

The trip that her mother was gushing about with such enthusiasm was not what Eleanor expected. She was hoping they would go by sea, pass by Gibraltar and then through the Mediterranean to Sardinia or Corsica or even land in Naples. Instead, they went overland through France in bumpy carriages, stopping only for food and overnight lodging. Her aunt wanted to only go as far south as Milan, which meant no Tuscany, no Venice. When they arrived in Milan, her aunt was not pleased. The city seemed filled with insurrectionists and protest. After staying only a short and uncomfortable time, the two made their way north.

Two weeks went by and Eleanor received not one word from Lieutenant Wentworth. Yet a day did not pass in which she did not think of him. She chastised herself for letting thoughts of him intrude on her, and then chastised herself again for quarrelling with him on the eve of his departure. She was comforted by the thought that she sent him a letter explaining all, and resolved not to send him another unless he replied. But why should he? A man like him, so worldly, so sought after, so handsome. He would be asked out to every ball, every garden party, and every dinner filled with young and lithesome heiresses all falling at his feet. And, of course, there was Julia. Julia was there and she was not. Eleanor had driven him away with her "prickly" exterior, and yet she yearned for him, with her body as well as her heart.

The silence from Lieutenant Wentworth was not the only trouble weighing on Eleanor's mind. From the time they left Lombardy, travelling north, Aunt Sophronia began to ail. She developed a cough that worsened every day, and despite Eleanor's entreaties that they return home, her aunt insisted on continuing.

"I believe this will be my last venture onto the continent, Eleanor. You would not have me miss it, would you?'

"But if you are ill, Aunt…" she began, but her aunt silenced her with a wave of her hand.

"Let me have one more small pleasure, Eleanor. You, of course, do not understand as you are young and at the beginning of your life. You have so much joy ahead of you. For me, life is behind me."

"Do not say that, Aunt." Her aunt's life was indeed behind her, but what joy was ahead for Eleanor? She would be Aunt Sophronia before she knew it, taking care of other people's children. As if her aunt had read her thoughts, she began again.

"I know whereof I speak, my girl. I see how you look at that Lieutenant Wentworth of yours. I too had such a love."

Eleanor did not know what shocked her more: that her aunt observed her infatuation with Lieutenant Wentworth or that she spoke of a long-ago love. Her curiosity got the better of her.

"What love, Auntie? You never spoke of him."

Her aunt gave a sigh that gave way again to a fit of coughing. When it subsided, she continued. "He was in His Majesty's army, fighting against Napoleon." She smiled at the remembrance.

"An officer?"

Her aunt shook her head. "No, that was what made it so impossible. He was a common infantryman. My family thought him unsuitable."

"So, you gave him up, then?"

"Oh, no. I eloped with him. We were married at Gretna Green, one week before he left for the continent. It was such a week."

Eleanor could not take her eyes off Aunt Sophronia's features, which took on an ethereal expression. Her mother had never spoken of an elopement, a scandal - never. Perhaps her aunt's mind was not as reliable as it once was.

"You think I am inventing this story, do you not? I can tell by your face, Eleanor. Don't deny it."

"But… but Mother never spoke of this. Never."

"Your mother never knew, and those in my generation never spoke of it after he was killed. It was as if he never existed for them. He existed, though. His name was Robert Fairchild and I loved him. He fell at Waterloo." Her aunt turned her beatific expression once more to Eleanor. "Now you and I have a secret. All who witnessed my scandal have long since passed to their reward." She patted Eleanor's hand. "You are my confidante. Do not let that splendid Lieutenant Wentworth get away, Eleanor. He is half in love with you already."

Eleanor was grateful, then, that she did not have a weak heart, for so many stunning disclosures in so short a time would fell anyone who did. She did not speak for a moment. Finally, she found her voice. “I will keep your secret, Aunt. But you are wrong about Lieutenant Wentworth.”

Aunt Sophronia continued smiling and shook her head at Eleanor. “You must reach out and grasp life, Eleanor. Do not wait. It is fleeting.” And she began coughing again.

Over the next few days, Eleanor sent off several letters to her mother informing her of her aunt’s worsening illness. She thought that perhaps a telegram would reach home more quickly but knew it would be delayed at country borders. In any case, a letter taken by rail would arrive home soon enough. Eleanor could feel a slowly rising panic as her aunt’s condition worsened. They were alone in a foreign land in which they were not able to speak the language fluently. If she had to speak to a doctor in German, she wondered if she could manage.

They stopped for a few days in Düsseldorf in Königreich in the German Federation, when Eleanor could stand no more and decided to confront Aunt Sophronia and convince her that it was time to return home.

“Aunt Sophronia, are you awake?” There was no answer.

“Aunt Sophronia?” Perhaps she had already left the room for the water closet. Eleanor eased the door open and peered in. Her aunt was still in bed, but a rasping, grating sound greeted her ears. Her aunt began to cough. She ran to her side. Trying to ease the coughing, Eleanor propped her aunt up in bed and handed her a handkerchief, but Aunt Sophronia could not speak for a time as the rough, grating coughing spell prevented her. Finally, she turned a rheumy eye to Eleanor.

“It is nothing, child, merely a cough.” Eleanor knew better. Touching her hand to her aunt’s forehead, she knew immediately that her aunt was feverish. She could wait no longer. A doctor was sent for, and with her barely adequate German, Eleanor determined that he wanted to send her a place called Kaiserswerth, a nearby hospital. English hospitals were places where one went to die, and if her great-aunt was indeed on the eve of death, Eleanor was inclined to let her pass into the next world in a clean hotel rather than some fetid hospital.

“Our infirmary is a training school for nurses. It is quite nice. We can care for her there. Do not worry.” At least, that is what Eleanor thought the doctor said. Her German was not as advanced as her French. When her aunt could not be roused, Eleanor made the only decision she could. She would entrust her aunt to this German hospital.

The long shadows of late afternoon were already present when they arrived. The building stood atop a hill, its long, two-story exterior interrupted by another two-story building with a roof that slanted in only one direction.

“We had an English lady study nursing here. Perhaps you know her?” the doctor asked. He tried to keep up a conversation, undoubtedly, to take Eleanor’s mind off her aunt’s condition. Why he would think that all English people know all other English people was a mystery to her. She merely shook her head and turned her attention back to her aunt. The carriage stopped. They were greeted at the door by a smiling, buxom, blonde woman all dressed in white. “I am Deaconess Gertrude,” she said, pronouncing the “e” at the end of her name.

“Eleanor Sherbrooke. My great-aunt, Sophronia, *sie is wirklich krank*.” She could at least say “very ill” in German. Two similarly dressed women had already manoeuvred Aunt Sophronia into a wheeled chair and were pushing her somewhere as she drifted in and out of consciousness.

“We know. We take care of her.”

“I need to stay with her. She will be upset if she is alone in a strange place.” Eleanor spoke in English but chose her words carefully, trying not to say anything beyond what someone with a rudimentary knowledge of English would know. It was not necessary.

“Have no fear. We are very competent here. You may come with her to the ward and see what is to be done.” The deaconess took Eleanor’s hand in both of hers reassuringly and then led her down a long corridor.

This place was not at all what Eleanor expected. Freshly painted hallways, floors scrubbed clean, and beds covered with fresh linen were a welcome surprise. The entire place smelled of carbolic soap. A kind of calm hush infused the ward and worked its magic on Eleanor. Her aunt was finally readied and put to bed. Her breathing still sounded rattled and gasping, but she seemed more comfortable than in the pension.

"You are in a hospital, Aunt Sophronia. I am here with you. Do not worry." Eleanor was holding her aunt's hand as the old woman turned her head towards her and struggled to open her eyes.

"She will sleep now. Come, eat with us and we will find you a place to rest."

At first Eleanor thought to refuse, but with her aunt settled, she finally felt her own fatigue. She followed the deaconess.

They ate in a large refectory, and in contrast to silence in the hospital itself, the room reverberated with chatter. Eleanor realised she was ravenously hungry, and the food was simple and filling. As she was being shown to her room for the night, she remembered that she had not sent word home about what had transpired.

"*Ich muss….*" She stopped a moment, trying to think of the words. "*Ich muss meiner Familie einen Brief schrieben.*" She made the motions of writing a letter.

"*Sehr gut.*" The young woman showed her into a room so simply furnished, it resembled a monk's cell. Paper, pen and ink, and the ubiquitous Bible were neatly arranged on a small table. The doctor must have arranged for their belongings to be brought here, for her and Aunt Sophronia's cases were sitting in the corner. The young deaconess left her, and for the first time, Eleanor let herself give way to the panic she felt. She was alone in a foreign country. Her aunt was ill and might die. No one knew where she was or could come to her aid. She breathed deeply to calm herself. There was no use in letting circumstances overwhelm her. Aunt Sophronia was depending on her, and for the moment, they were safe and well taken care of. Tomorrow, she would try to find a telegraph office or a post office and send word home.

***

In the days that followed, Aunt Sophronia rarely regained consciousness, and the doctor was adamant that she not be moved. Eleanor had to agree. For the foreseeable future, they were residents of the hospital and nursing school.

Since there was little for her to do for her aunt, Eleanor decided to make herself useful. She spoke to Deaconess Gertrude and offered herself as a volunteer. It would fill her days and provide her escape from her thoughts. The Deaconess agreed.

At first, the work seemed odious to Eleanor. There was much cleaning and emptying of pans and basins. This was work usually left to servants in her household, and every household she knew, but she did put herself in this position, and she would see it through. As she observed and learned, however, she was entrusted with actual nursing duties such as dispensing medicine and treating wounds.

One morning, a woodcutter was brought in with a fiendish gash to his lower leg. Eleanor's German was gradually improving, and she understood that a slight distraction led him to misaim his axe. She was to assist the physician in stitching the wound back together. She had to admit that merely looking at the gash gave her a chill and bile rose in her throat, but she resolved to steel herself. After all, if she was to become a doctor, such tasks would be expected of her.

As she helped the poor man up onto a long, reclining leather chair covered in linen, he let out a scream.

"Hold still, *Herr* Bruckner, or we shall stitch you to the bed coverings," Dr Wagner said as he and Eleanor got the man settled. The wound was still bleeding profusely. "Do not look at the wound," he advised, and *Herr* Bruckner looked from the doctor to Eleanor and then directed his gaze to the ceiling. "We will give him some chloroform. It will help us as well as him. Here, you do it."

Eleanor had never administered chloroform in her life. She shook her head rapidly. "I do not know how. I could not—"

"Nonsense. It is easy. I will show you." He opened a small, brown bottle and placed a few drops on a gauze mask. "Here, quickly. Put the mask over his face. Take care that you do not breathe it yourself."

Herr Bruckner did not resist, and she did as instructed. He took a deep breath and then another and slumped back.

"All right now, we have to work quickly." He took the mask from Eleanor's grasp. With the doctor's help, she lifted *Herr* Bruckner's leg over a long basin and poured water over the wound. The bone was exposed beneath the slashed muscle. "Here, hold his leg together while I stitch."

Eleanor took hold of the two chunks of flesh that used to be *Herr* Bruckner's calf muscle and watched with fascination as the doctor deftly knotted a white layer above the muscle in several places, and then went back to stitch the skin. Eleanor forgot her early discomfort and was fascinated. As he neared the end of his task, Dr Wagner looked up.

"Do you want to try? I will show you." How extraordinary. She could not pass up this opportunity. Eleanor nodded. She would learn how to stitch a wound.

With the doctor's careful guidance and explanations, she made the final three stitches in the woodcutter's leg. Rinsing the blood away once more, she sat back to admire her work. When she looked at the doctor, he was smiling. He took her by the hand. "Well done, Miss Sherbrooke. You could be a surgical nurse, I think. I will leave you to clean him up and bandage him. I will call for an orderly to take him to bed."

Eleanor stood and went to a clean basin to wash the blood from her hands. She returned to *Herr* Bruckner and slowly began to bandage his leg from the ankle, taking care not to make the bindings too tight. Before finishing near his knee, she stopped to admire her needlework.

She, Eleanor Sherbrooke, delivered chloroform to a patient. She, Eleanor Sherbrooke, stitched a man's leg. This was, by far, the most satisfying day of her life.

***

"Ah, Lieutenant, so good to see you again. Julia will be down momentarily." Mrs Sherbrooke attended to her needlework, as she usually did during his visits. The time was growing short, and Wentworth did not know how much longer he would be on these shores. He had been encouraged by his fellow officers to take some time at home before it was impossible to do so. He was suspicious, however, that they encouraged his trip because he was making the rest of them look slovenly by his constant drilling of his men. He stood awkwardly for a moment until she looked up at him again. "Do sit down, Lieutenant."

He sat and fidgeted with his coat, trying to retrieve a letter he had written to Eleanor. If there was one thing he disliked, it was writing letters. He felt, though, that he owed Eleanor some sort of explanation or something, and therefore he sat down and forced himself to write. Whilst he was thus engaged, he remembered why he hated it so much. It was difficult to gauge exactly what to say when one did not have the other person's reaction. Still, he did it for good or ill and he would deliver it now.

Mrs Sherbrooke looked up at him. "Is there something I can do for you, Lieutenant?" He smiled and brought forth the letter and handed it to her. "A letter? For our Eleanor? It is a shame you did not bring it yesterday. Her father could have delivered it to her himself. Now, I am afraid it is too late.

"Oh?" He was confused.

She adjusted her pince-nez and continued her needlework without looking up at him. "My Aunt Sophronia was taken ill on their trip. Eleanor fears the worst now and is marooned with her at a German hospital somewhere near Düsseldorf. Her father has gone to fetch them."

Oddly, he felt an acute desire at that moment to ride to Eleanor's rescue. "How long ago did Colonel Sherbrooke leave?"

"He took the four o'clock train to Dover yesterday afternoon. He should be across the channel by now."

It was too long ago for him to follow. Why should he follow? He would speak to Eleanor when she arrived home. Why did he bother with the effort of writing?

"Did she send a letter or a telegram? How did you know of her distress?"

"Indeed, she did send a telegram. Her father has taken it." Mrs Sherbrooke put down her needlework and removed her glasses. She looked about and then got up and went directly to the small secretary near the window. "I do believe I have one of her letters here if you would like to see it."

"Yes, very much." He was on his feet now. She retrieved it and handed it to him. It was dated nearly a month previous.

Dear Mama and Papa,

I will dispense the pleasantries and get right to the point, since I have little time to write. That sounded so much like Eleanor, he had to smile.

Aunt Sophronia is quite ill with pneumonia and in hospital here in Kaiserswerth, a nursing school near Düsseldorf . Her illness proved too much for me, so I followed Dr Wagner's advice and had her brought to hospital. The place is clean and well run and she is being cared for by the Lutheran Deaconesses. Many who care for her are nursing students.

Since she does not need me by her bedside every waking moment, the sisters here have been training me in nursing skills. I find their methods practical and effective and am learning much during my stay. It is good to be useful. Even Dr Wagner has let me assist him in surgery.

None of us are sure how Aunt Sophronia will fare. She is advanced in age and this disease is pernicious and cruel. The doctor is adamant that she not be moved until she improves, so I will remain here with her and let you know when we are able to travel again. Rest assured that all is being done for her that is humanly possible and that I am safe among these kind people.

Your loving daughter,
Eleanor

So, Eleanor did not mention him. No doubt, she had forgotten him already, and it was just as well. He handed the letter back to Mrs Sherbrooke. “And you say you received a telegram from her last night?”

Before she could answer, Julia entered the drawing room. “And what have you two been discussing?” She wore a light blue frock and her hair was down, with long ringlets framing her face. She looked a vision, as always.

“We were reading Eleanor’s letter.”

Julia raised her eyebrows. “Eleanor’s letter?”

“Yes, of course, my dear. The one that told us of poor Aunt Sophronia’s indisposition.”

“Oh, of course. It was so distressing to hear of Aunt Sophronia’s troubles.”

Wentworth studied her. Something had disturbed the atmosphere in the room, but he could not determine what it was. “Are you not concerned for your sister’s welfare?”

Julia looked at him wide-eyed. “Oh, Lieutenant Wentworth. We, in this family, have learned never to worry about Eleanor. She needs no one, and certainly not a man’s protection.”

"Your father thinks otherwise." Mrs Sherbrooke shot an annoyed glance at her daughter.

"Father is doing his duty, as he always does. As you read, Eleanor is quite happy learning nursing, of all things. It is so beneath her station. She cares not what others think of her. She never has." Without so much as a breath between thoughts, she turned to her mother. "Mama, would you like to move to the garden? The weather is so lovely today, perhaps the lieutenant would like a stroll. Would you, Lieutenant?"

It was a lovely day, and he was here with a lovely woman. "Yes, thank you, Miss Sherbrooke. I would like that very much." As he stood, his letter to Eleanor brushed against his skin from its place in his breast pocket. Then Julia beckoned to him. With a spring in his step, he joined her in the garden.

***

By the time Colonel Sherbrooke arrived in Kaiserswerth, Aunt Sophronia's suffering was over. The pneumonia, once it had taken hold, was not to be discouraged, and one night, with Eleanor by her bedside, she breathed her last. They had been at the hospital for nearly a month. In that time, Eleanor woke each morning with a renewed sense of purpose. It astonished her that her life had taken such an abrupt turn in so unexpected a direction.

Eleanor wanted to stay on in Kaiserswerth and complete her nursing studies, but her father was adamant. She was to come home at once and abandon this unsuitable vocation. As they sat in the first-class compartment waiting for the departure of the Paris train, her father broached the subject again.

"Only the lowliest women, the drunks, and the poor with no education work as nurses in hospitals. Why ever do you want to do something so unsuitable?"

Eleanor sat with her arms crossed, staring at her own reflection in the windowpane. "The women I met, the deaconesses, were anything but unsuitable. They were dedicated, efficient, kind. You were not there. You did not see how they looked after Aunt Sophronia."

"So, you are thinking of taking holy orders, then, and becoming a nursing sister? Perhaps you will become a Lutheran also."

Eleanor sighed and turned to look at her father. Why was he being deliberately obtuse? “No, of course not. I am just trying to make you see that your opinion of nurses and nursing is misguided. I wish you had let me stay.”

“I will not have you living in a foreign country alone and unprotected.”

“And who are you protecting me from now, Father? The good sisters?”

Now it was his turn to cross his arms and look out of the window. The subject was not brought up again.

***

The London Season was in full flower, but now the city was abuzz with the anticipation of war with Russia. There was a frenzy of social activity among the well born, as no one knew when their gallant officers would be called upon to embark for the Black Sea. Anyone in uniform was especially sought after at balls and dinners. It was as if they were providing a purpose for the entire nation.

During the previous week, Wentworth had travelled back to Sussex to complete his men’s training. As they galloped, lances down, to meet the sawdust dummies and spilled their wooden entrails on the ground, he arrived at an idea. During the next training, when they charged, and their lances met their inanimate foes, blood and gore splattered every man and dripped into the dust. The horses wheeled; the men cried out. He had the dummies filled with animal entrails so that the men would have a taste of what it was like to do battle. The bugle sounded retreat.

When they reached the opposite end of the training ground, Wentworth had his troop in formation. He faced them. “That is what warfare is about, gentlemen. It is the spilling of the blood of our enemies. Be prepared for it.” He raised his bloodied lance above his head. “Death or Glory, boys!”

The all shouted in unison. “Death or Glory.”

Now, again he was in another stuffy ballroom, awaiting what? Although he had only known her a scant six weeks, he was encouraged on all sides to marry the lovely Julia. Did he love her? Most would say that it did not matter. Love would come during marriage, or it would not. He could not deny that he found her desirable. Every man who ever met her found her desirable. They also looked well together, as if made for each other.

Julia's arrival was marked by heads turning on her entrance. She wore a gown of midnight blue, cut to expose her exquisite neck, and it just capped her shoulders. She crossed the ballroom to Wentworth at once. He filled in her dance card for all the Le Lanciers and waltzes for the evening. He was determined that no other man would hold her in his arms.

After she and Lieutenant Wentworth finished the first waltz, she asked for him to bring her refreshment on the terrace. He found her at the bottom of the steps leading to the garden.

"Thank you, kind sir." She took the drink from his hand and fluttered her eyes. Taking her fan from the small velvet bag she had at her wrist, she fluttered it before her face. The signal she sent could not be mistaken. She wanted him.

He took a long draught of his drink and set the glass upon the balustrade. He did not speak. She seemed to glow in the moonlight with an unearthly luminescence. Was it his desire for her that made her look so, or was it too much champagne?

"Shall we take a stroll through the garden?" She stared at him unblinkingly, her lips slightly parted.

"Unchaperoned?" he asked.

"Are you afraid of the scandal, Lieutenant?"

He did not answer but took her arm and entered the maze.

It was well past three in the morning as Lieutenant Wentworth loped home on Merlin's back, trying mightily to clear his head. When he and Julia entered the labyrinth, they were quite alone by his reckoning. Of course, his head was swimming with champagne, and the moonlight lay so softly upon Julia's shoulders that it was all he could do to contain himself. She stood so close to him and the soft puffs of her breath in his ear sent a shiver down his spine. She softly whispered endearments, her finger tracing his hand. Her touch bubbled through his body in time with the champagne.

"You know you want to kiss me, Joshua. Kiss me." Calling him by his Christian name acted like an aphrodisiac. He moved his head ever so slightly, and her lips were upon his. After that, he was all desire. His kisses were furious then, travelling down her neck and to those temptingly bare shoulders.

He heard her gasp, but the sound seemed far away. Then he realised it was not she who was gasping, but onlookers, catching them in this most indecent act. It was then that Julia fled from him. Were there tears? He could not remember. He ran after her, calling her name, but did not find her again. Many eyes were upon him as he entered the ballroom. He excused himself and took his leave. And now he was nearly home, Merlin carrying him. He knew what he must do. As an officer and a gentleman, he knew.

***

Julia awoke late the next morning and smiled, stretching her arms over her head. The plan she set in motion worked perfectly. Lieutenant Wentworth would not allow her to be ruined by scandal. She had no doubt in her mind he would be calling upon her by this afternoon. It was a shame her father was away with Eleanor.

"Julia, you do look well this morning." Her mother was buttering her toast at breakfast.

"I feel well, Mama. I do think this will be a day to remember."

Her mother's eyebrows arched. "Oh, really, dear? I doubt Eleanor will be back so soon."

"I am not speaking of Eleanor, Mama. I am speaking of me. I do believe, before too long, I will be engaged to be married."

Her mother's butter knife clattered to the plate. "What's this? To whom?"

Julia shook the ringlets that framed her face. "To Lieutenant Wentworth, of course. Who else?"

"Has he asked you?"

"He will."

"And how do you know that?"

"I know it because I know him. He is a gentleman and will do anything to preserve a lady's honour."

Her mother did not speak for a moment and then shook her head. "Oh, Julia. What have you done?"

Julia pushed herself from the table and went to the sideboard to partake of some eggs. "I did what had to be done, Mama. The men will soon be leaving for war, and I had to at least secure his promise if not the wedding." She sat down again and took a sip of tea.

"You have not spoken of love between you. Do you love him, Julia?"

Julia sighed dramatically. "I believe he loves me, and I am fond of him. He is awfully handsome, don't you think so, Mama?"

"But, Julia—"

"But nothing." Julia's voice rose in pitch and volume. "How often have you spoken to me of making a suitable match? You said yourself that a woman must find security in a good marriage. That is exactly what I am doing."

For a moment, her mother said nothing. Julia stole a glance at her and then deliberately concentrated on her breakfast, not meeting her eye. Her mother was not put off.

"What if he is killed, Julia? What then?"

Julia deliberately set down her knife and fork and looked directly at her mother. "I will have to marry him before he goes to war. If he is killed, then I will be his widow and inherit his share. If he survives, we will live a long and happy life together. Either way, I am decided." She rose from the table and pushed open the French doors of the breakfast room with deliberate force. Turning back to her mother with a dramatic flair, she said, "The next time you see him, Mama, he will be my intended."

Chapter 4

"Welcome home, dear Eleanor." Her mother, dressed in black, took her hands in hers and kissed her upon her cheek. "Was it awfully hard for you, dear? Come. Rid yourself of your bonnet and we will have tea."

Eleanor noticed her mother's eyes brimming with unshed tears. Was it the memory of her Aunt Sophronia that she saw there, or her own homecoming? Her mother's aunt was the last of her generation, and she was sure her mother grieved for her. It was an imperfect grief, however, since there was nothing with which to mark it. No wake, no funeral, nothing. Just a prodigal daughter returning.

"Was the journey tedious? Your father looks exhausted." Eleanor could not fathom why. When he was not eating or arguing with her, he was dozing in his seat.

Her father yawned. "That it was, my dear, long and tedious. Yet here we are."

They adjourned to the morning room where tea and scones were laid out. Eleanor had not said anything as to her experience in Kaiserswerth. It was tragedy marked by transformation. She was sorry for her great-aunt's death, to be sure. She was her aunt's confidant in those last weeks and became not only her niece but her friend.

The real wonder of the experience, though, was her eyes opening to an avenue in which she could realise her purpose in life. She knew it was beneath her station to desire this particular purpose, but she felt it was her destiny now. The sisters of Kaiserswerth were excellent nursing teachers. Eleanor wanted so much to tell her mother all her thoughts, but when she looked at her, her mother had such a weary expression on her face that Eleanor did not have the heart to begin what was surely to be a battle of epic proportions.

“Now, my dears, refresh yourselves and have a rest. We are having a guest for dinner this evening at Julia’s request. It is your mutual friend, Lieutenant Wentworth.”

Eleanor’s teacup clattered into the saucer and nearly upset itself. Lieutenant Wentworth. Why was her heart pounding at the sound of his name? The man abandoned her when she needed him most. No, that was not fair. He did not write to her, but then, excepting the first letter, she did not write to him either.

“Are you all right, Eleanor? This experience must have been an awful strain on your constitution. Perhaps we should tell the lieutenant to come another time.”

“No!” Eleanor’s answer came a little too suddenly and loudly. “That is to say… I am sure I will be myself by this evening. No need to change your plans, Mother. I am sure I will be all right.”

A few hours later, when Eleanor dressed for dinner, she gazed at herself in the mirror. Her time in Kaiserswerth had done her good. Despite the family tragedy, there was a change in her aspect for the better. Some of that change might have been attributed to that good and copious German food she was plied with every night. Her figure looked a little fuller… her cheeks a little rosier. She hoped Lieutenant Wentworth would notice. Perhaps all was not lost. Perhaps they could begin again.

She wanted to see Lieutenant Wentworth, especially tonight, for she suspected it might be the last time for a long while. The French papers she read on the train home were full of talk of a war with Russia. Troops were amassing in the land of their old enemy, France, and General Raglan, who fought against Napoleon, was ready to set sail from England. She knew Joshua would be among those who would fight. Whether he thought of her or not, she thought of him, and she wanted to see him once more before he left.

***

Lieutenant Joshua Griffiths Wentworth was bouncing on his heels before the Sherbrookes’ door. As he entered the foyer, Julia ran to greet him. She looked stunningly beautiful as always. Her skirt and bodice were a champagne colour, nearly matching her skin tone. It gave her a salacious look, as one could not tell exactly where the dress left off and her skin began. He had to admit that he was very much attracted to her, and even felt flattered that one so spectacular as she would set her sights on him. She took both of his hands in hers. From this gesture, he knew that she assumed an understanding between them. It would not be long before he must put an end to the whispering he caused from that night in the garden. Soon, he would ask for her hand.

He squeezed her hands for a moment and then began to remove his gloves when the soft crackling of skirts rustled above him.

There, on the landing, stood Eleanor.

He swallowed hard and removed his hat and handed it to Baxter without taking his eyes off Eleanor. He was suddenly aware that Julia was speaking.

"Oh, Eleanor, look. Lieutenant Wentworth is here."

"Hello, Lieutenant," Eleanor said from the landing on the staircase above them. As Eleanor began to descend the staircase, Wentworth, on an impulse, took the stairs two at a time to meet her.

"Eleanor…" He paused as he reached her and leaned upon the bannister. His gaze locked with hers and his smile widened almost to a grin. "Eleanor, how grand to see you." Looking her up and down from head to toe, he added, "How well you look." He offered her his arm. She took it lightly. As they reached the ground level, Eleanor discreetly removed her hand from his arm. Julia, at the same time, slipped her arm proprietarily in his.

"Eleanor has just returned from Dusseldorf this morning, Lieutenant." Although Julia had a grip on his arm, Joshua Wentworth did not take his eyes from Eleanor's.

"I am surprised that you did not write and tell me you were coming," he said pointedly.

Eleanor opened her mouth to speak, but before she could reply, Julia interrupted. "Come along. Mother and Father await with dinner."

***

It was not her imagination. Lieutenant Wentworth was genuinely happy to see her. She felt light and almost giddy sitting here with him after so many weeks. How she longed to tell him of her experiences at the nursing school, how she found a talent within herself, and a practical way to learn and practice medicine.

During Julia's charming and amusing patter, which Eleanor had heard variation of time and time again, she would steal a glance at Lieutenant Wentworth. Although their dining room was lit with the gas lights on the wall sconces, the flickering of the candlelight on the table threw his jawline into relief when he laughed, or it highlighted the creases near his eyes when he smiled. From time to time, he would discover her looking at him and once even winked. As they got up from the table to take coffee in the parlour, Julia addressed their father.

"Papa, I know Lieutenant Wentworth has not spoken to you yet, but I really cannot contain myself any longer." She threw a meaningful glance at Lieutenant Wentworth, who raised his eyebrows, but said nothing.

"For goodness sake, Julia, speak plainly," said her father gruffly.

Julia paused dramatically, looking at each of them in turn, but Eleanor noticed that Julia's glance did not rest on her for long. "Mama, Papa, Eleanor… Lieutenant Wentworth and I are engaged to be married."

Was it Eleanor's imagination, or did Lieutenant Wentworth give a visible start at the announcement? For her part, Eleanor felt as if everything she had just consumed for dinner was about to make a reappearance. The shock struck her with such force that she grasped the edge of the table to steady herself. Why did he flirt with her so brazenly the last few hours if he was already betrothed to her sister? She must have misjudged him from the beginning. He was just like all the others. She was only an object of fun and amusement.

The dining room became deadly silent for a moment, and then, through the blood thundering in her ears, Eleanor heard her mother's voice. "Oh, Julia, Lieutenant Wentworth, how very fine. Julia…." Her mother adopted a mock-scolding tone. "You should not have kept such a secret from us."

"Do we have your consent, Papa?" Julia now had one hand on Lieutenant Wentworth's arm and one on her father's. The old colonel snuffled in his moustache for a moment and then looked Wentworth up and down. "Are you asking for my daughter's hand, Lieutenant?"

Wentworth hesitated for a moment, his face working. "I do apologise for my hesitation, sir. I am afraid I had no idea that Julia was going to bring up this subject tonight… so soon."

"Well, you are a fine young man, and I give you my blessing."

Julia released Wentworth's arm and flew at her father, throwing her arms around his neck and kissing his cheek. "Oh, thank you, thank you, Papa."

"Shall we open a bottle of champagne to celebrate?" Mrs Sherbrooke no sooner had the words out of her mouth as her hand was upon the bell pull, summoning the servants.

Eleanor could abide the scene no longer. "No champagne for me, Mama. I am rather tired." She turned to look at Julia and then Lieutenant Wentworth. "Congratulations to both of you. I hope you will be very happy." She wanted to run from the room, to flee, but forced herself to walk slowly and deliberately out, not glancing at all in Joshua Wentworth's direction. As soon as she slid the pocket doors of the dining room shut behind her, the tears that mercifully merely shone in her eyes began to course down her cheeks. As she lifted her skirt slightly so that she could run up the stairs, the same doors swished open, and then closed again.

"Eleanor." It was Joshua Wentworth. She dared not turn and look at him. "Eleanor, stop."

She clutched the bannister and froze. Did she want to hear what he had to say? No, absolutely she did not. However, she would force herself to hear it. Hear how he loved Julia and wanted to make a life for her. How sorry he was that he hurt her so. Pity. Yet again, pity. Quickly removing her handkerchief from her sleeve, she dabbed her eyes and turned to face him.

"Lieutenant Wentworth…" Her voice broke slightly as she spoke his name.

"Eleanor, let me explain." He did not follow her up the stairs, but stood, his hand on the newel post, looking up at her.

She shut her eyes then and sighed. "What is there to explain? Whilst I was away, you fell in love with Julia. Everyone falls in love with Julia." She could not contain the bitterness in her voice. She paused a moment to gather her thoughts. Yes, she would ask him.

"Why did you not write?" They both said the words simultaneously as if rehearsed in a play. She looked at him in surprise.

Before either of them could speak, the doors slid open and they both turned to look at a smiling and exultant Julia. Neither said a word. Julia looked from one to the other, her smile fading momentarily but then reappearing again in a triumphant curl. “Whatever are you two talking about?” she said airily. Then, turning her attention to Lieutenant Wentworth, she again took his arm. “Come along, darling, Papa has opened the champagne.” She lifted her eyes to the figure on the stairwell. “Coming, Eleanor?” Eleanor turned on the staircase and scurried to the safety of her room.

***

“Go back to bed.” The stable boy at his father’s house groggily rose from his bed in the barn to attend to Merlin. Wentworth was not the least bit sleepy and wanted to brush his horse down himself. In fact, his brain roiled with discontent. He had ridden his poor steed at a faster pace than necessary, and now the beast was wet with sweat. After removing his saddle and harness, Wentworth began earnestly brushing his horse.

The last thing on God’s earth he wanted to do was hurt Eleanor, but that was exactly what transpired. Julia’s impulsiveness was the cause. Although it was a foregone conclusion, she should have waited to announce their engagement at least until he asked her. Then, he could have broken the news more gently to Eleanor. The evening was one unmitigated disaster.

“I suppose I will have to buy a ring now that all is settled.”

The horse snorted, and Wentworth continued brushing. Yet his thoughts again turned to Eleanor. Did he love her? How could a man love two women at once? No, there could be no vacillating now. Julia and he would be married. They had better do it soon. The impending war would soon change things for him forever. He resolved to think no more about it until the morning.

***

When Eleanor arrived at her bedroom, she did not retire. Her mind was so agitated that she knew sleep would not come. She sat for a long time staring into the fire. The evening that had started so clear and starry had turned to rain that pattered disconsolately against the windowpane. The clock chimed eleven, and she began to ready herself for bed, when a knock came at the door.

"Eleanor. Eleanor, are you awake?" Julia whispered. Eleanor quickly wiped away the tears that sprung to her eyes once again.

"I am quite tired, Julia. Could you wait until morning?"

There was a moment of silence. "No, Eleanor. I cannot wait. Open the door, please."

Julia entered, but Eleanor could not bring herself to look at her. She was afraid she might betray her own emotions to her sister. "I just wanted to see if you were all right, Eleanor. You behaved so strangely after dinner."

"Oh, Julia…" Did her sister genuinely not understand her distress? If she did not, Eleanor was not about to try to explain it to her. Then a thought suddenly occurred to her.

"Why did he say that I didn't write? I left a letter for him by the door. Baxter should have posted it. Surely, you saw it there?"

Julia squinted her eyes and then slowly shook her head. "I don't remember a letter there, Eleanor, but then, it was quite some time ago." Her sister's expression betrayed nothing. Julia must practice before a mirror to be able to appear so guileless. No, that was unkind. "Does it matter now? Are you not happy for me?" Julia peered at her.

She was right. What did it matter now? Was she happy for her? How could Eleanor tell her sister that she harboured affection for her fiancé? That thoughts of him made her time in Germany seem less lonely? How, from that first conversation, she was completely enamoured of him? Eleanor knew she could not confide any of these thoughts to her. Instead she said, "Of course, I am, Julia. I wish you all the happiness in the world."

***

"Ooh, that Julia. I could strangle her." Cordelia was quite red in the face. They sat head-to-head in Eleanor's bedroom. "I want you to know I did my best for you, Eleanor. Whenever she was invited to ours, I never sat her by Lieutenant Wentworth."

Eleanor had to smile at her friend. Cordelia always was fiercely loyal, and Eleanor appreciated it more than she could say. "There was nothing you could do, Cordelia. I believe it was written in the stars. Who can resist Julia?"

"I can, that's for certain." Cordelia crossed her arms and made such a face that Eleanor had to laugh. "What will you do now? The London Season is still upon us and spring is in the air. You must come with me to the Sheridans' this weekend. They are giving a lovely party and—"

"No, thank you, Cordelia. I don't think I am ready to endure any parties just now." Cordelia's sympathetic expression made her feel quite emotional, so she averted her eyes.

"Well, perhaps not, but you need to do something. Julia will be flouncing about, planning her engagement party and her wedding. Surely, that will be intolerable."

Eleanor hesitated for a moment, then changed the subject. "May I show you something?" When Cordelia nodded, Eleanor left her seat by the fire and opened the drawer of her writing secretary. She retrieved a few papers and set them before Cordelia.

"Whatever is all this?"

"Letters of recommendation."

Cordelia looked up in shock. "Oh, Eleanor, you are not thinking of becoming a governess?"

Eleanor laughed at the suggestion. "Of course not. What a notion, Cordelia. I want to become a nurse."

Cordelia looked at her friend and then down at the papers in her lap. She studied them for a time, turning each one over carefully. "These are from that hospital where you were with your Aunt Sophronia. You're serious, Eleanor."

"I am. I have been ever since I spent time there. I have a talent for nursing, Cordelia. I believe I truly do."

Cordelia shook her head. "Eleanor, if you told me you were considering being shot out of a cannon, you could not have shocked me more. Nurses, Eleanor… They are—"

"I know what their reputation is. That is why I need your help. I have found a place to work that I believe my father will allow me to go. It is here in London."

"But, nursing men, Eleanor. It is not suitable."

"This hospital admits only women and is run by a female superintendent."

A look of determination came over Cordelia's face. She rose to her feet. "On to the desk, my friend. Let us write a letter of introduction. We can surprise your parents once the deed is done."

***

The hansom cab pulled up in front of the Institution for Sick Gentlewomen in Distressed Circumstances in Cavendish Square just before nine o'clock in the morning. Eleanor hoped to be home before her parents or Julia noticed that she was missing but left a short note just in case. Her mother would be scandalised to know that she rode in a carriage without a chaperone, but it could not be helped.

Cordelia was right. If Julia could create her own destiny, then she could also. Eleanor learned of this institution from the sisters at Kaiserswerth. They informed her that the other English lady who had studied with them had learnt her lessons so well that she now was an administrator of a hospital in London. It was an accomplishment that Eleanor admired. Now she would apply for a position in that very same hospital. There certainly was nothing to keep her at home.

Once she was admitted to the hospital office, her heart pounded. What if this superintendent did not think her qualified? How would she make her case? She had little time to ruminate as the office door opened and she rose to her feet to greet her inquisitor. The superintendent walked with an upright gate and wore a modest white bonnet that revealed her centrally parted hair in front. Her skirt and bodice were equally plain. The woman, however modestly dressed, had the air of someone who was in charge. She looked Eleanor squarely in the eye before taking a seat behind her desk. Immediately, she took up the letters and documents Eleanor sent ahead of her.

"So, Miss Sherbrooke, you are interested in working as a nurse. I see you have a good education and have done much reading." The superintendent did not look up.

"Yes, miss."

"It says here you had nursing experience at Kaiserswerth. You say you were there for…"

"I was there for over a month. You see my great-aunt—"

"Yes, yes, yes." She waved her hand dismissively and then looked directly at Eleanor. "A month of training does not a nurse's certificate make, Miss Sherbrooke."

"No, I realise that, but I am very eager to continue working and learning. I have done extensive reading, and although I was not enrolled as a nursing student per se at Kaiserswerth, I did learn a great deal. The sisters there taught me how to do most of the duties required. I was even a pupil of Dr Wagner from time to time."

Eleanor could not tell if this woman was listening or not. She seemed to pore over the meagre letters of introduction and other papers from the good deaconesses. Finally, she looked up in Eleanor's direction.

"Does your family approve of your work here?"

Ah, therein lay the rub. She could lie, but if there were objections at home or if her father forbad her from engaging in this work, there would be no point in deception. "I have not broached the subject yet. I thought I would see if there was any need to do so."

For the first time, the woman smiled. "I see. You anticipate that there might be some objection to nursing. My family was not overjoyed at my choice either. They thought it the work of slatterns, drunkards, and… dollymops…." Eleanor swallowed at the word "dollymops." For a woman to use such an expression… "Do I shock you, Miss Sherbrooke?"

"No, miss…. Yes, miss. I will endeavour not to be shocked."

The superintendent smiled again. "I am inclined to accept you, Miss Sherbrooke, if only on the grounds that you studied nursing where I did at Kaiserswerth and I am well aware of the quality of their training. I will give you a month. If you satisfy, then you may consider yourself employed here." She stood and offered Eleanor her hand. She took it.

"Do speak to your people. If I do not see you again, I will know what happened."

"You will see me again; of that you can be sure. Thank you so much."

The superintendent showed Eleanor to the door. As she opened it, she handed Eleanor her calling card.

"Please, give this to your parents and tell them they may visit at any time." She smiled warmly.

Eleanor stood for a moment in the hallway, and then gave a little jump and clasped her hands together in sheer exuberance. Finally, she would be able to enter the field of medicine. She looked once more at the calling card in her hand before she secreted it in her purse. It was embossed with a tiny bird and next to it was written the superintendent's name: Florence Nightingale.

***

Armed with an offer of employment, Eleanor informed her mother and father in no uncertain terms that she had decided to become a nurse. She was pleasantly surprised at how easily her parents allowed it. After disappearing for a morning on her own to visit Miss Nightingale, she surmised they were so relieved that she came home at all, they were willing to mollify her with their permission. Perhaps her mother suspected her infatuation with her sister's fiancé and was happy for an excuse to have her engaged elsewhere. During the week, Eleanor stayed at the hospital and, at her parents' insistence, came home on Sundays and sometimes even a day earlier. This nursing business did create a bit of a scandal, but fortunately, the impending war was uppermost in everyone's minds, and her minor adventures did not hold the attention of the gossips too long.

Lieutenant Wentworth visited frequently at the Sherbrookes' now, and sometimes Eleanor would find him and Julia in intimate discussion over the plans for their impending nuptials. She tried mightily to avoid any time in which she would see Lieutenant Wentworth, for despite her resolution not to break her heart over him or envy her sister, seeing them together still distressed her greatly.

Spring was affording them some lovely weather: the delphiniums and cornflowers were already in bloom. Eleanor, Julia, and Lieutenant Wentworth were in the townhouse garden together. Eleanor ruminated on the fact that, unwittingly, Aunt Sophronia bequeathed her title of "chaperone" to her. She tried to make an exit, intending to leave the engaged couple together, but the lieutenant would not hear of it. Was he being deliberately cruel to her, or was he blissfully unaware of the effect he had on her? In an effort to remain unobtrusive, she set up an easel to paint. It was not her strength, but it did command her attention, which was a relief.

"The war should only last a few months, Julia. You needn't worry. By the time the 17th arrives, the whole blasted thing might be over and done, though I hope not." Lieutenant Wentworth took a sip of his gin and tonic and cast a glance at his fiancé.

"Nevertheless, Joshua, I believe we should have our engagement party as soon as possible. You have no idea what awaits you in the… what was it called again?"

"The Crimea, dearest. The Crimea."

Eleanor could not look at them, nor long endure Julia's pretence of ignorance. How could she keep that façade up, day after day? Eleanor contrived to make some excuse and find shelter in the house. After all, as an engaged couple, her sister and the lieutenant could now spend time alone with one another. The servants were about the house in any case.

"You know, you could resign your commission and avoid the entire thing altogether. Your father would welcome you into the business, I am sure of it."

"Do not *ever* mention such a thing again," Wentworth said with such force that it caused Eleanor to turn and look at him. At that exact moment, a crackling sound brought the lieutenant to his feet, broken glass falling from his open palm and blood dripping upon the table.

"Oh." Eleanor ran to him immediately.

Letting the crumpled drinking glass fall from his hand, he calmly remarked, "Oh dear. How stupid of me."

"I think I shall faint." Julia was fanning herself and rolling her eyes.

Eleanor could not contain her irritation at the display. "For heaven's sake, Julia. Run into the house and fetch one of the servants. Bring water, towels, and a basin…" Julia did as she was told in haste. Eleanor called after her, "And bring my sewing basket." The lieutenant already had his handkerchief out and was about to apply it to the wound. "Stop." Eleanor took the cloth from him. "There may still be glass in your hand, and you will only make it worse. Please, sit down, Lieutenant. I will attend to it." Eleanor gently opened his fingers and inspected the wound. Rather deep cuts incised his palm and the blood flowed copiously. One of the servants ran out, probably at Julia's behest, with a basin and some water. All the time, Eleanor was holding Wentworth's hand. She felt its smoothness and warmth as it lay in her own. She dared not look at him. There was only silence between them.

Eleanor placed the basin on the table and, still holding the lieutenant's hand upright, poured water over it. Some of the blood washed away immediately. "Well, there now. You do not seem to have any glass in your hand, Lieutenant." Eleanor looked up and saw Julia standing some feet away, clutching her sewing basket. "Julia, bring my needle and thread here forthwith." Julia scurried over, averted her eyes, and dropped the sewing basket in Eleanor's lap. She then retreated to a distance, clutching her handkerchief and pressing it to her lips.

Eleanor finally let go of the lieutenant and rummaged around for a suitable needle and white thread. She again took the lieutenant's hand, and with a towel on the edge of the table, laid his hand upon it. "This will hurt a little." His eyes met hers and it sent a shiver through her.

"Do what you will, Miss Sherbrooke."

Julia spoke up. "Eleanor, what do you think you are doing? Have you gone mad?"

"Certainly not. The lieutenant needs a stitch or two in his hand, and I will accommodate. It is not the first stitching I have done."

A grunt of disgust issued from her sister as she turned to Wentworth.

"Would you like me to proceed, sir?"

"I have every faith in you, Miss Sherbrooke." He gave her a playful wink.

Deftly, Eleanor began to close the deepest wounds on Lieutenant Wentworth's palm with the stitching she learned from Dr Wagner. The lieutenant held his hand still and did not flinch during her procedure. The bleeding was staunched, and, with the last of the wounds closed, Eleanor looked up from her work. "There. All finished. Now allow me to bandage your hand."

The lieutenant turned to Julia. "Come, Julia, see the marvellous job our Eleanor has done for me."

Julia shook her head vigorously. "I will not. I do not like the sight of blood one bit. It is not a sight for ladies' eyes." She turned her head away dramatically.

Wentworth looked down admiringly at his mended hand. "Then it is my good fortune that a lady in this household not only does not mind the sight of blood but is skilled as a doctor."

Eleanor proceeded to tear a few clean white cloths into a proper size for a bandage. "I certainly do not have the skill of a physician, but I am endeavouring to be a good nurse."

"And a jolly proper nurse you are." By this time, the bandage was around his hand, and he wiggled his fingers cautiously. "I should be able to hold a lance soon, is that not right, Miss Sherbrooke?"

"I think in a fortnight all should be well." He held her eyes for a long while.

It was Julia who broke the spell. "Eleanor, please have Gerard clear away that bloody water."

Eleanor looked at her sister in shock. "Julia, your language." With that, Eleanor began to giggle, and Wentworth, realising Julia's use of the word "bloody," joined her.

Julia looked confused for moment and then covered her mouth with her hand. "Oh, I did not mean… that is, I meant to say…. Oh, the two of you, having a laugh at my expense." She turned on her heel and began to walk swiftly towards the house.

The lieutenant gave Eleanor a wink, and then jumped up to follow Julia. "Oh, come along, my dear, it was all in good fun."

Eleanor watched him follow her sister as they disappeared into the house. She rejoiced that she could not see them as they embraced and perhaps as he even kissed her. These last few moments with him, the warmth of his hand, his praise of her skill, was all she would ever have of him. It was enough. It would have to be enough.

***

The British fleet had sailed more than a month previous for Varna, and Wentworth had to admit that he was anxious for Lord Cardigan to give the order for his brigade to set sail. The Heavy Brigade, including the Scots Greys and the Royals, had embarked to great fanfare in February, and here sat the Hussars and the Lancers, pawing the ground in anticipation. One of the "camp shaves," or rumours around camp, was that government had acquired two screw steamers which would cut their voyage time in half or less than the old sailing ships. He hoped that would be the case. Even as an officer, he had extraordinarily little knowledge of what the grand plan was for conquering the Crimea. In the meantime, Julia and her mother were planning an engagement party.

"I feel rather superfluous." Wentworth paced in his mother's room. He had just returned that morning from drilling his men in Sussex.

His mother laughed. "I am afraid you are, dear. This is a time for the bride and her mother. The most important day in a girl's life. You are merely an…accoutrement."

Joshua looked at his mother in shock. “Surely not. Wouldn’t be much of an engagement, or even a marriage, without me, would it?”

“Do settle somewhere, Joshua. You seem so anxious.”

He sat on the small footstool near his mother’s chair but could not alight long and sprang up again. His left fist clenched and unclenched, his right not quite healed. He noticed his mother’s eyes upon it and, realising he betrayed his anxiety to her, forced himself to stop. “Time grows short. We will receive our orders soon, and all these plans of Julia’s may come to naught.”

“I have a feeling that Julia’s arrangements are not what concern you most, my son.”

He turned to look at her, and she was possessed of that all-knowing expression he found so disconcerting. At times he did not know why he even bothered to talk to her. She already seemed to know exactly what was on his mind.

“It is war, Mother. It is my time to show what I am made of. My time to serve Queen and country. I hope I am ready for it.”

“Come here and sit with me.” She motioned to the chair opposite. He reluctantly took it. “I have every faith in you, Joshua. You should have the same in yourself. Your men are disciplined, are they not?”

“Disciplined but untested. Many are raw recruits. I do not know how they will behave under enemy fire.”

She leaned back wearily in her wingback chair. “No one knows how we will behave until the matter is at hand. I have faith you will acquit yourself bravely, my son. I pray each day that God will protect you, and that you will return to me.” She nearly did not finish, as the words seem to catch in her throat. She turned her head from him.

He rose and went to her. “Do not weep for me, Mother. I am very much alive, and soon it will be my wedding day.”

She could not speak then, but merely touched the crown of his head as she did when he was little, and then drew him into an embrace.

***

“You look tired, Eleanor.” Cordelia welcomed her friend into the morning room. Eleanor had not been able to come home for a fortnight as cholera swept through the second ward at the women's hospital.

"I am all right. You needn't worry about me." Eleanor removed her bonnet and sat down heavily, as heavily as one of her slight frame could sit.

"Cook has just baked scones. I will ring for tea, and we will restore your strength."

Eleanor leaned wearily back into the overstuffed armchair in which she was ensconced and closed her eyes.

"Perhaps you should be at home resting and not calling upon me." Eleanor opened her eyes to Cordelia's strained expression.

"I would rather not be at home just now. Julia really is too much to bear. I'm sure our dear Queen made less of a fuss over her own wedding to Prince Albert."

Cordelia had to laugh, and that made Eleanor laugh too. Cordelia's expression turned solemn again.

"Is your work very hard? You can give it up, you know."

Eleanor sat bolt upright. "Give it up? Never. I've never felt so alive in my life as I do nursing. Much of the work is taxing and even distasteful, but the rewards are more than anything I ever conceived of before. I think I was born to it."

Cordelia poured the tea and handed a cup to her friend. "And your Miss Nightingale. Is she a good mistress?"

Eleanor sighed. "She is decided in her ways and disciplined. She expects nothing less from her nurses. I do find her difficult, but one cannot argue with her results."

They sat in silence a moment, and taking advantage of the warm scones set before her, Eleanor buttered one with a satisfied air and commenced on her treat. "Oh, Cordelia, these are spectacular. We shall steal your cook."

"Many have tried, but we have always fought to the death for her."

Eleanor nearly choked at such a remark. She was suddenly overwhelmed with gratitude in having such a friend.

"All right now, tell me. When is the wedding?"

"Julia insists on a June wedding, but Lieutenant Wentworth keeps telling her he will be 'bobbing about on the Black Sea' by then. She will not listen. She thinks it is bad luck to be married in any month save June."

Cordelia shook her head. "She gets whatever she wants, does she not?"

"Perhaps not this time. Major General Cardigan and the Minister of War will not consult her, I should think. I am afraid she will miss her chance with Lieutenant Wentworth due to her stubbornness."

Cordelia's eyes narrowed and a sly smile crossed her lips. "Really, Eleanor. How afraid are you that Julia will miss her chance…really?"

Eleanor cocked her head. "Oh, Cordelia, you are wicked…" She partook of her scone once more and chewed thoughtfully. "I want them both to be happy. Genuinely, I do."

"And I wish you to be happy, dear friend." Cordelia reached out and clasped Eleanor's hand.

"I am happy. Truly, I am." She said those words and meant them, even though a part of her heart still ached for Lieutenant Wentworth.

***

It was decided that there would be no delay in the engagement party and there was much to be done. Flowers were ordered from the best florist in the city, and Colonel Sherbrooke even arranged for a marquee to be set up in the garden for guests. Both families had extensive friends and relations among the Ton and it was shaping up to be a spectacular affair.

Julia fluttered about the morning room with her mother, surrounded by bits of menus from every chef known in the city. This event would be talked about for years if Julia had anything to say about it.

"And what about Monsieur Robert, Mama? His gateau is legendary."

Mrs Sherbrooke adjusted the pince-nez on her nose and peered at the small pamphlet in Julia's grasp. "I don't know, Julia. This party is promising to be a sizeable sum. More than most people spend. I doubt your father will approve."

"Oh, but he *must*, Mama. He must. I will die if he does not."

Mrs Sherbrooke took a sip of her coffee and looked askance at her daughter. "You will not die, Julia. One does not die of the wrong sort of gateau."

"Let it not be said that we had the wrong sort of cake, Mama."

It was in the midst of these frenzied preparations that Baxter arrived with a card. Julia recognised it immediately and ran to the drawing room.

"Joshua, what is it?" Julia extended her hands towards him and he took them in his.

"It has happened, Julia. We are off to the Crimea. Cardigan has already sailed, and we are to follow."

Mrs Sherbrooke arrived in the drawing room just as Julia and Joshua broke their embrace. "You have news, Lieutenant?"

"We sail tomorrow, ma'am. Time is short."

"Ah, well. We were expecting this, were we not, Julia?" Julia searched her fiancé's face. This war became a real threat just at that moment. She never really considered it before.

"Julia?" Her mother's voice broke the spell. "Well, I will leave you two alone for a moment to say your good-byes."

The door clicked and she threw her arms around Joshua's neck. "Oh, my darling. Do be careful." His warm breath on her neck caressed her, and wondered if she would ever feel that again.

"I will be as careful as one can be at the front of the line."

She pulled back to look at him and could see his smile, but his eyes told another story. "Do not jest with me at a time like this."

"This is exactly the time to jest. It is better to jest than to weep."

Her throat tightened and her eyes filled with unexpected tears. She had wept before, many times, mostly for effect. Her body would do exactly what she asked of it. This time, however, tears coursed down her cheeks unbidden. He cupped her face in his two rough hands and brushed them away.

"Smile now, my darling. I want to remember your smile."

She threw her arms about his neck once again and held him fast. His arms encircled her waist, and after a time, he drew back and kissed her on the mouth as he did in that garden only a few weeks ago. Abruptly, he let go of her and stepped back.

"I must go. There is so little time and much to do."

She said nothing but bit her lip and nodded. As he walked to the door, she whispered, "Come back to me, Joshua."

He stopped for a moment but did not turn. The last she saw of him was his back as he shut the door behind him.

Julia let out a great wail and dropped to the floor. Her mother called out from behind the door and ran to her side. “My dear, my dear, are you all right?”

Julia covered her mouth with both her hands, tears still coursing down her cheeks. She then clutched at her mother’s sleeve. “Oh, Mama, the most awful thing has happened.” Her mother’s face was all concern. “Mama, I think I am beginning to care for him.”

***

The next morning, as Joshua descended the stairs and did his best to collect himself from his mother’s emotional farewell, he wondered if he would ever see her again. As he reached the foot of the staircase, his father called him from the study. “Joshua, is that you? A word, my boy.”

Wentworth closed his eyes and bit his bottom lip. He was not prepared to go head-to-head with his father today. Still, there was no alternative. He entered the study. His father stood by the marble fireplace, his arm resting on the mantelpiece.

“Yes, Father. What is it?” He regretted his tone immediately. He really did not feel impatient or hostile, but experience had taught him that most encounters with his father ended badly. His father’s eyebrows shot up, but he made no retort.

“Sit down, Joshua…please.”

He took a seat on the sofa and his father joined him. Mr Wentworth leaned his forearms on his legs and bowed his head.

“Is something distressing you, Father?”

His father glanced up. “Of course something is distressing me. You are going off to war.” He rose slowly and began to pace before the fireplace, his hands clasped behind him.

What an extraordinary thing to say. After all, he was in the army. It was inevitable that this day would come. “Yes, Father. I am going to war. It is what I have been preparing for all these years.”

Mr Wentworth suddenly stopped and peered at his son. “You are determined to do this, then.”

Now Joshua was on his feet. “Must we have this conversation repeatedly, Father? Really, I must go.” He began to stride towards the door.

"No, wait… wait." As Joshua turned back, his father suddenly seemed to have lost his vigour. He beckoned to him and Joshua sat down again. His father shook his head and spoke as if he was talking to himself. "I am sorry. I am making a dog's dinner of this. Your mother was so much better at talking with you boys…. I have something for you."

This was a surprise, and no doubt it showed in his face. His father reached into the pocket of his frock coat and retrieved a small box covered in blue velvet. He handed it to Joshua. He cleared his throat. "Here. Take it. For your travels."

Joshua slowly reached and took the box, staring at it for a few moments. "Thank you, Father."

"Well, open it." The sound of his father's voice so changed that Joshua had to look up at him. His father was expectant, even joyful.

Gently, Joshua opened the box. Encased inside was a very splendid-looking gold pocket watch lay in velvet. Embossed on the cover was the skull and crossbones and the ribbon reading "or glory." Death or Glory—the motto of the 17th Lancers. It suddenly became difficult for Joshua to swallow. He removed the watch and held it gingerly by the chain. "My word, Father. This is grand." He let the watch drop into his hand. It felt cool and heavy to the touch.

His father cleared his throat. "Open it, son. Read the inscription."

After flipping the cover back, he read inside. "To my son, Joshua. May God protect you. Your loving Father." Below those words was the date—1854. Joshua blinked several times, not daring to look at his father. His father cleared his throat again and walked away.

Fortunately, when he looked up, he saw his father leaning on the mantelpiece, his back to the room. Joshua quickly wiped both of his eyes and stood. "Thank you very much, Father. I will keep it with me always." He hooked the end of the chain on one of the gold buttons at the front of his uniform and tucked the gift into his sash. "I will have to get a pocket made in my coat for this watch."

"Indeed, you will." His father's voice broke slightly, and he would not turn. "Well then. Godspeed, son."

Joshua stood awkwardly for a moment, not knowing what to do. Then, decisively, he marched over to his father, lay his hand on his shoulder, and gave it a squeeze. "Good-bye, Father." Then, just as decisively, he walked out the door.

***

Eleanor was at work in the hospital. Today was her day to take patients who could bear to be moved out into the sunshine, if there was any. She pushed a Miss Merryweather about in her chair. The old governess was recovering from a bout with the ague, and Eleanor turned to face the sunshine.

"I thought for a time that the pneumonia would take me."

"It was not yet your time, Miss Merryweather."

"I suppose not, but I was ready. Lovely to be out here in the garden. Could you take me over there to look at the tulips, Sister?"

As she pushed Miss Merryweather's wheeled chair towards the tended gardens, a figure exited the hospital. She recognised him immediately and quite forgot what she was doing, when Miss Merryweather suddenly cried out that she was about to fall into the flowerbed.

"Oh, I do apologise, miss."

"Watch what you are about, Sister. My goodness."

With the elderly patient settled, Eleanor again turned her attention to that fine figure of a man. Many heads turned, and he strode down the steps and into the garden, looking about until his gaze fell upon her. She stood rooted to the spot and he fairly sprang towards her.

"Oh, Miss Sherbrooke, there you are." Wentworth smiled, his black moustache framing his perfect mouth.

"Lieutenant Wentworth, what an unexpected pleasure." She could fairly hear her blood beating in her ears. She breathed in slowly. "Whatever are you doing here?"

He was now only inches from her, his expression softening. "I am afraid I am here to say good-bye. We sail from Portsmouth tomorrow."

Eleanor knew in her heart of hearts that his departure for war was inevitable, but nonetheless it came as a jolt. She realised now that someone whom she cared for more than she dared would be fighting in it. "Oh." Something caught in her throat and she dared not speak for a moment, lest it betray her emotions.

"Can we sit together a while?" He cocked his head to catch her eye, and after checking on Miss Merryweather, who by now had dozed off, she nodded.

They sat on a nearby bench, looking out at the riot of colour in the hospital garden. "This is a pleasant place. I think you must enjoy it."

"Taking the patients here is one of the more pleasurable aspects of my duties here."

It was then he turned his head and met her gaze. "I want to show you something." He felt along his sash, and then retrieved a watch. "Here. Look at this." He dropped the object in Eleanor's palm, its chain still attached to his coat. She gently pulled it towards herself.

"Oh, my. This really is lovely." There on the cover, in relief was the symbol of the 17th, Death or Glory.

"Open it." She looked up and his expression reminded her of a little boy, delighted to show off a found seashell or a frog he caught himself. When she opened the watch, the inscription was so poignant that it was all she could do to contain herself.

"Oh, Lieutenant Wentworth, you must treasure this always." She closed the cover and handed the watch back.

"Indeed, I will. It came as quite a surprise."

"I am not surprised," she said, and he cocked his head to one side in confusion. "No, I am not surprised. Your father may not agree with you, and even be disappointed that you did not follow in his footsteps, but I am sure he loves you very much. He is your father after all."

Wentworth turned away and sighed. Finally, he spoke. "I did not come here solely to show you the watch. I have a favour to ask of you, Miss Sherbrooke… Eleanor. May I call you Eleanor? After all, we are almost family."

She nodded mutely.

"And you must call me Joshua."

"Perhaps one day I will…" He looked puzzled at her remark. How could she tell him that she needed to keep some distance from him, and this small formality would accomplish the task. "Is that the favour you came to ask?"

"No, there is something else…more important."

Oh, Lord, whatever could he have to say? How could he look at her like that?

"Eleanor, I so enjoyed our brief talks when we first met. Do you remember?"

Did she remember? They swam through her brain whenever she was alone with her own thoughts. "Of course, I remember. I very much enjoyed them as well. What is it you need, Lieutenant Wentworth?"

"I would like you to write to me, Eleanor. When I am away."

"But surely Julia will write—"

"Julia, indeed, will write, but I would be pleased if you would also. I do so enjoy your candour, Eleanor. I really do. I ask if I may be candid with you as well."

So, he wanted a friend and a confidante. One half of her rejoiced at such an idea; the other half thought it might be pure torture to be so close to him and yet so far away. It took her no time to decide. "Yes, yes of course I will write to you. You merely must give me an address, and I will begin. I will begin today so that a letter is waiting for you when you reach Crimea."

His face creased into a smile...one of gratitude, and perhaps even fondness. She did not care either way. There would be small fragments of his affection coming to her from the Black Sea.

Chapter 5

The voyage was mercifully quick as the *Himalaya* could travel at a steady six knots, wind, or calm. Sea voyages never agreed with Wentworth and agreed even less with Merlin. Only a few weeks out of Portsmouth, the two stepped on the bleak shore in the pounding sun not of Crimea but of Varna in Bulgaria. Rumour had it that the Russians had crossed the Danube, and almost from the time they bivouacked, Lord Cardigan took the 8th and the 13th out on a scouting mission. The rest of his troops were set to work setting tents and finding forage and water for themselves and their beasts. The Crimea was still a sea voyage away.

There was precious little to do in the weeks whilst they waited for their compatriots to flush out the Russians, if there indeed were any. Supplies were scant. Many of the officers left in camp organised hunting parties, coming back with wild boar. "Bloody good job we brought all this champagne along, wot?" Major Easton, the second son of the Earl of Something-or-Other, cracked open another bottle. Wentworth held up his hand in refusal. The wine and his head did not agree with this blazing sun, and he'd had enough. "Coming along on the pig shoot, then, are you, Wentworth?" Pork and champagne. It was a disgusting combination, but infinitely superior to hard biscuit and salt meat.

"I believe I will join the chaps organizing the races," Wentworth said distractedly as he cleaned the barrel of his carbine. "Old Merlin is in need of a bit of a run."

"Anyone taking wagers, old boy? I'd like to get in on the action." Easton swilled another glass of wine and then lay back on his cot. The sun beat down on them relentlessly, making the small tent like a sort of breezy oven.

"I believe Collins is handling that sort of thing. Do not wager against me, Major. You'll put your money in peril."

Easton yawned at that and, setting down his glass, drew his forage cap over his eyes and was soon snoring. Wentworth left to stretch his legs.

Wanting to be alone with his thoughts, he walked about the deserted part of the camp evacuated recently by the 8th and the 13th. As he passed by Lord Cardigan's marquee, which flapped in the desert breeze, an odd sound drifted from one of the tents abandoned by the Dragoons who were on their search for invading Russians. At first, he thought it a cat mewing, but on further investigation, determined it was the sound of moaning. Walking quietly among the deserted tents, he drew closer and closer to the sound. It nearly made his hair stand on end, so mournful was the noise. It conjured up stories his nanny told him of ghosts who walked the halls of the ancient castles of Britain.

Most of the canvas shelters were fastened down, but one nearby had a flap that waved about in the wind as if beckoning him towards it. His footsteps, no doubt, were heard by whoever was inside as the lament stopped abruptly.

"Who's there? Who is there, I say? Declare yourself." A high, tremulous voice emanated from the tent.

"It is I, Lieutenant Joshua Griffiths Wentworth of the 17th Lancers, sir," Wentworth shouted.

A hand appeared and clutched the errant flap, and then a slight youth peered out at him from the opening. He carried no weapon, but in his free hand was a bugle. Upon seeing Wentworth, the youth fell to his knees, clutching his abdomen. "William Brittain, sir, Orderly Trumpeter to Lord Cardigan, at your service, sir."

Wentworth rushed to the boy's side. "Good Lord, what is wrong with you?"

"I think it's the cholera, sir." With that, the young man's eyes rolled back in his head and he slumped against Wentworth. The heat of the day and the stench emanating from the private's soiled clothes confirmed to Lieutenant Wentworth that it was indeed cholera. He hoisted the young man in his arms and carried him through the camp to where the medic's tent was situated. It was not as large as Cardigan's marquee but had round walls and a top high enough for a man to stand. There were men in cots arranged around the sides like the spokes of a wheel, all looking a bit rough.

"I have a patient for you, Doctor," Wentworth said as he deposited the lad on the nearest empty cot. The doctor walked over slowly and took in the prone boy. "Another case of cholera, eh? Well, either we'll sort him out or we won't. Where'd you find him?"

"Among the empty barracks of the 13th Light Dragoons. He was there alone."

The doctor screwed up his face in disgust. "Major General Cardigan took all of them off on a Russian hunting expedition. Left this poor bugger alone to fend for himself." He shook his head and began to loosen the boy's clothing. "Thank you, Lieutenant. That will be all."

Wentworth was summarily dismissed but delayed his departure. Even though he had only known him a few minutes, he felt responsible for the lad. "May I come to see him tomorrow?"

"Suit yourself, Lieutenant. If he lives through the night, he will be here tomorrow." By then the boy was retching over the side of the cot and the doctor spent no more of his attention on Wentworth.

Wentworth saluted. "Thank you, sir." He turned on his heel and left.

***

"Julia, how are you faring?" Eleanor greeted her sister, who had not received any visitors nor attended any social functions since Joshua Wentworth's abrupt departure.

Julia sighed. Eleanor, observing her sister's expression, was genuinely surprised to see real melancholy there.

"Oh, I don't know, Eleanor. Some days I just sit by the window and watch it rain. I really cannot go out and socialise as before. I'm engaged, but my fiancé is not here to escort me. It puts me in a very untenable position."

"Is that what concerns you? Lieutenant Wentworth is somewhere in the Black Sea, thousands of miles from home, fighting England's sworn enemies. He may be engaged in a battle right now, and all you think of is attending balls. Really, Julia."

Julia turned upon her. "Of course I'm concerned for him, but you wouldn't understand. You spend your days emptying bedpans for women who are your inferiors. What would you know?" Julia tossed her curls and looked upon her with her doe eyes. She was infuriating. How did men find her so appealing?

"Perhaps you should come with me, Julia. We could always use some help at the hospital. It would take your mind off your troubles, since you are not making calls or dancing or—"

"What a revolting idea, Eleanor. You may want to disgrace the family name by engaging in such unsuitable activities, but I will not."

Eleanor sighed. "Julia, it's not Lieutenant Wentworth's fault that your engagement was never announced. He was called away and had to follow orders."

Julia's eyes grew wide as Eleanor spoke, her mouth expanding to a broad grin. "Eleanor, you are genius. No one knows of my engagement. Of course. I mean to say, the Wentworths know, but I will avoid all society that may include that Geoffrey Wentworth and his tiresome wife. I don't think his father goes out much… and isn't the mother dying, or something?"

My God, that sister of hers could be callous. "You are not thinking of socializing, are you, Julia?" Before her sister could answer, a thought then occurred to her. "You should call upon Lieutenant Wentworth's mother. She doesn't leave the house often and I'm sure that she would love to see you."

Julia looked askance at her and pouted for a moment. "I liked your other idea better, Eleanor, but I suppose it has to be done. You must come with me, though. You have so much more experience talking with people who are ill." She made a face.

"I would be happy to. We shall send word and await her reply." It did not appear to Eleanor that Julia was thinking of a visit to the sick. The delights of London society shone in her sister's eyes.

***

The drills began at four thirty in the morning, before breakfast. Even though Major General Cardigan was out with the scouting party, his orders were clear: the entire brigade drilled until 9:30. Wentworth shared his distaste for Cardigan with his brother officers but would not voice it directly. He did not mind the drills all that much. A good portion of his men were new recruits and needed to fully embrace the discipline of the service. It could mean the difference between life and death, glorious victory or tragic defeat. And the early hours saved all of them from the blistering heat of the day.

When his breakfast was finished, Wentworth walked to sick bay to visit his young charge. He found the boy alive, which was a relief, and able to take some nourishment.

"I am sending him back to his quarters tomorrow if he continues to improve. I believe the worst is over." The doctor indicated young William with his head as he stood preparing some noxious mixture for one of the other suffering men. "He was lucky. I have seen men walk in of their own accord with a stomach upset, and by the evening, they are dead as a doornail. Damned cholera."

Wentworth brought a camp chair to William's bedside and sat down. "You look better today, Brittain."

"Thanks to you, sir. Would be dead in my quarters if you had not come by."

"You are an orderly to Lord Cardigan, then?"

"Aye, sir. He left me behind, sir, when I started ailing. He said, says he, 'what use are ye to me now?' and I can't say I was any use, doubled over and retching…and worse." The lad looked away, embarrassed.

"Why didn't you come right away to the doctor?"

"Didn't think I'd make it without disgracing myself, sir. Couldn't hold anything in, if you get my meaning."

Wentworth nodded. "The doctor says you can go back to your quarters tomorrow."

The boy's face blanched. "Really? I do think I might need another night in hospital."

"There are too many men coming in with the same malady as yours, Brittain. They need your bed."

Wentworth knew exactly what the trouble was. The camp of the 13th Dragoons and the neighbouring one of the 8th Hussars were empty of men. The boy would return to a lost city.

"I was thinking, Brittain, since your commanding officer is away, perhaps you would like to be my orderly until the rest of the regiment returns. I have no one at present, and it would be a great favour to me."

The boy's eyes widened. "Do you mean it, sir? I would like that ever so much, sir. I'll do my best for you, sir."

"First you will regain your strength—"

"Oh, I am fine, sir, really."

Wentworth narrowed his eyes at the lad. "You will follow my orders, Brittain, is that understood?"

The boy cast his eyes down. "Yes, sir."

"Now, as I was saying, you will regain your strength and then resume your duties."

"Yes, sir." The lad saluted and then lay back on his cot, a smile on his face.

***

Good as his word, Wentworth moved Orderly Trumpeter William Brittain into his quarters along with his gear. William's physical condition continued to improve, but he did have a melancholy air about him. As he gained strength, Wentworth set him small tasks and within a week brought him along to stables in the evening. There was much grumbling among the officers about Cardigan's order that officers attend stables every evening, rather than leaving it to the enlisted men. It was no hardship for Wentworth. Attending to Merlin always felt more of a privilege than an obligation.

"He's a fine bay, sir. Does what you tell him, I'll wager." William brushed the horse's neck with long strokes. Merlin shook his head.

"He may appear to disagree, Brittain, but he does follow orders… better than some of the men."

William Brittain laughed. They continued in silence for a while. William spoke again from behind Merlin. "I miss home, sir. Do you? What I mean to say, sir, is… do grown men miss home and their mothers, I mean… from time to time, sir?"

Odd question for a military man. Wentworth knew he was young, though. "How old are you, Brittain?"

"Fifteen last January, sir."

Good lord, this was but a boy. Her majesty's army had many such "bugle boys" in her service. Wentworth considered his own condition as a fifteen-year-old. He was away at school, then home on holiday, not a care in the world. This boy was half a world away from his family, left alone to die by that blasted Cardigan. Bloody outrageous. "Did your mother encourage you to be a trumpeter, then?"

"I taught myself, sir. My uncle had one left over from the last war."

"The last war? You mean, with Napoleon?"

"Yes, sir. My great-uncle, really. Made a right nuisance of myself with it, my mother says. Thought they might take me in the army because of it, and I was right. Thought I might be able to be of some use, sending some of my pay home and all."

"And have you? Sent your pay home?"

"Not too much, sir. Seems like there is hardly enough to keep me alive. Still, one less mouth to feed at home, anyway, sir."

The boy finished with Merlin and began on the next horse in the stable. How many of his men had barely enough to keep themselves? How many needed to send pay home to a wife or children, or a mother?

"I wrote her about you, sir. My mum, that is. Told her how you saved my life and all."

Wentworth smiled at that. "I hardly saved your life, Brittain."

"Oh, you did, sir, and make no mistake, I'd have died alone and that's sure if you hadn't come along and helped me. I'll never forget it, sir. Not as long as I live."

Wentworth, in spite of himself, felt protective of this boy, rather like an older brother. "We all have a duty to look after each other in the Light Brigade. That is all I did. My duty."

William poked his head out from behind the horse he was tending and smiled a great grin. "Death or glory, right, sir?"

"Death or glory. Right."

***

"Eleanor, you should come along with me. Cordelia will be there and many others whom you know. It's not right that you should shut yourself up here at home during the height of the Season." Julia was twirling before a mirror in Eleanor's room. Why Julia bothered to come in here and harass her, she did not know.

"I am tired, Julia. I just arrived home this evening from the hospital. The last thing on earth I want to do is dance."

"But you are such a good dancer, Eleanor. Come along."

“Go, Julia. Mama is waiting.” Julia threw a look Eleanor’s way over her shoulder and then left her in peace. Eleanor breathed a sigh of relief.

The work at the hospital did tire her, but not as much as the balls and parties did. Her mother was cross with her that she did not make more of an effort to entice the young men of her class, but they all seemed less and less appealing as her work absorbed more and more of her time and spirit. Annie came in with a tray laden with tea and sandwiches and left without a word. Blessed silence. That was what she needed.

It had been a week since she and Julia called upon Lieutenant Wentworth’s mother. Eleanor felt that she did not look well, and Julia… Julia looked distracted. Eleanor did not ask if Julia had written to her fiancé since the visit. She would not be her sister’s keeper in this instance. No one could tell Julia anything, and to goad her was the surest way of having her do the opposite of one’s request. She promised to write to Lieutenant Wentworth when he came to say good-bye, and now she would finally do so.

Dear Lieutenant Wentworth,

My sister, your fiancé, has gone off to a ball without you. She finds this war very inconvenient to her plans. I do believe she forgot you as soon as you walked from her door. How she could forget you, I do not know, for I think of you daily and wonder as to your safety. I also wonder if you ever think of me. I have to tell you again that I love you and I think you are making a mistake in marrying Julia…

“Will there be anything else, miss?” Annie’s voice called across the bedroom and startled Eleanor so that she left a great blot of ink on her letter.

“No, Annie, thank you. I will ring for you later if there is anything else.”

“Very good, miss.”

Eleanor crumpled the letter and threw it into the grate, striking a match and immolating it at once. She really needed to stop writing her true thoughts, for one day they would betray her. Still, it felt wonderful to do so. She then began again.

15 July, 1854
Dear Lieutenant Wentworth,

I promised you that I would write immediately upon your departure, and I got as far as the envelope. You may chastise me when you return home. I hope this letter finds you well. All is well here.

I continue to work for Miss Nightingale at the Institution for Distressed Gentlewomen and have learned a great deal from her. She is a strict task mistress, but I am not averse to taking orders, so I believe that you and I have that in common. There are times when I chafe at the bit, but the work is satisfying, and I really do feel that I have found a way to put my interest in medicine to practical use.

Julia and I paid a visit to your mother last week and found her in good spirits. She was very gracious in receiving us, and I found her to be a forthright and wise woman. Although she did not complain, I do fear that the London air is not good for her breathing. She would not hear of travelling elsewhere. I believe she wants to be home when you arrive back after your adventure. She misses you very much. I am sure Julia will write at length about our visit.

The public here in England await news of your progress in the Black Sea. There is a reporter called William Russell who is there with you somewhere, sending reports via telegraph to The Times. The news of your exploits reaches us in a flash of lightning due to this wonderful invention. I hang upon each word he writes, always scouring the papers of news of the 17th.

Please do be careful. There are many here who wish you to cover yourself with glory, but not at the expense of your life. I pray for you daily.

With fond wishes,
Eleanor Sherbrooke

Eleanor read and reread the letter. She hoped it did not sound too cloying. She was careful not to mention her errant sister, who was off to a ball whilst her lieutenant risked his life on some foreign shore. She placed it in the envelope and sealed it. Papa could take it to the post tomorrow.

***

Cardigan and his troops returned from their reconnoitre having found not one Russian for a hundred miles. They did catch a glimpse of them once on the opposite shore of a river somewhere to the north, after which the Russian commander waved his hat to Cardigan and, with his troops, retreated. All of this effort, which accomplished nothing, took a terrible toll on the English troops. They returned half starved, as were their horses, and many were sick. Most were unfit for duty.

Wentworth visited the sick bay in the next days and found many more had contracted cholera and died. The troopers were challenged to dig the graves of the dead, but the soil in this godforsaken corner of Bulgaria was as hard as rock and the graves were shallow. It fell upon the 17th to stand watch at night and drive off the wild dogs that tried to scavenge. Wentworth was returning to his tent after such a night when he encountered his orderly.

"I'm returning to Major General Cardigan's service, sir." William Brittain gathered his things in the early morning hours. "He's called me back now that I'm fit for duty."

"Indeed. It was a pleasure to have you as my orderly, if only for a fortnight." Wentworth extended his hand to the young man, who eagerly pressed it with his own.

"See you at drill, sir." Brittain saluted, and Wentworth returned it.

"See you there, Brittain." When the young man left, Wentworth shook the dust from his coat and put it on again. After a night of burial duty, five hours of drill was about to commence.

Thus, the regiments waited, having little forage for the horses and dwindling rations for the men. Fighting broke out on more than one occasion and punishment and court-martials were frequent. Wentworth despised having to watch a man flogged in any circumstances, but here, where the men were subject to the combined burdens of illness, short supplies, and boredom, it was particularly infuriating.

The waiting and indolence soon came to an end when Cardigan received the orders in August to sail to the Crimea at long last. All in the camp were in very high spirits. They began their march back to the port in Varna and five days later embarked.

"See, Easton, they've sent the *Himalaya* for us. The journey will be swift." Wentworth could not contain his enthusiasm upon seeing the ships anchored in the harbour.

"With any luck, there will be food and water for us and for the beasts on board ship. The champagne ran out long ago. Ho, look there. It's Duberly's wife, Fanny." Easton cocked his head in the direction of chaos.

Hardly disguised, Fanny Duberly giggled like a schoolgirl at being hoisted aboard the *Himalaya* in an ox cart. She had come to Crimea with her husband. Rumour had it that Raglan, the commander-in-chief, forbad her to come any farther on the expedition, but he must have relented. It suddenly crossed Wentworth's mind that, had they been married, Julia could have followed him to the battlefield. He tried to picture it but could not. It was just as well. A battlefield was no place for women.

Once they were under way, Wentworth took the opportunity to seek out Merlin. The horse did not take well to sea voyages. To his surprise, he found Merlin well tethered in a stall, contentedly munching on some grasses. Easton was correct: there were more supplies for both man and beast aboard ship.

"You look a bit thin there, boy." Wentworth patted the horse's neck and inspected his general condition. He had to admit to himself that his clothes fit quite a bit more loosely than they did in London. The stallion shook his mane, and Wentworth slipped him a carrot he pinched from the ship's stores. "Tell no one of this meeting," he whispered. Merlin nuzzled his great head against Wentworth. The lieutenant took his brushes out of his knapsack and happily commenced his stable duties.

When Wentworth emerged on deck, he was accosted by none other than William Brittain.

"Oh, there you are, sir. I've been looking for you." The lad looked a great deal better than when Wentworth last saw him. The voyage was doing some of them a lot of good, although many in the hold were still sick and dying by the day.

"You have found me, Brittain, out with it."

"A letter for you, sir. One of the ships coming from England brought it." William rummaged inside his coat and produced an envelope. "Here you are, sir."

Wentworth was sure that the letter was from Julia, but then saw the handwriting was Eleanor's. She was a loyal friend, to be sure. The letters from Julia must have been delayed. "Thank you, Brittain." Upon arriving in his quarters, he tore open the envelope.

He read and reread the letter several times, almost committing it to memory. ... *Please, do be careful...I pray for you daily...* Such words had so much more meaning so far from home. Good, kind Eleanor. He would write to her at the next opportunity.

Within a week, the 17th landed upon the beaches at Kalamita Bay in Crimea. By day's end, it was called "Calamity Bay" by most of the regiment. They were joined by the French and the Turks, and within days nearly sixty thousand men with their horses, dray animals, and supplies were unloaded on the beach. Soon, the shore was filled with thousands of men and horses, but no water for either. They were north of the city of Sebastopol. Soon the search for wells began.

It took five full days for the British force to disembark. Many men came ashore on litters as they were ill with cholera. The infantry embarked first, as they all expected resistance to their invasion. It never came. By the time the cavalry came ashore, the sea was again rough, and poor Merlin clambered off his raft on shaky legs. Wentworth had to admire the French expeditionary force. Whereas the British seemed completely unprepared to move supplies and guns and had to send out foraging parties to the nearby Tatar villages for oxen and carts, the French brought everything they needed with them. At first, Wentworth and his men did not even have their kitbags or tents, so they all slept rough in the night rain and roasted in the sun for days.

On the morning of the fifth day, Wentworth rode out with some of his fellow officers to higher ground. It was quite a sight—columns of soldiers arranged in gigantic squares across the wide valley, the British and French cavalry at their flanks. For the first time in months, his heart rejoiced at the sight. Perhaps this war would be over in a month. With the privations he and his men endured on Varna, it felt like they had been gone years.

As they began their southward march, there seemed to be little evidence of the Russian army or the Cossacks. The band struck up a tune, and for the first mile or so, all seemed well. By midday, though, the water had run out and the sun was baking the troops.

Discipline among the infantry began to break down as soldiers broke rank in search of water in nearby villages. When they reached the Bulganek River, which in the height of summer was merely a muddy stream, discipline broke down altogether and many soldiers rushed forward to drink from the sullied waters.

A volley of gunfire reached his ears as they moved along the valley floor. There, on the high ground, above the banks of the Alma River, at least a thousand, perhaps two thousand Russian cavalry assembled in formation. They opened fire on the 13th Dragoons scouting party who retreated to the line.

"We're a bit outnumbered, eh, Wentworth?" Easton had ridden up on his right from the flanks of the 11th Hussars.

"We can take them, I'll wager. There's Cardigan. It won't be long now." Wentworth repeatedly opened and closed his fist on his lance, and Merlin pawed the ground in anticipation. This would be the first taste of war for both of them.

A shout rang out, and then the bugler blew not "charge" but "retreat." Easton swore and galloped off to join his men. The entire army turned to the jeers of the Russians on the ridge.

After all the hardships his men had already faced, after all the death they had experienced before one shot was fired, Wentworth needed an explanation about why, after coming all this way, they sat idly by and gave the Russians a chance to regroup. Alas, generals need not explain anything to the lower ranks. They were merely to follow orders. As soon as their encampment was established, Wentworth obtained paper and pen and poured out his frustrations to Eleanor.

22 September, 1854
Dear Eleanor,

Thank you for your letter. You have no idea how much a letter from a dear friend means to me. I will endeavour to keep up my end of the bargain also.

By the time this letter reaches you, I am sure you will have already read in the London papers what has been transpiring here in the Crimea. Our supplies are short and our medical care for the wounded and sick is woefully inadequate. For the moment, I am well, if a little thinner than when last we met.

There was a large battle on the Alma River here not too long ago. All of us in the 17th were ready for the charge, but General Raglan saw fit to order us back, and we did nothing, nothing, as our own fusiliers fought valiantly from the valley floor and up the hillside to face volley after volley of Russian shot. The boys who lived to tell the tale said that Prince Menshikov, the commander of the Russian forces, was so confident of victory that he invited the elite of Sebastopol to a picnic on the ridge near his forces to watch the Russian victory. Our boys scattered them all like a flock of doves.

This is the second time we were not allowed to engage the enemy. My friend, Major Easton, lost a foot at a small skirmish at the Bulganek River. A Russian shell exploded near his horse, and the next thing anyone knew, he was trotting about, his foot hanging only by a piece of skin. He kept his mount, though, and calmly asked to be directed to the medic. That is the stuff we are made of.

After our victory at Alma, I was hoping that we would advance on Sebastopol immediately, and put an end to this conflict. We have the Russians on the run and could take the city easily if we move quickly. If the cavalry does nothing but observe and flank the real combatants, I fear my time in the army has been a waste.

I do hope you are keeping well, and that Julia is not too lonely in my absence. I have written to her as well but have not been as candid in my remarks as I have with you. I do not want to alarm her. The sight of a broken glass was too much for her sensibilities, so I do not think regaling her with the scenes of battle and hardship is wise.

Give my best wishes to your parents, and always my best to you, dear Eleanor. Please continue to write with all your news from home. I do not know when I shall have the opportunity to write again. I hope it is after we have won this war and the 17th has distinguished itself.

Yours,
Lieutenant Joshua Griffiths Wentworth

Wentworth deposited his letter with the rest that would be sent via the French packet. Tomorrow he would write to Julia in less brutal terms. There was no reason to distress her. After all, the Lancers were only witnesses to this conflict so far.

***

Eleanor pored over all of William Howard Russell's accounts of the war in *The Times* with an interest based on obsession. How was it that the greatest fighting force in the world, the army that defeated Napoleon, could be so ill equipped and badly managed? She read the account of the aftermath of the Battle of Alma once again.

"*One who has not seen cannot conceive the relics of a great fight, especially on such a field as that of the Alma. There was an immense accumulation of camp litter on the hillside. There was a sickening, sour, fetid smell everywhere and the grass was sloppy with blood.*"

Eleanor stopped reading aloud and looked up at Julia and her mother. Both gazed at her with open mouths.

"Eleanor, really, do you have to read such things at breakfast?" Julia raised her teacup to her lips.

"Your fiancé, Lieutenant Wentworth, was at this battle, Julia. Does that not move you at all?"

Julia began buttering her toast. "Oh, for goodness sake, Eleanor. You read to us just a moment ago that the cavalry was kept out of it. I am sure he is all right. He is probably writing a letter to me at the very moment and will be home within the month. That General Raglan or Cardigan or whoever he is does not seem to want to use the cavalry at all."

Eleanor shook her head in disbelief. "So, now you are a military expert."

"Ladies, please…" Her father finally looked up from his breakfast. "Perhaps we should leave discussion of the war to a more appropriate time, Eleanor." Julia gave her sister a self-satisfied smirk. "And Julia, you could be more sympathetic to our brave boys overseas. Eleanor is correct in that. I am sure the generals did not include the cavalry in their expedition to function merely as witnesses." Eleanor was tempted to return the smirk but refrained from doing so. She rose from the table.

"Duty calls. I shall probably be late returning tonight." She avoided looking at Julia again.

"I will send a carriage for you at six," her father said as he retrieved the morning paper from Eleanor's spot at the table.

***

After the completion of her rounds, Eleanor was summoned to Miss Nightingale's office. If she knew her father, a carriage was outside already waiting.

"Have you seen the evening paper?" Miss Nightingale was not one for greetings or small talk.

Eleanor took a seat. "No, miss, I have not."

Miss Nightingale handed her *The Times*. "Read… read and tell me what you think." Eleanor began to scan the page, and Miss Nightingale, in her usual brusqueness, jumped up from her seat and pointed to a passage. It read:

"*The commonest accessories of a hospital are wanting; there is not the least attention paid to decency or clean linen; the stench is appalling; the fetid air can hardly struggle out to taint the atmosphere, save through the chinks in the walls and roofs; and for all I can observe, these men die without the least effort being made to save them.*

There they lie, just as they were let gently down on the ground by the poor fellows, their comrades, who brought them on their backs from the camp with the greatest tenderness, but who are not allowed to remain with them. The sick appear to be tended by the sick, and the dying by the dying."

"This is appalling." Eleanor handed the paper back to Miss Nightingale. "It is the Crimea, I presume."

"Indeed, it is. Yes, appalling and the Crimea."

"My sister's fiancé is there with the Light Brigade under General Cardigan."

Miss Nightingale did not appear to be listening. In the lamplight, she searched her desk crowded with correspondence and papers and finally pulled a letter from one of the piles and handed it to Eleanor. It was from the Secretary of State at War, Sidney Herbert. She scanned it and, wide-eyed, handed it back to Miss Nightingale.

"He wants you to lead a group of nurses to this Scutari place in Turkey? Is this the place described in the newspaper?" Eleanor did not know if she was feeling excitement or trepidation. Why was Miss Nightingale confiding in her?

"It is. I already sent a letter to Mr Herbert's wife, asking her to intercede for me so that I might lead a private expedition. It seems the government and I are of like minds."

Eleanor's mouth went dry. "And what do you want of me, Miss Nightingale?" At that moment, Eleanor did not know if she wanted her superintendent to ask her to remain here in London and oversee the Institution in her absence, or if she wanted an invitation to what sounded like hell on earth. Her thoughts immediately veered to Lieutenant Wentworth….

"So, Eleanor, what say you?" Miss Nightingale had asked her something, but she was so absorbed in her thoughts that it deafened her ears.

"I am sorry, miss. What did you say?"

Miss Nightingale set her lips and narrowed her eyes. "Are you deaf, Miss Sherbrooke? I asked if you would accompany me as one of my nurses to the Crimea."

***

"The Russians must think us mad." Lieutenant Wentworth and Merlin trotted ahead of the 17th Lancers as they moved south of the city.

Captain Waverly of the 11th Hussars trotted along with him, shaking his head. "You think we could have taken them after Alma, do you?"

"Don't you? Now we have to take Balaclava. Could have finished the whole thing in one fell swoop."

"We are fighting a war against Napoleon, my friend." Captain Waverly laughed. "These commanders are from a different era. Raglan keeps calling the French 'the enemy.' Good God. Surprised we haven't fired on our own men."

"We did." Wentworth shot a look at his companion, who raised his eyebrows. "Over at Varna. Our pickets arrived in the middle of the night when we were expecting Russians. Cardigan had to get up on his horse, with bullets flying, to get all of us to stop. It was a right circus."

"And now we move south to dig in. At least that is the infantry's job, not ours."

"So what are we, only guards for the flanks? When will we get our day to fight?"

"We do what we are told, Wentworth. We do our duty, nothing more, nothing less. Always champing at the bit, aren't you, you Death or Glory Boys, eh?"

Wentworth said nothing. They approached the great valley that led to the supply depot at Balaclava. No doubt, the Russians had taken the high country again. Whatever were these commanders thinking?

***

"Oh, Mama, surely you are not considering letting her go." Julia stood, arms outstretched as a seamstress took another tuck on her new ball gown.

"I do not see how we can prevent her, Julia. She seems adamant. If the reports are correct, the minute she gets there and sees that it is no place for a lady, she will return forthwith."

Julia looked down to observe the work going on around her. Two women were furiously pinning seams. "Really, I should be the one going. After all, my fiancé is there."

Mrs Sherbrooke made a rather unladylike snort and then recovered herself. "Julia, you are no camp follower and you are no nurse. Whatever would you do there?"

"Fanny Duberly is there with her husband. She rides her horses behind the lines and spends her evenings in the harbour aboard ship. I believe she is having a grand time."

Julia's mother walked around her daughter and pulled on the skirt from the back. "Here, I believe the seam needs a tuck." The seamstresses took note and began to fold the fabric back. "You are not married to the man yet, Julia. I am sure they will not run out on the battlefield and fetch him for a wedding."

Julia harrumphed. "Well, if I cannot go to the Crimea, I will not sit and pine at home waiting."

"You have shown no desire to do so yet, my dear," her mother said ruefully. "I do so hope your sister will be careful. She is so single-minded. I fear for her sometimes."

"Nothing will happen to Eleanor, Mama. She has that Miss Nightingale with her. Both madwomen, in my opinion."

"Mad and brave… mad and brave." Her mother was almost whispering now and left off with the seamstresses and stood gazing out the window.

***

Eleanor did her best not to surrender to tears as she bade good-bye to her mother and father at the station. Her mother did not fare as well, but Julia was dry-eyed…dry-eyed and distracted. As usual, she behaved as if she had something better to do. The old colonel demonstrated his stiff upper lip as she embraced him. His only words to her were, "Do take care of yourself, daughter."

The accommodations aboard ship were a far cry from any Eleanor had experienced when travelling abroad with her parents. Even then, she found shipboard accommodations to be rather cramped and dark, but here she and her companions were consigned almost as cargo, deep in the murky and odorous bowels of the vessel. Rarely were they able to emerge from the hold and breathe in the fresh sea air. Eleanor wondered if they would be in any fit state to help anyone once they arrived. She also feared what they might find there.

The only bright spot on the voyage was a young nurse, like herself, called Mildred Potts. She came from a cottage hospital in Surrey. She was short and sturdy with a ready smile and an unflappable disposition. Eleanor took an immediate liking to her.

"You may call me Millie," she said on the second day of their voyage. "Seems to me we were going to get to know each other pretty well, confined as we are belowdecks."

"And you may call me Eleanor. I wish we had enough light in here to read."

Millie gave her a knowing look. She disappeared out of the pool of swinging lamplight and soon came back with a deck of cards, which she began to shuffle expertly. "If we can read, we can play. Are you in?"

Eleanor had to smile. Perhaps this voyage would not be as dismal as she thought.

***

The British and the French set up their positions south of the city of Sebastopol. The French were to the west, with their supply port at Kamiesh, and the British on the southeast hoping to supply their lines from the southern port of Balaclava. The Light Brigade, the Heavy Brigade, and the 93rd Lancers were all encamped on the valley floor. The infantry of both the French and the British began their trenchwork and building of their earthen work redoubts south of the city. It fell to those on the valley floor to keep the supply roads open from Balaclava.

Lieutenant Wentworth stepped out from his tent to greet the late afternoon sun. Row upon row of closely pitched, round tents with their pointed tops stretched along the dusty floor on the far end of the great valley. On either side, the cliffs rose from the valley floor, and ahead, a mile and a half of empty desert that led to the high ground. His stomach churned at the thought that the Russians might already be there.

"Good afternoon, Lieutenant." The voice came from behind him and was familiar. He spun around to greet his visitor.

"Good afternoon, Mr Brittain." The young bugler smiled and saluted. "Does the Major-General have no need of you this evening?" Wentworth turned away to observe Cardigan's marquee in the distance.

"He has no need of me for a few hours, sir, so I thought I would come by and see if I could offer you my services."

Wentworth could think of nothing pressing.

"Perhaps a shave, sir, or a haircut. It's been a long march, sir." Wentworth ran his hand over his chin and then through his hair. The boy was right. He had not looked at his own image for a week at least, having too many duties to see to moving his company around the city of Sebastopol. The young man continued. "We might be in it for sure tomorrow, sir. Want to look your best."

Death or Glory. Perhaps by this time next evening, he would be a well-groomed corpse. And then there were the onlookers. Some were wives of the enlisted men; some were officers' wives like Fanny Duberly. Some were just hangers-on who came along with the army from England. Even the Russians proved to have their own claque as they did during the battle at Alma. Blood and gore and an audience.

"All right, Brittain, I will get my razor and strop." He turned back to the boy momentarily. "Only trim the moustache, there's a good lad."

Soon Wentworth settled in a camp chair, his head leaned back as Brittain deftly scraped a fortnight's whiskers from his chin, and just as deftly cut the black, unruly ringlets from around his neck and ears. The boy brought the major-general's looking glass with him and, once he had brushed the hair from Wentworth's collar, showed him the result.

A familiar voice sounded nearby. "So, you are as beautiful as ever, eh Wentworth?"

Joshua leapt from his camp chair in response to the arrival of his commanding officer, Captain Morris.

"Sir." Both Wentworth and Brittain snapped to attention.

Wentworth admired Morris. The man was sensible and had combat experience in India. It showed. It also had crossed his mind that a man like Morris should be commanding the cavalry, not a scandal-ridden aristocrat like Cardigan who had never seen a battle in his life.

"At ease, men." He smiled slightly and looked Wentworth over. Then, turning to Brittain he said, "Don't suppose you'd give me a nice clean-up like Lieutenant Wentworth, here?"

"It would be my pleasure, sir." With that, Morris took Wentworth's place in the camp chair. His shave took considerably more time as the captain regaled them with his opinions for the entire procedure.

"The Russians are no fools. They have sunk their own fleet and bottled up the harbour. We will have to keep the buggers off the Wolzonoff Road if we want to keep the lines open from Balaclava." Wentworth only half listened. The gold-red sheen of the setting sun glowed above them on their flank, reflecting off the half-finished earthworks the Turks began on the far-right ridge.

"So, Brittain. You know our Lord Cardigan's mind better than either of us. Will he finally use the cavalry?"

The young man sputtered. "I am sure I don't know, sir. I am not in his confidence."

Morris laughed. “But you hear what he says to Raglan and Lucan, and they to him, do you not? Come along now. We are all on the same side.” Wentworth looked at the boy’s troubled face as it was thrown into relief by the setting desert sun.

“I am sure I don’t know, sir.” He wiped the last of the errant soap from Captain Morris’s chin. Holding up Cardigan’s looking glass, he showed his work to Morris.

“Not half bad, Brittain.” He searched in his pocket for a coin with which to reward the boy.

“Oh no, sir. That is not necessary.” Wentworth could see the agitation in the boy’s movements. No doubt he desperately wanted to be free of Morris’s prying questions.

“Nonsense, here, take it.” Morris pressed the coin into the bugler’s hand. “Use it to buy a sweet from one of those French *vivandière*s whenever they come over the ridge.” Brittain coloured from the base of his neck to his forehead but took the coin and stuffed it into his pocket. “Must be getting back, sirs. Lord Cardigan may need me.” He threw the remainder of his supplies in his kitbag and turned to salute. Morris and Wentworth returned it.

“I will walk with you a way.” Wentworth fell into step with Brittain. When they were out of earshot, Wentworth clapped the boy on the shoulder. “Do not pay the captain any mind, Brittain. He is legitimately concerned. Lord Cardigan is reputed not to favour officers who have served in India, no matter how excellently. I believe the captain feels the sting of it.”

“Thank you, sir. I understand.” They walked companionably in silence for a while, until Brittain broke the silence.

“Sir?”

“Yes, Brittain?” Wentworth could barely see the young private’s face in the fading, golden light.

“I am frightened about tomorrow.”

“All men fear death, Brittain. It’s natural.”

The boy was silent for a time. “I am more afraid that I will disgrace myself when it is time to do my duty.”

Wentworth grasped him by the shoulder. He could barely make out the young man’s features in the fading desert light. “You are a brave man and true. I have every confidence in you, Brittain. Every confidence.”

The bugler's shoulder straightened, and then the boy saluted him in the near darkness. Wentworth returned the salute. "Until tomorrow, then, Brittain."

"Yes, sir." The youth spun on his heel and walked towards the fires of the 11th Hussars.

When Wentworth returned, Captain Morris was gone, so he retreated to his tent to read the letter he had just received from Julia. How far away she seemed. It was as if he existed in one world and she in another. At that moment, he longed for that world—one in which there was enough to eat, a soft bed to sleep in, a lovely woman on one's arm. The letter was filled with ballroom intrigues and society gossip. One short sentence included his mother. *I visited your mother and she is as well as can be expected.* Whatever did that mean? He had not received any communication from his mother. She must be ill, or perhaps dying. He swallowed as the dust of the Crimean valley stuck in his throat. Perhaps his father was right all along. What was he doing here? He immediately banished such thoughts from his mind. Now was not the time to waver in one's purpose. From the sound of Captain Morris, tomorrow they would be in the thick of things if Lord *Look-On* Raglan could be persuaded to make good use of his cavalry.

Chapter 6

The next morning, the Light Brigade assembled at the far end of the valley. To the south, on their left flank, lay the expanse of the Causeway Heights. On their left flank towards the end of the valley, the bombardment of the Turkish position could be heard. The Heavy Brigade assembled on the other end of the Heights, and from their position on the valley floor, Wentworth could see the Russian cavalry moving along the Heights towards the Heavy Brigade's position. At least he thought that was where they were. They were at the bottom of the valley and could not see what went on behind the ridges. Raglan was on the high ground behind them, and no doubt could see everything. Wentworth's agitation increased as he watched the Heavy Brigade come up over the hill above them into the waiting arms of the Russians.

The Light Brigade, still in formation on the floor of the valley, stood awaiting orders. Captain Morris, to Wentworth's right, mounted on his steed commented, "Can't wait to get into the fray, eh, Wentworth?" The captain stared at Wentworth's lance and Joshua realised immediately that he must be opening and closing his fist upon it.

"Death or Glory, sir."

Morris gave him a wry look. "Good man. Some of us will see both today. Today is the day for the cavalry."

At the far end of the valley, a thin, red line extended at the far end of the Causeway Heights. The distance was over a mile, but Wentworth surmised it must be a line of 93rd Highlanders standing their ground in the path of the advancing Russian cavalry. A lump formed in his throat. That red streak on the horizon was the only thing standing between the advancing Russians and their supply port at Balaclava. They were vastly outnumbered, and no doubt would be slaughtered where they stood. There was a report of guns, and then another, and Wentworth watched in astonishment as the entire mass of advancing Russian cavalry turned and abandoned their advance. A great cheer went up amongst the Light Brigade. Merlin pawed the ground in frustration. They must receive orders soon. They must.

As the Russians retreated from their routing by the Heavy Brigade, Morris pointed to their cavalry retreating into the North Valley. “We should attack them now, by George. This is our moment.” With that he broke formation and galloped to the spot where Lord Cardigan stood mounted at the head of the regiment. Wentworth could not hear what was being said, but they all watched as an animated Morris gestured and shouted at the immovable Major-General. Wentworth waited as Morris trotted back to his position at the head of the 17th Lancers.

“What an opportunity we have lost,” he said to Wentworth, shaking his head. “We needed to reach them before they took shelter behind those guns, there on the ridge.” He pointed to the far end of the valley. The entire regiment could see the Russians make for shelter. Then as Morris turned his attention to their flank, he heard Morris’s sharp intake of breath. “Good God, they are taking the Turkish guns with them.”

On the distant left flank, the Russian cavalry swarmed the ruins of the Turkish redoubt. The Turks had abandoned it early in the battle, and now all would be lost if those guns fell into the hands of the enemy. Surely, now, now that they had waited so long, held back in every battle, the Light Brigade could plunge into the fray. Surely now they could save the day that their comrades had fought so bravely to win.

The sound of hooves behind them had every man turn and follow the horse and rider. He had just descended from Raglan’s position on the Sapouné Hills behind them. It was Captain Lewis Nolan, young, outspoken, furious champion of the cavalry come with a message from the battle commander. Nolan handed a message to General Lucan. Wentworth was close enough to the general to see him unfurl the paper. All eyes were upon them both. All Wentworth could hear was the general asking, “Guns? What guns?”

Nolan, forgetting his place, in fury shouted, “There is your enemy. There are your guns, My Lord.” And Nolan pointed to the Russian positions, not at the Turkish redoubt, which was attainable, but at the entrenched Russian positions at the far end of the valley. Captain Morris shifted next to Wentworth in such a manner that it caused his horse to buck slightly, bumping into Merlin. The two men looked at each other in shock. It was a mile or more across the open valley, with Russian guns on three sides. Such an attack was suicide.

Every eye of the men in the front line followed Lord Lucan as he rode ahead of the regiments and conferred with his hated brother-in-law, Lord Cardigan. With an all-too-brief discussion, the mounted 11th Hussars, Lord Cardigan's men, broke into two lines and took their places behind the 17th. Wentworth heard General Cardigan's shout, and the Light Brigade began a calm, orderly trot down the centre of the valley.

Wentworth swallowed but his throat was as dry as the dust filtering up from the horses' hooves. This was his first battle and, he was convinced, also his last. His heart pounded his blood into his ears and his stomach twisted in a fear he would show no one. He pictured his mother reading of his heroic death on the field of glory. He thought of Julia, a widow before she was even a bride. And he thought of Eleanor, his friend and confidante. He touched the gold watch secreted in the special pocket he had made in his field uniform. *I will make you proud today, Father.* He remembered the inscription "God protect you". They would need divine intervention this day.

Still they trotted, trotting, trotting, trotting, as if they were again drilling on the Sussex Downs, a drink waiting for them at the officer's club. They were mercifully short of the Russian guns for a time, leaving each man to make his peace with God as best he could. At least, that was what Lieutenant Wentworth was doing. *God help me and God comfort my mother.*

The 17th led the left flank of the advancing cavalry, and Captain Nolan joined them. Wentworth wanted so much to break formation and ask him, "In God's name whatever are we doing?" Then Nolan himself suddenly broke rank and galloped ahead, screaming. He rode before the lines of the advancing 17th, pointing to the Causeway Heights, not the far end of the valley where they were headed. Was he warning them of a mistake? Wentworth could not make out a word the man was saying, and before Cardigan or Lucan could take heed of his warning, a shell broke above Nolan, the shrapnel flying, killing him instantly. His horse lay wounded and he motionless in the dust. No one stopped. They all merely rode around their prone bodies and reassembled the relentless line. The hellish rain of Russian cannon fire broke all around them.

The cannon fire became heavier now, and men were falling, horses screaming, disembowelled on the ground. They left them where they fell, closing ranks around them, all the men in silence, calling upon the discipline of the service. Deadly debris choked the air all around with the stench of brimstone. It then occurred to Wentworth that, if they reached the Russian guns, he would have to kill a man. He would have to kill many men. He had never killed a man before. He spoke soothing words to Merlin as the gunfire erupted around them. His stomach was in his throat.

Wentworth choked on the smoke and dust from the almost constant cannon fire that intensified with every hoofbeat, and still they were trotting, trotting. Was he to die on this Sunday walk? More than half a mile of desert floor still stretched between them and the enemy. Through the smoke and the ash, Captain Morris rode out to Cardigan, several yards ahead. He travelled at a gallop, and they all picked up their pace behind him. Finally, they would charge. Cardigan, however, did not budge. Morris returned, and the regiment slowed again to a gentle canter.

The cannon fire was heavier now, and men beside him disappeared in a cloud of black smoke and screams. A man, headless, blood splashing from his decapitated body, rode up next to him, and for an interminable moment sat atop his horse as if he still directed it. Finally, mercifully, his body fell. Wentworth pulled Merlin out of harm's way and endeavoured to return to the line when, through the dense smoke and shrapnel, Morris screamed, "Charge!" In an instant, William Brittain with his trumpet, galloping ahead, sounded the order. What a sound it was! The Lancers of the 17th broke into a furious gallop, the deadly barrage raining upon them. The horses' hooves thundered as they charged into the enemy cannon's roar.

"Hold steady, hold steady!" Morris cried out in the acrid fog. Now the gunfire was relentless, men falling forward as their horses somersaulted before the merciless barrage. Wentworth was still atop Merlin, his lance lowered. As they neared the rise, the firing intensified. He could hear the voices of the Russian gunners shouting as the first of them, himself included, rode past the deadly cannons to breach the enemy line.

The men of the 17th rode past the shocked and scattering gunners, who they left to the Dragoons, and attacked the Russian cavalry behind. There Wentworth's lance found its mark and men crumpled in agony before it. They were in the midst of a great melee, and after pulling his mameluke sabre from its sheath, he stabbed and hacked his way through the Russian cavalry. Merlin reared and turned with great alacrity, and man and beast were one and the same warrior.

When Wentworth was finally able to fight his way out, he saw what was left of the Light Brigade, returning at a gallop from whence they came. He took a moment to try to see his chance to make it back to the British lines. A small window opened in the uproar and, jubilant at having survived unscathed, he turned Merlin back.

As the beast turned homeward, Wentworth heard a cracking sound and, falling forward on Merlin's neck, heard nothing more.

***

Wentworth awoke in what he believed was a tent. He tried opening his eyes, but the one on the right would not obey him. Still, he could see men lying on the ground on either side of him. Nearly in a seated position, he was propped up against something and someone pressed up against him. The man had a bandage on his head and a bloody stump where his right arm used to be. A cold panic overwhelmed Wentworth, and he quickly pulled his hands up to his face to inspect them. Both were there. He then felt for his legs. They were there too. He breathed a sigh of relief. Still, how did he get here? Where was "here"?

He tried calling out, but his throat was so dry he could barely make a sound. "Water," he croaked. "Water." Someone pressed a cup to his lips, and he drank.

"Oh, awake now are ye, sir? Good on ye. Ye boys did England proud, ye from the Light Brigade. Never seen nothin' like it in my life, no sir." Before Wentworth could address this man, pain shot through his face. It radiated from his forehead down his cheek to his chin. He reached up to touch the right side of his face and realised it was covered in a bandage.

A soldier in the blue, braided uniform of the 11th Hussars passed in front of him. He shouted out, “You there, Hussar. Stop. Stop, I beg you.”

The man stopped in his tracks and knelt next to Wentworth.

“What happened? Where am I? How did I get here?”

The bewhiskered face broke into a smile. “You lived through it, as I did, sir. We were behind ye. Do you remember?”

The memory came flooding back. He was on a ridge, slashing through the Russian cavalry. “The charge. The charge to the guns.”

The Hussar was nodding. “Lost a lot of men that day, sir. You and I, we were the lucky ones, I’d say. Escaped with our lives.”

Yes, he remembered now. That fool charge. “My horse. My horse, Merlin. Is he all right?”

“A cavalry man through and through, aren’t ye, sir? What’s your name, sir, and I’ll inquire after your horse for ye.”

Wentworth’s mind was working. “And Captain Morris? What of him?”

“Wounded badly, sir. Horse shot from under him twice, but we got him back, sir.”

Wentworth sighed. “I thank you for that, Sergeant. The name is Wentworth. Lieutenant Joshua Griffiths Wentworth.”

Wentworth felt suddenly weak and lay back again. Despite the bright sun baking canvas over his head, Wentworth fell into a deep and troubled sleep.

***

“Can you stand, sir?” A private from the 17th was helping Wentworth out of his field cot. “You are off to Scutari, sir.”

Wentworth was unsteady on his feet but could walk to the bullock cart provided for the wounded to be taken to the Balaclava harbour. How many days had passed? He felt for the bandage on his face. It was no longer soft and pliable, but stiff and crusted. He still could not see out of his right eye. Many men in camp were unable to walk or were unconscious. Some were vomiting copiously, and the stench of the filth in which the men lay filled the air. Wentworth was grateful that, so far, cholera passed him by. It made swift work of many of them.

Wentworth was put in a hammock in the hold of the transport ship, and there he remained, save for attending to his bodily functions. He burned with fever and slept a great deal, troubled by feverish dreams. When he awoke, he was always thirsty. Attempting to eat was painful, his face swollen and infected. He still had not seen it.

When they arrived at Scutari, Wentworth was put in a fever ward. There were hundreds of men there with him. Through his blurred and feverish vision, he could see them lying upon litters or on the floor with no one to come to their aid. It occurred to him that he could have avoided death in that damnable charge, and now was fated to die as so many others had before him, in his own filth, neglected and unable to help himself.

***

The nurses' arrival at Scutari was met with little fanfare and a great deal of hostility. Eleanor could smell the place a mile off and, with each passing moment, prayed that the fetid odour of excrement and offal was disappearing behind them and not greeting them at their destination. Alas, her fondest wish went unanswered. The Scutari barracks looked quite grand from a distance: a great, white square building of two stories. Each side looked a quarter mile long and had a turret on each corner. It was set upon a hill, looking over the sea. From the size and shape of it, Eleanor surmised that there was a large courtyard within, if for nothing else, to let in the light.

It did not take them long to arrive. A weary-looking and scant medical staff greeted them. At the head was a rather short man, clean shaven with receding brown hair. He was solidly built and had and air of authority. "I am Dr Walsh. We will see what we can do for you ladies now that you are here." The army surgeon gazed at them with mild irritation. The man looked consummately weary.

"Florence Nightingale, sir. We need only to be shown where we may deposit our gear and will begin work at once."

"Oh, you will, will you?" It appeared as if it took his last bit of strength to puff out his chest in defiance. "You will not go into the cholera wards, is that understood?" His voice was louder now, and he raked all of them over with his withering gaze. "Is that understood, Miss Nightingale?"

"I do not see why you ban us admission when we are only here to help." Eleanor had to admire Miss Nightingale's fortitude. Men, even men in authority, did not intimidate her in the slightest.

"You will do as you are told, Miss Nightingale."

Eleanor waited for the explosive response, but there was none.

"For the time being. Show us our quarters, and we will begin."

They were led by an orderly in an infantry uniform through the hallways to their quarters. As they walked, what greeted Eleanor's eyes was nearly beyond her comprehension. Beds were few, and many men lay about on the floor, some in their own filth, wounds open and gaping, many filled with writhing maggots. She gritted her teeth and swallowed, keeping the bile from rising to her mouth. The place was running with rats. They scurried in front of them, and one of the sisters gave a howl when a great fat one ran over her feet as she walked. Eleanor tried not to stare, but it was a sight worthy of Dante's Inferno. The unshaven men were crawling with lice and fleas, and flies buzzed about in thick clouds. One of the good sisters was retching.

"Now, we will have none of that." Miss Nightingale did not even turn in their direction while giving her reprimand.

The orderly picked his way through the prostrate bodies, as if he were crossing a small stream on stepping-stones. How could he be so unmoved? The most shocking of all, besides the horror of the men's condition and the putrid smell, was the silence. All these men just lay there in silence. Eleanor wanted to scream.

Finally, they stopped at a dilapidated door, and upon opening it was a rather large room with about a dozen beds. "'Ere it is, ladies. 'ome sweet 'ome." The orderly grinned, two of his front teeth missing.

"There aren't enough beds for all of us." Miss Nightingale observed the young man over the bridge of her nose.

"There ain't enough beds for nobody, miss. Just the way it is 'round 'ere."

Eleanor set the small bag she carried with her on the floor and wondered how she would sleep tonight. The rest of their belongings had yet to arrive from the ship. She pondered the possibility of sleeping in her trunk that night. At least it would save her from being overrun by rats. She shuddered at the thought.

Most of the women in their little group belonged to a religious order. She and Mildred Potts, and of course, Miss Nightingale were the exceptions. Although Eleanor wondered about Miss Nightingale. She belonged to a small sect of liberal Christians called the Universalists and seemed to have a shining religious fervour about her work that transcended medicine and bordered on a spiritual crusade. All of them needed every bit of strength and commitment to their duty now. Scutari was in worse condition than even the London papers described.

When they all assembled in their little barracks, Miss Nightingale made an announcement. "I am setting you all to work, ladies. This place is filthy, and therefore men are dying. Our first order of business, then, is to clean the wards."

"But, begging your pardon, miss, where are we to sleep?" Mildred was no shrinking violet either.

"No time for sleeping, ladies. Time for work."

Eleanor did precious little nursing in those first few days at Scutari. Miss Nightingale, in a flurry of activity, sent orderlies and nurses on buying sprees in Üsküdar and Kadıköy for soap, basins, clean shirts, towels and all other manner of supplies to help with the sanitation of the Scutari barracks. They began with what little they had on hand.

"Ye see that, miss?" Private Robinson pointed out one of the windows in a hallway where Eleanor had the privilege of scrubbing.

"What exactly am I looking at?"

"That, miss. That mess. It comes from under the building. It is the cesspool, miss. That's where the awful smell comes from."

"I don't doubt it, Mr Robinson."

"Miss Nightingale says some blokes is coming all the way from England to drain it."

"I will bless the day." Eleanor returned to her scrubbing. Miss Nightingale was strict in her expectations for work. That was as it should be. The task of setting this place to rights, however, was beyond overwhelming.

The cesspool was not the only thing visible from the row of windows. Sometimes Eleanor would look up from her duty to watch the daily procession of burial details carrying litter after litter of the dead from the halls of Scutari. Cholera and typhus were killing more soldiers than the war. If they could just have enough time to do their work cleaning this appalling excuse for a hospital, there might be a chance they could change that relentless procession to the graveyard.

At the end of another interminable day, Millie, back in their sleeping quarters, disconsolately pulled her bonnet off her head and flopped back on the makeshift bedroll on the floor. "I should never have come," she said wearily. "I cannot even write home to tell them of my days. It is all too appalling. My mother would faint."

Eleanor had to smile. She could not imagine her mother's reaction. Already this place was giving her nightmares. She was weary to the bone, but it did not keep her from thinking day and night of the fate of Lieutenant Wentworth. He could already be dead from a wound or disease, but she felt in her heart of hearts that it was not so. She began to remove her bonnet also but changed her mind.

"Eleanor, where are you going?" Millie's voice rang out in the hallway.

Eleanor needed to speak at once to Miss Nightingale. She found her in her makeshift office.

"All right, Miss Sherbrooke. You may come with me on my rounds and help some of the soldiers write letters home. You say this man is your sister's intended?"

"Yes, miss. We also are friends. I just need to reassure myself of his well-being."

Miss Nightingale sighed. "That may not be possible. There are so many here and we have no idea what is transpiring across the water in Crimea even as we speak. He may already have died of cholera or wounds. Perhaps even in Varna."

"No, miss. I know he has not. I have a letter from him as he was leaving Varna and I have seen the rolls of the dead from this place. His name is not among them."

For the first time, Eleanor saw a light of sympathy in Florence Nightingale's eyes. Gone was the strict disciplinarian and superintendent, and in her place was a woman who would cross the ocean to the bowels of hell to help her fellow countrymen.

"You have been thorough in your search for this man."

"I have not neglected my work, I assure you."

Miss Nightingale smiled. "I did not say that you had. All right. Come along. We will see what comfort we can bring."

They went together, the pair of them, checking most of the wards where the present military medics allowed them to enter. Men would look up as the lamplight approached, their hollow eyes fixated upon them. From what Eleanor could see on the three nights she accompanied Miss Nightingale, Lieutenant Wentworth was not among the wounded. Her heart rejoiced, but it was to be a short-lived peace.

In less than a week, all hell descended on Scutari.

***

The boats came, one after the other. Men shot to pieces—gangrenous legs, stumps of arms, bullet-shattered faces, gaping sword wounds. All infected. All filled with maggots. Day after day they arrived. There were not enough supplies, medicine, or nurses to attend to them all. Their work at trying to clean the hospital had to stop as they did what they could for the wounded.

"You, you there, nurse, come with me." It was Dr Walsh. Eleanor worked in the reception area where the doctors sorted the men as they arrived. Some were critical and needed treatment immediately, some could wait, some were already dead, not having survived the two- or three-day journey from Balaclava. The number of them was overwhelming.

"Yes, doctor."

He waved her towards him, and she entered a room with a table that was already crusted with blood. Men were on litters or on the floor with ghastly wounds to their limbs. "Rumour has it you do not sicken at the sight of blood."

"I do not believe any of us do, sir." Eleanor found his tone demeaning and she was too worn out to make any pretence of politeness.

The doctor harrumphed. "Come here and help me." Private Robinson and another of his regiment hoisted a groaning man onto the sticky table. His leg was no more than strips of flesh and bone below the knee. "Robinson, you administer the chloroform. You, nurse, I need you for more delicate work."

Eleanor nodded.

The doctor turned his attention to the young soldier on the makeshift table, whose pale face barely registered what was being said. "Don't worry, son, I will make this as quick as possible." Robinson placed the cone and sponge over the young man's face and began dripping the chloroform. The young man began to twist and moan, crying out, "No please. Don't cut off my leg. Please."

The doctor lay his palm on the soldier's forehead and pushed his head back onto the table. "Lie still if you want to live beyond this day." The soldier let out a sob and lay back. Soon, he made no more protestations.

"When I pull the vein out, I need you to wrap it with this thread and then let it go. Don't want the poor devil to bleed to death. Have you done any of this work before?"

Eleanor shook her head mutely and took a deep breath.

"You will learn. I will guide you."

She looked about for a basin and some water. Finding it, she dipped in her hands and then scrubbed them with soap.

"What are you doing, woman?" The doctor's surgical tools were laid out, already sticky with blood, and he had a scalpel in his hand.

"Miss Nightingale requires us to wash before doing any work with the men, sir. She thinks it helps ward off infection."

The doctor laughed. "Oh, she does, does she? Damn nuisance."

"It does seem to work, sir. It did in London."

Without being asked, Eleanor moved the basin to the table and offered it to the doctor. He scowled at her, but she did not retreat. "Oh, very well, then." Dr Walsh narrowed his eyes, but he dipped his hands into the basin and, taking up the soap, methodically scrubbed his hands. Then, one by one, washed the instruments as well. Muttering, half to her and half to himself, he said, "It will give me a better grip on things anyway."

The doctor worked swiftly, and Eleanor soon became an expert at tying off blood vessels the doctor held out for her. After each operation, she did her best to rinse the surface of the improvised operating table with soapy water and aided in washing Dr Walsh's hands and instruments for him between each of the surgeries.

In the corner of the room, a stinking pile of severed limbs began to accumulate, and as the sun set, the rats made a meal of the soldiers' discarded extremities. When it became too dark to work, Dr Walsh dismissed her. Robinson and the orderlies still had burials. The operating theatre had to be cleaned and readied for work to commence at first light. She watched the orderlies begin the gruesome work of disposing of the soldiers' severed limbs. Almost unseeing, she walked wearily back to the nurses' quarters.

Mildred greeted her as she entered the newly claimed refectory that Miss Nightingale had procured for them. “Oh, Eleanor, you are covered in blood.”

It was the first time Eleanor had a moment to think. She looked down at her blue, cotton skirt and bodice and at the apron tied neatly around it. All of it was soaked and crusted with blood. She stared at it a moment, her exhaustion slowing her movements. She then raised her hands and examined them. “My fingernails too, Millie. Look. Blood.”

“Come along.” Millie put her arm around her friend and led her to the sleeping quarters. “We will get you out of this and into a clean gown for sleeping.”

Eleanor felt as helpless as a child again. Millie helped her out of her clothing, which was soaked through to her corset. “Now, that’s better.” Millie’s voice came to her out of a fog. “Lie down for a moment and I will bring you some broth.”

Eleanor did not hear another word until they were all roused in the morning. Dr Walsh had already sent for her. She was to aid him again. Millie, bless her, brought her a cup of tea and a biscuit.

“No water for washing as yet, Eleanor.” She pointed to the blue dress, caked with yesterday’s blood.

Eleanor wearily stepped into the stiff and gory material, and like a sleepwalker, joined the doctor once again in the rough and ready operating theatre.

***

It was a day or two later that two men from the medical corps came to move Lieutenant Wentworth into a ward for the “walking wounded.” To his shock and surprise, a nurse in a white bonnet and plain brown dress came to change the bandage on his face. He could smell the stink coming off the rest of his body. When he sat down in the camp chair, he addressed the young woman.

“I say, miss. Is there any possibility of a bath?”

She smiled and patted his hand. “I will inquire for you, sir. I have only just arrived myself, and we are truly short of supplies. I believe there are only a few baths and more than a thousand men. Just sit up now, and I will see to your face.”

The removal of the bandages was a painful process. The fabric stuck in several places and pulled pieces of his damaged flesh off with it. When it was finally removed, the young nurse took out some instruments, including a razor and a pair of tweezers. She looked him in the eye.

"What I am about to do will undoubtedly hurt you, sir. We do have chloroform if you want to wait for the orderly to bring it. I can come back."

Wentworth braced himself. "What are you going to do?"

"There are pieces of metal still in your cheek and in your chin, causing them to fester. I am going to remove them."

He did not want to wait. From what he had seen, there were so many wounded, she may not return for days. "All right. Do what you must. I will endeavour not to move.... Oh," he added as an afterthought. "See what you can do about opening my right eye."

The nurse's eyebrows shot up. "Your right eye, sir? You have no eye."

***

After four days of shattered men, the relentless parade of wounded bodies finally eased. Eleanor requested to be sent to the wards for a time. She approached Dr Walsh with her request.

"Yes, Miss Sherbrooke, I believe you might try to rest a bit. You look quite worn out."

"As do you, sir." She cocked her head to one side and looked at him askance. "Physician, heal thyself."

The doctor blinked at her, wide-eyed, and then let out a great guffaw. "You have become quite cheeky in the last few days, Miss Sherbrooke. I am shocked."

Eleanor smiled through her weariness. "You are not the least bit shocked, sir, and that's the truth of it. I would like to visit the wards, though, and see how our patients are doing."

"*Our* patients?" Dr Walsh's smile played upon his lips.

"Indeed, *our* patients, sir. You may be the surgeon, but without me and the orderlies, you could not have saved so many."

The doctor clucked his tongue. "You do not wait for compliments, Miss Sherbrooke, but take them of your own accord."

"I have learned not to wait for compliments, as you put it, but to speak the truth whenever I am able."

"The truth it is, Miss Sherbrooke. Go and visit *our* patients."

The small lull at the hospital, if one could call it that, afforded Eleanor a moment not only to rest and take nourishment, but also to hear the news of the battlefield. She sat with Millie in the refectory, eating the first vegetable soup she had since leaving England and relishing every drop.

"Miss Nightingale is transforming this hellhole." Mildred dipped her bread into her soup and gazed frankly at Eleanor.

"Millie, your language."

"Hell is hell, Eleanor. We had better be forthright about it. That battle at Balaclava nearly wiped out the Light Brigade, and then on its heels, these men from Inkerman. There are not enough supplies, the place is filthy—"

"What do you mean, wiped out the Light Brigade? The 17th Lancers? Oh, Millie, please tell me."

"Have you not heard? Well, I suppose not, as you are helping the surgeons and away from the wards."

"Millie, tell me." Eleanor was nearly frantic.

"Oh, of course. I am sorry. The 17th were right in front. Slowly cantered a mile and then charged straight into the Russian cannon fire. Straight in, unflinching. It was magnificent, they say…. But so many were killed. So many wounded. The Heavy Brigade too, and the Scottish Fusiliers. All of them but the Light Brigade was decimated." Millie finally looked up from her soup and blinked at Eleanor.

"Oh, Eleanor. I am sorry. Your friend is in the Lancers. Oh, I am sorry."

Eleanor stood up wordlessly and went to the wards to search for news of Lieutenant Wentworth.

***

On the morning of the third day since his arrival at Scutari, Lieutenant Wentworth awoke without a fever. Sweat soaked his filthy clothing, but he felt cool. His appetite had also returned. He then remembered what that nurse had told him. He lost his eye. He could believe it save one thing: he could still feel it moving in his head. She could be mistaken, but he doubted that. She seemed so competent. Whatever that nurse had accomplished must have worked a miracle. Now, however, he must find a looking glass and see what those Russian guns did to him. Touching his upper lip, he could still feel his moustache. He had escaped with that and his life.

After arising from his cot, he sought the water closet and, upon finishing, walked about trying to find a drink of water, some food, perhaps a basin, soap, and a clean shirt. And a looking glass. At the moment, though, he was still stinking filthy. Running his hand through his hair, he could feel the lice. Shuddering, he walked on through the ward.

"You there. Eh, you." It was an elderly man who Wentworth assumed was in the Ambulance Corps. Why anyone thought these feeble old pensioners fit for such taxing duty as caring for the sick and war wounded was anyone's guess. Obviously, the man did not know whom he was addressing.

"Are you speaking to me, sir?" Wentworth asked, and when he turned, the old man stepped back on his heel.

"Oh, I am sorry, sir. I did not know you were an officer. A Lancer too. Fought at Balaclava?"

Wentworth was a bit taken aback, but the man had apologised for his rude salutation. "Yes, we routed those Russians on the cliff, well and good…. Did we not?"

"Oh, yes, sir. Soundly defeated those hairy cretins… well and good. Yes, sir." The man then commenced to look at his feet as if he had run out of conversation.

Wentworth took pity on him. "Wanted to ask me something, then?"

"Uh, no, sir. Well… yes, sir. Any able-bodied men are requested to help with the wounded and the sick, sir. More coming in, sir."

Wentworth sighed. "For the love of God, man. Is there anywhere I can have a wash first?"

The elderly gentleman nodded and then led Wentworth down a long hallway to an indiscriminate door. He rapped on it and a woman answered. Whatever was this?

Motioning Wentworth to follow, the Ambulance Corpsman led him into a large room with a clean floor, scrubbed walls, and tubs of various sizes. There were men lying in them, the soapy scum floating on filthy water filled to their chests. Some lay back, their heads lolling over the tall backs of the same sort of baths he had at home. Some were sitting cross-legged in laundry tubs. Younger men Wentworth assumed were regimental orderlies were scrubbing these poor creatures, while a young woman in a starched bonnet, plain dress, and pinafore supervised the bathhouse. How incredibly extraordinary: a woman in a room full of unclothed men. The woman seemed nonplussed as if this was something she did every day.

"Brought you a walking wounded. Do you have room for him, miss?"

The sister looked up from her duties. "Oh, an officer. There's a tub behind the screen, sir. Take off your clothes and hand them over. I'll be giving them to the launderesses."

Wentworth raised an eyebrow and opened his mouth to speak, but before he could form a thought, the woman walked over to him with clean shirt and freshly laundered trousers and undergarments. A woman, handling a man's undergarments. Still, he said nothing and slipped behind the screen. There was a large round tin laundry tub with almost six inches of water in it, and next to it a cloth, a scrub brush, a bar of soap, and a clean towel. He stood for a moment, and oddly, tears came to his eyes. He was so filthy and in so much pain. A bath was an act of mercy. A miracle. Before long, he was scrubbing the lice from his hair and gently washing the wound on his face. The soap stung his cheek and his eye socket, but no blood appeared. He must be on the mend. When he finally emerged from the tub and towelled himself dry, his uniform was missing. Someone had come and taken it while he was in the bath. It slowly dawned on him that the rules he had lived by so far in his life had all been broken or at least suspended in this foreign place. The feeling of clean clothes against his skin was exhilarating.

The woman in charge sent two privates from the Dragoons to clear up after him. He enquired about his clothes and another orderly took his name and assured him that he would see his uniform again. Miraculously, he still had his watch, which he slipped into the pocket of his newly acquired trousers.

"If you would sit down, soldier, I will fit you with a new bandage." It was one of those nursing sisters he had seen before. However did these women come to be here?

"Is there a possibility of a looking glass first? I have not yet seen the extent of my wound."

The woman grimaced for a moment and then nodded her head sagely. "I suppose you must. Prepare yourself. It might be a bit of a shock at first…." She looked at him with pity. That was it. Pity. He could feel his teeth grinding. Crossing the room to where some soldiers were shaving, she procured a cracked piece of mirror and handed it to him. He was not prepared for what he saw.

The right side of his face was raw and burned, and where his eye had once been gaped a pinkish empty socket. Some of the scattered wounds on his face were still festering. Must have been a blast of a shot. He suddenly had a flash of that Russian's face and the barrel of a shotgun. He felt his stomach heave. The nurse reached for the mirror and he clutched her arm.

"Wait. Let me look once more." He closed his good eye and, taking two deep breaths, looked at his face once again. "All right. Thank you."

"Stay there, sir. I will bandage your face." That was a small mercy. At least bandaged, his face would not look so ghoulish. He then thought of Julia… how perfect they looked together at that summer ball. Perfect.

With his face bandaged again, he made for the door. The old man who brought him there snagged him by the sleeve.

"Must get to work now, sir. More's comin' in. They had another tussle on Inkerman."

***

After having been greeted with such derision and even open hostility when they first arrived, the nurses of Miss Nightingale were reluctantly accepted. The casualties of the Balaclava battlefield and now the wounded from two battles on Inkerman so overwhelmed Scutari that the army medics were only too happy for an extra pair of hands, even if they were female. Eleanor continued in the improvised operating theatre with the surgeon. She was worked from early morning until the sun set with only time for tea and bread or some soup.

She was grateful that supplies of soap, towels, and other necessities were finally being delivered to Scutari. The conditions, though, were still appalling. Hundreds were dying of disease or wounds inadequately treated on the battlefield. Eleanor had never seen so many maggots in her life and wondered how the men could lie so still with them crawling through their flesh. After the first day, she was no longer squeamish and was thankful for her strong stomach and stoic nature. As she finally closed her eyes each night, she wondered how could men feel themselves superior to women? She did the work of a man day after day.

The clear morning in November dawned, and she reported to the operating room. Dr Walsh was not there, and a young woman she had not seen before entered, collecting cloths and towels that were left from the night before.

"Who are you?" Eleanor asked, as the woman went silently about her work.

"Mrs Grace Abernathy, ma'am."

"I have not seen you before. Are you among the nurses?"

Eleanor immediately knew that this girl was not a nurse. Her demeanour, her clothing, even her way of walking bespoke of a different social class. The woman laughed. "Oh, no, not me, ma'am. I'm the wife of Sergeant Abernathy of the 11th Hussars, come to collect the laundry."

It then dawned on Eleanor that the skirt from that first day that was so encrusted with blood and gore, and each one after that, were returned to her now in clean condition. Her mind being on the terrible work she did every day, she did not pursue the source of this miracle. "The wife…?"

"Of Sergeant Abernathy, yes, ma'am. Well, we were married legal sure, but the army don't think so."

Eleanor knit her brows together in disbelief. "Did you follow him here… here to Turkey… here to the battlefield?"

The young woman, her arms filled with soiled linen, stopped a moment. "Would 'ave been wit' him at Balaclava if I could, but they won't give me passage, so I does laundry 'ere for Miss Nightingale and I waits for 'im. I needs to go now, ma'am." She bustled out the door that Eleanor held open for her. Dr Davis approached from the far end of the hallway.

"Go to the wards, Miss Sherbrooke. We have no need of you today." His voice echoed over the bare walls. Eleanor wove her hands together and pressed them to her lips. As she shut her eyes, she made a fervent wish that they had seen the last of the carnage.

The ward work was as challenging, if not more so, than the operating theatre. Most of the day, she went from one bed to another, some only inches apart, giving water, or broth or tea to desperate men. There was little time for more than a cursory word or introduction, and then she was called upon to set a man upon a bedpan or bathe him best she could. There were still not enough beds for all, so she went about on the floor, trying to minister to each one.

There were so many of them, and although she scanned each crowded ward the minute she entered, she found no sign of Lieutenant Wentworth. As the sun sent its last rays through the large, newly washed windows, she came upon a young man on a litter, wearing the field uniform of the 17th Lancers. He was really no more than a boy, and from the smell of him, his wounds were severe. Attached to what was left of his tunic was a bugle. She scrutinised his face and wondered if she and Dr Walsh might have operated on him sometime during the last few endless days. Unfortunately, emanating from his prone body was that sickening smell of rotting flesh that came with gangrene. He was feverish and, she suspected, delirious. Nevertheless, she sought out a basin and cloth and applied a cool compress to his brow. He opened his eyes immediately.

"Is that you, Mum?"

"No, dear. It is Miss Sherbrooke. I am a nurse here. You are at Scutari."

The boy screwed up his face in confusion and shook his head. "No, Mum. I am home with you."

It was no use. The poor fellow was like so many others. He was nearing his time and his mind went back to the comfort of his home even if his body remained in this stinking sewer. She decided to take another tack. "Did you do your duty well, my son?"

He grew animated at this suggestion and even smiled. "I blew the charge, Mum. I was not afraid. I heard the command of Captain Morris and I blew the charge strong and clear. They followed me, Mum. For a time, I led the Light Brigade." His face then contorted, and he looked off into the empty air, his eyes seeing something Eleanor could not fathom.

Eleanor swallowed hard. She must not give in to sentimentality. If she should weaken and give way to emotion, she could never serve so many and witness all the death that she had been sent here to witness. “I am proud of you, son. Lie back now.”

He would not lie back but continued to talk. “Did you see Lieutenant Wentworth,Mum? He was there. I gave him a shave. I did. He saved me from cholera, so I gave him a shave.”

Now Eleanor knew the boy was delirious because what he said made no sense at all. But a cold chill ran through her when he talked of Joshua. He might have known something of his fate. “Does he live, son, Lieutenant Wentworth?”

Now the boy lay back and seemed to search the ceiling with his darting eyes. He closed them then and began to breathe evenly. Eleanor raised herself up wearily and went to seek out Dr Walsh. Perhaps he could do something for this poor boy before the decay and filth claimed another victim.

Chapter 7

The days dragged on with more wounded or sick arriving every day. The halls and wards were filled to overflowing, but unlike when they first arrived less than three weeks before, there was a great deal more organization. As the sun set and Dr Walsh dismissed her, Eleanor made her way again through the crowded hallways. Before she reached the nurses' quarters, Miss Nightingale came out to greet her.

"I have heard good things about you, Miss Sherbrooke. Dr Walsh is singing your praises."

Eleanor jerked her head back in surprise. "Really? Really?" It seemed incongruous with his gruff manner in the operating room.

"Dr Walsh even admits that you would make a fine doctor if not for the fact that you are a woman." Eleanor opened her mouth to reply to this extraordinary comment, but Miss Nightingale continued. "Well done, Miss Sherbrooke. Carry on."

Yes, she would carry on, exhausted as she was. It was then she thought of the young lad in the wards. Before she lay her burden down for the day, she would seek him out. Although she informed Dr Walsh of his condition, he was not brought to the operating theatre where she worked, but that did not mean he was unattended. There were other surgeons. He could have been seen to elsewhere.

The sun was fading, and she would soon need a lamp if she did not hurry. Finding the ward where the boy lay was not difficult, but it was now filled to overcrowding with newly arrived wounded from the Crimean battlefields. Picking her way carefully among the prostrate men, she arrived at her destination, and was surprised to see a soldier in the coat of the 17th Lancers bending over the boy. A bandage wound around the back of his head and again around his neck. From where she stood, she could not see their faces but could hear their conversation.

"Good to see you, sir." The young bugler was not delirious now, and that was a good sign. Perhaps he was improving.

"I have been looking for you for days, Brittain. Wanted to say you did well. A brave man and true."

The voice was unmistakable.

At first, Eleanor could not speak. She could not even swallow, and her heart pounded so that she felt it would knock itself to pieces.

"Tell my mother, sir, when you get back. Tell her... please, sir..." Brittain clutched at Joshua's coat.

"You may tell her yourself when you return."

"No, sir. I will never see her again. Tell her I did my..." The boy's voice faltered, and his arms went limp.

"Brittain.... Brittain. No...." Wentworth turned around and looked desperately for help. Eleanor could hardly breathe when he looked upon her.

"Eleanor," was all he said at first. He looked completely astonished for a moment then said, "Please, please, help him."

Eleanor knew before she reached the prostrate figure that the boy had already passed from this world to the next. Wentworth jumped up to get out of her way and stood at the boy's head whilst she felt for a pulse in his wrist and his neck. The poor child stared lifelessly at the ceiling. She closed his eyes and pulled the tattered blanket covering him over his face. There was no sound from Lieutenant Wentworth, and she raised her gaze to his.

A tear slipped from his eye, and he turned immediately away from her. His fists opened and closed, over and over again. Oddly, tears brimmed in her own eyes. On the first day of her arrival, she vowed that she would not give way to tears no matter what she saw or heard, but the sight of this dying boy and the tears of her beloved lieutenant wormed its way into a chink in her armour. She quickly wiped her face and, standing, called for an orderly to remove the body. Wentworth stood stock-still for a time, and then, when they raised the body to move it for burial, he rushed forward and took the bugle from Brittain's belt. "For his mother."

He stood leaning against the wall, bugle in his hand, looking at her. She did not move. Finally, he said, "My God, Eleanor." Taking a few steps forward in a most determined manner, he engulfed her in his arms, pressing the uninjured side of his face to hers. She threw her arms about him. How thin he felt, but the energy of life pulsed strongly through him.

"Oh, Joshua, Joshua," she said, forgetting herself completely. "I—"

"Dear Eleanor," he whispered as she lay her head against his chest and felt him breathing. Joy flooded her.

One of the injured men give out a feeble hoot, so she pulled away from him slightly. Reaching up, she gently ran her fingers along the bandage. "You are wounded."

"Lost an eye, turns out." He smiled at her, his mischievous expression flickering for just a moment before being replaced with sorrow once again.

She embraced him once more. "I am so sorry about your friend."

He said nothing, but his arms tightened around her. How many friends had he lost already?

"*Miss* Sherbrooke. Whatever do you think you are doing?" It was Miss Nightingale. "There is absolutely no fraternising with the wounded. Is that clear? I am surprised at you."

Eleanor was instantly abashed. She let go of Lieutenant Wentworth immediately and stood facing her superintendent, who strode determinedly towards her. Miss Nightingale was quite right. The nurses they encountered upon arrival at Scutari were a brazen and drunken lot. Miss Nightingale's nurses were to be an example. She hurried over to Eleanor, lamp in hand.

As she reached them, Lieutenant Wentworth spoke up. "I am sorry. Miss Sherbrooke is not to blame. We were both so surprised to see each other that—"

Miss Nightingale held the lamp up to Wentworth's face. "You are from the 17th… the Light Brigade."

"Indeed I am."

Miss Nightingale took in a deep breath, almost a sigh. "Then you must be Lieutenant Wentworth." She still was not smiling, but her demeanour seemed to soften. Eleanor remained quiet and waited. "This young lady has been scouring the wards for you, Lieutenant. I am pleased to see you are still among the living, for Eleanor's sake."

Eleanor bit her lip. This was the first time Miss Nightingale used her given name. There was a momentary, awkward silence, but in his usual, competent manner, Lieutenant Wentworth breached the chasm.

"I was here visiting my friend, Mr William Brittain. He blew the charge that set us upon the Russians. Unfortunately, he…." Wentworth's voice broke slightly.

Miss Nightingale held the lamp so that she could observe Eleanor. "Was this the boy you recommended to Dr Walsh, Miss Sherbrooke?"

Eleanor nodded. "I thought perhaps he could do something about the gangrene."

Miss Nightingale shook her head. "There is so little we can do. Poor lad."

This was an evening of miracles. In the last few minutes, Eleanor saw more warmth from the formidable Miss Nightingale than she had seen all the months she had known her. No one said anything for a few moments.

"Come along, Miss Sherbrooke. It is time for you to return to quarters." Miss Nightingale inclined her head towards Joshua. "Lieutenant Wentworth." Then, lamp in hand, she led the way for Eleanor, as they left Lieutenant Wentworth to the encroaching darkness and his grief.

***

6 Nov, 1854
Dear Eleanor,

How are you, sister? How do you fare in that awful place? Father insists on reading the papers and then tells me about the reports from Crimea. I cannot bear to read them myself; they are so distressing. Neither Lt. Wentworth's family nor I have heard word of him since that disastrous yet glorious charge down some awful valley. So many were killed. So many. Tell me, Eleanor, do you have news of him? I know that the Crimea is a big place and there are thousands of soldiers there, but if you have news, good or ill, please tell me. I cannot sleep for not knowing.

Cordelia sends her love and I have enclosed a letter from her for you. The London Season has ended, and Father talks of Lancashire and the shooting there. How can anyone think of shooting birds when there is a war on? Can you imagine?

Still, a weekend away from London would do wonders for my nerves...

Eleanor stopped reading. She knew the rest would be of people she did not care about in the first place and others that she did not know. They were going about their privileged lives as if nothing was happening. Still, there was a glimmer of concern in Julia's words, and Eleanor was glad of them. It was always good to hear from home. Putting Julia's letter away, she sought out Cordelia's.

3 Nov, 1854
Dear Eleanor,

How are you, my friend? I think of you often. Is there anything you need? Father says I can send you crates and crates of things. Whatever you want, Eleanor, to help you in your work or to give you some comfort. I feel so helpless here. The opinion of the war has turned considerably from the early days of cheering and singing and bands playing. I can barely force myself to read the papers anymore, the news is so overwhelmingly dire. Do you think of coming home, Eleanor? How can you bear it?

We have read of the disastrous charge of the Light Brigade and I tremble for you. Have you news of Lt. Wentworth? I fear for him. I fear for you. I know that you love him, Eleanor. I write this to you as you cannot deny it to my face. I pray that he was one of the few who survived.

As to news from home, I am still blissfully unmarried, much to my father's chagrin. Sometimes, when he is haranguing me, I tell him that I will go off and be a nurse in Crimea like you. The discussion of my future plans then ends abruptly. I know I am wicked, but I cannot help it. You see, Eleanor, you are helping me from afar. Dear, brave Eleanor, I do admire you so.

Again, please tell me of anything you want or need, for yourself or for your soldiers. I can send you heaps and heaps of champagne and caviar if that is what you desire. Write when you have a moment. We all think of you daily.

Your dear friend,
Cordelia

How different these two were. *Julia thinks only of herself and her misery. Well, she may think of Joshua, but does she really love him, and is that the source of her concern?* Eleanor shook her head to banish such thoughts. It was not her place to judge her sister or Lieutenant Wentworth. And then there was dear Cordelia. She was hilariously cheeky, and her letters always brought a smile to Eleanor's face. Since she offered, Eleanor would ask her to send some provisions, but certainly not champagne. She would ask for bandages, canned meat, soap, linens, medicine, perhaps even a surgical kit…and all manner of supplies the British army, in its infinite wisdom, did not think to bring on a campaign.

***

Lieutenant Wentworth exercised his privilege as an officer to procure an assignment as a litter bearer to the operating room where Eleanor was assigned. The alternative was scrubbing filthy walls and floors in the cholera ward. How women did such work was beyond his reckoning. He heard the cries of the wounded men emanating from the operating room well before he got there. The poor sod from the Royal Fusiliers who lay on the stretcher he was carrying looked at him in the most imploring manner.

"Don't take me in there, sir. I'll be all right. No need to cut." He was breathing heavily, and his eyes rolled back in his head as he tried to keep his gaze steady. The plaintive sound of the wretch nearly did Wentworth in. He needed to harden himself against the suffering if he was to be any service to these men at all.

"Dr Walsh knows what he is doing. It will all be over before you know it."

The man leaned his head to the side and looked down at his shattered leg. "How will I be any good without my leg, eh? How will I?" Tears began to roll down his cheeks. Wentworth had to look away. Perhaps scrubbing walls would have been better. He was rescued by the door opening and a call for the next man. Wentworth and Robinson lifted the stretcher, and Eleanor and the doctor pulled the man onto the crude operating table. The floor was sticky with blood. Eleanor momentarily looked into his eyes and then set to work cutting away the burnt fragments of the man's trousers.

"Don't just stand there, man. Go get the next one," Dr Walsh admonished him. "And clear away some of these maggots before you bring them in. Can't see what I'm doing."

As they shut the door and carried the empty litter between them, Robinson began to whistle. Wentworth could hear the groans of the unfortunate patient they had just brought in.

"How can you whistle with all this going on?"

Robinson looked at him quizzically. "Don't know, sir. Get used to it, I suppose." He began whistling again as they walked to the reception gallery.

It turned Wentworth's stomach. He would rather be on the battlefield than watch all this agony. Eleanor might be able to help him return there. She could look at his wounds and pronounce him fit for duty, or even get one of the doctors to do so. Perhaps he was well enough to return to his regiment. He had been at the hospital for more than a week.

As darkness fell, Wentworth and Robinson returned for the severed limbs the good doctor and Eleanor had separated from their owners. They had a small, wheeled cart that looked as if it had been commandeered from some unfortunate Tatar farmer. Wentworth insisted on covering the gruesome mess with a cloth so as not to further distress the men who still lay scattered about in the hallways. The casualties and sick were coming in wave after wave. It was unfathomable to him how the nurses and Miss Nightingale were coping with this relentless onslaught.

When he returned to deposit the empty litter, Eleanor was there, scrubbing the wooden table they used for their grisly work. Men were on their hands and knees scrubbing the floor. The sound of the door opening elicited a response.

Eleanor did not look up from her industry. "There are no more to be taken, Robinson. Thank you."

"Is there anything else I can do for you, Sister?" Wentworth said.

At the sound of his voice, Eleanor looked up from her scrubbing and smiled. "Yes, Lieutenant. You can help me empty these buckets."

He picked his way carefully over the wet floor and took hold of both buckets.

"Oh, you needn't do my work for me, sir. I can carry my share." As she took one of the buckets from his hand, she spoke lightly, but the intensity in which she met his gaze was disconcerting.

He leaned in close and whispered to her. "I must speak to you, Eleanor."

They exited together and walked to the ground floor. Eleanor led them to a drain on the outside of the building. "Pour it in there…but watch out. The rats."

He looked at her disbelieving, and as he began to discard the bloody water, at least twenty rats scrambled from the sewer and scattered over their shoes. He jumped back with a shout and she giggled.

"Did I not warn you?" She threw the contents of her bucket swiftly down the drain. The rats did not repeat their frenzied exit.

"How ever did you do that?" he asked, astonished.

She laughed. "You disturbed them, and they fled. Now, there aren't any more."

"You did that on purpose to watch me jump."

She touched his sleeve. "I do apologise, Lieutenant. No more tricks, I assure you."

The harbour lay below them in the distance, the sparkling shafts of light glittering on the calm waves. As evening settled upon them, the red sun slowly sank into the sea.

"Come along," she said after they stood in silence for a time. "Miss Nightingale likes to account for us when darkness comes."

They returned to the stone stairwell and did not speak until they reached the entrance to the second floor.

"Could you change my bandage, Miss Sherbrooke?"

The wound beneath had been weeping as it was stained yellow in patches. She hoped she could remove the bandage without hurting him.

"Of course. Come with me." As they walked, Eleanor wondered if he had requested to work with her. She must stop thinking such thoughts and quickly reminded herself that he was her sister's intended. "Here, sit down, and we will see what we can do."

She stopped near a window on the west side of the building that caught the last remaining rays of light. A table with dressings on it held a lantern. Eleanor lit it and then fetched a pitcher of water and a basin. Wentworth sat down in a camp chair, and Eleanor bent over the basin, soaking a clean cloth in water. She then pressed it against Lieutenant Wentworth's face to loosen the encrustations of his wound below.

Three weeks ago, there was no such cloth to be found. Slowly, incrementally, things were improving at Scutari. There was more fresh water than a fortnight ago. The sanitation people arrived from England and began draining the cesspool beneath the building. All these things were the doing of Miss Florence Nightingale, and Eleanor felt a certain pride in knowing that she was part of her work.

As she tilted his chin upward towards her, the soaked cloth warmed in her hand as she held it to his cheek. His eyes were closed. How he trusted her. She wanted to lean down and touch her lips to his, but thoughts of Julia and his attachment to her cooled her ardour. Besides, she had work to do, and she was also preparing herself for what she might find beneath those bandages.

As soon as the cloth on his face had soaked enough to remove it without tearing away the healing flesh beneath, she began to undo the knots that held it to his forehead and his neck. As she touched the top of the cloth to pull it away from his face, he grasped her hands in his and stopped her. "Whatever is the matter?"

"I fear I shall be hideous in your eyes, and I do not think I could bear it. Perhaps another sister could assist me."

Eleanor let go of the bandage and sat down in a rickety camp chair, facing him. "I will get someone else, if you insist, but there is no need. Whatever your wound, you will always be the handsomest man I have ever met…." She stood again, moving close to him. "And the bravest."

He said nothing but let his hands fall to his sides. She took hold of the bandage and slowly peeled it away. Surreptitiously biting her lower lip, she gazed upon the wound, conscious of every twitch and shift in her expression. Even if horrified, she would not betray her feelings to Lieutenant Wentworth.

The sunlight had faded to black, and the flickering lamplight threw the slashing scars that ran the length of his face in sharp relief. She had seen wounds similar to these before, usually caused by fire. The skin was pockmarked and stretched from his forehead to his chin. To her relief, he retained all of his nose, and even most of his moustache. His eye socket, however, was empty.

"The wound is disfiguring, is it not?"

She nodded without saying anything. "But I have seen worse. Much worse. Your face is healing nicely. I believe we shall leave it open to the air, but you must keep it clean until all the skin has healed. I will put a patch over your eye and will have Cordelia send you a silk one from London." She forced herself to smile.

"You mean Julia. Julia will send me one."

Eleanor turned to lather a cloth with soap and to hide her expression. *Julia, ha! Julia who faints at the sight of blood. Julia who complains only of her own worry and loneliness. No, that is not fair. Surely, if she knew, Julia would send anything he needs to him. She, someday, will marry him.* Eleanor began washing the wound. In a day or two, he would need no more ministrations from her.

"Time to go back to the front. What do you think, Sister Eleanor?"

Those words pierced Eleanor like a dagger through the heart. The front? No, no. He could not put himself in harm's way again. She wouldn't have it.

"What will you do at the front? You cannot see."

He jerked back from her touch and glared at her. Of course, she immediately regretted her words, and now, after finding him again, the last thing she wanted to do was make him angry. But someone would say those words to him. If not her, then some regimental captain. In an instant, she decided not to soften the blow for him, but soldier on.

"Sit still and let me finish." She soaped up the side of his face, and then sponged it off twice with clear water. He was healing and, if they wanted him back, he could go back. She knew it and it terrified her. Some minutes passed, and she fixed a bandage to his eye. He still had not spoken to her.

"Damn it, Eleanor," he said finally, "you are right again. What use am I to them now? I am sure I will be invalided back to England."

"Would that be so terrible?" She was close to his face now as she affixed the patch over his eye.

"Who would take care of Merlin?" He sounded like a little boy just then, asking after a puppy dog.

"Merlin? Merlin survived the fray?"

Wentworth became animated again. "Oh, indeed he did. As soon as I regained consciousness, I asked after him. They told me that he brought me back to the lines himself. Must have gone through the gap the French tried to make for us. I suppose he did. I don't remember. You should have seen him, Eleanor. Never balked. Cannon fire all around him, men and horses falling in agony, smoke choking us. Never faltered, never even flinched. And the charge, Eleanor. You should have seen him. Like a shell shot from a gun, he thundered down the valley and right up into the fire of the Russian guns. Magnificent. Incredible."

Yes, you are, Lieutenant Wentworth. You are magnificent, incredible. Eleanor gazed at his suddenly enthusiastic expression as he told the tale and wondered how a man who had thrown himself into the jaws of death like he did could attribute all the glory to his horse.

"There. All finished. Keep it clean, and I believe you will be right as rain soon enough."

As she moved to step back and admire her handiwork, Lieutenant Wentworth grasped both her hands in his. "Please speak to the doctors for me, Eleanor. I need to get back to my men, and to Merlin. We have to finish this."

She said nothing but stared at the hands enfolding hers. He followed her gaze to their clasped hands but did not release her immediately. Instead, he brought her hands to his lips and, ever so gently, kissed her fingers. A thrill like a feather being brushed lightly against her skin ran up her spine and down again and trembled there between her legs. Looking up at her, he suddenly let her go.

"I do not know what came over me. Forgive me." He would not meet her eyes.

"Never." She laughed. He looked up at her and that mischievous smile she had so missed returned to his face.

His expression turned serious again. "Speak to the doctors for me, Eleanor. I must go back."

***

Wentworth knew that Merlin would be happy to see him, but he was surprised that the horse reared up whinnying and snorting and shaking his mane at the sight of him.

"How are you, old man?" Wentworth patted the horse's neck. "Brought you a treat from Eleanor…a carrot." He opened his hand

and the horse greedily accepted the delicacy. "That is thanks for saving my life."

Upon his return to Crimea, he was greeted with sick men, short supplies, and low spirits. Merlin looked decidedly thin. It was raining relentlessly, a cold, never-ending downpour. The siege seemed to be going nowhere. Men were stuck, day after day, in the trenches surrounding Sebastopol as they filled with water and mud. Wentworth, on stable duty, occupied his time making an earthen and rock corral for the horses. Perhaps today he could fit it with a roof. No doubt snow would be on its way soon. There was hope, though. Rumours of a great fleet bringing food and winter clothing to Balaclava were flying through the camp. The cavalry had saved Balaclava. Now it was time for the port to save them.

For the next few days, the rain never seemed to cease. The cold November weather was wearing on everyone. The men, so many of whom were stricken with diarrhoea and confined to hastily constructed hospital marquees, shivered in the damp weather—their summer uniforms inadequate for the worsening climate.

As the morning of 14 November dawned, the rain finally ceased, and the day dawned bright and sunny. For the first time since his return, Wentworth left his tent with a light heart. The aroma of roasting coffee in the officers' mess drifted up, and an orderly set a steaming cup in front of him.

"Breakfast, sir?"

"Salt pork and biscuit?"

"Aye, how did you guess?"

"I have been to this restaurant before."

The orderly laughed and presently lay before Wentworth a plate with not only salt pork and biscuit but also two fried eggs. Joshua looked down on them as if they appeared by magic.

"How ever did you come upon these?"

The orderly put his finger aside his nose. "I have me ways, sir. Now enjoy. Nothing too good for the 17th."

It was a rare treat to have fresh eggs for breakfast and Wentworth would not turn it down, even if the origin was a chicken stolen from some hapless Tatar farmer. For the first time in a long time, Wentworth did not dread the day ahead. Something good was going to happen, he could feel it.

As the morning turned to afternoon, however, the weather betrayed them. A front of bloodred clouds formed on the western horizon. It did not bode well. He was crossing from the tents to his corral when all the furies of hell descended on them.

The first barrage of the great storm was a driving rain that beat the ground so heavily that it seemed to be fired from a million pistols. The horses gave up a whinnying cry, and the wind came at all of them with such force that tent pegs were torn from the ground and everything from canvas shelters to pots and pans were sent flying. Men lost their footing and crawled upon the ground, seeking shelter. Wentworth's first thought was of Merlin.

He could not stand upright against the onslaught, so clawed his way along the ground towards the unfinished shelter where he kept his horse and those of the other officers. Unexpectedly, he saw coming towards him at a great speed a tumbling bullock cart that was being tossed along the ground as a child would toss a toy. Wentworth flattened himself immediately in the mud as the cart rolled head over heels over him. The force of the gale was incredible. He mused for a moment at the irony of it all. What if he survived the Light Brigade's charge through the valley and was subsequently killed by a flying frying pan?

The horses whinnied in fright, and now soaked to the skin and covered in mud, he made his way towards them. The wind was howling so and had uprooted everything in the camp to such a degree that he had no idea if he was headed in the right direction. For an interminable time, he tore his way along the ground, and lifting his head from time to time, finally arrived at the partially finished shelter he built.

Now he wished mightily he had finished it, but again, no roof could withstand the force of the wind. As he threw himself behind the low wall of the corral, he tried to stand and take hold of Merlin's bridle in an attempt to force him to lie down.

"Come on, old man, come down here with me. Don't be stubborn." He shouted with all his might, but the wind seemed to swallow his voice. Debris flew, and the rain stung like nettles assaulting his face and hands. Wentworth leaned against the horse's side and tried to think. The panic in him subsided a bit, and he stroked the horse's back and neck. Merlin was well trained, and not just to verbal commands. He tried to place himself before the horse's head so the animal could see him clearly and obey his commands. The wind was at such a force and the ground so greasy with mud that he lost his footing more than once and slipped, sliding some distance from Merlin. If the situation had not been so dire, his predicament might be comical. After some time, he was able to soothe the horse enough that he obeyed his command to lie down. When they were both sheltered as best they could behind the half-finished wall, he gave the beast a friendly pat.

Now, he had to try to save the other horses. To his relief, he did not have to attempt to stand again, as the other animals followed Merlin's example. Before long, they were joined by men of the 11th Hussars and the 4th Light Dragoons… what was left of them. Some attempted to talk to him, but he shook his head. The wind carried their words away. All took shelter next to the prostrate horses, the warmth of their bodies welcomed in the driving rain.

Wentworth did not know how long they lay there together in the wet and the mud. The sky was still imbued with some grey light, so he knew that evening had not yet fallen. One thing he was sure of as the wind eased: the temperature dropped. Soon they were lying in a foot of mud, soaked to the skin, watching the newly arrived snowflakes descend.

When he could find his footing, Wentworth stood up and gave a command. "All of you, see if we can find some tents and get ourselves some shelter."

The men's teeth were chattering, as were his. They all rose and trooped out to retrieve whatever canvas or boards remained that had not been blown miles away. Darkness gathered.

***

Eleanor was working in the wards when the great storm slashed at the barrack windows. The rain came down in sheets, and the men, usually so stoic in their suffering, began to moan and cry out. She stood at the head of the ward to speak to them.

"It is just a storm, gentlemen. There is nothing to fear. Lie down and rest. We will take care of everything."

In her month at Scutari, Eleanor had become an adept liar. She was sure of nothing. When the cannonade of wind flung itself at the windows, she was sure they would shatter and leave all of them, medical staff and patients alike, in the rain and the cold. Miss Nightingale arrived in her ward and organised the walking wounded and the orderlies to do what they could to stop up the chinks in the western windows. They were somewhat sheltered on the south side of the vast building, but the windows rattled, and the rain beat down. Eleanor had to admit to herself that she was unnerved.

"Do not show your fear to the patients, Miss Sherbrooke." Eleanor jumped at the sound of Miss Nightingale's voice. "Remember, we are their solace in their time of need. I do not need my nurses going to pieces over a winter storm."

Eleanor took breath. "Yes, miss. I will endeavour to be calm. You can rely on me." Even as she said these words, she knew them to be false. Every nerve burned with fear. What would they do if this hurricane breached Scutari? They were already without enough medicine and supplies to adequately care for these poor men. She leaned against the cold stone wall and forced herself to take long breaths. Her nanny would advise such a thing when she was so angry that she was hysterical. She felt on the verge of hysteria now. The long hours, the inadequate supplies, day after day of sickness, death, and suffering all stretched every nerve. Now, the weather was adding to her despair. She must stop thinking such thoughts. There were people who depended on her. She could not fall sick with nervous exhaustion. There was no provision for it.

She did not know how long she stood there, immobile, trying to get hold of herself. She knew she had to move but could not. Then a friendly voice called through the howling ruckus.

"Eleanor, I brought you a cup of tea. Here, drink it." Millie came over.

With shaking hands, she took the cup and raised it to her lips.

"It will be all right, Eleanor. You will see. It will be all right."

The warm liquid and the imperturbable Millie seemed to have a transformative power over her, and she forced herself to take a step away from the wall. A few more followed, and she felt that she would soon be able to resume her duties.

"At least we have a roof over our heads. Imagine those poor souls in Crimea. Whatever will they do?"

Eleanor put the teacup down and put her hand over her mouth. He had just returned to his regiment. What had become of Lieutenant Wentworth?

***

How they managed to find and then pitch three tents in the snow and the mud, Wentworth would never know. All the men were soaked to the skin, and there was no dry fuel, no fuel at all, with which to build a fire. Wentworth had never known such misery.

He could have commandeered a tent for himself as an officer, but truth be told, he preferred to sleep in the open with Merlin. The heat from the horse's body was more than a tent could afford him. The snow fell rapidly now.

Lying next to his horse, he fell into a fitful sleep.

There was a mighty crash, and he awoke with a start. Then another booming report and another. Someone was shelling someone in Sebastopol despite all this misery. He hated the Russians at that moment. He hated them. His only comfort was in knowing that ships waited in the harbour, filled with warm boots and greatcoats and food for his men and their horses. They would endure until those things could be procured.

The next few days were filled with reconnaissance. The horses were too sick and too thin to be of much help, so the cavalry, who were not in the trenches, went about the countryside to search for whatever was left of their tents and cooking pots. Some men were put to work burying the dead. When the hospital marquees took off like great, billowing kites, the wind spilled the sick and wounded into the mud. Many, who were barely hanging onto life, lost it during the storm. As the men came back with scavenged fuel, some salvaged canvas, or by some miracle blankets, Wentworth built fires and dried the blankets first. The men then removed their clothing and wrapped themselves in them while their clothing dried. It was slow and painstaking, but little by little, men were restored to some modicum of comfort. Where were the supplies from the port?

There was precious little to feed the horses, and any forage that could once be found was now under a blanket of snow. Some of the poor beasts took to eating each other's tails to stave off starvation. Wentworth could stand it no longer. He sought out his captain.

"I don't see the harm in it, Wentworth. See if you can get something from the old man. I was going to try myself, but do not want to leave the men in such a state. Go."

After slogging through the mud for hours, he finally arrived. "Lieutenant Joshua Griffiths Wentworth, sir." He saluted Lord Raglan in what was left of his quarters. It was an old farmhouse that had lost its roof in the storm. Some soldiers were put to the task of patching it back together. "Sir, I have been sent by my captain to request permission to take a troop of men to Balaclava for supplies."

Raglan looked up from his makeshift desk and regarded Wentworth without emotion. "Ah, yes. Supplies. Supplies from the harbour." Wentworth did not know what to make of him. Was the man addled? The old general's jaw worked as if the words were inside his mouth and he was endeavouring to keep them from escaping. His eyes seemed to wander upwards, past Wentworth to a corner of the farmhouse.

"I will tell you something, Lieutenant, in the strictest confidence. May I have your word?"

Wentworth squared his shoulders. "You can rely on my discretion, sir."

"Very good, Wentworth…." The commander-in-chief sighed and stood up from the table. He walked to a cold fireplace devoid of wood or coal and took a pipe from the mantel. Slowly and methodically, he filled it, turning every few seconds to gaze at Wentworth. The lieutenant felt as if he was being scrutinised, perhaps for his trustworthiness.

"Your face there, Lieutenant. Battle wound?"

"Yes, sir, Balaclava."

This news seemed to slow the general down to nearly a standstill. Men were freezing to death without shelter. Men were sent uncomplaining, soaking wet and cold, back into the trenches. The horses and mules were starving. All he wanted was permission to retrieve what they all needed. Why was the general hesitating?

"Ah, yes. Balaclava. What unit did you say you were from?"

"The 17th Lancers, sir."

The general raised his eyebrows. "Light Brigade, eh?"

"Yes, sir." Now, in the general's presence, he wanted badly to ask him what he was thinking when he ordered the Light Brigade to charge straight into the Russian guns. Unfortunately, it was not his place to do so.

"Bloody fool thing, that charge. Even the Russians thought we were mad."

Wentworth could not believe his ears. A fool thing? How could he say that when he, himself, had given the order? After hearing that remark, Wentworth decided to press the general on that very matter. "Begging your pardon, sir, about the—"

"Yes, yes, yes. The harbour… Balaclava…." The general seemed to wake from his reverie momentarily. They were back to the subject at hand. "There is no way to tell you this but plainly, Lieutenant. The Great Storm sunk the fleet. Most of it, that is. Three hundred lives lost. Sixty thousand greatcoats lost. All the munitions and guns for the winter campaign—lost. Fodder for the horses—lost. Nine thousand gallons of rum—lost. The only thing that wasn't lost was that blasted Duberly woman. She seems to have nine lives."

Fanny Duberly—Wentworth had heard of her. She followed her husband to the Crimea and lived on ship in the harbour. He tried to picture Julia following him to war but could not. But blast Fanny Duberly. Whatever was he saying about their supplies?

"Pardon me, sir. Are you sure that we have lost everything?"

"Lost nearly everything. I received word this morning. The storm crashed the blasted ships onto the rocks or smashed them together in such a fashion that they splintered into a thousand pieces and sank. Sank with everything… everything I need to win this bloody war."

"Is there nothing left, sir? There must be something. I can take my men and—"

"If you think you can get through the mud, you are welcome to try. Heaven knows the poor souls in the trenches need whatever we can give them…." Raglan finally took a drag on his pipe. "Go, Wentworth. See what you can do."

The general lay down his pipe and scribbled an order and handed it to Wentworth. "Good luck."

Chapter 8

News of the disaster at the harbour at Balaclava reached Scutari in a few days. It came to them along with the newest casualties of war: men with frostbite. Eleanor was again assigned to Dr Walsh primarily, as his skill in amputations was unsurpassed in the hospital. Having received no word from Lieutenant Wentworth after he left to rejoin his regiment, she was again filled with anxiety as to his safety. The word brought back by the men she treated was anything but encouraging. The first of the patients arrived in the operating theatre during the last days of November.

"Unwrap the bandages, Sister." Dr Walsh prepared his instruments with his back to Eleanor. The soldier's foot was encased in mud-crusted rags, and with sunken eyes, he lay silent upon the table. The men she saw now were quite different from those with battle wounds. These were half-starved, some just emerging from drunkenness, their clothes in rags, damp and fetid. She carefully undid the bandage, and the man's foot fell off into her hand. He made no sound nor moved in any way.

Eleanor was not one, after all she had seen, to be faint of heart or easily appalled, but this was a fresh horror for which she had not prepared herself. She ran from the operating table and retched in the corner. Upon recovering herself, she washed her hands again and resumed her place at the operating table. Dr Walsh said nothing but turned to the faithful Robinson, who stood at the ready with the litter.

"Go fetch nurse a cup of tea, there's a good man."

Eleanor began to cut away the soldier's trouser leg. After a cup of tea, Robinson took his place at the soldier's head and administered the chloroform. The doctor began to cut.

Many more cases of frostbite arrived that day. After the first gruesome case, Eleanor was mentally prepared for the rest. *So, this is the new abyss into which these poor soldiers have been cast.* And still, they bore their suffering with so much stoicism. Eleanor could not help but admire them.

As the last case of the day was taken back to the wards, she addressed Dr Walsh. “Sir, do you have any medical books with you?”

Dr Walsh deposited his instruments into a waiting basin where she would clean them momentarily. “I do have a few here, why?”

“I am interested in reading about frostbite. Do you have any that address that condition?”

Dr Walsh’s expression softened. “I expect there is a little in each of the volumes. I will send them on to the nurses’ quarters for you.” He removed his apron, which bore the bloodstained evidence of their day’s activities, and began to roll down his sleeves. “What do you hope to learn, Miss Sherbrooke? By the time these men reach us, the damage has been done.”

“Yes, I know, but perhaps we could make recommendations to the commanders in the field if we knew more about the condition.” She was being earnest, but he looked amused.

“I cannot imagine a military commander taking any heed of what we have to say, Miss Sherbrooke, but you are welcome to my books. I would like to discuss anything you discover there.”

Eleanor scrutinised his face for a hint of teasing or sarcasm but found none. She finished preparing the theatre for the next day and took advantage of the remaining light to dash down the stairs. After reaching the large entry doors, she pushed one of them open and stepped outside. For the first time that day, she filled her lungs with fresh air. It smelled of the sea. Miss Nightingale had accomplished her goal and drained the fetid cesspool beneath Scutari.

Her mind was not on the vast improvements that she and the other nurses had made. It was consumed instead by a theory she was forming about the cause of this rash of frostbite cases. The weather was cold, to be sure, but not so cold as to cause the limbs of these men to freeze solid—at least not on most nights. Something else was at work, and she would discover it.

***

When Wentworth made his first trip to Balaclava, the track that had not been reinforced or paved in any way was a sea of mud. The poor mules trying to navigate it were stuck after only a few steps, and the cartwheels were turned by men walking behind them as well as animals. General Lucan received the command from Lord Raglan to mobilise the cavalry to transport the sick and the wounded from the front to Balaclava. There they would bring back as many supplies as they could for the men fighting in the waterlogged trenches around Sebastopol.

Upon finally reaching the harbour, the backbreaking physical exertion was replaced by incessant haggling. Men appointed by Her Majesty's government wanted reams of paperwork signed by officers who were miles back at the front in order to release basic goods needed by the troops. Wentworth, clothed in a ragged, muddy uniform, found himself facing one of these bureaucrats.

"You bloody bastard." Wentworth fished around in his jacket and produced the hastily written order of Lord Raglan's. "I have this order, signed by the commander-in-chief himself."

The little man gingerly took the folded note and carefully straightened it out on his desk. Wrinkling up his nose, he disdainfully brushed the mud from the edges. He perused it carefully, and then pushed it back in Wentworth's direction. "I am afraid this won't do."

Wentworth lost his temper. "You will release these goods, or I will have you put under military arrest."

The official, who was well dressed, had pomade in his hair, and was freshly shaven, looked up in horror at Wentworth.

"You cannot do that. I am an official of Her Majesty's government. You will be court-martialed."

Wentworth set his jaw and then pointed to his face. "Do I look like a man who is frightened by the likes of you? Do I?"

"Now, now, sir, let us keep our heads. Perhaps it would be all right if you filled out the forms here for me and signed them, then I…"

Wentworth snatched the papers from the little martinet and on the bottom of each, wrote his signature. Within the hour, the brave men of the Light Brigade were loading charcoal, fodder, victuals, and blankets for their arduous journey back to the trenches. Some, he hoped, would fall to the men and beasts behind the lines, the men of the cavalry.

As the crates were being loaded, Wentworth scanned the harbour. Evidence of the destruction of the British and French fleets was in evidence all around. Ships lay partially submerged, some were dismasted. Most telling of all was the masses of floating timber and bodies still bobbing about in the water. His winter boots and greatcoat were at the bottom of the sea. It would be months before new provisions were sent, and by then the winter would be over. Perhaps even the war.

While they were loading their bullock carts, a platoon of Dragoons from the Heavy Brigade arrived. They were leading a band of bedraggled men, many afoot, some in carts, all with the look of dead men. Wentworth hailed them, and one of their officers made his way over. Never forgetting his military discipline, Wentworth saluted and introduced himself. The Dragoon offered his hand.

"Lieutenant Kelly at your service, sir."

"Always happy to see the Heavy Brigade."

Kelly laughed. "I thought I would never live to hear those words from your lot…sir."

"We are all on the same side, and now doing the same duty, are we not?"

Kelly sighed and looked about. "That we are, Wentworth. For all the misery, I think we have the best of it. Look at those poor sods." He pointed a thumb toward the wounded infantrymen being unloaded from the carts. "Most of them with rotten feet, swollen into shoes that don't fit, frostbit hands and toes." Kelly shivered. "Bound for that rathole, Scutari."

Wentworth's eyes lit up. "Not such a rathole anymore, I should think. Miss Nightingale and her nurses were cleaning up the place when I was there."

Kelly arched his brow. "You were there then and lived to tell about it? Perhaps there is some truth in what you say. Well, I must go, I—"

Wentworth took hold of Kelly's sleeve. "Wait. I would like to send a letter to Scutari, to one of the nurses there."

Kelly slapped Wentworth on the back and guffawed. "Why you sly devil, you. Good on you. I can send it with the boatman. Do you have it?"

Wentworth patted his jacket and shook his head. "I have neither paper nor pen, but I have a 'friend' in that office there who would be ever so glad to accommodate me. Also, I have something for you." He reached into his inner pocket and retrieved the order from General Raglan.

"It might prove useful in prying the goods from Her Majesty's officials that you are charged with obtaining."

Kelly undid the document and looked at Wentworth with admiration. "From old 'Look-On' himself. Well done."

With that, the two men returned to Her Majesty's Commissariat to pry loose pen, paper, and a few more provisions left rotting on the docks of Balaclava.

***

Julia sat in the drawing room of George Shaw's Lancashire hunting lodge, smiling wryly in his direction. She knew he was smitten with her. The longer the months of the war dragged on, the less she was convinced that her engagement to Lieutenant Wentworth should go forward. The man hardly wrote to her. Was it so difficult to pick up a pen and paper? He could not be fighting all the time. Having all this time to think made her wonder if she had made a mistake.

That incident in her garden when he cut his hand to pieces played over and over in her mind. What made him break that glass? He crushed it in his hand the moment she mentioned his going into business with his father. Despite her charms, she may not be able to persuade him to give up the army and join the family business, guaranteeing their continued prosperity. Was she looking forward to living on an officer's pay and a small allowance? Would his father make good on his threat to cut him off from the family fortune? Or heaven forfend, would they have to live on her money?

George was talking grouse with one of his cohorts, but turned periodically to give her a knowing glance, or lift his glass to her. She was playing coy. Men loved a conquest, and she knew how to put them through their paces. As she talked of the new fashions from Paris with the other young women assembled, she took time to look him over carefully. He was not as handsome as Joshua Wentworth, but then, who was? He also was not as honourable. That particular quality was becoming less and less attractive the longer Joshua was gone. George also had one brilliant quality that Julia truly admired. He came from old, aristocratic money.

"Julia, you seem so pensive these days. Is something wrong?" Amelia Southerland ran her finger around the edge of her glass and looked pointedly at Julia.

"This war. It just drags on and on. Lieutenant Wentworth promised to be home in a few months and look now: the new year has passed." She fixed her expression in a little pout and aimed it at George.

William Mosley knocked the tobacco from his pipe into the fireplace. "I do not expect that he has much to say about it. Have you read the papers? The conditions there are appalling."

George Shaw raised his eyebrows but did not take his gaze from Julia. "You should not fret so over Lieutenant Wentworth. I am sure he can take care of himself. He survived The Charge of the Light Brigade after all. Brave man, wot?"

What was Mr Shaw on about? Was he trying to endear himself to her by complimenting Lieutenant Wentworth? She knew they all heard of their assignation in the garden last spring, but she was deadly quite about any engagement. Did they all assume the two of them were engaged? She did wear the ring that Joshua gave her, so she benefited by the assumption everyone made of their engagement, evidenced by the ring, and the small doubt as to the arrangement between them because of her reticence to make anything public. No army general was better at strategy than she.

It was then that William Mosley began to recite. The entire company fell silent, all eyes turned upon him as he spoke.

"Half a league, half a league,
Half a league onward,
All in the valley of Death
Rode the six hundred.
"Forward, the Light Brigade!
Charge for the guns!" he said:
Into the valley of Death
Rode the six hundred.

"Forward, the Light Brigade!"
Was there a man dismayed?
Not though the soldier knew
Some one had blundered:

Their's not to make reply,
Their's not to reason why,
Their's but to do and die:
Into the valley of Death
Rode the six hundred.

Cannon to right of them,
Cannon to left of them,
Cannon in front of them
Volleyed and thundered;
Stormed at with shot and shell,
Boldly they rode and well,
Into the jaws of Death,
Into the mouth of Hell
Rode the six hundred.

Flashed all their sabres bare,
Flashed as they turned in air
Sabring the gunners there,
Charging an army, while
All the world wondered:
Plunged in the battery-smoke
Right through the line they broke;
Cossack and Russian
Reeled from the sabre-stroke
Shattered and sundered.
Then they rode back, but not,
Not the six hundred..."

At the last few words of the verse, Julia let out a muffled cry and broke the spell William Mosley had created. She covered her mouth with her hand, and George Shaw erupted.

"For God's sake, Mosley. What are you about? Look how you have upset Miss Sherbrooke."

Julia read Tennyson's poem when it was published the month before. Now, reminded of it, she was struck with a sickening feeling that turned her taste sour and, to her surprise, brought tears to her eyes. She was reminded at that moment, quite vehemently, of her pledge to Joshua Wentworth, and now she was ashamed of herself.

With every ball, with every shooting weekend since his departure, she was betraying him. He, who was prepared to give his life for his country. He, who bravely rode into the Valley of Death. Looking down at the ring he gave her, she could remain among them no longer. She stood up quickly.

"I do believe I will go to my room. I suddenly do not feel very well." A murmur went up in the assembly, but she did not hear what anyone was saying. Finding the staircase, she stopped and closed her eyes, breathing rapidly. Then, quickly ascending the stairs, she resolved to write a long letter to her fiancé.

***

Dr Walsh was as good as his word, and after the evening meal, Eleanor sat by candlelight to pore over anything she could about frostbite and gangrene. Millie came upon her, already dressed for bed.

"Eleanor, whatever are you doing? Miss Nightingale will be well and truly cross if she sees you using candles in so cavalier a manner."

Eleanor barely acknowledged her; she was so engrossed in her reading. Finally, she looked up. "I am sorry, Millie. What did you say?"

"The candles, Eleanor? We are not to waste them."

"I am not wasting them, I assure you. It is for the benefit of the men that I make my study." She smiled mischievously at her friend. "Besides, Miss Nightingale is up and about with that lamp of hers, checking the wards. By the time she returns, I shall be tucked up in bed."

Millie shook her head, but the gleam in her eye reassured Eleanor that she was safe in her confidence.

"The men think Miss Nightingale a visiting angel, you know."

"Oh, I know. I suspect, though, that some of her purpose in prowling about at night is to keep those women who were here before us from molesting the patients or drinking themselves into a stupor."

Millie's mouth dropped open. "My goodness, Eleanor, you have become quite cynical."

Eleanor sighed. “I believe you are right. I do think Miss Nightingale does bring a modicum of comfort to the men. I am rebuked.” With that, she gave a rueful laugh. “Now, go to bed. I have work to do.”

Millie did not go to bed but put her hand upon Eleanor’s shoulder. “You will overwork yourself, Eleanor. Do not stay up too late. It will do no one any good if you fall ill yourself.”

Eleanor nodded, but was already engrossed in her reading once again. Only when she heard the door of the nurses’ quarters open to admit who she assumed was Miss Nightingale did she blow out the candle and trundle off to bed.

The next morning, Eleanor arrived at the operating theatre with a small notebook and a pencil. After she prepared the instruments for another day’s service, she began writing. Dr Walsh crept up behind her and peered over her shoulder.

“Whatever are you doing, Miss Sherbrooke?”

The sound of his voice made Eleanor stiffen. “Oh, Doctor Walsh. You startled me.” She turned her head towards him. He was so close to her that their lips nearly touched. He stepped back from her immediately.

“Oh, I do beg your pardon.” The man was obviously embarrassed, but there was not time to discuss anything. Robinson and his partner had already arrived with the first patient. As they transferred him from the litter to the operating table, Eleanor continued writing.

“With your permission, Doctor, I would like to take down the details of each patient’s injury, whether from frostbite or from wounding in the field. Then I want to see how each progress after treatment.”

“Details? For what purpose?” He was already tying his apron around his waist and rolling up his sleeves.

“I think that perhaps the conditions in the trenches, the men’s all-around physical condition, their nutrition, their clothing, might be factors in how susceptible they are to frostbite.”

Dr Walsh scoffed. “I do not see how, but if you must, you must. I do not want your note taking to interfere with the efficiency of our work here, Miss Sherbrooke.”

“Oh, no, Doctor. Rest assured that I will not cause any delays.” Ironically, instead of cutting away the man’s bandages and clothing, she asked his name, his regiment, the condition of his diet, and many more questions about life in the trenches. She dared not look up at Dr Walsh as he stood, arms crossed, tapping his foot as he waited for her. To her surprise, he said nothing. Eleanor's scientific experiment had begun.

***

Lieutenant Wentworth requested an audience with Captain Morris. He hadn't seen him since he rode on his left at the Battle of Balaclava. Morris was not a well man, having barely escaped with his life from the sabres of the Cossacks. After Morris's return from Scutari, he was not fit for duty but remained with the Light Brigade suffering through the Russian winter. The men had managed to secure lumber for a hut for him, so he was sheltered more than most. Certainly, more than the infantry in the trenches.

What prompted his visit was the state of poor Merlin. Every time Wentworth returned from those long treks delivering the sick and the dying to Balaclava, he was shocked at the state of his faithful friend. Every rib was visible, as was the horse's pelvis and backbone. His tail was nearly gone. He had that hollow-eyed look they all bore. Wracking his brain, Wentworth came up with a bold plan that had little chance of working and an even smaller chance of being approved.

"Ah, Wentworth, come in, come in." Captain Morris was sitting in a camp chair, covered by a blanket. It appeared he had not shaved in some time. What skin on his face that was visible looked ashen and the man was thin. Of course, they were all thin…starving really. "My *aide-de-camp* tells me that you would like to make a request."

"Yes, sir." Wentworth took the seat opposite his commanding officer. "It is rather unorthodox, but I am a desperate man."

Morris shook his head. "We are all desperate men, Wentworth. Tell me, what is it you want?"

"You see, sir, my horse is dying." Wentworth stole a glance at Morris to see if he would laugh at him. Everyone's horse was dying or dead already. Everyone was dying of disease or frostbite, or even shrapnel wounds from the pounding Russian guns.

Morris said nothing but shook his head slowly. "It is a crime, Wentworth. It truly is. Feel sorrier for the poor beasts sometimes than I do for the men. After all, a horse really has no idea what we are doing here…." He sighed. "So, what is this request?"

"Sir, we are well behind the front lines here, and I thought that perhaps I could cross over to our French allies and buy some fodder and supplies from them. The camp shave is they did not suffer as much from the great storm and have more provisions. I know it is not protocol—"

"No, Wentworth. It goes against all protocol, but desperate times call for desperate measures, eh? Couldn't let you take anyone with you, you understand. Don't want the whole army deserting to the frogs, now do we?" Morris began to laugh, and the laugh turned into a hacking cough.

Wentworth got up and brought the captain a glass of water. Morris looked up at him when he caught his breath. "All right. I cannot see how it would do any harm. You can take a cart with you and any dray animal you think could pull it and head for Kamiesh. I can only get you a limited amount of script and don't know if the French will take it."

Wentworth's spirit soared. He never thought he would get this far with his scheme, and here was Captain Morris granting his request and offering him money besides. "Thank you, sir," was all he could manage to say.

***

"All right, Miss Sherbrooke. It is time you shared your notes with me. Perhaps together we can make some sense of things."

Eleanor could not have been more surprised. Dr Walsh really wanted to see her notes. She was already drawing conclusions of her own and was anxious to see if a trained physician and surgeon would agree with her.

"If Miss Nightingale and the other nurses could spare you this evening, perhaps we might have dinner together and talk about your findings."

She could not imagine Miss Nightingale consenting to her sitting alone at dinner with any man, even the good doctor. "I will ask her, but I do not hold out much hope."

He smiled at her. The long hours they worked together, the suffering they had witnessed together, made her feel close to him in a way she had never felt before, not even with Lieutenant Wentworth. She heard of soldiers developing such bonds with one another and thought that perhaps this was the same thing. The only difference, of course, was that Dr Walsh was a man and she was a woman.

It so happened that Miss Nightingale agreed that the two should meet, but immediately after surgery was finished for the day, and only if the two orderlies were still about doing their work. It did not matter to Eleanor when or where they met, just that Dr Walsh really wanted to hear what she had to say. It was as if they were equals. She was getting ahead of herself. It was a start, nothing else.

So, in the waning light, the two of them sat down at a table in the corner of their operating room near the large windows that overlooked the bay. Eleanor spread before the good doctor the chart she had composed while in surgery.

"You see here, Doctor, the longer the men remain immobile in the trenches, the greater their injuries from frostbite."

"Mm-hmm."

Eleanor looked up from her notes to find the doctor was not looking at them, but at her. "Are you too tired to continue?"

He shook his head vigorously and gave her a sheepish smile. "No, no of course not. I find all of this fascinating."

"And as you may have noticed, the injuries usually happen *not* when the limbs are first exposed to extreme cold, but later, once the temperature warms. It seems that fluctuating temperatures are a factor."

There was no response. Eleanor then realised that the two orderlies were both out of the room, probably to take their grisly load outside to the burial detail, and she and Dr Walsh were alone. She lit the lamp as the sun slipped over the horizon. In the fading, orange sunlight, she lifted her head, and again, Dr Walsh was not looking at the notes, but at her. "You look lovely in this light."

She jerked her head back as if she had been struck. At first, she did not know how to respond. He reached up and gently stroked her cheek covered with the birthmark. "I think I find this the most endearing part of you, Miss Sherbrooke."

He kissed her there at that table, and she did not resist. When she did not, he kissed her again. Robinson's voice then rang out in the corridor, and they pulled apart. As the orderly entered the theatre,

Eleanor gathered up her notes, and with all good speed, nearly ran back to the nurses' quarters.

***

"Have some dinner, Eleanor. You look done in." Millie offered up a bowl of thin soup. Since Miss Nightingale had not made provision for dinner, Eleanor realised suddenly that she was hungry. The other nurses were already clearing up, and she and Millie were left in the refectory together alone. While she ate, Millie scrutinised her.

"All right, Eleanor. Out with it. What happened?"

It struck Eleanor then how much Millie and Cordelia were alike. Both seemed to be able to see right through her. It was most vexing. "Whatever do you mean, Millie?"

Millie clamped her lips together and screwed up her face. "All right. If you do not want to tell me, that is your prerogative. Just remember, dear Eleanor, Dr Walsh is a married man."

Eleanor's spoon clattered into the bowl. "A married man? How do you know?"

Millie shook her head. "Eleanor, Eleanor, Eleanor. We all live in this prison one atop the other. Everyone knows everything."

"Well, there is nothing to know about me and Dr Walsh. Our relationship is purely professional. The man is a gentleman."

Millie gave her a sceptical glance. "If you say so, Eleanor. Finish your dinner and come along. I am done in."

Not wanting to sit alone, Eleanor quickly finished her soup and followed Millie into the dormitory. As she lay her head on her pillow, she thought she would never sleep, but her weariness soon overcame her.

***

In the morning, Millie shook Eleanor's arm. "Come along, sleepyhead. Time to get up." Eleanor tried lifting her head, but it felt too heavy to move. She could not even summon the energy to open her eyes. "Eleanor, come along now." Millie took her by the hand and then dropped it. She placed her hand on Eleanor's forehead. "You are burning with fever. Stay where you are. I will fetch Miss Nightingale…"

***

"Eleanor, Eleanor, are you awake? How are you feeling today?" Millie carried a pot that Eleanor hoped against hope was tea.

"There is no milk, of course, and no sugar, but my family sent me an entire tin of tea and you, my dear friend, are the first to enjoy it."

Millie helped her sit up in bed and handed her the steaming cup. It was absolute ambrosia, not the watered stuff they were used to drinking. How many mornings at home, or even at the hospital in London, had Eleanor taken her morning cup of tea for granted? Now it seemed like the nectar of the gods.

"Oh, thank you, Millie. I feel guilty drinking your tea."

Millie patted her hand. "It is my gift, and I may share it with whomever I like, and there is nothing you can say about it. Now hush, and drink."

Eleanor did what she was told. "I must have overslept. What time is it?"

"Overslept? What time is it? You should be asking what day is it. I believe it is Thursday, but I am not sure. You have been ill for four days."

"Four days? That cannot be so." Eleanor screwed up her face, trying to remember. "I feel as if I have slept one night. Poor Dr Walsh. I must go and help him." Eleanor tried to swing her legs over the edge of her bed and felt the room spin around her. Millie snatched the cup from her grasp before it crashed to the floor.

"Dr Walsh will make do until you are well, Eleanor Sherbrooke. You do no one any good by fainting in the operating room. Now, lie back and drink your tea." She handed the cup back to Eleanor after filling it to the rim again. "Oh, I nearly forgot. A letter came for you. From Crimea." Millie dropped the missive on the blanket.

Eleanor breathed a sigh of relief. It could only be from one person, which meant he still lived and was not lying moribund in a trench somewhere as his limbs rotted off in the cold. She involuntarily shuddered.

"Are you cold, Eleanor? I could try to find more coal for the fire."

"No, don't bother. The fever keeps me warm." She laughed weakly.

Millie put her hand to Eleanor's forehead and nodded. "It is still with you, but much reduced from yesterday. I do believe you are on the mend." Millie patted her friend's hand and then rose. "I must get back to my scrubbing or letter writing or whatever else Miss Nightingale has in store for us today."

"Thank you for the tea, Millie. It is a godsend." Millie smiled. As she reached the door, she turned back and, with a mischievous expression, said, "I am sure that letter is also."

Before Eleanor could reply, she was gone. Immediately, Eleanor set down the cup and tore open the letter.

27 Dec, 1854
Dear Eleanor,

I have little time to write but wanted to assure you that I am still living. Since we promised to be honest with one another, I will tell you that circumstances here are desperate. All of our winter supplies, huts for the men, medicine, winter clothing, fodder, all of it, went down into the bottom of the sea during the great storm. I am sure the hurricane passed over you as well. We, however, had no strong building to protect us and are now sleeping in the open. I am grateful that I am in the cavalry, as we are charged with bringing the poor, sick souls from the trenches near Sebastopol all the way to the port of Balaclava. Once we are there, we try to negotiate with the bureaucrats for whatever provisions were salvaged. It breaks my heart to see crates of goods on the docks that these little Napoleons will not release to us because of government rules and regulations! It is enough to drive a man mad.

I am most concerned about poor Merlin. The horses and mules die in alarming numbers every day. They have taken to eating each other's tails just to stay alive. I am at wit's end how to save them. As for me, my face has healed, and I still await the silk eye patch you promised. I think that I do appear quite horrible. I can see it in the eyes of people I meet for the first time. My vanity, though, is not at issue here. We are at death's door, all of us, man and beast. I despair of what to do.

Pray for me, dear Eleanor. If you have occasion to write to Julia, be as gentle as possible about my condition. I will explain all to her upon my return, if I return. I think of you often and bless you and all of Miss Nightingale's nurses for the work you do.

Yours,
Joshua Wentworth

Eleanor read the letter over twice. It did more to add to the anxiety about Lieutenant Wentworth than to assuage it. Would that she could sail across the bay and pluck him from the Crimea. The feeling of helplessness overwhelmed her and she was exhausted by fever. After laying the cup and letter beside her, she fell into another fevered and disturbed sleep.

***

The French Headquarters lay downriver from the British, so Wentworth set off in search of provisions with a small bullock, and a cart he repaired himself.

"Now, do not despair, Merlin, old friend, I shall return shortly, and all will be well." The horse did not stand as of old, but spent much time on the cold ground, which worried the lieutenant to no end. He patted his faithful companion's neck, and the horse neighed softly. It was going to be all right. Wentworth had the means now to save his friend from the fate of so many of the cavalry's animals. He had some army script to trade and a means of transport for the goods. Now it was just a matter of scaling the ridge to reach the French positions.

He had travelled most of the day and knew he would not reach his destination before dark. Bedding down in the back of a cart would have served him, but the rain began to pelt unmercifully, so he spent the night shivering beneath the cart rather than on it. Sleeping in the mud was not new to him, and it had to be endured. He awoke the next morning to hoofbeats.

Clutching his pistol, he peered out from under the cart. The likelihood that there were Russians this far from Sebastopol was unlikely, but he was not taking chances. What greeted his eyes was like a vision from heaven.

He heard of these young, French women, the *vivandières*, who provided provisions and even nursing to the French soldiers. Now one of them had come upon him, on horseback, tight-fitting jacket reminiscent of the uniforms of the Zouave regiment, leather bag slung across her body, and sitting astride her horse in trousers. Trousers of all things. It was quite a sight.

She called out to him in French. "Come out and show yourself." Wentworth scrambled from beneath the cart with as much dignity as he could muster. "*Mon dieu*! You are British. What are you doing here?" When he did not speak immediately, she repeated her question in English.

"I am Lieutenant Wentworth of the 17th Lancers. I am seeking provisions for my horse and my men."

She seemed amused. "You are seeking such provisions from us, *monsieur*? We have nothing to spare."

He dug into his jacket and produced the script. "I am not begging. I will pay." He handed her the paper. She flipped it from one side to the other and then handed it back to him.

"This is nothing to me. *Adieu*, *monsieur*." She pulled the reins, and her horse's head followed.

"Wait. *Wait*." He was shouting now. "Wait. I have something else."

The horse made a full circle and she faced him once more. "Well. Let me see." He again put his hand into his jacket, feeling about. He had no money, only useless army script. The only thing left in his pockets was the watch his father had given him when he went off to war. He pulled it from his pocket and turned it over and over in his hand. He still had not shown it to her.

"Well, *monsieur*. I do not have, as you say, all day. Do you have something to trade, or do you not?"

It was the watch he took when he rode into battle. It was a legacy he hoped to hand down to his son one day. It was also the difference between life and death for Merlin, and perhaps even himself and his men. He hesitated a few seconds longer, holding it in his grasp. Then, decisively, he held it out to her. "It is a gold watch. Worth quite a bit of money. Will this do?"

She did not take it from him but looked down from her perch as he held it up for her perusal. "This is much better. What is it you want?"

"First, fodder for horses. Then whatever food you can spare for my men."

She cocked her head to one side and then nodded. "Very well. Follow me. I will take you to my stores and we will make a bargain." She snatched the watch from his palm.

He scrambled up onto the bullock cart and gave the reins a slap on the bullock's rump. Slowly, they made their way up the rise to the French camp.

***

"So, you are decided to grace us with your presence, eh, Miss Sherbrooke." Dr Walsh seemed in the mood for hectoring, but Eleanor did not mind. This type of banter was only permitted among the closest of colleagues, and she felt welcomed by it. It had been a full two weeks since she had taken ill, and now felt strong enough to begin again.

"After taking my holiday in Tuscany, I thought I might drop by for a visit." She endeavoured to make her cheekiest expression. Robinson, ever faithful stretcher bearer, tried vainly to suppress a laugh.

"Well, then. We are happy to have you back." Dr Walsh inclined his head, and when his eyes met Eleanor's, she could see the sincerity in them. The poor man looked so weary. All the time she was abed, he was here, trying to save men whose limbs had turned stiff and black with frostbite. He held her gaze for a moment, and then impatiently turned to the litter bearers. "All right, Robinson, don't stand there gaping. Go and get us a patient."

The day dragged on. So many men, most from the trenches near Sebastopol, arrived with atrophied feet and legs from sitting in flooded trenches with only their summer shoes. So many of the shoes were without soles, worn away from overuse. So many were without any shoes at all, walking about in the frozen mud and the snow barefoot. These were worse conditions than those felt by any poverty-stricken street urchin in London. Yet, the boys never complained, and sang the praises of their country and queen.

When that first day of her return finished and Robinson and the new man left with their grisly cargo of limbs for burial, Dr Walsh called Eleanor to help him clean the instruments.

"You see, Miss Sherbrooke, that Miss Nightingale's peculiar habits have rubbed off on me." He was using carbolic soap and water to clean the scalpels and saws.

Eleanor nodded approvingly. "I knew we would wear you down, sir. The patients have fared better since our arrival, have they not?"

He made a mock scowl and then smiled. "You know that they have, Miss Sherbrooke. Here, dry these things and put them in the case there."

Dr Walsh dumped his instruments into a towel Eleanor held out. She took the instruments, and one by one, rubbed off every droplet of water. As she worked, Dr Walsh moved to stand in front of her, the small, tallish table between them. Without warning, he lay his palm on Eleanor's cheek. She looked up at him in surprise.

"I've missed you, Eleanor," he whispered.

The gesture caught Eleanor unawares and she dropped what she was holding, the surgical equipment clattering to the table below. Instinctively, she jerked backwards, breaking his hold on her.

"I thought…." He did not finish his sentence.

"You are a married man, sir." Eleanor looked straight into his eyes.

Now it was he who looked startled. "Widower, actually. My wife passed away while I was here."

Eleanor's heart went out to him. Millie and her rumours were off the mark. He really was a lovely man, but she had no more affection for him than one comrade has for another.

"Oh, I am so sorry for your loss."

"Thank you, Eleanor…." He still held her gaze and went on. "You see, I thought perhaps…."

She knew then that she should have resisted him when he kissed her. It was her fault that he was misled. It was time to set everything right. Not knowing what to say, she merely shook her head. Her expression and this gesture met their mark.

As her eyes met his, humiliation burned in his. He turned his back on her. "I apologise for my behaviour," he said softly, looking off into the distance.

"No need, sir. We are all under a great strain here. You more than most. You did nothing wrong…really." He turned to look at her and stroked his chin.

"There you are wrong, Miss Sherbrooke. I feel I took advantage of you… I am sorry."

She struggled to think of something to say to him. Slowly, it occurred to her. "There is no need. We will forget all about it, all right?"

"I am a foolish old man," he said. He would not look her in the eye and turned on his heel. "I will see you tomorrow." Before she could say another word, he was striding down the hallway.

She stood motionless for a long while, watching his retreating figure. This place, where nothing was as it should be, where all the rules they lived by seemed to bend and flex, this place made fools of them all.

***

Wentworth's mission had borne fruit. He drove and cajoled that poor bullock along the track back to the Lancers' camp, with fodder for the horses and provisions for the men. The *vivandières* had storehouses full of supplies: hay, potted meats, canned vegetables and fruit, and wine and liquor aplenty. As the cart bounced along the track, Wentworth sang songs from his childhood, he was in such high spirits. His only regret was parting with his beloved watch. Every time the thought of it entered his head, a lump formed in his throat.

Upon reaching the pickets guarding the entrance to camp, he greeted them heartily and handed them a bottle of French wine. The two bedraggled soldiers looked at it as if it had descended from heaven of its own accord. "*Vive la France*," Wentworth shouted as he drove the bullock cart straight for the makeshift stables that contained Merlin, the other horses who still lived, and what was left of the Lancers.

As he approached, he called out, and men came to greet him, his sergeant at the lead. "Thank goodness you're back, sir. Frenchies didn't give you much trouble, eh?"

Wentworth climbed down, his back to his men. "No, no, those *vivandières* are something to behold. Women in trousers, men. Imagine." He grinned, but his men were sombre. They should have been rejoicing, clambering over the cart looking for good things to eat and bottles of brandy. Instead, they stood in a formation of sorts, the bewhiskered sergeant forward as spokesman. Wentworth kept talking, even though he could feel a twisting in his innards. Something was very wrong. "Well, don't just stand there, boys. Let's unload this fodder for the horses. Poor things need nourishment, eh?"

Before he could move to the back of the cart, the sergeant moved forward and caught him by the sleeve. "About the horses, sir."

Wentworth turned and looked into the man's eyes. All of them had the hollow, sunken look, but this man's expression tore into Wentworth like no other. "What is it? Out with it, Sergeant."

The men looked back and forth at each other, thin shadows of men, rags hanging off their bones. Wentworth knew what they were trying to tell him, but he did not want to believe it. "Sir…" the sergeant began, but Wentworth was already running.

He reached the half-finished stable, and inside he found him. Merlin. Lying on his side, pelvic bones visible through his stretched skin. Flies crawled across his open eyes, and he did not blink. He did not breathe.

The breath came out of Wentworth's body in short bursts, and he fought to control his emotions. He turned his head quickly and glanced back at the men. They had moved off now, leaving him alone. None made a move towards the cart filled with provisions. Wentworth knelt next to Merlin and closed his eyes. The poor beast was a mere shadow of his former self. Wentworth stroked his nose and patted his neck. "We nearly made it through, eh, old boy? Nearly made it." Wentworth's tears slid down his cheek and he made no move to wipe them away. He knelt there in the mud for a long time. Long enough for the tightening in his throat to ease, and his silent sobs to cease. The men never came near.

When he finally got up, he ordered a burial detail, and his men mutely followed him to a spot near the river where the ground was soft enough to dig. There, he and his men buried Merlin. Shaking himself from his sorrow, he organised the feeding of the remaining horses and began to distribute the bounty he accrued at the hands of his French allies. A gold watch bought a great deal of food and liquor. There were even a few bits of wood and some coal to build a fire that lasted throughout the night. It was the first time Wentworth had been warm and dry for weeks.

As he staggered, half-drunk, to his pallet in the stable, something broke inside him. Throughout the trials of Varna, the deaths of his comrades in the relentless Russian fire during the charge, the loss of his eye, the loss of the young bugler, Brittain, through all of these trials, Merlin was there. He touched the empty pocket that had contained the only thing his father ever gave him out of love. Nothing was left. Nothing.

Chapter 9

News from the front reached Scutari every few days. The Sardinians had joined the war on the allied side, which brought some relief to the British siege. The conditions in the trenches were still appalling, and men were continuously arriving at Scutari with wounds, but more were sick with cholera, typhus, and frostbite.

Eleanor continued her work in the operating room with Dr Walsh for a few more days. Then, one morning, as she was leaving the refectory, Miss Nightingale took her aside. “I am relieving you of your duty in surgery. Report to the west ward and ask Miss Stanhope what your duties will be there.”

Eleanor asked the question but knew in her heart what the answer was. “Why am I not needed in surgery anymore?”

“It was Dr Walsh’s request that you be replaced.”

“Did I not satisfy? I thought—”

“Dr Walsh had no complaints about your performance as a nurse, Miss Sherbrooke. He just feels that he has no more need of your services.”

Eleanor did not want to give up her position as a surgical nurse so easily. She had learned so much, and the work revived her ambition to train as a doctor. “Of course he needs my services. This is completely unfair.”

Miss Nightingale looked at her aghast. “Miss Sherbrooke… Eleanor, you are to do your duty here, as I see fit. Report to the western ward and commence your duties there. Understood?”

“Yes, miss.” Eleanor was seething, but she did not argue. *This must be what it is like in the army. No one cares for your opinion. You are to do as you are told.* Once she arrived at her new post, Millie was there. Having her friend on duty with her removed some of the sting of her reassignment.

“Eleanor, I am so glad to see you.” Millie approached her at once. Miss Stanhope, however, intercepted the reunion.

“Miss Sherbrooke. You are assigned on the other side of the ward. Go and begin emptying the bedpans. When you are finished with that, you may begin bathing the patients and changing the sheets. Miss Potts, I believe you have some scrubbing to do.”

Millie shot a look at Eleanor and then made a hasty retreat. Miss Stanhope glared at Eleanor, and she finally managed a feeble, “Yes, Sister.” She then retreated to the end of the ward and began her new duties.

***

He was not quite sure when the fever began. They were taking another group of wounded soldiers to the port at Balaclava, which was a nightmare in itself. Dazed and wounded men staggered about; more were on stretchers. From where he stood, trying to unload the wounded and get them safely to the boats, a stench hung in the air from tons of rotted vegetables that were never distributed because of lack of paperwork. The constant, endless trek back and forth from the trenches to Balaclava were taking its toll on everyone, and now on Wentworth in particular.

While Merlin lived, there seemed to be one bright spot in all this death and confusion. Now, he was gone, and every day seemed more pointless than the next. After delivering his charges to the harbour, he began the long, homeward march with his men. When they were no more than a mile distant from camp, his strength failed him altogether and he sank to his knees and vomited profusely.

***

He awakened on a camp bed in a hut constructed of planks. For the first time in a long while, he was warm and not revolted by the rank smell of his own unwashed body. He tried to recollect what had transpired but knew nothing from the time he collapsed on the trail. His throat was parched, and he did his best to call out for water. Soon, an older, matronly figure approached. She wore the white, starched bonnet of the nurses belonging to Miss Nightingale.

“Feelin’ a bit rough, are ye, sir?”

Wentworth did not feel he even had the strength to answer but nodded mutely.

"'Ere. Got ye a cup o'tea, believe it or not. Not the strongest, mind you, but somethin'." She held Wentworth's head up slightly and he partook of the nearly scalding liquid. When he was finished, the woman laid him back on the cot. "You just rest now, sir."

"Am I in Scutari?" he asked, even though this place did not look like Scutari.

"No, sir. You are in Balaclava. We've started a new hospital here. I will go and fetch…" But he heard no more. Feverish sleep overtook him again.

***

As winter slowly released its grasp on the struggling armies, goods from all over England began to pour into the Crimea. Investors from England, hearing of the army's dire predicament, undertook the building of a railway from Balaclava to the British lines at the front around Sebastopol. It opened near the end of February. The relentless reporting of William Howard Russell created such an outrage among the citizenry that the entire country mobilised to bring their soldiers some semblance of safety and succour.

After losing her position as a surgical nurse, Eleanor became increasingly dissatisfied with her work at Scutari. More nurses had arrived, admittedly, with less endurance for the work demanded of them, but Eleanor felt confident that Miss Nightingale would bring them to heel soon enough.

For a time, she had been communicating with a Welsh nurse called Elizabeth Davis, who defied Miss Nightingale and took herself off to Crimea on her own. She was matron of a make-shift hospital in Balaclava. There were times she even took her nurses to the trenches at the front. By now Eleanor was completely disabused of the notion of the "glories of war" and therefore had no desire to thrust herself in front of Russian sniper fire. The idea of returning to her important work in surgery, however, compelled her to make serious inquiries of Miss Davis.

"I am going to Crimea, Millie." Eleanor just finished a bowl of porridge when she looked up at her friend to gauge her reaction.

Millie sipped her tea and shook her head. "What are you talking about? You are in Crimea."

"No, we are in Turkey. I am going to Balaclava to nurse. I have been writing to Miss Davis, you remember?"

Millie's mouth hung open. "That mad Welsh woman who broke with Miss Nightingale? Have you considered the implications? She takes nurses straight up to the front. What will Miss Nightingale say?"

Eleanor got up to wash her bowl. "It does not matter. I am resolved. I cannot stay here scrubbing walls and writing letters while wounds go septic and men die of cholera and typhus in Crimea."

Millie rose and put her hand on Eleanor's shoulder. "What is this really about, Eleanor?

It is about that Lieutenant Wentworth, is it not?"

Eleanor turned on her friend, her voice strident. "No… I mean partly, perhaps. I am a surgical nurse. I should be in surgery, and… I have not heard from Lieutenant Wentworth in over a month. Something is wrong…"

Millie took Eleanor's hand in both of her own. "He may be dead. You know they never tell us anything. The only person I know who writes letters to the families of these brave men is Miss Nightingale. If the men die in the field…."

After pulling her hand from Millie's grasp, Eleanor turned away from her. She was afraid her friend would read every thought upon her face. "I know what I am doing. I know he might be dead. I know Miss Nightingale will be angry. I know there is great danger from our enemy to anyone near the front. I know all these things, but I must go. I discovered something about my abilities, my calling, if you will, that I must act on." She turned to look at her friend, whose entire body seemed drained of its energy. Eleanor embraced her. "I will write. You'll see. All will be well. You'll see."

Millie broke Eleanor's grasp and held her out at arm's length to look at her. "You are the bravest person I know, Miss Eleanor Sherbrooke."

"Don't be silly," Eleanor said, and they turned, arm in arm, towards the door. As they stepped through, they nearly collided with none other than Miss Nightingale herself.

"So, you are leaving us, Eleanor."

Millie disentangled herself and left Eleanor to face the superintendent. "Yes, miss. You see, I feel that my skills—"

"I heard all, Miss Sherbrooke. I understand your frustration, but you need to understand my position as well. I have built up a certain trust with the doctors, and if that trust is violated by any of my nurses, it falls to me to repair the damage."

Eleanor's eyebrows shot up. "Violated? It was not I who violated anything. I—"

"It does not matter. What is done is done. I must choose my battles carefully, Miss Sherbrooke. Certainly, you can understand."

Eleanor opened her mouth to speak but refrained. The die was cast and the result the same whether Miss Nightingale received her side of the story or not.

"I am sending you to join Miss Elizabeth Davis in Balaclava. General Raglan—"

"Miss Davis. I thought you and she—"

"Miss Davis and I had our differences, to be sure. As I was saying, General Raglan deems Balaclava safe enough to send a nursing staff. Miss Davis took a few nurses, but I am sure they will welcome one more. I will send a letter for you with the next tide. Gather your things, then resume your duties. You leave in two days."

***

The port at Balaclava was not at all what Eleanor expected. The landing itself was difficult, and the scene at the port beyond comprehension. How did anything get accomplished in all this confusion? All sorts of flotsam floated in the water, and she was convinced that she saw dead bodies among the debris. There was a mix of languages being shouted in every direction, and no one seemed to be in charge of anything. As her foot finally touched dry land and she waited on the pier for her small trunk, she realised she had absolutely no idea where she should go or how she was to get there. A slowly rising panic engulfed her. She was a woman alone in a strange port in a foreign country. No one knew her here, nor could anyone at home ever find out what became of her. Then a swarthy man in a Turkish army uniform stepped forward.

"Are you the Miss Cher-broo?" he asked. It was close enough.

"Sherbrooke. Miss Sherbrooke." She nodded.

"Good. Good. I take you to hospital. Miss Davis wait there."

Eleanor nearly hugged the poor man in relief, but that would certainly have created a scandal. Of course, there was someone here to meet her and to take her to the Balaclava hospital. Miss Davis knew she was arriving. All was well.

The Turkish soldier secured her meagre luggage to a flat oxcart that was already loaded with goods from the port. He indicated to her that she should take the seat next to him. Such an arrangement would have created a raging scandal at home. If she did not wish to bounce about in the back with the sundry goods, she had only one choice. She smiled at the thought of her mother watching her climb next to this swarthy fellow. He extended his hand, and he pulled her up next to him on the rickety seat. After making their way through the crowded streets, the wheels crunching through the snow encrusted mud, they finally arrived at what looked like a few hastily strung together wooden buildings quite near what looked like the beginnings of railway lines. She was grateful they were buildings. She was expecting tents.

She insisted on disembarking without his help, and he began to unload her small trunk and case. There was a larger third case that he put alongside her two.

"No, no, that is not mine." She shook her head at the Turk, who nodded at her.

"Yes, yes, yours. See. Look." He pointed to a label on the handle, and although she did not recognise the crate, it indeed was labelled with her name. He then began to unload the rest of the supplies.

Before long, a portly woman in a plain brown dress came running out to greet them. She scurried past Eleanor, waving her arms.

"Hakan, Hakan, no, no. Not in the mud. Wait for the sergeant major." Hakan stopped immediately and crossed his arms, scowling at her.

She finally took notice of Eleanor. "These Turks do not like to be ordered about by women." She then gave a hearty laugh. "No men do, do they, dearie? You must be the new nurse. Welcome. Welcome."

By this time, the sergeant major arrived to see what the fuss was about, and he and his men began unloading the cart. A steady parade formed while packages of all sizes entered the building. The sergeant major was left in charge of her things. The portly woman, after making sure supplies were delivered in the proper place, extended her hand to Eleanor.

"I am Mrs Norton. You look familiar to me. Come from Scutari?"

"Yes, Eleanor Sherbrooke. I was a surgical nurse there."

Mrs Norton nodded sagely. "Mrs Davis will be mightily glad to see you, then. A good surgical nurse is worth her weight in gold, but then, that wouldn't be too much gold, now, would it?" She poked Eleanor in the ribs with her elbow as they walked and laughed again.

She showed her to the nurses' quarters, which, to Eleanor's delight, was a small, square building that Eleanor had to share with only three others. It also contained the luxury of a camp stove.

"This bed is yours, and you have this corner for your things. We don't have much room here, so you will have to live out of your trunk. I will give you a few minutes to sort yourself out and see if I can find you something hot to eat." Mrs Norton then disappeared and left Eleanor to her own devices.

Overwhelmed with curiosity, she picked up the extra case. It was quite heavy, but she managed to swing it, bouncing on the bed assigned to her. Yes, the label on the top had her name on it. How odd. She clicked open the latch and lifted the lid.

At first, it appeared that the entire case was packed with the cloths that they all used at Scutari for each soldier, but then Eleanor realised that some of the cloths were used as wrapping for bottles. Carefully, she undid the fabric and was astounded to find six bottles of chloroform secreted there. There were more towels and bandages, and to her delight, the entire bottom of the case was neatly arranged with bar after bar of carbolic soap. She was about to close the case and seek out Mrs Norton once again when she noticed another wrapped package. Upon opening it, she discovered to her delight a box of tea. Miss Nightingale may strike some as tough and unyielding, but Eleanor now knew her to be kindness itself. She added some of her newfound supplies to the bag she always carried at Scutari and went in search of Mrs Norton.

A small refectory stood near the nurses' quarters, and Eleanor found Mrs Norton there amid the smells of cooking. She had little to eat on the ship during her three-day voyage from Scutari and was again surprised to be offered a stew of not only meat but also vegetables. It was the first decent meal she had since she left England.

"Where are the wounded?" she asked as soon as she finished.

"That's what I like to see. Ready to work. There are more sick than wounded these days, but I don't have to tell you. It was the same at Scutari."

Eleanor followed Mrs Norton out of the refectory to a long, wooden building patched together with odd pieces of lumber and even bits of metal, but it looked sturdy enough. A brazier with a small coal fire was set up in the centre that gave off a bit of warmth. The men lay on cots along the walls, quite close together, in a manner similar to Scutari.

For all of Mrs Davis's objections to Miss Nightingale's methods and authority, she emulated her here in Balaclava. The men were clean, each one had a basin and cloth to himself. There were even chamber pots about, and all were empty as far as she could observe. She was about to remark about these things when a voice sounded behind them. "So, there is the new nurse."

Eleanor turned and there stood Elizabeth Davis. She recognised her from Scutari. Over sixty, with white hair bristling out beneath her bonnet, she was vigorous and sturdy with an open expression. Immediately she reached out and shook Eleanor's hand most heartily. "Miss Sherbrooke. So glad to have you with us. You are familiar with surgery and battle wounds, are you?"

"Yes, ma'am. Very familiar. More than I care to say."

Mrs Davis's face suddenly became solemn. "Yes, indeed, aren't we all. We have some new arrivals from the front. Are you ready to get stuck in?"

"That is why I am here."

"Very good, then."

Mrs Davis led Eleanor to the far end of the building where there were two entry doors that opened from the middle. She assumed that facilitated bringing in the wounded and the ill on whatever conveyance they arrived on. The doors were open, and orderlies of various regiments were unloading men from donkey carts. They were set upon camp beds without linen, and Mrs Davis sorted them according to the severity of their conditions.

"That one, over to the C ward. Leave that one here. Can you walk, private? All right, take him to the A ward. Pick him up and aid in his walking. Be quick about it. That one can go to Scutari…."

There must have been a hundred new arrivals, but Mrs Davis seemed unperturbed. She had, obviously, done such work before, and Eleanor marvelled at it. She was soon assigned to a group of men who just arrived from the trenches. They had their wounds dressed in the field. It took days for them to reach Balaclava. Eleanor was assigned an orderly and set out to clean and dress wounds from the new arrivals.

The first man she attended to lay silently breathing, a bloody rag wrapping his shoulder over his coat and shirt. This looked like a hastily made field dressing at best. As she undid it, the putrid smell of decay assailed her. She looked to the orderly.

"Bring me a camp chair, Mr…?"

"Bradley, Sister."

"Mr Bradley. Please bring me an empty bucket or something and some clean water. Can you do that?"

Mr Bradley stood stock-still, wide-eyed in horror at the wounded man. This would not do. "Now, Mr Bradley."

Her tone of voice seemed to awaken him, and he rushed off. Within a few minutes, he returned with a bucket of water. It was not what she asked for, but she made do. After emptying the water into the basin near her patient and in all the others nearby, she returned with her empty one and began to unwrap the layers of cloth on the shoulder wound. Between each layer, a writhing mass of maggots fed off the rotting flesh. This was not work she relished, but not anything she hadn't done before many times. Her skin prickled with the odd feeling that she was being watched, and Eleanor turned. A young recruit gazed at her, transfixed.

She immediately returned to her work. "Have you been in Crimea long, Mr Bradley?"

"Just arrived a week ago, Sister." His voice wavered, and he nearly whispered.

"I am sorry this is such an inglorious introduction into war, but you need to come and assist me with this man." She turned to look at him again and to assure herself that he hadn't bolted. The private looked about as if searching to find someone else whom she might be speaking to. Having found no one, he stepped forward. Eleanor washed her hands and had him wash his. They looked like they had not been washed since he arrived.

Without many words, Eleanor and the private relieved the wounded man of his spoiled clothing, and Eleanor began removing maggots from the wound. She dropped them with a sickening plop into a bucket below the bed. Then, washing the wound and applying a fresh bandage, she covered the man as best she could.

"Go and find him some broth or gruel."

As Bradley darted out, Eleanor began clearing away the debris from her first operation in the Crimea. The wounded soldier turned his glassy gaze towards her.

"You are an angel." He closed his eyes and sank back on his pillow. She brushed his filthy, matted hair back from his forehead.

"Rest now," she said, and rose to examine her other patients.

***

Julia Sherbrooke and George Shaw sat by the fire in her parents' drawing room. Her mother sat opposite them, knitting, looking daggers at Julia, who was doing her best to ignore her.

"Well, I don't know, George. Mother and I are organising a benefit to raise money to send food and medicine to our dear boys at the front." Julia looked as pointedly at her mother as she could, but to her frustration, her mother took the opportunity at that moment to look down at her work. Julia waited and then tried again. "Isn't that right, Mother?"

Her mother reluctantly glanced up and made some sort of face that looked like a smile at the bottom and a murderous squint at the top. "Yes, Julia, you are quite correct. I am afraid we will be quite busy all weekend."

"Oh, that is a shame. All the best people will be there. I think you know them all - the Mosleys, the Cruikshanks, the Pettigrews, well, you know. We shall certainly miss you, Julia. You are always the life of the party." George Shaw swirled his brandy casually.

That comment drew another murderous look from Julia's mother. George seemed quite content to nestle down into the armchair by the fire and continue being oblivious to Mrs Sherbrooke's disapproval. "Odd that you are so gay when your

Lieutenant Wentworth remains in those horrible conditions in the Crimea. Have you received another letter from him, Julia?"

Both of their heads spun towards her in an instant. The consequence of not taking a hint from her mother was certainly quick and pointed. She seemed determined to discourage Mr Shaw, when it was he who had the greater fortune. Joshua Wentworth seemed a rather distant memory now, having been gone nearly a year.

"Yes, Mother, I did receive a letter, but it was dated more than a month ago. He does not mention any hardships. I think, perhaps, the newspapers exaggerate."

"I suppose Mr Fenton's photographs exaggerate as well."

Julia peered at George, who seemed finally to wake up to the fact that this visit was not going well. Whenever Julia's mother mentioned Lieutenant Wentworth, Julia knew it was a signal that it was time for George to depart. He raised his eyebrows at Julia, and she made such a face at him that he had to stifle a laugh.

"Well… then… this has been pleasant." George swirled the last of his brandy, swigged it, and rose from his chair. Deliberately turning his back on Mrs Sherbrooke, he leaned in towards Julia. "I will see you soon," he whispered. Then, turning to Mrs Sherbrooke, he made a low bow. "Madam." With that, he strode through the French doors.

"Oh, Julia, I do not know how you can abide that man," her mother said stridently the second the doors closed.

"Mama, I like him. He amuses me *and* he has a sizable fortune that he takes pains to increase."

"You are an engaged woman, Julia. You need to act like one."

"Oh, Mama!" Julia jumped up from her seat and made two fists that she punched towards the ground. "No one knows that I am engaged. They assume so because of…." She did not continue.

"They assume so because of the scandal you created. Oh, Julia, I despair of you. You engage in a dangerous game, playing both sides towards the middle."

"I did not create that scandal by myself. Joshua Wentworth had a rather large part in it."

The clacking of the knitting needles increased in frequency and volume, and Mrs Sherbrooke took a deep, deliberate breath. Finally, without looking up, she spoke. "Read me Lieutenant Wentworth's letter, Julia. I would like to hear it."

"Mama, there are some intimate parts of that letter. After all we are an en—"

"Ha!" Mrs Sherbrooke dropped her knitting and shook her finger at her. "You were about to say that you are an engaged couple. This will not do, Julia. Either break off your engagement with Lieutenant Wentworth or stop your flirting with George Shaw. It isn't decent."

"Isn't decent? What isn't decent is Eleanor off being a nurse to all those men. Imagine what she sees and what she *does* every day."

"You have no right to bring Eleanor into this." Her mother returned to her knitting. "You have always done so. Try to change the subject when you know you are losing an argument or you know that you are wrong." Julia made no reply, so her mother continued. "I am quite proud of Eleanor."

Julia could feel the conversation veering away from her own concerns, so she interjected. "I am not changing the subject. I will not break off our engagement. It isn't fair to Joshua, off fighting as he is… a member of the Light Brigade…."

Her mother shook her head. "And you bask in the glory of that accomplishment too, I suppose. Oh, Julia. I despair of you. I really do."

"I do not know why, Mama. I know exactly what I am doing." Julia picked up her skirts with a flourish and glided from the drawing room.

***

A week had passed, and Eleanor sent an inquiry up to the 17th Lancers by way of the newly running railway. She addressed one letter to Lieutenant Wentworth himself, and a second to whoever might be commanding the regiment. She hoped one of them would bear fruit.

The work at the Balaclava hospital was difficult but rewarding. There were still too many cases of frostbite coming from the trenches, as well as horribly neglected wounds. The new surgeon assigned to the hospital was called Dr Farley. He had been in attendance at the battle of Alma and was skilled in amputations. Eleanor was assigned to him at once. He was tall and sinewy, with thinning blond hair and a haunted look. Most of the doctors or nurses who had been in the Crimea for any length of time bore that look. A man of few words, he worked well with Eleanor and she took care not to become overly familiar with him.

Opening that box of tea from Miss Nightingale and sharing it stood Eleanor in good stead among her fellow nurses. Most of them were older than she, so she was the recipient of much counselling and advice. She missed Millie, but felt she landed in a nest of mother hens and was quite enjoying their attention. They all seemed as independent and strong-willed as Elizabeth Davis. It occurred to her then that all the nurses Miss Nightingale sent to Balaclava were older and matronly. She suspected that Miss Nightingale wanted to remove the temptation of romance between soldiers and their nurses by doing so. Why, then, had she allowed Eleanor to come? It took her a few moments of contemplation, but then the realisation came to her. It was something she had not thought about for months because it no longer seemed to matter. Miss Nightingale considered it, though. It was the mark upon her face. That mark removed her from temptation.

Eleanor waited yet another week for word from the 17th. It arrived after breakfast, before she had to report to Dr Farley. Left alone, she tore open the letter that held the regimental seal. It was not from Lieutenant Wentworth, but from a Captain William Morris. Within the envelope was yet another letter. It was addressed to Lieutenant Wentworth and bore a London postmark.

7 March, 1855
Dear Miss Sherbrooke,
I am writing regarding your inquiry as to the fate of Lt. Wentworth. I regret to inform you

Eleanor stopped reading immediately. Her blood ran cold. Closing her eyes, she breathed slowly, trying to stem her rising panic and the tears that quickly puddled in her eyes. This would not do. If he was dead, the sooner she accepted the fact, the better. Not knowing would not change his fate. Blinking away the tears, she continued reading…

I regret to inform you that I am, at present, unaware of his exact whereabouts or even his condition. He was put on sick list two weeks ago when his men left him in Balaclava. I believe he was ill with typhus. If he survived, he is at one of the hospitals in Turkey or perhaps the new one in Balaclava.

I am soon to be invalided home, as my health fails me as well. I have enclosed a letter that came for the lieutenant from home. I thought it best to entrust it to you, as I am sure it would lose its way if left here near the front lines.

I do hope you find him alive and well. I am a great admirer of his courage and initiative. If you do see him again, give him my condolences on the loss of his horse, Merlin. I realise this might sound silly to you, but a good cavalryman has no better friend than his faithful steed.

Thank you for your kind concern. My best wishes to you and the other nurses doing so much for our brave men.

With deepest regard,
Captain William Morris, 17th Lancers

Her heart slowed to its normal pace the farther she journeyed into the captain's letter. There was still hope that Lieutenant Wentworth was alive. He might even be here, in this hospital. Her pulse quickened again. As soon as Dr Farley was no longer in need of her services, she would begin her search.

***

Joshua Wentworth was having the most peculiar, feverish dream. He sat on the dock at Balaclava, having tea with Eleanor. She fed him cakes. Then he was riding Merlin and cannon shot exploded all around. A headless rider passed him and handed him his head. When he turned it in his hands, it bore the face of his father. He woke with a start. The heat from his body was still pouring off him, but the oddest thing happened. He was awake but could still hear Eleanor's voice. Unconsciousness soon followed.

When he woke again, he took a deep breath. The smell of unwashed bodies, vomit, putrefaction, and faeces were gone from the air. He gingerly pulled his hands from beneath the bedclothes and looked at them. They were clean. Through his fevered vision, he could see that he was in a clean shirt. Touching his face, he was clean shaven. Then he realised what had happened. He died during the night. No, that could not be true. If he was dead, he would undoubtedly feel better. A moment later, he tried to sit up but was too weak.

"'Ere now, sir. Lie back.... Unless you need to use the chamber pot. I could 'elp you, sir." The young sergeant from the Dragoons looked familiar, but Wentworth could not clear his head enough to think how he knew him.

"Yes, Sergeant. I believe I do. Can't quite seem to get my bearings."

"It's the typhus, sir. You got it pretty bad. That's what the sister said, sir."

Wentworth could barely move. His muscles ached and did not obey his mind, but in short order, he was able to relieve himself. "So, how did you get such a duty, Sergeant?"

The young man smiled as he tucked Wentworth back in bed. "Orders, sir. Prefer it to the trenches, sir. Don't mind at all." Although the man was younger than Wentworth, he had the old eyes of one who had seen much suffering and death.

Wentworth realised that he was thirsty. Nausea still kept his hunger at bay. "Might I bother you for a drink of water, Sergeant?"

"Only get tea, sir. Sister says so. Don't know why, but tea seems to keep off the cholera no matter how weak it is. Funny thing, eh?" He disappeared from Wentworth's sight for a moment and then returned with a cup of rather anaemic tea. Wentworth was so shaky that he could not even sit up alone, but the sergeant wrapped his arm around him and held a cup to Wentworth's lips.

"Does this have sugar in it?" Wentworth asked incredulously.

"Does indeed, sir. We 'ave more of everything now, sir. Things started comin' in from 'ome."

Wentworth lay back. The tea and sugar made him feel much better, and he did not immediately retch this time. He vaguely remembered doing quite a lot of that lately. He dozed off again, or at least he thought he did, for he began dreaming. Again, Eleanor's voice sounded in his ears, or was it his imagination? He kept his eyes closed for a moment, relishing the sound of it.

"Lieutenant Wentworth, can you hear me...? Well, I suppose I will have to wait. I believe he is unconscious again."

"Aye, Sister. I'll call ye again when 'e wakes." He recognised the sergeant's voice. Immediately, Joshua opened his eyes. Eleanor was indeed there, turning away from him.

"Eleanor."

She rushed back to his bedside, kneeling next to him, concern showing in her face.

"Am I dreaming again?" He reached up and touched her face. "Are you really here, Eleanor?"

For a moment, she did not speak. She bit her upper lip, and her eyes filled. Blinking, she wiped them quickly and then whispered softly, "I am here, and I am pleased to say that you are too. We thought for a while that we would lose you."

He closed his eyes again and took a few shallow breaths.

"You are tired and need your rest. I will come back later."

"No." His voice quavered. He took hold of her arm, but his grip felt weak. "No, please. Sit with me a while. Can you?"

"Of course." He released her, and she placed her hand upon his brow. Her touch felt cool and soothing. "Your fever is still strong. We need to get more tea and broth into you."

"I am so glad to see you, Eleanor. I thought I would die alone in this place."

A cloud passed over her face, and then it became serene again. "You are not dying at all if I have anything to say about it."

When Merlin died, he'd felt all the life drain out of him. Perhaps that was all the typhus needed to take hold. He wanted to tell her that he nearly lost the will to live another day in this hopeless abyss, but something shone in her eyes when she looked at him, and he could not speak of such things. It occurred to him then how unfair life was to instil in each of us such a will to survive that we would endure almost any amount of pain just to live another day. Seeing her here, feeling her touch, hearing her voice, it made a dying ember in him flicker into a flame once more.

They did not speak for a time, and she gave his arm a gentle squeeze. It made him smile. Suddenly, her face brightened as if she had an epiphany. "The letter. I have a letter here from your mother."

"She lives, then." Relief flooded him. He thought perhaps his final loss would be his mother, but it was not so. "Would you read it to me, Eleanor." He blinked several times. "My eyes… my eye… will not do what I ask of it."

Eleanor began to read…

24 February, 1855
My dearest son, Joshua,

First and foremost, I hope this finds you well. We hear such grim and nearly unbelievable reports from Crimea that it fills all my days with terror. How you survived that fateful charge into the Russian guns, I will never know, and I thank God every day for having spared you. Now, with reports of food shortages and lack of medicine and shelter, I fear for your life once again. Please write to me and tell me you are safe.

Eleanor stopped reading and looked up at Wentworth. His jaw was working, and he turned his head from her when their eyes met. "You must write to her, Eleanor. At once."

Eleanor patted his arm once more. "It has already been done. The moment I found you here, I wrote to your mother and father and told them that you were ill, but I had confidence that you would survive. Once you are stronger, you may write to her yourself. I am sure she will feel much better getting a letter directly from you."

He still would not look at her but whispered, "You are an angel, Eleanor Sherbrooke." He swallowed hard and then looked at her again. She took his cloth from the basin next to his bed and, squeezing the water from it, dabbed his cheeks and then lay it across his forehead. Then, taking up the letter again, she continued…

Your father, Geoffrey, and I have packed a box for you and sent it overland. The Russians have retreated from the Danube, I am told, and these goods should reach you soon. Papa had a new field coat made for you, and I have packed some of cook's biscuits and some Darjeeling tea. As I write this, I find it sounds so trivial and your trials are so great that I fear we can do little to alleviate your suffering. Still, I hope these goods find you and that you are able to make use of them.

Do write, dear Joshua, and let me know that you are still with us. Please thank Miss Sherbrooke for her letters. She has assuaged our fears more than once and I bless her for it.

I think of you and pray for you every day. God bless and keep you, my son.

Your Loving Mother"

"You have been writing to her, then?" Wentworth asked.

"Whenever I had news of you or of the 17th, I sent it along to her. I did not know if she was receiving your letters, so I thought I could allay her fears in some small part."

He patted her hand, but his weariness was so great, when he opened his mouth to speak, no words would come. Her image swirled before his eyes and he resigned himself to slumber.

Chapter 10

A steady stream of wounded and sick were being transported daily from the trenches around Sebastopol. Men talked of long days of boredom, sitting in the trenches, interrupted from time to time with a comrade falling from Russian rifle fire or explosions from the heavy guns. The Russians had constructed large earthen bastions resembling rooks in a chess game all around the city early in the fighting, and now they were fortresses. The English and the French bombarded them constantly, and on every occasion, they were completely rebuilt overnight by the enemy. This astounding feat confounded the allies. With General Winter in retreat, the war had dissolved into a stalemate.

Eleanor's new position at the hospital at Balaclava was at once satisfying and draining. Dr Farley was the consummate professional, doing his work efficiently and never criticising unfairly, but also quick to recognise good work. The hospital was smaller by far than Scutari, which had four miles of beds less than two feet apart. When she was there, Eleanor had little time to walk among the wounded as her services were needed from sunup to sundown in surgery. Here, however, it was different. Surgery did not take up all of her time, so she did have duties that brought her among the men. Keeping them clean, dressing their wounds, talking with them, writing their letters home were part of her daily routine now.

The most heartbreaking were the men in the cholera wards. Some came in early morning, feeling they had been sent to hospital by mistake for they were not that ill, and by evening they were dead. It took so many, driving every drop of water from their bodies in only a few hours. Working so closely among the sick and wounded, her tears were becoming harder and harder to contain. The emotional strain was so great that she felt it a relief to serve in surgery. At least there the men were sedated and the tasks were clear, if somewhat gruesome. She could brace herself against the horrors of gangrene and shattered limbs, but not against the daily losses of men that she now could number among her acquaintance.

It had been a fortnight since she arrived, and Lieutenant Wentworth was slowly recovering from typhus. His fever was gone, but he was still weak. Eleanor made time every day to visit him. The patients' beds were not as close together as Scutari, but conversations were still overheard. The men on either side of Lieutenant Wentworth kept their eyes closed and feigned sleep most of the times she came to visit, but they did not fool her. This place, however, gave Eleanor a certain license in her behaviour that she never dared take before.

As she entered his ward, Mrs Davis accosted her. "Going to visit your young man again, I see?" The woman was nothing if not blunt.

Eleanor was momentarily taken aback. "He is not my young man, Mrs Davis. There could never be anything between us."

Mrs Davis scowled and took Eleanor by the elbow, leading her to the doorway, out of earshot of the patients. "Miss Sherbrooke, listen to me. Your personal involvements are your own, but let me give you some advice. Do not reject this man based on his disfigurement. After all you have seen, I must say I am surprised at you. All of his subordinates say he is a fine officer and an honourable man. Think again. Beauty is in the eye of the beholder, you know." With that, she let go of Eleanor's arm and left her without waiting for a response.

Eleanor stood, dumbfounded, at the doorway. What an extraordinary thing to happen. She found herself nearly laughing at the irony of it. As she approached Lieutenant Wentworth's bed, he was sitting up and reading something. He smiled broadly at her approach. After putting down the papers, he held up one finger.

"Watch and be amazed, Miss Sherbrooke." He swung his feet off the cot and put them on the floor. Then, struggling to stand, he held his arm out to her. "Perhaps 'amazed' was too strong a word. Do give me your arm."

She did, and leaning heavily on it, he struggled to his feet. "See, I am able to stand. Soon, I will be able to return to my regiment."

The momentary joy disappeared, and it was as if a large stone had dropped into Eleanor's stomach. He wanted to return to the front. Was he determined to get himself killed?

"Return to your regiment?" She helped him lower himself back into bed and continued talking while she arranged the blankets over him. "I thought you would be returning to England."

"Not yet, I am afraid. I doubt any of us in the Light or the Heavy Brigade will see much fighting, but they do need us to transfer the wounded and such."

She pulled up a camp chair and sat next to him. "I think that is a terrible idea."

His expression took on a look of amusement. "Well, I will be sure and inform Lord Cardigan of your displeasure." She was not amused, and her face must have shown as much, for he dropped the smile and took one of her hands in both of his. "It is dear of you to worry for me so, but this is the life of an army officer. I cannot abandon my post because I am concerned over my own safety. Surely, you understand."

She said nothing but turned her face away from him. She did not, however, let go of his hand. The emotions that she had so far been so adept at hiding all bubbled to the surface and tears began to roll down her cheeks. She pulled her hand from his and quickly wiped them away, again turning from him. "I do not know what has come over me these days. Perhaps it is the strain."

He touched her cheek and turned her head to face him. "My dear. Of course, it is the strain. I do not know how you do the work you do…any of you sisters. It is all right, Eleanor." His expression was so sympathetic that Eleanor feared she might begin to cry again if she continued looking. Taking a deep breath, she pointed to the papers he had on his blanket.

"Letters from home?" she asked.

He did not look down immediately but touched her face a few moments longer as he held her gaze. "What?"

"That." She pointed again to the papers.

"Oh, yes," he said absently. "A letter from Julia."

Of course, Julia. There were times when she forgot completely about Julia and their engagement.

He continued. "She speaks of all her social engagements, of people we both know and their goings-on."

"She writes me of the same things. I find it all quite trivial, don't you?"

He looked at her quizzically. "Actually, I find it quite a comfort. Somewhere in the world, life goes on in a peaceful, ordered way. No one is ill or wounded. No one falls asleep to the pounding of guns. All is right with the world. I cannot wait to return there."

Eleanor was taken aback. She did not expect such sentiments from Lieutenant Wentworth. "I suppose I feel just the opposite. Even with all the death and sorrow here, I feel for the first time that I am doing something worthwhile."

He cocked his head to one side and took on an amused expression. "You never cease to surprise me, Eleanor Sherbrooke, and that is the truth."

"Well, then. I must go. Give my love to Julia when you write again."

"That I will."

She stood to go, and he was once again engrossed in his letter. Mrs Davis did not understand why she could not call Lieutenant Wentworth "her young man." It was not his scarred face at all. It was her sister, Julia. Lieutenant Wentworth was Julia's young man, and if he survived this conflict, he would soon be her husband.

***

After ten more days of recuperation, Lieutenant Wentworth was finally released for active duty again. The package promised by his mother had arrived, and in it a rather fine eye patch that was larger than most and hung down in a triangle to cover some of his disfigured cheek. He had yet to see his face since it healed but did not give it much thought. One got used to seeing disfigurement in Crimea. It was a fact of life.

The new railway that connected Balaclava with the trenches surrounding Sebastopol was finished. Before Wentworth boarded the train that would take him back to the front, he sought out Eleanor. She was most faithful in seeing to his care and, more importantly, keeping up his spirits. He saw many men die who just could not take the suffering and deprivation any longer. He was fortunate in many ways. The weather had finally broken, and spring brought forth carpets of flowers over the very battlefields where he and his comrades once fought. Many of them lay buried in that very ground.

The coming of new life filled him with a long-abandoned sense of optimism.

Lieutenant Wentworth found Eleanor with the other nurses having their noon meal in the refectory. He requested an audience with her, and she soon appeared.

"How do you like the eye patch, Miss Sherbrooke?" He swivelled his head one way and then another.

"Very smart, I daresay."

He had to admit that he felt a certain warmth come over him every time he was in her presence. "I am off, then. To the front." He endeavoured a jaunty attitude that he hoped would mask his unease. Her expression became solemn, and was it his imagination, or did her lower lip quiver a bit? Many people moved about near them, so he kept a discreet distance, but had an overwhelming desire to take her in his arms and comfort her. "Do not worry about me. I will be careful."

"Are you sure you are strong enough to return to duty?"

"The doctors and my captain certainly think so."

A cool breeze blew steadily, so she reached up and buttoned the top two buttons on his tunic.

"You must take care of yourself. Do not come back here with typhus again or cholera or I will be very cross with you."

Her eyes seemed deep enough for him to lose himself. They betrayed a concern not reflected in her words. He clasped both her hands.

"And no more wounds," she said. "I will never speak to you again if you get yourself wounded." Her words faltered, and he was undone. It suddenly did not matter if there were people about or if they would talk. He encircled her with his arms and let her head rest upon his shoulder for just a moment. She tightened her grip around his waist, then let go.

"Good-bye, Eleanor." He said the words quickly and spun on his heel, walking away. He dared not turn and look at her again.

***

22 March, 1855
My Dear Friend Eleanor,

How good of you to find time to write to me amidst all your duties. I truly marvel at your courage and your fortitude. I know I could not survive one moment in Crimea, much less five months. I know you are shielding me from the worst that you are enduring, but we do have Mr Fenton's photographs and the relentless articles in The Times, so you needn't lie to protect my delicate sensibilities. I do not know from whence you derive all your strength, but I can tell you it is much admired by me and all of us at home. Miss Nightingale has become legend here, and no doubt, you will as well.

Now to the express purpose of my letter. I have debated with myself many times as to how indiscreet I should be regarding your sister Julia, but I feel I must speak. I know you have seen Lt. Wentworth and you may decide what to tell him if anything. I know soldiers feel that they need someone to come home to, but the more I watch your sister, the more I am convinced that she is not the one.

I can tell you now, Eleanor, she does not behave as if she and Lieutenant Wentworth have an understanding. I know it is difficult to have the object of one's affection so far away for such a long time, but her behaviour is really beyond the pale. Almost from the beginning, from the moment Lt. Wentworth stepped on the ship, she has been flirting shamelessly with George Shaw.

Eleanor put Cordelia's letter down for a moment. Was she appalled or relieved? If Julia intended to break off her engagement, could she dare hope? Lieutenant Wentworth treated her more as a friend or a sister. But then, he knew nothing of what was transpiring behind his back. Of all the men Julia could have taken up with, did it have to be George Shaw? The man was, what was the word for it…a scoundrel. That's what he was…a scoundrel. Eleanor read on…

I know the man is rich, but he is so arrogant and even cruel at times that I just do not see what Julia sees in him, except perhaps, his fortune. We all must marry well, I suppose. The only reason I tell you any of this, Eleanor, is that I know of your affection for Lt. Wentworth. I thought from the beginning that the two of you suited one another better than he and Julia. There, I have said it and will not retract it.

Do take care of yourself, Eleanor, and come back safe and sound. I hope this awful war will end soon and all of you may return to our shores. I am glad that my box of supplies arrived unmolested. The surgical instruments looked absolutely horrifying. I cannot imagine how you use them every day. Write again soon and tell me of all your adventures.

Your Friend,
Cordelia

Eleanor decided then and there she would not say a word to Lieutenant Wentworth. It was not her place, and with the time it took for a letter to travel from England to Crimea, everything with Julia and Mr Shaw might have changed. No, Lieutenant Wentworth was better off concentrating on his duty and staying alive. Home would take care of itself when the time came. Eleanor chastised herself for secretly rejoicing in this bit of news. Spring had arrived at last, and with it came hope for the future.

***

To say that Wentworth was disappointed with his duty when he returned to the front was an understatement. The Light Brigade that had shown itself so valiant and steadfast in battle only a few months before was now relegated to burial and ambulance duty. An empty plain stretched between the Russian redoubts and the Allied trenches that men from both sides were ordered to try to breach despite the artillery and rifles aimed at them. Therefore, after each skirmish, many wounded and dead lay about in the open. From time to time, the gentlemen officers from each side would call a truce so that they could gather up the bodies for burial. Occasionally, one of those bodies moved or cried out and was taken off to hospital.

The first time Wentworth participated in this strange play, he was sceptical that the truce would hold. As soon as men emerged from the trenches to retrieve the bodies, they were vulnerable to shot, but the gentlemen's agreement between the Allies and the

Russians always held on both sides. He found himself standing with the French and even the enemy officers, trading tobacco or even a drink whilst their men went about scavenging the dead or the dying. It was then his job to supervise the burials. He took to bringing a notebook with him to try to keep a record of the dead so that he might notify their families. There was no system by which this was done, but he knew from Eleanor that Miss Nightingale took it upon herself to inform family members of their loss. He believed the army should do the same. If he was lucky, there were letters or pictures from home carried in the pockets of the dead, and although his men were reluctant, he ordered them to go through the uniforms of the fallen so that they might be identified. It was a grim task, but one that Wentworth deemed necessary.

After weeks of this gruesome task, Wentworth was granted leave. His first thought was to return to Balaclava to see Eleanor, but one of his fellow officers in the 18th Hussars told him of the British Hotel.

"It is between Kadikoi and Balaclava, right on the way to the hospital. You can stop there first and then travel on. You must see the place, Wentworth."

"Whatever are you talking about, a British Hotel?" Wentworth asked as he pulled on his boots and readied his kit.

Lieutenant Chapman scratched his woolly beard. "There is plenty of food and drink. Even a store of sorts. You could buy a gift for your nurse there." He laughed heartily, waggling his eyebrows.

"Do shut up, Chapman." Wentworth stomped his foot into his boot. "And who runs this hotel, then?"

"A Jamaican woman called Mary Seacole."

"A Jamaican? Really?" Wentworth could scarcely believe his ears.

"Came here to nurse 'her boys' and give us a place to rest. I have not been there myself but hear that Mrs Seacole is a proper nurse and will go straight into the trenches with all manner of nursing and comfort. You must come, Wentworth, if only to see such a wonder."

Wentworth reluctantly agreed and, taking his two-month pay in the pocket of his new field coat, he prepared to set out. His father had had the tailor make a small compartment for his watch in his new uniform, and he felt the seam along the edge of it.

"Come along, Wentworth. Don't dawdle." They walked together to the stable. More horses had arrived in Crimea but were used now for pulling carts and carrying the wounded. There were no more glorious and murderous cavalry charges now, only trench warfare. He had not been on horseback since Merlin died.

His Hussar friend climbed into the saddle and held the reins of a fine chestnut mare for him. She was already saddled. "Good God, Wentworth, you are slow. Are you ill?"

Of course, he was not ill but overcome. Swallowing hard, he grasped the saddle horn and swung himself up. He patted the horse's neck.

"That one's called Folly."

"I don't want to know her name. Let's go."

Lieutenant Chapman kept up a steady banter all the way to Spring Hill, which helped rescue Wentworth from his thoughts. As they approached the British Hotel, Wentworth had to admit what he saw was not what he expected. The place looked less like a hotel and more like a hovel being made of scraps of iron and wood that were haphazardly thrown together. Still, by the time they reached the corral outside, raucous singing and laughter assailed their ears.

As soon as they entered, a dusky-complexioned, robust woman dressed in the most colourful costume bedecked with ribbons and sporting a straw hat upon her head greeted them.

"Do come in, my sons. Come in. Before you take your ease, would you like a shave?"

"See, what did I tell you?" Chapman said, elbowing Wentworth in the ribs. Then, turning to Mary Seacole, he made a slight bow. "That would be most welcome, ma'am."

"Don' call me Ma'am, my son. Call me Mother. Everyone do."

"All right, Mother. Do you think your barber could help my friend here as well?"

Mrs Seacole peered at Wentworth's disfigured face. "De barber, he a talented one. I am sure he do your frien' a good service." She led them away to another part of the ramshackle structure.

After Chapman had his shave, which much changed his appearance, he retreated to the canteen. The barber intimated that copies of *The Times* were available there as well as various comestibles and a welcome drink. Wentworth watched as locks of his curly hair hit the floor. As he lay back in the crudely constructed barber chair, the Jamaican barber lathered up his face.

"Now, be still, sir. I don' wanna cut you."

"Spare me the moustache, will you, my good man?"

The uninjured side of his face took no time at all, but the barber laboriously worked on the other side. Finally, the man finished. "Dere, sir, all finished. Moustache trimmed and all."

"Give me the looking glass. Let me see."

The barber gave him a quizzical look. "Never see your face before, eh, sir?"

"Of course I've seen my face before, just not since it healed." Wentworth made a grab for the mirror in the man's hand.

"Well, den, sir. Let us put this patch on firs' and…."

It was not what Wentworth wanted to hear. The wound must have been hideous if this stranger was trying to mitigate its effect on him. "Give me the looking glass. I have seen it before."

The barber reluctantly handed the mirror to him.

My God, what a sight. Yes, there was an empty socket where his eye had once been. His cheek and chin were no longer smooth and flawless but marked with skin pulled and stretched over the bones of his skull. At least the infection and bleeding were long gone. He held the mirror there for a time. The barber then, wordlessly, picked up the eyepatch and fastened it to his injured face. He had to admit, that device mitigated the horror of his wound somewhat. Wentworth handed the mirror back to the barber. "I believe I need a drink."

***

When Wentworth woke the next day, for a moment he did not remember where he was. Raising his head from the pillow was a painful endeavour. He did remember polishing off a bottle of something the night before, which in his still-weakened state made him roaring drunk within a short time. He was grateful for his Hussar friend for getting him a bed for the night.

When he washed and dressed, he made his way to the canteen where Mrs Seacole was doling out coffee and eggs. Eggs. When was the last time he had an egg? Before the Great Storm, was it? Mary Seacole put his breakfast before him and handed him a cup of coffee.

The smell of it took him back to his father's house. "Are you all right, sir?"

Wentworth looked up into the kindly face. "Yes, Mother. I am quite all right." She patted him on the shoulder and went about tending to her other guests.

In a few moments, Lieutenant Chapman joined him. "How is your head this morning?"

"A bit larger than it was last night, no thanks to you."

Chapman laughed. "I hope you have some of your pay left, or there will be a very disappointed nurse in Balaclava." Chapman gave him a wink and joined the others among the newspapers.

After breakfast and a perusal of *The Times*, Wentworth was on the road to Balaclava, a precious bar of chocolate from J. S. Fry and Sons in his shoulder bag. It cost him twice what it would in England, but it did his heart good every time he imagined the look on Eleanor's face when he gave it to her. These small things, minor luxuries at home, took on a monumental significance in this outpost of hell. He hoped she would be pleased.

By his reckoning, it was Easter Sunday. Spring had awakened the wildflowers on the hillsides. He resolved to obtain permission from Mrs Davis to take Eleanor for a ride in the hills. They were far enough from the front to be out of harm's way. The only minor irritation was the constant pounding of guns in the distance. Yes, that was exactly what he would do. He dismounted at the Land Transport Corps hospital and inquired after Eleanor.

"Is Miss Eleanor Sherbrooke about? Tell her that Lieutenant Wentworth is here to see her." He stood at the doorway to one of the wards. One of Eleanor's colleagues looked at him with a sorrowful expression.

"Oh, sir. You are too late. Mrs Davis, Miss Sherbrooke, and a few others left this morning."

"Left? What do you mean left?" Had she gone home to England without telling him? No, that could not be.

"Well, sir. They've gone to the front."

***

The bombardment of Sebastopol began in earnest on Easter Sunday. The report of the big guns could be heard night and day all the way to Balaclava. Mrs Davis roused Eleanor from bed before dawn.

"Get up, Miss Sherbrooke. We are going to the trenches."

Eleanor had only time to wash quickly, dress, and drink a cup of tea before she and Mrs Davis and two of their fellow nurses boarded the train to the trenches before Sebastopol. Mrs Davis took the opportunity to prepare them on the way.

"I chose you women because I believe you will not panic under fire. There will be a great deal of noise, the cannon fire and all, but you must keep your heads. If we are able to dress the worst wounds in the field, we may save the limbs of some of these poor lads, and keep the maggots off them. The kit bags I gave you are filled with bandages, sutures, and your own instruments. If you can, set up a small field hospital in the trench and treat the wounds as best you can there. I was assured that the army would cooperate with us. If you get separated from the rest of us, make your way back to our nurses' camp before dark."

The three of them looked at each other furtively. Eleanor had never been under fire before; she had experienced many of the horrors of war but never this one. She was not convinced that she was up to the task, but she would endeavour not to disappoint.

They were transferred to oxen carts from the train. Mrs Davis did not exaggerate. The booming of the cannons was quite deafening. The clanging of metal against metal as the guns recoiled after each discharge was enough to nearly split one's skull. Nothing in Eleanor's experience prepared her for this onslaught; no thunderstorm could ever reach the bone-shattering level of this hellish noise. Eleanor was unnerved before she even reached the trenches.

The infantry met them and brought their small company forward as far as the frightened bullock would go. Eleanor disembarked with her kit, and then soldiers, their heads down, ran to fetch her as the earth splintered around them. After scrabbling down the sloping path, she reached the bottom of the trench. It was wider and deeper than she had imagined, like an underground complex of wide roads. In fact, it was wide enough for four men to stand abreast in it, not that anyone would dare stand. Bullets whizzed by, and above them cannons belched fire and shot and clanged incessantly. She was among the 90th Light Infantry, and they had sustained casualties.

Before setting up any sort of hospital, she moved along the trench, looking for men who had been wounded. Before long, she arranged for two privates to follow her with casks of water and basins, so that she might treat men where they lay. Many had stuffed whatever fabric they could find into their injuries to staunch the bleeding. She tried to steel herself against the constant barrage from their own and enemy cannon.

She stooped before a fair-haired youth, and his grimy face grimaced in pain. “Let me see the wound, soldier,” she shouted. The youth did as he was bidden and took his hands from the laceration in his abdomen. After opening his jacket and cutting away his shirt, she determined that shrapnel had perforated his stomach and intestine. Cleansing the wound as well as she could, she wrapped it tightly. “I will send a stretcher for you,” she shouted, and the soldier nodded mutely, his face twisted in agony. There was not much hope for him unless he could be brought to a surgeon within a few hours. She ordered men about, sending them for stretcher bearers and organizing them to bring the badly wounded to a staging area where they would be evacuated.

Several times, as she was working, a bullet buzzed by her ear. Once, it impacted itself in the trench wall mere inches from her head. There was no time to stop and contemplate her lucky escape from death. Everywhere scores of maimed and moaning men were strewn about like so much human flotsam, and she had all of them to herself.

Later afternoon the guns began firing with less frequency. Eleanor had no idea how far she had travelled from her starting position and had lost track of her fellow nurses. In the fading light, she felt she could stand up for a time and stretch. Up ahead she saw a remarkable sight. A woman, at least fifty, with dark skin and a flamboyant multicoloured dress, tended the men in the trench. Eleanor had no idea who she was. She certainly was not one of her band of nurses.

The woman looked up at her as she approached. Eleanor held an oil lamp over her and the suffering soldier she was attending. “May I assist you?” The woman smiled and nodded.

Eleanor watched as this remarkable apparition expertly cleaned the bullet wound in the soldier's shoulder and dressed it in a clean bandage. "He need to get dat bullet out, or they be fever." Her accent was of the Caribbean. Eleanor was sure of it. "We try and get 'im to Balaclava tomorrow."

The older woman pushed herself to her feet and then extended her hand to Eleanor. "I am Mary Seacole. Are ye 'The Lady of de Lamp'?" She had a wry smile on her face, and Eleanor shook her head.

"I am not Miss Nightingale, if that is what you are asking, but I did work for her at Scutari. Eleanor Sherbrooke."

Mary shook her hand heartily. "De guns be dyin' down now. Come along wid me."

"Oh, I couldn't possibly. Mrs Davis will be searching for me."

"Dey fin' you wid me. It be all right." Mrs Seacole had an open and kind face, and when she offered Eleanor her arm as support, Eleanor gladly took it.

Mary Seacole had a roofed wagon set up not far from the nurses' tents, and she hustled Eleanor into it. It was a marvel. Shelves of food and medicine lined the walls and not a few bottles of whiskey and port. Without asking, Mary poured a glass of port for each of them. "Here, dearie. Drink dis. It'll do ye good."

Eleanor reached for the glass, but to her surprise, her hand was shaking so violently that she could not grasp it without spilling the contents. Then her whole body began to shake, and she was helpless against it. The older woman sat next to her and put her strong arms around Eleanor until the fit subsided.

"Dere, it stop. Ye be all right now." She handed Eleanor the glass, and they both partook.

"That has never happened to me before." Eleanor felt quite faint. She leaned back heavily on the cushions.

Mary poured her another drink. "I seen it many time among my sons on de battlefiel'. It quite normal. Don't take alarm."

"I believe I may be of a weaker will that I first imagined." Eleanor dabbed the sweat from her upper lip with her handkerchief.

Mary shook her head. "Ye very strong to do the work ye do. No one should say udderwise…not even yerself." She patted Eleanor's cheek.

Before Eleanor could comment, a knock sounded on the side of the wagon. Mary peered out. “Yer comrade come for ye, Miss Sherbrooke of de Lamp.”

Eleanor rose shakily to her feet. Mary held her hand until she stepped onto solid ground again. “Thank you for your hospitality, Mrs Seacole.”

“Ye come to de store sometime, miss. We have a cup o’ tea and talk.”

Eleanor nodded wearily and accompanied her fellow nurses back to their quarters amidst a barrage of questions she was too weary to answer.

***

Unlike the men in the field who were left in the trenches indefinitely, Mrs Davis did not allow her nurses to stay under constant bombardment. Within a month, Eleanor was ordered back to the field hospital. She objected strenuously at first but was used to obeying orders. Her first few nights back in Balaclava were sleepless ones. Even though the cannon fire eased at night or sometimes ceased altogether, her nerves were on edge in anticipation. Any sound, a basin knocked to the floor, a rat scurrying outside the walls, a cough from a fellow nurse, awakened her with a start.

“Ah, Miss Sherbrooke. Please, sit down.” Mrs Davis indicated a seat near her makeshift desk she maintained at the end of the first ward. A partial wall concealed them from the patients and afforded a modicum of privacy. “You look tired. I am afraid that time in the trenches unsettled you.”

Eleanor shook her head vigorously. “Oh, no, Mrs Davis. I could go back tomorrow.”

Mrs Davis looked at her sceptically. “On the contrary. I am thinking of sending you home.”

Eleanor jumped up from her seat. “Oh, please do not do that. My work here is not finished.” She leaned forward on Mrs Davis’s desk and her hands were shaking.

“All right. All right. Do not agitate yourself, Miss Sherbrooke. Perhaps you just need some time to rest. I am relieving you of duty for a week.”

“But, Mrs Davis—”

"You will rest, Miss Sherbrooke, or you will be on the first ship to Constantinople."

Eleanor nodded mutely and sat down in a heap. She knew that her strength was failing. Exhausted, she returned to her quarters and changed back into her nightdress. Within a few minutes of her staring at the ceiling boards, Dr Farley arrived with a syringe.

"I have heard of your indisposition, Miss Sherbrooke. I have come with a tincture of opium to help you rest."

Eleanor sat up in bed and shook her head in protest. "I do not believe that…."

The doctor said nothing, but gently eased her back onto her pillow. "For once, Miss Sherbrooke, allow me to be the doctor."

There was no more resistance in her. She offered up her arm, and soon a welcome darkness engulfed her. When she awoke, the faint pink light of daybreak filtered through her window. Still drowsy from either sleep or the sedative, she swung her legs heavily to the side of the cot, and with great effort, stood and stretched. She must have slept nearly a day. Upon rising and performing her morning ablutions, she was famished. The other nurses were still asleep when she left her quarters and entered the refectory. Mrs Davis was already there.

"You look much better, Miss Sherbrooke." She motioned to one of the Turkish women who cooked for them, and soon a cup of tea and bowl of gruel were before her.

"I feel much better. I believe I can return to my duties now."

"You will do no such thing. I have a few sundry items that I would like you to purchase from the British Hotel if you would. I will send an orderly with you. I know you have a friendship with that Mrs Seacole, and perhaps she will give you a good price. Finish your breakfast, and you can start out."

This was a relief. Eleanor wanted to see Mrs Seacole again and thank her for her kindness. She also longed to see the famous "Iron House" that the soldiers talked of so fondly. There were reports that one could even read *The Times* there. She had not seen a newspaper in months.

Before long, with Mrs Davis's list securely tucked away, and whatever English money she had saved over the past few months, Eleanor and a private called Weatherly embarked on their journey by donkey cart.

***

The ramshackle buildings came into view. Chickens and other farm animals nosed about the yard, and a few horses stood tied outside, no doubt belonging to British officers. All seemed quiet enough as it was still early morning. The place had a reputation for wild and boisterous drinking parties, but those were at night, no doubt. There were also reports of rampant thievery, so despite the young private's objections, Eleanor entered the establishment alone and left him outside to guard the horse and wagon.

A few officers sat about in the canteen, reading the papers and smoking. One looked up at her and rose from his seat to accost her. "Well, now. What is an English rose like yourself doing in a place like this?" His eyes were bloodshot, and he smelled of gin.

Eleanor was quite taken aback by his boldness, but before she could open her mouth to reply, Mary Seacole appeared from the depths of the storeroom behind the bar.

"Now, now, sir. Ye don' wan' be chasin' 'way my customers, do ye? Go and make yourself comfortable and I'll send Johnny wit' more coffee."

The unkempt officer wavered a bit, giving Eleanor a sinister look, but retreated from his position and wobbled back to his seat.

Mary was shaking her head. "Some o' dem can't hold de drink." She then turned to Eleanor with a smile. "Now, what can I do for ye?" She squinted at Eleanor. "I know ye from somewhere, is it not so?"

"The trenches. Easter Sunday."

Mary did the most extraordinary thing: she stepped forward and embraced Eleanor. "Yes, indeed. We were helpin' de boys togeder. I remember."

That motherly embrace was exactly what Eleanor needed. "Mrs Seacole—"

"Call me Mother, like my boys do, all right?" Mary was now patting Eleanor's back. Eleanor broke the embrace as her emotions began to rise.

"Mother, then. I have a list—"

"All right. Dat's good. Come in de back and we see what we can do."

Mary had a large storeroom with everything and sundry that anyone could possibly want. Eleanor's first order of business was collecting the things Mrs Davis needed, but as she looked through the shelves, she began to think that perhaps she should buy something for herself. A bar of chocolate might not go amiss.

"Now, go an' have a sit down and I will bring ye a nice cup o' tea. You can read de newspaper. Dose men be gone now."

Eleanor peered into the canteen and the officers had departed. It would be nice to sit for a while and do something ordinary like read the paper. "Could you bring a cup of tea and perhaps a copy of *Punch* for the young man waiting for me outside?"

"I send Johnny for it right away."

Eleanor settled down in the only chair that retained any padding and began to look through the newspapers. Many of the articles concerned the war. One titled "The Army in Crimea" from April 4 caught her eye and she set to reading. Soon, Mary appeared with her tea. Eleanor was blessedly alone, the booming of the artillery fire sounding only as loud as a distant thunderstorm. After nearly an hour, she lay her paper down, having exhausted the teapot's contents. No doubt Mary would have customers soon, and she really should not keep the young private from his duties much longer.

As she rose, Mary came from the back storeroom, carrying an iron box with a massive lock on the front. It was so heavy that Mrs Seacole could not lift it to the counter, but grunting, struggled across the bar with it and laid it at Eleanor's feet.

"I never show no one what I got in here, miss. But I trus' ye." Eleanor was indeed intrigued. "Dese some o' my bes' t'ings I get from tradin'. Wan' see?" Mary had captured her imagination, so she readily agreed. After taking a key from a chain around her neck, Mrs Seacole reverently opened the box. It contained many fine pieces such as a pistol with an ivory handle, a silver chain, a polished cigarette case. Mary laid each one on the table and told the story of how she acquired them.

After reaching in again, she pulled out something that fit in the palm of her hand. "Dis my favourite. Mus' belong to one de boys who got killed I'm t'inkin'."

She held the treasure out for Eleanor to examine. What she saw made her gasp involuntarily. It was a gold watch emblazoned with the insignia of the 17th Lancers: the skull and crossbones of death and under it, the ribbon inscribed with the word "Glory". Death or Glory. Before she could ask how Mary came upon such a treasure, she was offered the explanation.

"Oh, ye like dat, eh? I traded for it w' one o' dem French ladies on horseback."

Eleanor looked at her enquiringly.

"You know. Dey in biznis like me. But dey sell t'ings to de French army, not ours, and ride about in trousers."

"You are joking."

"I am not. Dey come here sometime to trade t'ings dey don' wan'. I suppose dey don' wan' dis watch because it say somet'ing inside."

Eleanor opened the case…

To my son, Joshua. May God protect you. Your loving Father 1854.

She'd held this very watch in her hand so long ago, in a garden at a hospital for gentlewomen on Harley Street. It did not seem possible. How did some French, trouser-wearing canteen girl get it? It did not matter. Eleanor must have it back.

"How much do you want for this?" she asked.

"You know who belong to? He still livin'?"

"He is very much alive. His father gave him this watch before he left London. He showed it to me. How did this French—"

"*Vivandière* I t'ink dey call dem."

"Yes, yes. How did it end up with one of them?"

Mary shook her head, laughing. "I can tell ye dat many t'ings come to me. Here, take it. Give it back to 'im."

Eleanor shook her head vehemently. "No, I cannot just take it. I must pay you for it."

Mary patted Eleanor's hand and then grasped both of them in her own. "I give away more dan I sell. Officers owe me more money dan I can tell ye. If I make it from dis place wit' a penny to my name, it will be only due to God's will."

"Even so. I must give you something for it." Eleanor dug in her small bag and collected every penny she brought with her. She had saved most of her pay since there was little to spend it on while at Scutari. "Here," she said, pressing the coins and bills into Mrs Seacole's hands, "it's nearly ten pounds. I know it is not enough—"

"No, it more dan nuf. More dan I pay for it, but I don' wan' yer money. Ye give dis watch back to my son." Mary pushed the money back at Eleanor and thrust the watch into her hands as well.

After a brief struggle, Eleanor could see the determination on Mrs Seacole's face. "Mother" would not take a penny for the watch. Then an idea occurred to her. "Those officers who were here. Did they pay their bill?"

Mary smiled slyly at her. "I know what you tryin' to do."

"I merely want to do something for our brave men. How much do they owe you?"

Mary did not even have to consult her ledger. "Twenty shillings thruppence, but—"

"I will not hear another word… for our brave men in the field." She began counting the money out, and this time Mrs Seacole did not object. "Well, I must be going. I do hope we see each other again…Mother."

Mrs Seacole patted Eleanor's cheek. "Oh, I t'ink we will."

Chapter 11

Lieutenant Wentworth emerged from the trenches on the twenty-second of May. English ears and Russian troops were subject to the incessant pounding by the French batteries of the western side of the siege works. The casualties were enormous, but the French prevailed. Slowly, the allies were making headway in capturing Sebastopol. Joshua Wentworth had received his orders, and now, saddling his mare, Folly, he set off for Spring Hill and the Iron House.

Securing a room for the night, he sent word ahead to Eleanor that he would come for a visit the next day. After his surprise visit on Easter Sunday ended in disappointment and anxiety for her safety in equal measure, he resolved to announce himself. In the morning he treated himself to a bath, shave, and clean clothes. Since the French dealt with their own casualties, he was hoping against hope that the English hospital would not be desperate for her services and, more importantly, that she had not been sent again to the front. Like him, her life and fate were bound up in other's decisions. At any rate, he had not received word that she was elsewhere, and that was good. He had important news. Arriving just after breakfast, he requested an audience with Mrs Davis.

"And you want to take Miss Sherbrooke away for a picnic for the entire day without a chaperone. Is that what you are proposing, Lieutenant Wentworth?"

Wentworth cleared his throat and pulled on the collar of his field jacket. "It does sound like the height of impropriety when you say it, Mrs Davis, but I can assure you that Eleanor and I are old friends and that my intentions are entirely honourable."

Mrs Davis let him struggle on a bit before her eyes crinkled up in an amused grin. "If Miss Sherbrooke would like to accompany you, I have no objection. Frankly, I feel she is working too hard and could use some amusement. I need your word, sir, that you will treat her like a lady at all times."

Wentworth raised his hand as if swearing in court. "Oh, you absolutely have my word."

"I am not jesting, Lieutenant."

The smile fled from Wentworth's face. "Neither am I. I have the highest regard for Miss Sherbrooke and would do nothing to besmirch her honour."

"Very well, then. I will find her and ask her if she is willing to go with you."

***

There was no question that Eleanor would accept Lieutenant Wentworth's invitation, no matter what tongues would wag. As soon as Mrs Davis left her quarters, Eleanor dug to the bottom of her trunk. She slipped the gold watch bearing the emblem "Death or Glory" into her day kit and rushed outside to meet him.

She wondered at their mode of transport, and once outside the hospital, a mare appeared to be fitted with an elongated saddle.

"Have you ever travelled thusly?" Lieutenant Wentworth made a short bow and indicated the elegant but strange contraption. His face indicated much amusement whenever he looked at her.

"I confess I never have."

"It is a Spanish saddle. The man sits astride and his lady on this cushion behind him."

Was she to sit with her legs dangling over the side of the horse, with nothing to anchor her there? She would have to hold on to the cantle just behind Lieutenant Wentworth's…. Oh, dear. He must have seen the uncertainty in her eyes for he spoke reassuringly.

"No need to worry. I will help you mount." Once he was seated, Eleanor took Lieutenant Wentworth's hand, placing her right foot in the stirrup, and stepped off the mounting block he provided. She pirouetted into her seat behind the good lieutenant. Arranging her skirts, she took hold of the back of the cantle to steady herself.

Eleanor felt quite wicked at that moment. It was a delicious feeling, really, to be riding off alone in the company of a young man.

"All set?" he asked, and Eleanor assented. They moved off in a gentle walk towards the Balaclava road. Soon, the hospital was out of sight, and they began their ascent to Spring Hill. She had to admit to herself that she did not feel completely at ease in her present position. It was especially precarious as they began to climb the steep hillside. She cried out suddenly as she slid precariously. Lieutenant Wentworth stopped the horse at once.

"Are you all right, Miss Sherbrooke?"

She endeavoured to seat herself more securely, but to no avail. "I am sorry, Lieutenant. I feel as though I may slip from my seat."

He said nothing but turned the horse around and descended to even ground. Her body bounced against his once or twice, but he did not seem to notice. "We are not returning to the hospital, are we?" She realised the disquiet at once in her voice.

"Oh, no. Far from it." The mare halted, and he seemed to slide effortlessly from the saddle. "I was never fond of these contraptions." On the ground now, he looked up at her. "Would you be ever so scandalised if I were to ask you to ride astride?"

The look on her face must have been most comical for he threw back his head and laughed. "I assure you, Miss Sherbrooke, I am not trying to compromise your honour. I am trying to secure your safety to the top of this hill."

She raised her head to look ahead. The climb was quite steep. He proffered his arms up towards her. "Here. Hop down and we will install you astride." She put her hands on his shoulders and slid off the mare into his arms. He looked down at her with an intensity she had not seen in his countenance before. Momentarily, he broke her gaze and put his foot in the stirrup.

"When I am mounted, I want you to give me your hand. I will leave the stirrup free. Put your left foot in it and swing your right leg over the horse."

That manoeuvre did not sound ladylike in the least. "But—"

"Either you must ride astride, or we must return from whence we came."

She looked up at his face and that mischievous grin was there. He was challenging her, and now she was determined. She did as she was bidden, and soon was seated behind him, one leg on either side of the horse in a most scandalous and undignified manner.

"Now, take hold of my waist and we will endeavour to climb this infernal hill."

She gingerly took hold of his waist. Every fibre of her was on fire. Without warning, he shouted, "*Hold on*," and kicked the horse in the flanks. The beast began a gallop up the hillside. Without any thought to modesty, Eleanor clasped herself tightly to Lieutenant Wentworth, who gave forth a great whoop as they clambered up the hillside. For the first time since she arrived in Crimea, all thoughts of pain and suffering, all thoughts of suitability and propriety, all thoughts of anything but the warmth of his body in her arms took flight out of her head. She was flying over rough ground, grasped tightly to the man she loved above all others.

They arrived, breathless, at the corral outside Mrs Seacole's hotel. A few enlisted men were about, and seeing them enter the corral, all ran to Eleanor's side. "Let me help you down, miss."

Before she knew it, she was standing in the midst of a group of unshaven, beaming scarecrows.

Lieutenant Wentworth dismounted forthwith. "Thank you very much, gentlemen. You are dismissed."

They gave a collective groan and began to make their way to the canteen. Eleanor was exhilarated. Upon securing his horse, Lieutenant Wentworth turned to her, a gentle expression in his eye, and a smile flickering across his face.

"Are you too scandalised, Miss Sherbrooke?"

"I am endeavouring not to be scandalised, Lieutenant Wentworth." She knew she was grinning like one who had taken leave of her senses, but she could not help it. This day was like an unexpected ray of sunshine amid a relentless grey and rainy day. She would enjoy this day, whatever came after.

Mary Seacole bustled to and fro when they entered. Her man, Johnny, poured drinks and brought food. Eleanor was the only woman there, save Mary and her daughter. She felt no consternation, however, for she was with an officer of the valiant Light Brigade, and everyone knew it. Mary had prepared a basket of victuals, which promised to have a bottle of French wine in it. After settling accounts with Mother, Wentworth led the mare Folly by the reins in search of a picnic spot. On a bluff nearby, a gnarled pine still stood despite the trampling of all the armies past, and Lieutenant Wentworth proceeded to lay a blanket on the hard soil and bid Eleanor sit. The day was flawless, sunny, and warm with a gentle breeze that felt like a caress on one's skin.

"Are you hungry, Eleanor?" He had tied the mare securely to a nearby clump of brush, and she seemed to be happily munching on some sort of grasses.

Eleanor was not hungry. She merely wanted to hear his voice and feel the sun upon her face. Then, the echoing sound of a barrage tore into her reverie. She started and he reflexively took her hand. "It is all right. It is the French, I think, from the sound of it." Here in the sunshine, she suddenly noticed how he had aged over the past year. He had the look of a man ten years older than he was. Then, of course, there was the injury to his face. The eyepatch, and its fellows that he had made here in Kadikoi, did hide much of the damage but gone was the flawless beauty that was his only a few months ago.

"Let us be wicked and have a glass of wine." She smiled at him and he leapt to his feet to fetch the basket.

"I have a surprise for you." He ran to the horse and produced two wineglasses from the saddlebag.

"However did you—?" As she spoke, she opened the basket, and as she reached in for the wine bottle, a great, fat rat poked its nose out at her. She screamed and dropped the basket. The rat, startled, leapt out of the basket and ran off. By this time, she was on her feet, shaking her hands and crying out. Lieutenant Wentworth ran to her side and, without thinking, took her in his arms.

"Now, now, Eleanor. It is all right. Shhh." She lay her head against his shoulder and then, realizing that they should not be thus engaged, she stepped away from him.

"I am sorry. It just startled me so."

Wentworth walked carefully over to the basket and, lifting the lid, looked back at Eleanor with an impish grin and then looked carefully into the basket. His expression changed to irritation.

"Oh, damn and blast." After reaching in, he pulled forth a half-eaten carcass of a fowl. "He's mangled the duck. Damn and blast." He held it out in front of him, shaking his head sorrowfully. He then looked up at Eleanor. "I don't suppose—"

"No. I am not eating any of that." She shivered.

With a great effort, he flung the carcass into the brush. "Ah well, let us partake of the wine and see what we can salvage of our picnic."

The rest of the comestibles seemed intact, and neither of them, after all they had been through, were particularly squeamish. They unwrapped the rest of the delicacies packed by Mrs Seacole and began their repast.

"Do you remember our first dinner, out on the terrace? No rats there." He was lying on his side, smiling his playful smile at her again.

"I do. You were quite dashing and gallant."

"I was, wasn't I?"

"And modest too, as I recall." She attempted to make that remark with composure but began to laugh.

The joke did not fall flat. He laughed as well and then looked off into the distance. "At least I can still be gallant. My looks, however—"

"Anyone who knows you will think you handsome despite and perhaps because *of* your war wound. How could they not?"

He turned back to look at her again with such tenderness that it sent a radiating heat through her. He leaned forward, and she knew he intended to kiss her. How could she betray Julia in such a way? It was true that Julia, at this very moment, was probably betraying him, but that did not justify—

A rifle shot rent the air. Wentworth flung himself on top of her and flattened her to the ground. Another shot sounded, and then the bullet whistled past, too close for comfort.

"Stay down, Eleanor. Stay down," he whispered close to her ear. His body, so thin and yet so strong, pinned her to the ground. She was aroused and terrified at the same time. He crawled away from her and, moving behind the tree, stood and peered out in the direction of the shots. He cursed again.

He stepped out and began waving his arms.

"Joshua," she called out to him. What was he doing? It was suicide.

"Halloo. Hello there. You are firing on us." He was shouting down the valley. A man called from a distance, and then Joshua ran in the direction of the shooting. Eleanor remained on the ground.

In a short while he was back. He did not look amused. "You can get up now, Eleanor. I've put a stop to it." Apparently, a pair of young enlisted men were playing at some sort of target practice in a ravine near their picnic spot. A pair of stray bullets found their way over the rise and nearly killed the two of them. "I sent them packing.

The fools. They will have enough to shoot at once they are sent to the trenches."

He did not approach her but grasped the trunk of the tree to steady himself. Her blood ran cold. "Have they shot you? Are you all right?" She ran to his aid, and instinctively propped him up with her body clutching his back as she did one hundred times before with men wounded in the trenches. He leaned heavily on her and then sank to the ground. "Where are you hit?" Her voice was shrill and betrayed her panic.

He shook his head vehemently. "I am not wounded, just a bit unsteady, is all. I do apologise."

She knew exactly what it was, for the same malady affected her. The sound of artillery when unexpected, the crack of a rifle shot—all set one's nerves aflame. One never grew used to such things. Most of the weakness occurred after the danger was over. It was logical to think that these things should affect one less and less the more one was exposed to them. Yet she observed that many men, and women for that matter, were eventually worn down by the constant threat of peril. The sounds of war were the trigger.

"No need to apologise. You saved my life."

He looked at her and smiled weakly. "Yes, and afterwards, my knees gave out from under me."

She sat very close to him now but dared not touch him. Her feelings were quite jumbled and overwhelming, and she could not put them in their place.

"That is what I wanted to speak to you about, Eleanor."

She peered at him. "What do you mean?"

"They are sending me home. Invalided to England. I suppose I am no use to the cavalry anymore."

She did not know what to say. Her first thought was for herself. She took a great deal of comfort in the fact that he was there with her, close to her. Still, the army should have sent him home after he was injured in the Battle of Balaclava, but no, they tortured him through the winter and then left him in the trenches for all those months. It really was too cruel. She did not want him to go, and yet she did.

"You deserve to go home to rest on your laurels."

He did not speak for a moment, and then his sombre mood seemed to evaporate. She was surprised to see a smile steal its way across his countenance. He patted his bottom. "So, Sister, are these my laurels?"

Her mouth dropped open in surprise. "Lieutenant Wentworth…shame on you." She laughed along with him, but his news seemed to seep back into her mind. "When will you go?"

He shrugged. "I don't know. Soon, I expect. I will not return to the front but will wait in Balaclava. I could leave in a week's time, or tomorrow." He stared off into the distance again. "Will you miss me, Eleanor?"

He was sitting so close to her, too close. She wondered if he could hear her heart pounding. She struggled to master her emotions, so she rose and stood a few feet away from him.

"Of course, I shall miss you." Why did he insist on hearing her say those words? They immediately brought tears to her eyes. She looked away from him and wiped them away. Before she could turn and meet his eyes again, he stood behind her, his hands grasping her arms. She wanted to lean into him. To surrender to him.

"Come with me, Eleanor. Let us return together."

She could not believe her ears. What was he asking her?

"And what of Julia?" She spun around to face him. She could not read his expression. It was as if he was just hearing her sister's name for the first time. "What of the life you planned with her? The life without any memory of the war? That is what you want, is it not?"

A myriad of emotions passed over his countenance, but he said nothing for a time. She could not read his expression.

"Do not ask me such questions, Eleanor. I cannot think. Do you not remember how life was before we left? This place is not real. It is not life. Life is back home."

She released herself from his grasp and put a bit of distance between them. "If that is how you feel, then you must return to that life you left behind. I cannot. My work here is not finished."

He closed the space between them. "The war will not last forever, Eleanor. You will come home eventually."

"I have been thinking of that, Joshua. I believe I will stay with the army. Perhaps go to India."

He stepped back from her as if she had struck him. "India? India? Oh, Eleanor, you cannot."

"I can and I will if I so choose, for what is left for me in England?"

To that he made no reply. In silence they packed the remnants of their outing. The journey home was sombre and silent. Eleanor sat sidesaddle and did whatever she could to keep her distance. She must surrender him now to her sister. It was already decided before the war. It was what he wanted.

On returning to the hospital, one of the orderlies helped her down onto the mounting block, so she did not feel even the touch of Joshua's hand before they parted.

"Good-bye, Eleanor." He held her gaze from atop his mare. She returned it.

"Good-bye, Joshua. Safe journey home."

He chucked the reins and gave Folly a nudge and they trotted off. It was then she remembered, but it was too late. She pulled it from her pocket and shook her head. She had forgotten to give him his watch.

***

8 June, 1855
My Dearest Julia,

I am returning home. I will be on board the Himalaya, the ship that brought me here. The army has sent me home an invalid, but I do not feel like one. I can still walk about and use my hands, but as I told you before, my right eye is gone and there is significant scarring to that side of my face. I do have some trouble sleeping and have some melancholia, and the army has seen fit to discharge me of my duties. You will not meet the same man coming home as you sent off to war.

There is nothing that I look forward to more than seeing your lovely face, having tea in your sitting room, and hearing all your news. For now and ever, I want to put the war behind me and never think of it again. I suppose that will not be possible, being one of the fortunate surviving members of the Light Brigade, but you will help me immensely, I think. The Season is in full flower now, and we will partake together. Then, we can begin our plans for the future.

Before I close, I must tell you how brave and steadfast your sister Eleanor has been throughout this ordeal, not only in regard to myself, but to all who fell under her care. She is reputed to be a fine surgical nurse, and if you ask me, or any of the men she aided in the trenches, she could easily become a remarkable surgeon in her own right. She has also been a great comfort to me and has encouraged me to write to you in all honesty, as I am doing now. Soon, Julia, we will meet again. I look forward to it with all my heart.

Your,
Joshua

"The chickens have come home to roost." Mrs Sherbrooke peered over her pince-nez and laid her needlework in her lap. "It is a lovely letter, Julia. You have promised your hand to this man, and now he is coming home to claim it."

"Oh, Mama. What am I to do? Invalided. There must be something wrong with him. And that scar on his face, Mama. What if he is hideous to look at?"

"Nothing in your sister's letters says that he is hideous. Really, Julia. You had to be prepared for such an eventuality. The man went off to war. He is a hero. What more do you want?"

Julia looked at her mother incredulously. "Really, Mama. You know what I want. I want to make the best marriage that I can. George's prospects are so much—"

Mrs Sherbrooke shook her head. "You made a pledge, Julia. You should honour it. I do believe that Lieutenant Wentworth needs you now."

Julia stood before the cold fireplace and struck a pensive pose. "Did you hear how he goes on and on about Eleanor? I believe she might be better suited to care for an invalid than I."

"Julia, you need to welcome him home, first and foremost. After that, you must share what is in your heart. He deserves that much."

Julia did not speak for a long while. "Of course, you are right, Mama. I will do what needs to be done. I will not disgrace you or Papa."

"Do not disgrace Lieutenant Wentworth either, Julia. He deserves better."

***

Being relieved of duty with as yet no date of departure, Lieutenant Wentworth had time to visit Mary Seacole's again and to ride into the abandoned hills behind the lines. The spring had turned to summer, and the flowers vanished to be replaced with dry scrub and dust. Still, in the few days he had before he left Crimea, he took time to be alone with his thoughts. He did not see Eleanor again after the day of their picnic. Truth be told, he did not know what to say to her. He did not know anything.

He sat on the hillside, on the massive root of an ancient pine, and looked out over the sea. The harbour at Balaclava was to his left, but if he turned his head, he could obliterate it from his view and look out over nothing but descending scrubland and a turquoise ocean. The thunder of the cannon fire at the French line was somewhat muffled by the distance, and he could almost pretend he was at the seaside at home. The breeze blew through his hair like a woman's gentle touch. How he longed for home and to be away from this war. His thoughts returned again to Eleanor. Why would she prefer to continue witnessing this relentless parade of death and human agony to returning to the bosom of her family? It made no sense. There was a hollow place in him now that she created when she left him that day. He had to admit to himself that the only joy he felt in this place was when he was in her company. It suddenly struck him that he may not find such joy in Julia.

In less than a week, he was aboard the *Himalaya*. The slow, seeping reality of his return to home soil began to dawn on him. Just walking about the deck that first day on the ship told the tale. People took one look at his face and turned away. There was so much injury and death in Crimea that his deformity was hardly noticed by his fellow soldiers. Here, even on a ship filled with invalids, there were those who gaped at him as they would a circus animal. He hoped that he could mitigate the shock to Julia and his mother. His father would take it in stride, as he did everything. His brother, Geoffrey, would likely be constrained by his impeccable manners.

On board ship, his rank as an officer afforded him a cabin that he shared with only one other: a brother officer with one arm. Fortunately, his cabin mate was on deck a great deal of the time, which gave Wentworth time to be alone with his thoughts.

One night, he woke to his cabin mate shaking him violently. "Good God, man. What are you doing?"

"You were screaming in your sleep, old boy. Something about Merlin."

Wentworth lay back on his cot. They lay in nearly total darkness, with only the reflected moonlight illuminating creaking, swaying cabin. "I do apologise." Sweat soaked his nightshirt. "Still dreaming about that winter over there."

The other officer's voice reached him through the darkness. "Nearly didn't make it, did we? No need for apologies. You'll probably be shaking me awake before this voyage is over." The officer gave Wentworth's arm a squeeze and then returned like a spectre to his bunk.

Joshua involuntarily still trembled.

The other man spoke again. "Lost my arm in the Siege of Sebastopol."

Feeling that he should say something, Wentworth replied, "Light Brigade. Charged the Russian guns."

The other man sat up. "By Jove. You don't say. Lost mine in the trenches from frostbite. Nothing so glorious as yours."

Wentworth sighed. "Nearly made it unscathed but caught a blast when I was already up the hill cutting through their cavalry. Surprised them, though."

"Surprised everybody, old man. Old Raglan couldn't believe his eyes, they say."

"He gave the order."

"Ours is not to reason why…"

"What?"

"Tennyson's poem, old man…. Ours is not to reason why, Ours is but to do and die."

"Haven't read it."

The other officer laughed at this remark and lay back in his bunk. "You should get a copy and have Tennyson himself sign it for you…. Good night, then."

"Good night." Wentworth stared into the enveloping darkness. No one would let him forget this war. No one.

***

Eleanor returned to her work at the field hospital and attempted to think of nothing else. Surely, there was enough to occupy her mind.

The thrust of both the French and the British was now to take the great earthwork rooks that surrounded Sebastopol. The bombardment was incessant, punctuated by infantry charges by both sides. Both strategies resulted in hundreds if not thousands of casualties. More were dying on the battlefields than were returning wounded.

By the 18th of June, Eleanor found herself back in the trenches. General Eyre led two thousand men into a place called Picket House Ravine, a large gulley with a few stone houses and a cemetery that the infantry held under terrific shelling by the Russians. The nurses in Eleanor's detachment were quite close to the engagement, just on the other side of the hillside. They developed a kind of pantomime to communicate with one another since talking under the deafening din was impossible.

The nerve-shattering, bone-shattering onslaught went on for hours. At one point in the afternoon, Eleanor looked up, and seeing a nimble, sinewy frame from the back, gesticulating and shouting orders, she, just for a moment, thought it was Lieutenant Wentworth. In the next moment, however, she remembered that he was gone. She turned her attention once again to a newly arrived patient and immediately began work with the field surgeon attempting to staunch the bleeding in the man's leg.

A deafening explosion interrupted their efforts and sent Eleanor flying off her feet. The raucous report of cannons ceased. She heard and saw nothing. When she opened her eyes again, she was bouncing along in a bullock cart next to some wounded men. She called out, but she could not hear her own voice, only an incessant ringing. There was a screaming pain in her left shoulder. Her head swam. She closed her eyes.

When she opened them again, she heard a familiar voice. "Well, well, Miss Sherbrooke. We welcome you back to the land of the living."

Eleanor blinked and Mrs Davis came into focus, peering down at her. Eleanor attempted to sit up, but her strength failed her.

"Now, now, lie back. You foolishly got yourself hurt, and now we have to take care of you."

Her shoulder throbbed. She surveyed her body: her arm was wrapped in a sling, and feeling with her other hand, she determined that she still had her legs. She then touched her face All her features seemed to be where they belong. A throbbing pain enveloped her chest and bandaged arm.

Mrs Davis smiled. "Some shrapnel in the shoulder. We got you out as fast as we could. Did not want the flies to get at you."

Eleanor shuddered at the thought of maggots. Now that she was wounded herself, she had a vision of what it must have been like for all those wounded at Scutari who came to her.

Dr Farley appeared behind Mrs Davis. "Can you wiggle your fingers, Miss Sherbrooke?" Mrs Davis moved to make room for him. She wiggled her fingers from both her hands. "Very good. We did a good job, did we not, Mrs Davis?"

"We always do a good job, Doctor. At least I do." With that, Mrs Davis set off and Dr Farley laughed. He sat on the edge of Eleanor's bed and felt her forehead. "No fever. That is a good thing…a miracle, perhaps. You rest now, Miss Sherbrooke. We will take good care of you."

By the time Eleanor could leave her bed, General Raglan was dead. He succumbed to a bout of cholera, but most thought the grotesque number of casualties from the attacks of the 17th and 18th of June put him in his grave. The war was over for him, and despite her protestations to the contrary, it was over for Eleanor as well. July had just begun, and the new Renkioi hospital was finally finished. It was built of prefabricated walls manufactured at home and had all the things that Scutari did not—proper sanitation, ventilation, and they even thought to build it above the malaria line. The best part about the hospital was that it was staffed by civilian doctors and nurses. The army and its ineptitude and neglect were not part of it. She so wanted to be part of its staff. It was not to be.

"Go home, Miss Sherbrooke. Live to fight another day." Mrs Davis's expression softened. "There are plenty now to take your place. Rumour has it that the war will be over by autumn."

"I would like to stay." Eleanor was digging in her heels. Above all, she did not want to be home for her sister's wedding.

"I am afraid it is decided. You will leave by the end of the week. Be grateful. You are to go home aboard the *Simla*. The voyage will be less tedious than the one in which you arrived."

Eleanor knew she was defeated. As she rose to go, Mrs Davis stepped around her desk and offered Eleanor her hand. "You are a fine nurse, Miss Sherbrooke. Many lives were saved because of you." She took Mrs Davis's hand, but said nothing. Another chapter of her life was over.

***

Lieutenant Wentworth arrived at his parents' house by carriage. It felt odd not to be on horseback. He wore his eyepatch that obscured a great deal of his face, but still received recoils from most he encountered. He hoped his altered appearance would not be too much for his mother.

"Lieutenant. Oh, so good to see you, sir." His father's butler met him at the door, and Wentworth offered him his hand.

"Good to be home. Is my mother…?"

"Upstairs, sir."

Wentworth used to take these stairs two at a time, but now he felt disinclined to do so. Standing a long moment before his mother's door, he braced himself for her reaction to his disfigurement. Finally, he knocked.

"Come in." Her voice sounded reedy and weak.

"Hello, Mother." He stood for a moment in the doorway. Perhaps the shock would be less if he was farther away. She raised her head to look in his direction.

"Oh, Joshua. You're home. Come here, come here." She sat in a wheeled chair and opened her arms to him. She looked as if she had aged ten years since he saw her last. When he reached her, he knelt beside her and let her enfold him in her arms. "I wanted to live to see you return."

There was nothing to say to that. He fell silent. Her body seemed shrunken and fragile, but there was a strength in her arms. She did not let him go for a long time. Finally, she loosened her embrace and quickly wiped her eyes.

"You feel very thin, my son."

"Cook will fatten me up, I am sure."

She laid her hands upon his shoulders. "Let me look at you." He wore his best uniform, which swam on him now. Her eyes darted around his face and swept over his body, but they always returned to where his eye had once been.

"I look quite grotesque, do I not?" He tried to smile.

She shook her head. "You do not. You could never be to me. I am so happy you returned. When we heard of that fateful charge, your father was convinced we had lost you, yet I knew you would come home. A mother knows these things."

She, quite unconsciously, put her hands on either side of his face. "I cannot believe it. You are here." She embraced him again. When she finally released him, she asked, "So how is our Eleanor?"

He started at the mention of her name. "She was well when I last saw her. Talked of going to India with the army."

His mother screwed up her face. "Surely you are joking."

Lieutenant Wentworth jumped to his feet. "Exactly. Exactly what I said. Stupid girl. Why would she go to India, for God's sake?" He clenched and unclenched his fist.

His mother bit her lower lip, but her eyes sparkled. "So, you do care what she does."

He looked at her incredulously. "Of course, I do. She was the only bright spot in the whole ordeal."

"And yet, you are determined to marry her sister. Are you determined to marry Julia?"

"Mother, I am engaged to Julia. It is the only honourable thing to do. Besides, Julia knows nothing of the war. She will help me forget." He looked at his mother again. Her expression changed to one of displeasure. "What?"

"Have you seen Julia yet? Have you spoken to her?"

Wentworth walked to the large window overlooking the garden and gazed out. "I have not. I have to admit, I am a bit reticent in that regard."

"And rightly so. I have met Julia on only two occasions, and I cannot say that I am overly impressed with her character."

Wentworth squared his shoulders and turned to make an argument, but his mother seemed so frail sitting there that he had not the heart to do it.

"I think you misjudge her, Mother. She may surprise you."

"She may," his mother said ruefully, "but she may surprise you as well."

***

Julia paced the drawing room in uncharacteristic agitation. "Oh, Julia, do sit down. You are wearing on my nerves."

"I cannot, Mama. I could not sleep last night. What am I to do?"

Mrs Sherbrooke patted the spot next to her on the settee. "Sit, Julia, and calm yourself. You may find that you have made more of this in your mind than actually exists. In any case, if you find that you and Lieutenant Wentworth have changed your minds, gossip has faded and there is no harm done. He is an honourable man and now a war hero. I am sure he would not want a scandal."

Julia did not sit down but fussed with her hair in the looking glass. "I do not think I ever loved him, Mama. It was just a passing fancy."

"You could be married to him right now if you had your way all those months ago."

Julia scowled at her mother, who looked quite serene sitting perched on the sofa. The bell sounded and Julia jumped with a start.

"I will leave you alone, then."

"Oh, Mama. You will not."

"You are an engaged woman. It is perfectly proper." With that, her mother sailed from the drawing room, passing Baxter as she went.

"A Lieutenant Wentworth to see you, miss."

Julia tried to swallow but her mouth had gone dry. "Please show him in, Baxter."

She could hear him approach and braced herself against the mantel of the fireplace on the opposite side of the drawing room. Baxter opened the French doors and he entered.

"Julia?" he said, his arms outstretched. She closed her eyes for a moment, trying to gather herself. His face. His beautiful face now a ruin. She could not even see the whole of the damage, for he wore a patch over what had been his eye, and it covered a great deal of his cheek. Still, one could see quite hideous scars beneath it running down his neck and chin. Opening his arms to her, he expected an embrace, and she crossed the room, holding her arm out in front of her. A confused look passed over his face, and he took her offered hand and kissed it.

"It is so good to see you, Julia. You look radiant."

And you look absolutely appalling. "Oh, thank you, Lieutenant Wentworth."

That perplexed look did not leave his face. “Joshua, surely. We are engaged to be married.” He looked down at her hand. She still wore his ring. Conscious of his gaze, she gestured to one of the chairs by the empty fireplace, and he took a seat. She took the one opposite. It would take her some time to accustom herself to his appearance and she needed the distance.

“Yes, of course we are. Engaged to be married.” She tried to look elsewhere than his face but was compelled to stare at it.

“I suppose I am much changed,” he said finally, when she could muster no more words herself.

“Indeed.” The speeches she had rehearsed before he arrived seem to dry up and blow away.

“You have not changed at all, my dear. Have you missed me?”

I have hardly thought of you at all, really. No, she could not say as much. “Of course, I have. Did you not receive my letters?”

“I did… and you mine?”

“Yes.”

Julia looked down at the floor. She really did not know what to say to this man. This man so changed from the dashing officer in the garden the night she decided that he was the man she wanted to marry. The silence was so profound, she could hear the clock ticking.

He stood suddenly. “Well, I must be off. We will meet again soon, I trust?”

By the time she stood to look at him, he was halfway to the door.

“Joshua.”

He stopped and turned to her.

“Joshua… I am sorry.” He tried to put up a brave front, but she could see that he was crestfallen. She turned her head.

“Perhaps we both need a little time. I will call again, and we will talk.” With that, he left.

Chapter 12

Eleanor did not even have time enough to write to her parents apprising them of her arrival. She still had pain in her shoulder, but Dr Farley assured her the damage was made chiefly to her muscles and that they would heal with the proper care. As soon as she was aboard ship and away from her companions at the field hospital, she removed her arm from the sling from time to time and began to move it about. She had seen enough in Crimea to know that lying still was only for the very ill. The minute one could, it was advisable to begin moving and doing things.

The voyage was quick enough since they did not have to depend solely on the wind, and before she knew it, she was in Portsmouth. Stepping onto English soil brought with it a remembrance of who she once was. Before Crimea, she would be dependent on her father to meet her at the ship, make arrangements for her tickets to London, even to hire a taxi to her house. Now, she did all these things herself, and when met with the slightest scepticism or disrespect from the men she encountered, she used the voice she did with the orderlies under her supervision. That set them to rights easily enough.

She reached her home near sunset and paid the cabby. For a time, she stood upon the pavement and listened. Even with a few carriages going by, she basked in a peaceful silence. The fact that she was really home engulfed her for the first time. The excitement of seeing her family and Cordelia was marred only by the nagging thought that her sister might already be married to Lieutenant Wentworth.

Standing by her scant baggage under the front portico, she knocked. Baxter opened the door. He stood for a moment, gaping at her, and then turned, shouting, "*Miss Eleanor is home. Miss Eleanor is home.*" Turning back to her and recovering himself, he looked sheepish. "Oh, I do beg your pardon, miss, come in, come in. It was just such a surprise."

"That is quite all right, Baxter. Could you have someone bring in my things?" Before the words were out of her mouth, her mother came running from the drawing room. She stopped within a few feet of her and covered her mouth with her hand. Tears sprang to her eyes.

"Eleanor. My goodness. Eleanor. I can't believe it." She seemed rooted to the spot, so Eleanor walked slowly to her. Her mother's eyes fell upon the sling on her arm. "You are hurt."

"It is not too bad, Mama. They sent me home."

Her mother seemed to recover from the shock and embraced her, kissing her cheek. She held her at arm's length and looked at her again. "You are very thin, Eleanor. We will have cook remedy that straight away."

"Where is Father…and Julia?"

Eleanor braced herself for the reply. The entire voyage home she argued with herself as to the inevitability of Julia and Joshua's wedding.

"Oh, Julia is at the Bickford-Allens' for some sort of do, and your father is at his club. I will send him a message at once. We will surprise him, shall we? He missed you, you know."

"I missed him too. I missed all of you, Mama."

Her mother's expression was the softest she had ever seen. All it took was a year and a half of hell on earth to produce it. It did not last long, however. She began to pelt Eleanor with questions almost immediately. "Why did you not write and tell us you were coming? How did you arrange your passage? How did you get from Portsmouth? Did you take a hansom cab alone? Oh, Eleanor…."

How could she explain to her mother that less than six weeks ago she was ankle deep in blood, sewing gaping wounds in men's groins? No, it was impossible. The experiences she had in the Crimea were beyond anything this poor woman could possibly understand. Taking a taxi alone? It was laughable. She suddenly thought of Aunt Sophronia and her father's trip across Europe to fetch her after her aunt's death. Now she believed she could have made the trip easily without him.

When tea was brought in, it was accompanied by the entire contingent of household servants. They all behaved like shy children, wide-eyed in Eleanor's presence.

"Have I much changed?"

Faithful Annie broke the spell. “You look like a right, good nurse to me, Miss Eleanor. Did those Russians hurt you?”

“Just enough to send me home.”

“Well, we’re all glad to see you, Miss Eleanor,” cook said. “I have a nice lamb stew ready for when your father returns. We’ll put you to rights soon enough.”

All of this outpouring of goodwill was working itself into Eleanor’s emotions, and she excused herself on the pretence of resting before she completely broke down into an embarrassing display. Every nerve seemed raw and exposed, and tears constantly bubbled just beneath the surface. She did not understand what was happening to her. It was probably returning home after all she had endured in Crimea.

Ensconced in her old room, she opened the wardrobe in an attempt at unpacking and saw all of her old dresses hanging there. She would be expected to dress for dinner. How peculiar it seemed. It was as if she was playing a role in a play. Her mind and heart were still back in the Crimea, all except the part that belonged to Lieutenant Wentworth. She pulled his watch and chain from around her neck and placed it in her jewel box. Before long, she would return it to him.

***

Lieutenant Wentworth sat alone in the garden, absently flipping the invitation from the Mosleys back and forth between his fingers. His mother’s condition was worsening, and the sunny summer weather could not lighten his ever-sinking spirits. The romantic reunion between Julia and himself had not materialised. Although they saw each other on one other occasion, she kept well away from him physically, as if she could not bear to be near him. He asked her if there was someone else, but she denied it. He began to eschew company, even that of his family. Long walks in the park or through the city, even in the pouring rain, became the only balm to his worsening frame of mind.

Although he told Eleanor that he wanted to forget about the war, he could not keep himself from reading every word of its progress in the papers. *The Times* lay next to him on the table near his coffee, and he put down the invitation and picked up the paper. *Those poor devils in the trenches.*

The butler's voice interrupted. "A Mister Mosley to see you, sir."

Oh, good God. What was he to say to him? Must be that blasted invitation that brought him here.

"Well, Mosley, good of you to come by." The look on his friend's face was one that he had learnt to expect: a mixture of revulsion and pity. That look disappeared quickly, and a smile took its place. William Mosley was extending his hand.

"So good to see you, Wentworth. Can't believe you made it back alive."

Joshua did not really feel alive since his return. He felt as if he was walking in some misty underworld that only he inhabited. Still, his friend had made the effort to see him, and he would do his best to be cordial. "Good of you to come, Mosley. To what do I owe the honour of your presence? Do sit down."

William Mosley took a seat and stared at his friend for just a moment too long.

"It is pretty ghastly, isn't it?" Wentworth gestured towards his face.

"Are you in pain?"

"Only when someone looks at me. I can see the horror in their eyes." Wentworth gestured to the butler. "Bring Mister Mosley some coffee, will you?"

As the butler scurried off, Mosley grimaced. "It is a bit of a shock at first. I won't deny it."

Wentworth relaxed into the garden chair. "It is a relief to hear you say so. No one else will admit it." Wentworth fell silent.

A few moments passed and Mosley spoke again. "I've come about the dinner invitation. You have not answered. Since we heard from Julia, we thought it odd."

"Julia replied? Well, I suppose she would. If it is a social occasion, Julia will be there."

Mosley nodded. "And you will be relieved to know that we did not invite George Shaw."

Wentworth frowned. "I have no particular quarrel with George Shaw."

Mosley was taken aback, and his face showed it. "That is big of you, old man, considering…." The coffee had arrived, and Mosley was absently stirring sugar in his cup.

"Considering? Considering what?"

Mosley looked up, his eyes wide. "Well, nothing really." His voice faltered.

Wentworth could feel his ire rising. "What are you implying, Mosley?"

"Nothing, nothing really. Let us talk of something else."

Wentworth was angry now, but it was not with William Mosley. He could not sort out if he should direct his fury at Julia for betraying him, or at himself for being such a fool. After a few more awkward moments, William Mosley left, and Wentworth took a horse from his father's stable.

It was time to confront Julia.

***

When he arrived at the Sherbrookes', he was shown to the garden. Julia was outdoors gathering blooms. She looked like an oil painting from a bygone era, but a cloud of suspicion spoiled Wentworth's reverie.

"Julia." His voice was a bit too loud, and she dropped her basket as she turned towards him.

"Joshua, how nice." A smile curled her lips, but her eyes were wary.

"We must speak frankly, Julia."

"Would you like some tea? I could ask Baxter—"

"No, nothing. I want nothing from you but your honesty." By this time, he was close enough to touch her. She looked up at him and her eyes were cold. He felt her forearm under his grip.

"Let go of me, if you please."

A hot fury boiled up inside him that he had not felt before. His first instinct was to grip her tighter, but his sense of gentlemanly honour prevented him. He let her go but continued searching her eyes. "What is this I hear of George Shaw?"

There was a fleeting look of fear in her expression, and then it hardened. "What is it you want to know?"

"Do you love him, Julia? Has he taken my place in your heart?"

She looked upon him half in amusement, half in pity. "You really are determined to force me to hurt you, Joshua. Things have changed between us. Can you not feel it yourself? You are not the man I promised to marry."

"You have not answered my question." His voice had a slight edge of rage in it, and the fear returned to her eyes.

"All right, then. Yes, George and I have developed an…attachment. Is that what you wanted to hear?"

No, of course that was not what he wanted to hear. He wanted to hear a denial. He wanted to hear that all would be well between them and that the dream he had for a life with her would come to fruition. He suddenly felt weary and sat down heavily on the garden bench.

"I release you from your promise, then, if that is what you want." He was not looking at her but staring at the stones of the garden path.

Her voice softened when she spoke to him again. "I am sorry, Joshua. I wanted to tell you, but I thought it best to wait until you were home again. Here." She took one of his hands and deposited the engagement ring into it. He did not look up again but heard her running footsteps recede towards the house.

***

When Eleanor entered the drawing room, her sister and mother abruptly ceased their conversation. She looked from one to the other. No doubt they were making wedding plans and were endeavouring not to do so in front of her. She needed to put them at ease at once.

"It's all right, Mama, Julia. You may continue with your planning. I was merely looking for some writing paper and will leave you momentarily."

The oddest look passed between Julia and her mother. "I think you owe your sister an explanation, Julia." She then laid down her needlework and walked briskly towards the door.

As the door closed behind her, Eleanor gave her sister a quizzical look. At least, that was what she was endeavouring to do. "Whatever does Mama mean?"

Julia tossed her hair and sighed dramatically as she rose. She walked determinedly to the fireplace and then made a brisk, theatrical turn. In times past, this type of showmanship made Eleanor bristle with irritation. Now she just felt weary.

"For goodness' sake, Julia, please just say what you have to say."

Julia rolled her eyes and then spoke rapidly. "I am no longer engaged to Joshua Wentworth. I broke it off."

For a moment, Eleanor could not speak. She felt a lump rising in her throat and then rapidly swallowed it down. When she could finally make a sound, all she uttered was, "What?"

Julia tossed her head again. "Oh, Eleanor. Surely, you can understand. He is much changed since he has returned. He is no longer the dashing young officer who left for Crimea. Not to mention his—" She stopped suddenly and put her hand over her mouth.

"His face? Is that what you were going to say, Julia?"

It always amazed Eleanor how quickly Julia could recover from some awkward situation that she had created. Her standard manoeuvre was to brazen it out, and she did so again.

"Oh, really, Eleanor. I will admit it. It *is* part of the problem. But there is so much more. So much more."

Julia made another dramatic turn towards the mantelpiece.

Eleanor would not let this matter drop. All that time in the Crimea that she held herself aloof from Joshua in deference towards her sister, and now to find out it was all for naught. It was too much. She crossed the room and, taking Julia by the shoulder, turned her so that they were face-to-face.

"Who is he, Julia?"

Julia looked a bit shaken for a few seconds, but then arched one eyebrow. It was like looking into the countenance of a bird of prey. "I don't know what you mean, Eleanor." She tried a frivolous tone, but it shattered in the air.

"I know you too well, sister. You do not give up a good prospect of marriage unless there is a better one in the wings."

There was a play of emotions on Julia's face—offence, surprise, and finally amusement. "Oh, all right. I am soon to be engaged to—"

"George Shaw," Eleanor said wearily.

Now Julia really did look shocked. "How ever did you know?"

Eleanor shook her head. "Really, Julia. You two must have been obvious because all of your social circle was well aware. Well aware."

Julia merely smiled and waved a hand as if batting away an annoying insect. With this gesture, Eleanor felt all her resentment and fury and energy leave her. She moved to the settee and sat down in a heap.

Julia was silent now. For a time, she said nothing. Then, gliding towards the door, she looked back at her sister. "Don't be angry with me, Eleanor. I think it is for the best, don't you?"

Eleanor gazed at her with weary eyes and said nothing. Julia tripped off, unscathed.

***

"So, you've not seen him, then?" Cordelia and Eleanor strolled through Hyde Park arm in arm.

Eleanor shook her head. "He made it quite clear that he wanted to forget everything about the war. I am the war to him, Cordelia."

"It was quite dreadful, then, was it?"

"Cordelia, I wish I could explain to you the sheer horror of it all. I would try, but I am afraid I would shock you. When we first arrived at Scutari the conditions…. And then, before we could barely begin to address the neglected wounded, the filth and the disease, more injured men came pouring in. Miss Nightingale called it The Kingdom of Hell. It was beyond comprehension."

Eleanor began to shiver, and then a more profound shaking of her limbs began. She had no control. Cordelia hustled her off to a bench at the side of the path and put her arm around her shoulders.

"Is there something I can do?" An elderly gentleman in a silk hat stopped with a bow. "Fetch a doctor, perhaps?"

Cordelia shook her head. "No, sir, thank you. It will pass. My friend was a nurse in Crimea and sometimes—"

"Ah… I will stand here and block the view of passers-by for a time, if you like?"

"Yes, thank you, sir."

The shivering subsided in a few minutes, and Eleanor sighed. The gentleman tipped his hat, and as he withdrew, he addressed Eleanor. "Bless you, child. We all owe you a debt."

Her nerves were raw after these episodes, and the stranger's kind words brought a flood of tears. Cordelia provided a handkerchief and her arm remained about Eleanor's shoulders. Gulping air, her breathing finally settled into a normal rhythm. When she felt she had resumed control over herself, she rose and the two resumed their walk.

"It is the war, Cordelia. You can see why he wants to forget."

"I do not see how he can… how either of you can. Now that Julia and he are no longer engaged, perhaps he has changed his mind. You must go and see him."

"Let him come and see me, Cordelia."

"Does he even know that you have returned? You should at least let him know."

For some moments, there was silence between them. "I am quite tired, Cordelia. It is time for me to return home."

***

A week went by and there was no communication of any kind from Joshua Wentworth. Eleanor knew that she could never call upon him no matter the pretext, and it occurred to her that he likely wanted to avoid Julia at any cost, so he would never call at the Sherbrookes'. A letter seemed the only recourse.

10 August, 1855
My dear, dear Joshua,

I hope this letter finds you well and your spirits mending. Julia has told me of your broken engagement and all I can say is hallelujah. She does not deserve a man of your calibre and is only interested in money and social position. I knew all of the goings-on between her and that snake, George Shaw, some months ago but did not have the heart to tell you. You are well rid of her and can now turn your attention to someone who really loves you, me.

Now that paper and ink were readily available, Eleanor returned to her habit of writing her true thoughts first and then writing the letter she would send afterwards. She reread what she had written and smiled. She could write a second paragraph telling him of Julia's engagement to George, but she had not the heart to write it, even as an exercise. As she crumpled the paper and set light to it in the empty fireplace, she wondered how he really felt about Julia and her betrayal. Perhaps his heart was broken, as Julia maintained. Perhaps he was relieved. Perhaps both. She resolved not to speak of Julia at all as she watched the paper turn to ash. Then she began again.

10 August, 1855
Dear Lieutenant Wentworth,

You likely heard that I am home again as well, also invalided. I was in a trench during General Eyre's taking of the Russian stronghold when I found myself flying through the air like a windblown leaf. I did not regain myself until I was in a cot back at the hospital in Balaclava. Mrs Davis was adamant that I recover at home, so here I am.

You asked me once to write and be honest with you, so I am doing so now. I have to confess that I have been experiencing some distress since returning to England. There are nightmares and these odd bouts of shaking that I cannot predict nor control. I expect I may experience these things because I am a woman, but I suspect that these episodes are more the result of war than of hysteria. Are you bothered by such things? You have been in battles and endured that awful winter, so I am imagining that you may be suffering as I do, perhaps more so. I feel quite alone sometimes, as I cannot speak of what happened in Crimea to anyone who was not there. They simply do not understand. I know you wanted to forget your time there, but for the life of me, I cannot. I suppose time will tell.

Please do write to me when you feel you can. I am in need of a friend. Cordelia does her best, but I can see the revulsion in her eyes whenever I speak of Crimea. As for my mother and sister, I dare not broach the subject. It also distresses my father to no end. I believe he feels he did not protect me sufficiently, although it was my decision to go with Miss Nightingale.

Please give my best to your mother. If she feels well enough, I would like to call on her soon.

Always,
Eleanor

She waited, but there was no answer from Lieutenant Wentworth.

***

The London Season was winding to a close and so was the war in Crimea. By the 15th of August, the Russians had been forced into a retreat across the Tchernaïa River. The British public was imbued with a great sense of optimism that they, and their French and Sardinian allies, had the enemy in retreat. Many balls were held to celebrate what had yet to be accomplished.

Julia readied herself for her first excursion as a newly engaged woman with her fiancée, George Shaw. They would make the official announcement of their engagement at the ball. His father was the host, as their house was considerably larger than the Sherbrookes' and could accommodate more guests. Nearly everyone knew of the change in her circumstances, and many did not approve. The Shaws, however, had enough money and enough influence to mitigate any chink in the armour of their social position.

"You must come, Eleanor. It is my engagement party. At least stay until we make the announcement."

Eleanor sighed. The last person she wanted as part of her family was George Shaw. Take away his money, and he had nothing to offer. Still, her sister seemed taken with him and she would do her best not to put a damper on the festivities.

"Very well. I'll go, but I will not stay long. I've still not recovered my strength."

Julia held up one pair of earrings after another to her ears as she tried to decide. "You do make a fuss about the Crimea, Eleanor. Please try to talk of something else at the ball. Perhaps the weather?"

The weather would be a fair subject indeed on such a night. A late summer storm blew up that afternoon, and the winds reached nearly a gale force. All preparations had been made, however, and the ball would go on despite nature's rude behaviour.

Eleanor retreated to her bedroom, then to dress. Julia insisted that a new gown be made for her, one that covered the scars from the shrapnel that had torn through her shoulder. All her other dresses were last year's fashion or older, not that Eleanor gave it much thought. Tonight, though, she was merely a reflection of her sister and must do her best to look presentable. For the first time since she returned from Crimea, she put powder on her face to hide her birthmark.

Cordelia waited near the door for her with a dance card that was partially filled in. "You are much sought after tonight, Eleanor," she said as she whisked her from her parents. Julia was already on George Shaw's arm. "Come along. We will try to tame your hair. The wind has mussed it so."

As they sat in the ladies' parlour, Cordelia retrieved the errant strands on Eleanor's coif. "What do you mean, I am much sought after?"

"Everyone knows you were with Miss Nightingale and she is now a national heroine. That makes you a national heroine too."

"Oh, don't be ridiculous, Cordelia."

"I tell you, Eleanor. There is a line of young men who want to make your acquaintance."

It was an odd feeling. If such a thing had happened before she left for Crimea, Eleanor would have been filled with excitement and pleasure. Now every experience seemed to be muted at best, and meaningless at worst. She tried to smile and look pleased, but Cordelia saw through her pretence as she always did.

"Do try to enjoy yourself, Eleanor."

"Now you sound like my mother." Cordelia gave her a playful slap with the comb and laughed. Soon they joined the festivities. Despite herself, Eleanor did enjoy the dance. The movement itself seemed to lift her spirits.

It was nearing eleven. All the guests were present. The orchestra hushed, and the servants did their best to herd the guests into the great hall near the staircase. Everyone knew that it was time for the announcement to be made. Eleanor stood near the edge of the crowd near the foot of the staircase. She had been instructed by Julia to do so. George's father climbed to the centre of the sweeping staircase where Julia stood with her soon-to-be fiancé. She looked, as usual, like a goddess. He merely appeared smug. The servants bustled through the rather close crowd with glasses of champagne.

"Ladies and gentlemen. Thank you all for being here tonight. It is a joyous occasion for our family. Please raise your glasses and drink a toast to the engagement of my son, George, to the lovely Julia Sherbrooke."

The crowd lifted their glasses and then, as if on cue, a roll of thunder gave its approval. Some in the crowd tittered in amusement, which was stifled in the next moment, as the front doors blew open with a cold, sudden gust of wind. A great battle cry sounded from the gaping entryway. With all eyes turned toward the doorway, a figure rushed in, sabre drawn. Women screamed and the crowd parted like the Red Sea.

After rushing to the stairway, a dishevelled, wild-eyed Lieutenant Wentworth ran upwards, taking the stairs two at a time. He shouted something unintelligible. He was hatless and his hair was a tangle. He wore his field coat, trousers, and boots, just as he had in Crimea. His face contorted in rage. George's father jumped well out of the way, clinging to the bannister, his mutton chops trembling. George, in an attempt to flee, tripped and slid down the stairs to land at Wentworth's feet. Julia was nowhere to be seen. Wentworth swung his sabre in the air, and George crossed his arms across his face in a futile attempt to protect himself.

"*Lieutenant*," Eleanor shouted at him as she ran up the staircase until she was close enough to touch him. He turned to her, his right hand in the air, sabre still raised. The crowd gasped and then a deafening silence descended.

No one moved. Wentworth's face contorted in confusion. "Eleanor, what are you doing here?" He looked about him. "We have them on the run, Eleanor. We captured the guns, didn't we? Ran like rats. Thought they'd kill us."

Her mind was working furiously and, in that instant, achieved clarity. He was reliving the charge. This was not about George and Julia. "Yes, Joshua. The Light Brigade made it through." She extended her hand towards him in a kind of entreaty, and then tried to approach him, but he shook his head vehemently. The crowd watched silently, the only sound the rumbling of thunder. Eleanor held her breath.

In his altered state, what would he do? Would he turn upon the staring crowd? What did he see in his wild state?

Joshua looked all about him, his expression changing from rage to utter confusion. He lowered his sabre and then dropped it with a clang on the stairway. Spinning on his heel, he ran past the quivering George Shaw until he reached the landing. Then, looking about quickly, he disappeared into one of the hallways.

The crowd and George Shaw suddenly sprang to life. He recovered himself and, standing, said, "After him."

To their discredit, not many of the men immediately rushed to Mr Shaw's aid. Once a few thawed themselves from their frozen positions and began to run up the staircase, Eleanor threw her arms out and faced them. "No, no, stop. Do not hurt him. He is ill. *Stop*."

The few in front hesitated a moment, and then they dashed past her en masse and she had not the physical means to stop them. Scattering over the landing and down the hallways, they began searching the upstairs rooms. She ran up the stairs after them, but then stood upon the landing, turning this way and that, not knowing what to do. Someone grasped her by the elbow, and turning, she came face-to-face with a concerned William Mosley.

"Oh, William. Please help me." Not even in Crimea had she ever felt such desperation.

He leaned in and whispered in her ear. "I believe I know where he's gone."

Somewhere off in the distance, her mother and Julia called to her. She ignored them and took off running with William Mosley.

Taking her by the hand, he pulled her to the back of the house to the door leading to the servants' quarters. Once inside the narrow hallway, William led her to the back stairs. Before they reached it, Eleanor noticed a few drops of water dripping from the ceiling into the hall. Eleanor gave William a quizzical look.

"Just as I thought," he said.

"What do you mean?"

"He is on the roof."

A rising panic engulfed her. "The roof?"

William pointed to the ceiling and there, embedded in it, was a trapdoor of sorts. "It is the access stairway. It leads to the attic, which in turn has a door to the roof. Shaw brought us up there from time to time to have drinks on the roof and look at the stars. The door has been opened. That's why the floor is wet."

The thunder of the storm was still rolling over them. Her heart pounded in her ears.

"Open it. I must talk to him," she implored.

"I will go with you."

"No," she said forcefully. William did not argue but took hold of the rope that hung from the trapdoor. Pulling it, he opened the hatchway, and an attached stairway revealed itself. Eleanor clambered up, shouting over the storm to Mosley.

"You stay here and waylay them. I will bring him down." She did not turn to hear William's assent or dissent but tore up the stairs. There was, indeed, a small doorway to the roof, and she clambered through it.

The rain lashed her face, blinding her for a moment.

There he stood, drenched to the skin and leaning over the stone parapet that ran the width of the roof. Below them, the stone drive.

"*Joshua*," she shouted, and he held up his hand to her.

"Do not come any closer." The thunder gave another tremendous clap and he clutched both his ears and bent nearly double. "The guns. The guns…" he repeated, shaking his head violently. While he was in this state, she took a few steps closer to him. Looking up, he straightened himself and stepped up onto the stone railing, wobbling slightly. Eleanor's heart was in her throat.

"Joshua, *please*."

He looked over his shoulder at her and shook his head. The way his body was swaying, the storm and gravity would make his decision for him if she did not intervene. She waited for a flash of lightning and quickly closed the distance between them. Taking hold of his coat, she pulled him from the railing. He lost his balance and fell backward, his back slamming into a chimney. She flew at him, closing him in her embrace and pinning him against the brick of the chimney.

For a moment, he was limp in her arms, and she could scarcely support his weight. His mouth was very near her ear, and he whispered, "Why did you do that, Eleanor? Why?"

She pulled him to her, and with her lips near his ear, she said, "Because I love you." Lightning flashed as she pulled away to look at his face. His eyes were closed, and he would not look at her. The thunder rolled again, and he jumped, startled. Clutching her closely, he said, "I am a broken man, Eleanor. Whatever do you want with me?" He pulled back to meet her gaze.

Then Eleanor's trembling began. First in her hands and then it spread like a wave throughout her body. She opened her mouth to explain, but she could not speak.

He waited for no explanation but wrapped his arms around her and held her to him. "It is all right, Eleanor. I am here. I am here." He held her for a long time, not saying another word.

The shaking subsided, and she was finally able to speak. "I am all right now."

He held her close for a few moments longer, the rain cascading over them in sheets. "Come along," he said finally, and put his arm about her waist to support her. Neither said another word as they descended into the house.

William was there waiting for them. "Come along this way," he said curtly, and the two of them, dripping with rain, followed him down the servants' back stairway. When they reached the kitchen, William signalled them to stop, and he looked about first. No one was there. No doubt they were still scouring the house for Lieutenant Wentworth.

Beckoning, but not saying a word, he led them outside the kitchen door. Mercifully, there was a small overhang before the threshold where they could stand out of the driving rain. "Wait here. I will get my carriage."

No sound issued from Lieutenant Wentworth. Eleanor tried to slip her hand into his, but he would not take it. Soon, the carriage arrived, and they climbed in with William. Eleanor could not take her eyes off Joshua. All the fight and the fury had gone out of him. He sat, his head bowed, in the silent carriage until it reached its destination. When they rang the bell, they were surprised to see Mr Wentworth open it, and not the butler.

"Oh, thank God, thank God. Come in. Come in," he said as William and Eleanor walked Wentworth through the doorway. "Thank you for bringing him home." Mr Wentworth looked from one to the other, his face working with emotion. "I do not know what came over him. He was not himself. Was anyone hurt?"

Eleanor spoke up. "No, thankfully."

The elder Wentworth sighed in relief. By this time, the butler and a footman were on hand. He noticed them and gave his instructions. "Take the lieutenant to his room, please."

Joshua would not look up at any of them. When he was out of earshot and they all turned to take their leave, Mr Wentworth said one more thing. "You will have to forgive him. His mother died this morning."

***

"Now, get out of those wet things and I'll have cook make you something to eat." Her mother had hold of her arm as they brushed past Baxter. Eleanor dragged her sodden skirts up the stairs. Annie insisted on drawing a bath for her, and as she sank into the hot water, she felt immeasurably fatigued. All that happened that night played over in her mind. She may have gone too far, telling Joshua of her love for him. The more she ruminated, the more she doubted that he felt the same. Was it even fair to speak of such things when he was so overwrought? Neither of them was the same as they once were. All that took place in Crimea twisted about in their brains. Would he ever be whole again? Would she?

The tea and sandwiches combined with a hot bath worked their magic, and Eleanor slipped into her nightdress and pulled the bedclothes over her. Exhaustion overtook her.

When she awoke the next morning, she knew that she had to see Joshua and speak of all that transpired. She could not call upon him. It would not be proper. The social chains that bound her now that she returned home seemed not only onerous but completely ridiculous. Before she had a chance to dress, Annie arrived with a breakfast tray. On it lay an envelope in a hand she did not recognise.

26 August, 1855
Dear Miss Sherbrooke,

Thank you so much for your invaluable aid during my son's difficulty yesterday. I really was at my wit's end as to what to do. The fact that he came home safely, and no one was harmed during his indisposition, is a great relief to me. We have you and Mr Mosley to thank for that.

It would mean a great deal to Joshua and our entire family if you would attend his mother's funeral in two days' time. I will send a coach for you if you assent. Our footman waits at the door for your reply.

Gratefully yours,
Mr Albert Wentworth, esq.

***

As promised, the coach arrived at two o'clock in the afternoon two days later. It was a torment to wait that long to see Joshua again, but Eleanor thought it best to give him time to mourn his mother and collect his thoughts as to what passed between them. She was properly draped in black. Her mother accompanied her. Nature also seemed in mourning for Mrs Wentworth as the sky was nearly black with rain. The coaches met at the Wentworth house and they were escorted inside. The smell of damp clothing, cut flowers, and the unmistakable scent of death assailed her as soon as they entered. The coffin was displayed in the sitting room, and Eleanor and her mother approached. Joshua stood stiffly in the dress uniform of the Lancers, sabre at his side. Although she only met his father once, she recognised him immediately. The other man, sporting mutton chops rather than a moustache, stood with a rather matronly looking woman, probably his wife. She surmised it was Geoffrey.

Joshua was greeting people, extending his gloved hand, abiding by the rituals. He then looked up and saw Eleanor.

"Oh, you have come." He broke free of the receiving line and greeted her, holding both her hands in his. Then, turning to her mother, he said, "Thank you for bringing Eleanor, Mrs Sherbrooke."

Eleanor's mother mumbled the proper words of condolence, and Eleanor looked up into Joshua's face. He wore a weary and pained expression that she recognised. "I am so sorry, Joshua. I know how you loved her."

He bit his lip and his eyes shone. He squeezed her hands and then let go. "Thank you, Eleanor."

The funeral procession soon began with each coach lining up behind the hearse. Eleanor could not help but pity the poor mourners walking outdoors at the lead, the rain soaking the black ostrich feathers hanging limply from their top hats.

The grave had been prepared, but it was puddling with water. The service was short, and Eleanor watched as each of the family tossed a handful of soil upon the lowered coffin. The rain kept up a steady stream of tears as the mourners, under black umbrellas, dispersed one by one. Eleanor waited to speak to Joshua once again, but his brother trundled him off into the coach. It was his father, then, who approached her. He bowed slightly to both Eleanor and her mother. The umbrellas kept them from standing too closely.

"My son wanted me to deliver this for him." He handed Eleanor an envelope sealed with a blue wafer.

"May I not speak to him?"

His father sighed wearily. "This letter will explain all. Thank you again for coming." He did not wait for a reply and turned and quickly walked back to his waiting carriage.

Eleanor and her mother stood for a moment, watching the carriage pull away. "Come along, Eleanor. Let us get out of this rain."

They retreated to their carriage. The letter from Joshua was fairly burning her hands, she was so anxious to read it, but refrained from doing so in front of her mother. On arriving home, she nearly threw off her cloak and bonnet and rushed up the stairs to the sanctuary of her room. Finally, she had time to examine the envelope. It contained only her first name and the handwriting was unsteady. She turned it over and broke the seal.

26 August, 1855

Dear, dear Eleanor,

I find myself in such a state of uproar and confusion, I do not know where to begin. First, I want to apologise for my inexcusable behaviour at the Shaws'. It must have been the storm that worked its way into my mind, for I truly believed I was back on the dusty plain before Balaclava, riding to meet the enemy. I know from that incident that my mind is no longer sound and that I need time to recover myself if that is indeed possible.

As to what transpired on the roof,

Eleanor stopped reading. She dreaded what he might say to her next. No doubt, he would try to be kind in responding to her confession of love. That kindness would perhaps be the greater cruelty. She took up the letter again and braced herself.

...As to what transpired on the roof, I must admit that I was quite prepared to take my own life. I do believe that I went mad at that moment and have you to thank for saving me. You said something to me, Eleanor, that changed everything. You told me that you loved me, and those words

were like an awakening for me. If I tell you now that I love you also, what does it mean? I can tell you that I certainly did on that hilltop in Crimea when the rat ate our picnic. Do you remember? My heart was filled with love for you that day and I longed to tell you. I would have if I had not made that promise to your sister.

Eleanor let the letter fall into her lap and closed her eyes. He did love her. He loved her. No matter what he said after that, she had those words to hold in her heart. She picked up the letter again.

It is for your sake, then, as well as mine, that I have decided to go away for a while and try to heal what the war has torn asunder. You know as well as I how the war lives on in us despite the fact that we are now home and safe. I felt it in you yesterday, but you are so much stronger than I, Eleanor. Whether or not I will ever be whole again remains to be seen. I cannot predict the future, so I tell you now, make your plans without me. I cannot, in good conscience, ask you to wait for me because I cannot tell if I will ever be the man you deserve. I know, in my present state of mind, I am not. I tell you to leave me because I love you and want you to be happy.

Whatever happens, you will always have my heart. Think of yourself now, Eleanor. You are one of the bravest people I have ever known, which includes the brave men of the Light Brigade. Your dreams lie ahead of you. Pursue them. In spirit, I am always at your side.

With love,
Joshua

No, no, no… this will never do. She helped him the other night, she could do so again. They could be help to one another, for who better understood the hell that was Crimea than the two of them? There was no time to lose. No doubt, the Wentworths were still at home and she would persuade Joshua to reconsider. What good would come from his facing his demons alone?

"Father, please. I need you to accompany me to the Wentworths' immediately. It is most urgent."

Her parents exchanged a look of alarm, but her mother nodded, and her father acquiesced. Within the hour, she pulled the bell at the Wentworth house.

"Ah, please come in." The butler looked almost as if he was expecting them. They were shown into the drawing room, and before long, Joshua's brother, Geoffrey Wentworth, opened the door.

"Miss Sherbrooke—"

"This is my father, Colonel Sherbrooke…" Eleanor said by means of introduction. The men shook hands and exchanged pleasantries. Eleanor was ready to crawl out of her skin. As soon as she could inject a word in, she asked, "Your brother, Lieutenant Wentworth, is he at home? I would like to see him."

Geoffrey's face was all confusion. "You have read his letter?"

"Yes, of course. He said something about going away. Surely, he is not gone already? Where has he gone?" Her voice took on a shrill quality and she endeavoured to calm herself. "Please, tell me."

"Ah, I thought you knew. My brother has gone for a rest to Hanwell. I imagine he will be there for some time. Their coach was waiting for us when we arrived home from the funeral. My father accompanied him."

Hanwell. Hanwell. Eleanor searched her brain. "Hanwell?"

"Yes, Miss Sherbrooke. My brother has committed himself to an asylum."

***

The war in Crimea was finally grinding to its bloodstained close. The great battles for capturing the bastions around the city, the Malakov, the Redan, the Flagstaff, and the Little Redan, took place at the beginning of September and fighting was reported to be savage. By 11 September, the Russians burnt what remained of their fleet in the Black Sea and were in full retreat. Eleanor busied herself with the papers, reading every word of news and poring over Mr Fenton's photographs. She also received a letter from her friend Millie, who remained at Scutari. Although conditions greatly improved there thanks to Miss Nightingale and her nurses, men's names were added to the rolls of the dead every day after every siege.

12 September, 1855
Dear Eleanor,

We do so sorely miss you these days. The influx of the wounded from whatever they are doing over there in Sebastopol has us running off our feet. A good surgical nurse would be most welcome if you decide to come back. Of course, I am joking. They will be sending us and many of our wounded home soon ourselves. The war is all but won now with the Russians in retreat and Sebastopol captured. I confess that I will not know what to do with myself once I am home. I hope the hospital in Chichester will take me. Perhaps I will meet a young man and give up all this "glory" and settle into domestic life. Whatever papers we receive here say that Miss Nightingale is much celebrated back home. They will remember her, but I doubt they will remember us.

I am sorry to hear of your Lt. Wentworth and his troubles. Many men we see who have been in the trenches exhibit the same sort of symptoms as you describe. It is as if they are wounded not on their bodies, but inside of themselves. I do not suppose women are susceptible to the same sort of malady since we have not been fighting. We have seen a great deal of death and suffering though, have we not, my friend? More than anyone should see in a lifetime.

Thank you so much for your invitation to come and visit. I will call upon you if I am ever in London. I suppose the army will send us directly to Portsmouth. My family will easily be able to come and fetch me home from there. Home seems like a dream to me now, although I have not been gone quite two years. You will write to me, dear Eleanor. We "comrades in arms" must stick together.

My best wishes to you and your family and to your Lt. Wentworth. I do hope he recovers himself for your sake as well as his.

Your friend,
Mildred (Millie) Potts

***

Hanwell Asylum was an imposing structure with a great arched stone gate that, once crossed, revealed a large complex of brick two-story buildings arranged in a square. In the centre was a large, well-tended garden. Mr Wentworth sat in silence for most of the journey as Joshua leaned his head against the wall of the carriage. Once the guards let them through the main gate, however, he spoke.

"Are you sure this is what you want, son?" he asked.

Joshua raised his head wearily and nodded. "It has to be done, Father."

"We could care for you at home… no need for this…." His father gestured out the window as the carriage veered to the right and finally came to rest at the back of the huge complex. A tall, lanky man with high cheekbones and a mop of light hair exited the imposing building at their approach and was at the carriage door as it came to a halt.

"Welcome, welcome. I am Dr Conolly," he said with enthusiasm as he opened the carriage door. Joshua was the first to exit, followed by his father.

"Lieutenant Wentworth, welcome to our little hospital. I hope you find your stay here restorative."

Wentworth barely looked up and shook his head. His father offered the doctor his hand.

"I am Mr Wentworth, the lieutenant's father."

"Of course, of course, welcome." Dr Conolly, after giving instructions to the staff who were accompanying him, gestured towards the building, and both Joshua and his father followed.

They sat for a time in a panelled office filled with comfortable furniture. The doctor did not sit behind a desk but rather sat with them in overstuffed chairs as he explained his philosophy. Joshua tried to attend to what he was saying, but his entire being felt numb. He almost felt displaced from his body.

"…and so we believe plenty of exercise, good food, social interaction, and, of course, rest and quiet, can do wonders for the unsettled mind. This is not the asylum of old with inmates in restraints under appalling conditions. I have had much success in healing mental illnesses." He then turned to Joshua, who spent his time staring at his two hands. "I understand, Lieutenant, that you are coming to us of your own free will."

Through the fog of his consciousness, he became aware that he was being addressed. "What? I am sorry—"

"You are coming here of your own accord, is that right?"

Joshua nodded. The doctor continued. "And am I to understand that you were a member of the famous Light Brigade recently of Crimea?"

Joshua's heart began palpitating rapidly and his breathing became shallow. He began clenching and unclenching his fist. His father's worried expression added to Joshua's distress. The doctor interceded. "Never mind. We will talk of such things later. Would you like to see your room?"

The doctor rose, and with a few more shallow breaths, Joshua's heart slowed. He stood and addressed Dr Conolly. "I beg your pardon. I have not been myself lately. Please, do show me my quarters." He and his father followed the doctor. They walked along a hallway of white doors until they reached one that was open. As Joshua entered, a single bed, a wardrobe, a washbasin and pitcher on a small table, and a large window letting in streams of sunlight were the only accoutrements. The room was simple, but clean and cheerful. His trunk already sat next to the wardrobe. Joshua listened, but heard nothing but the birds chirping outside in the garden. He had expected the screams of the insane, but nothing of that sort accosted his ears.

"I will leave you to unpack and settle. One of my staff will send for you at luncheon. Does that suit?" Dr Conolly was addressing him again.

Joshua roused himself from his thoughts. "Yes, sir. That is fine."

"I'll leave you to it, then. Mr Wentworth, if I could have a word before you leave? When you are ready, please join me in my office."

With that, Joshua was left alone with his father. He felt his throat constrict. How humiliated his father must be to have a son who put on such a display as he did yesterday, and now to have to deliver him to an asylum. He could not raise his gaze to meet his father's, but sat down heavily on the bed, and with his elbow on his knee, rested his head in his palm. His father was talking as he unpacked the trunk.

"I brought your uniform, son."

That roused Joshua enough to look up. “No, no. Take it back. Do not leave it here with me. I have disgraced it.” He was looking off into the corner of the room, shaking his head.

“You have done nothing of the sort. I will not hear it. I am leaving it with you.” His father hung the jacket in the wardrobe and smoothed over the epaulets.

“Brigham’s Dandies, that’s what they called us.”

His father turned ’round upon him. “They would not dare say such a thing after Crimea.” His father was springing to his defence against an invisible, anonymous enemy. It nearly made Joshua smile.

“All right, Father. Leave my uniform here. It does no harm hanging there.”

“You will wear it when you come home to us.” His father brushed unseen dust from the back of the jacket.

“If I ever come home to you,” Wentworth mumbled under his breath. From where he sat now, he could not see any way forward.

Chapter 13

"Married when the year is new, he'll be loving, kind and true," Julia trilled as she fussed with her wedding gown during the fitting. "Did you just roll your eyes at me, Eleanor? Jealousy does not become you."

Eleanor directed her gaze away from her sister as the seamstress worked on her bridesmaid's gown. "I will not dignify that remark with a response, Julia. When will I be free to go? I have things to do."

Julia glared at her. "If it did not create a scandal, you would not be part of this wedding party at all. You are lucky George is such a kind and forgiving man and didn't have Joshua Wentworth arrested for his unprovoked attack at our engagement party."

Eleanor opened her mouth to speak but thought better of it. It was fortunate for Joshua that George didn't file charges against him. It was also to George's benefit that he did not appear so heartless as to jail a member of the Light Brigade. In any case, kindness had nothing to do with it. Always, always it was about appearances.

Eleanor sighed with impatience. Julia gestured to the seamstress pinning Eleanor's gown. "Fix the veil on her, please. I would like to see it."

Eleanor grimaced, but said nothing. First a tiara was applied to Eleanor's head and then the veil affixed. "Pull it down over her face." Eleanor knew from her expression exactly what Julia was thinking. The veil hid her birthmark. She nodded in Eleanor's direction. "Yes, that is perfect. Now, let me try mine."

Julia haughtily ordered the seamstresses about. Everyone was at her beck and call. No one opposed anything she asked. Julia turned to look in the mirror. "Ah, lovely. Now, pull it back to reveal my face." The seamstress did as she was told.

"You look splendid, miss. Just splendid." The seamstress was all admiration.

"See, Eleanor. Splendid."

Eleanor bit her lip. The endless dinner parties, teas, and other social occasions wrought by this engagement had left her fatigued. The worst of it was being in the company of George Shaw. He never managed an entire evening without some biting remark directed at Eleanor that was either meant as a joke or as an ill-aimed compliment. She detested him. The thought of having him as a member of her family turned her stomach, but she tolerated his presence as it was expected of her.

The minute the seamstress released her, she escaped to her father's study. Julia's wedding was to be at the new year. Eleanor had plans of her own for the year of our Lord, 1856. The letter she was working on was to a school in the United States, in the state, but not the city of New York - Geneva Medical College. The school had already graduated Eleanor's idol, Elizabeth Blackwell, and she thought that perhaps she had a chance at being accepted as well. Miss Nightingale was still at her post at Scutari, staying until the last of her charges were repatriated to England. Despite their falling-out, Eleanor requested a letter of recommendation from her, which she duly received. Now, merely a week before Julia's wedding, all was in readiness. She had not heard from Joshua save that first letter. In it, he told her to look to her own dreams and not to pin all her hopes on him and his recovery. Before she met him, she dreamt of being a medical doctor. After her work in Crimea, she refined that dream. She wanted to be a surgeon. Her application, sitting before her on her father's desk, was ready.

The fluttering and giggling of Julia and her entourage floated down from the upper chambers of the house. Sealing the envelope addressed to the admissions department of the college, Eleanor called Baxter in. It left with the afternoon post.

***

Joshua Wentworth scrubbed himself from head to foot with strong soap and dumped the basin of tepid water over his head. As he towelled himself off, he took stock of himself. The emaciated frame he had entered with over four months previous had been replaced by taut muscles. Dr Conolly put him to work almost immediately in the stable, and his care and training of the horses restored both his mind and his body. The nightmares were less frequent now, but he still jumped at loud, unexpected sounds. Still, the slide back into the war that occurred the day of his mother's death had not been repeated. He was not the man he was before the war, for that man was gone. He had no regrets on that score. Now was a time for new beginnings. He felt strong… he felt better.

After opening the wardrobe in his room, he stared at the dress uniform of the 17th Lancers. The black plume on the helmet was covered in dust. As he reached for it, his hands no longer trembled. After taking hold of it, he shook his uniform, and the fine particles of dust floated like snow in the sunlight. He set it back on the shelf and took the trousers and jacket from their places and laid them across the bed. He ran his hand along the two rows of brass buttons that ran the length of the coat. Someone knocked at the door.

"May I come in?" Joshua recognised the voice of Dr Conolly. He threw back the door.

"Yes, indeed. Do come in."

Dr Conolly's attention was immediately drawn to the uniform Wentworth laid across the bed.

"Thinking of trying it on?" Dr Conolly said jovially.

Wentworth's eyebrows went up. "I don't know, actually. I have been taking it out and looking at it for some days now. I suppose that means something."

Dr Conolly shrugged his shoulders. "It does not disturb you, then, to remember?"

Wentworth looked at him askance. "I have spoken of it so often, now, that it seems to have less power over me." He smiled at the doctor. "I suppose that is what you intended all along."

The doctor laid his hand on Wentworth's shoulder. "I came to tell you that you might begin the new year at home… that is, if you feel you are ready." Wentworth did not look at the doctor, but again ran his fingers over the uniform of the 17th Lancers.

Yes, he was ready.

With every hoof stroke that brought him down the London streets, Wentworth felt a surge of energy. Doubts, however, began to assail him. He hoped that his long hiatus from Eleanor did not drive her away from him. He would not let his doubts prevail. He was resolved.

Come good or ill, he would declare himself.

***

New Year's Day and all its tumult finally arrived. The wedding was to take place in the morning, and all the revellers would return for breakfast at the Sherbrookes'. Eleanor dutifully marched along behind the other bridesmaids and took her place at the altar. All of them were resplendent in white, just like the bride. Each wore a pair of white kid gloves, with white roses about their tiaras. Then, veiled and regal, Julia began her slow procession down the aisle on her father's arm. Her veil was adorned with orange blossoms. Truth be told, she looked quite magnificent, and a collective gasp went up among the attendees.

The rhyme *"Marry Monday for health, Marry Tuesday for wealth..."* occurred to Eleanor as she cast a glance at her future brother-in-law. It was a Tuesday, and wealth is what Julia was indeed marrying. She had to admit to herself that George looked quite handsome with his pomaded hair and his claret-coloured frock coat. He glanced around the chapel rather like a nervous peacock. It was such a shame she disliked him so. She took a breath and promised herself to be more charitable. As George took Julia from her father's arm, the ceremony began. Eleanor, watching the couple take their vows, said a small prayer of thanksgiving that the groom was George Shaw and not Joshua Wentworth.

A coach waited to take them to the Sherbrookes'. As the church disgorged the happy couple and the bridesmaids, Eleanor was reminded of a flock of scattering chickens, white feathers flapping. She dismissed the thought again as being uncharitable. She affixed a smile to her face as her father handed her up into the carriage.

By the time Eleanor reached the house, George and Julia were tucked away in the "bride's corner." After her parents congratulated the groom, the other guests formed a line to give their best wishes to the happy couple. Everyone then adjourned for breakfast. Eleanor, balancing her plate in one hand, kept the smile on her face as people made their small talk around her. "Oh, when will it be your turn, Eleanor?" or "Doesn't she make a beautiful bride?" or occasionally, "You worked with Florence Nightingale? That must have been thrilling."

She did her best to keep up her end of the myriad of conversations. It was Julia's day, after all. For all her faults, Julia was still her sister, and Eleanor resolved to play her part of bridesmaid cheerfully. It was not difficult to be merry at such an occasion. She had a more formidable job keeping up morale in the hospitals of Crimea. Someone was speaking to her. She turned to smile.

***

As Lieutenant Wentworth approached the Sherbrooke house, he could not help but notice a great many carriages lining their street. Someone must have been having a celebration. It took him a moment and then he remembered it was New Year's Day. He rang the bell, and no one answered. Removing his chapka and tucking it into the crook of his arm, he rang it again. Baxter opened it, and his eyes widened. He then did a most curious thing. He stepped out onto the snowy stoop and shut the door partially behind him.

"What are you doing here, sir?" His expression was most distressed.

"I have come to see Miss Eleanor Sherbrooke.... Whatever is wrong with you, man?"

"It is Miss Julia's... that is to say... Mrs Shaw's wedding day, sir."

Wentworth stepped back. The crowded street. The carriages. "Oh, this will never do. I shall come back tomorrow." Wentworth turned to go, and Baxter caught his sleeve.

"Please, sir. Wait. Miss Eleanor will be ever so cross with me if I turn you away. Just a moment." The butler opened the door slightly and peered inside. Motioning with his head, he opened the door for Wentworth and they quickly crossed the vestibule. Baxter deposited Wentworth in the drawing room.

"I will go and fetch her, sir."

***

Eleanor just tasted her glass of champagne after her father's toast when Baxter wound his way through the crowd and drew her attention. "There's someone here to see you, miss."

"Today? I cannot see anyone today. We are in the midst of a wedding."

At that moment, Eleanor's mother motioned to her. She joined the other bridesmaids standing on the sides of the main table. They were cutting the small cake belonging to the groom. Eleanor had been dreading this moment. Baked into the cake were small favours, each of them having a meaning. All the attendants, groomsmen, and bridesmaids alike were given a small piece. The bridesmaids began to chant as they and the groomsmen each searched through their piece of cake for the token.

"The ring for marriage within the year,
The penny for wealth, my dear,
The thimble for an old maid or bachelor born
The button for sweethearts all forlorn."

Eleanor did not join in the chant. It was all she could do to keep a smile on her face. Shaw's best man got the button, and the crowd sighed collectively. Eleanor was praying that she would not have anything in her cake, as she was loathed to be the centre of attention. Then she found it. It was the thimble of all things. She held it up, and some people looked away, and others shook their heads. Casting a glance at Julia, she noticed a slight smirk, but her attention was soon taken up by her maid of honour, who obtained the ring. A groomsman found the penny at nearly the same moment and the crowd cheered and clapped.

The line of bridesmaids dispersed, then as another toast was forthcoming, Baxter took the opportunity to touch Eleanor's sleeve.

"Please, miss, you must come with me." His face had such an earnest expression that Eleanor became quite alarmed.

"Is someone hurt?"

Baxter's face broke into a grin. "No, miss. But it is important. Please."

***

The doors to the drawing room opened, and Eleanor entered. Wentworth, in his dress uniform, sans sabre, crossed the room in wide strides to meet her. Baxter discreetly closed the doors and left them alone.

"Oh, Eleanor, I am so sorry. I had no idea that Julia's wedding was today." The words were barely out of his mouth and she was in his arms.

"What are you doing here? Are you well?"

He brushed the veil away from her face and touched her cheek. "I love you, Eleanor. I came to tell you." Then, not able to restrain himself, he kissed her. Kissed her longingly, passionately. Her body rose up to meet his and he kissed her again, covering her face with kisses and tracking the curve of her neck with his mouth. She sighed… no, it was a groan of pleasure. He finally pulled away and gazed at her. "You look luminous."

This time, it was she who drew him close and kissed him. He did not need any encouragement. He felt as though he could devour her, that he could not get enough of her. He was lost in desire.

"Eleanor…." he said breathlessly.

"*Eleanor*." Mrs Sherbrooke appeared in the drawing room and stared at the two of them. Instead of jumping apart, Eleanor clung to him with one arm and turned to face her mother. There was a long silence. Eleanor's mother broke it. "Lieutenant Wentworth. You are back."

"Indeed." It was all he could think of to say.

Mrs Sherbrooke looked from one of them to the other. Julia's voice could be heard calling her through the open door. Mrs Sherbrooke shut it immediately.

"Eleanor…" she said in a loud stage whisper. It nearly made Eleanor laugh. "You need to return to the reception. We are cutting the wedding cake." She turned to leave and then thought better of it. "I am sorry. I am being rude. You are welcome to join us, Lieutenant…."

Wentworth could tell by Mrs Sherbrooke's pained expression that the last thing on earth she wanted was his presence at this wedding.

"No, thank you. In fact, if I might exit surreptitiously—"

"Take the door at the far end of the room, through the breakfast room, and out the kitchen. I'm afraid it is the only way." She motioned then to Eleanor. "Come quickly."

He nodded and then turned his attention back to Eleanor, who looked up at him with shining eyes. He bent down and whispered in her ear. “Tomorrow, then?” She nodded. “I know we have not discussed it, but …. May I speak to your father?”

She touched his cheek again. “Speak to my father.” He let her go, and with a spring in his step, retrieved his helmet. He turned to watch her retreat out the double doors into the vestibule, and he, to the surprise of the kitchen staff, escaped out the back door.

***

“I find it very odd that you were engaged to one of my daughters, and now ask me for the hand of the other.”

Joshua Wentworth rocked on his heels, clenching and unclenching his fist. Mr Sherbrooke was not making this interview any easier, and in truth, he did not have an explanation ready for Eleanor’s father other than that he had been a dolt and now was slightly less of one.

“I do love her, sir, and she loves me. We have been through a lot together. More than most.”

“I must be frank with you, sir. You have been in an asylum and that causes me great concern.”

Now Joshua knew where Eleanor learned her frankness. He needed to meet the challenge head on. “Yes, sir. That is true. You have only my word that I am well and whole again, for I do feel it. I can only give you the assurance that I will do everything in my power to make your daughter happy.”

Mr Sherbrooke raised his eyebrows and pressed his lips together so that they disappeared beneath his most prodigious moustache. “And you believe you have enough money to keep her and any children you may have.”

“Yes, sir. I do have my pension from the army…” Mr Sherbrooke looked at him askance. “…which I admit is not much, but I have an inheritance from my mother.”

Mr Sherbrooke nodded sagely. “And you will have Eleanor’s money. What she has will be yours as her husband.”

Joshua drew himself up and faced Mr Sherbrooke. “I assure you, sir, I am not marrying Eleanor for her money. I hope you are not insinuating—”

Mr Sherbrooke laughed and slapped Joshua on the back. “Enough, enough. Of course, you have my blessing. I have never seen Eleanor happier. You will have your hands full with her, you know. She still talks of medicine and nursing and the like." He extended his hand to Joshua.

"Welcome to the family, my boy."

"Thank you, sir."

As Lieutenant Wentworth clicked the door of the drawing room shut behind him, Eleanor waited in the entry hall. She nearly burst with excitement.

"Well, what did Father say?" She searched his face. He frowned.

"He said I am too mangled and ugly and mad for you and you could do better." The look on her face was so priceless that he had to relent. He sniggered and then burst into laughter. "You should have seen your face, Eleanor. It really was a picture."

She gave him a playful slap on the arm. He looked about for witnesses, and then drew her to him. Before he kissed her, with her face close to his, he asked, "Is it very hard to look at me, Eleanor? I know that my face—"

"Beauty is in the eye of the beholder." As if to punctuate what she just said, she caressed the injured part of his face. He could not stop himself now and kissed her and then kissed her again. Her hands pressed his back and her body went soft in his arms. He kissed her forehead and then looked into her eyes. "We must be married soon. I cannot wait."

"Soon," she said and kissed him again.

***

Eleanor took Wentworth by the hand and led him to the morning room. "Now that we are engaged, we can be alone together."

He raised his eyebrows most provocatively, but the playful expression on his face faded rapidly. "We have much to discuss, Eleanor."

Not letting go of his hand, she sat facing him on the sofa. "Why so serious?" she asked.

He let go of her hand and stood with his back to her. His hesitation caused her thoughts to run wild. *He has come to break things off with me. I just know it.*

"Eleanor." He turned to look at her. Her heart was in her throat. "Eleanor, I want you to know that I never asked her."

Whatever is he talking about? Then it dawned on her… Julia. *What a relief. He is talking of Julia.* "Are you saying you never asked Julia to marry you?"

He looked up towards the ceiling and did not meet her eyes. "I feel such a fool now. There was this episode… between us…."

Since he was not looking at her, she let herself smile at his discomfiture. "Yes, yes, in the garden. I know…."

Then he did look at her, the shock evident on his face. "You know? But—"

"Everyone knew, Joshua. But you were saying… you never asked her?"

"She just assumed, I suppose. I would have, as a matter of honour… but then she announced it at dinner to your parents and well…."

She could not contain herself any longer and burst into giggles. With a quick bound, she was in his arms. "Oh, it is all right. It is in the past…." She then became quite pensive. "You know, Joshua, you never asked me either."

His mouth dropped open, and he looked as if he was about to speak, then screwed up his face in thought. A smile crept over his lips. "You are quite right, as you always are. Well, then, I must remedy that situation immediately."

He broke from her embrace and, falling to one knee, looked up at her, the mirth gone from his countenance.

"Eleanor Sherbrooke, would you do me the honour of becoming my wife?"

Eleanor was filled with the most exquisite feeling of joy and serenity, as if every interlocking piece of her life had suddenly fallen into place. "I would be honoured, Lieutenant Wentworth."

He rose and kissed her, and she nestled herself into his arms. She pulled back and looked at him.

"I have something for you." She retrieved a small box from the fireplace mantelpiece and set it before him.

"No, it is I who should have something for you—"

"Later. I have been waiting to give this to you for a long time."

He lifted the lid and stared into the box, then returned his gaze to her. "This cannot be. How…?" Gently, he lifted his pocket watch and held it in his hand. "However did you have this made? Did you speak to my father?"

She said nothing but waited as he opened it. He turned it over and over in his hand.

"This is not a replica. This is my watch."

"It is your engagement present. I have been keeping it."

He shook his head as if shaking off disbelief. "Thank you, Eleanor. Thank you." He leaned over and kissed her quickly, and when he drew back, she could see the tears starting. He rose and quickly wiped his face with his handkerchief.

"Do not thank me. Thank Mary Seacole."

"Mary Seacole?"

"She traded for it with one of those French, trouser-wearing *vivandières* or whatever they are called. I tried to pay her for it, but she would not take money. She told me to give it back to you. It was by the merest chance that I saw it at all. I would have given it back to you sooner, but—"

"But I was in no condition to receive it, and you were quite right." He continued speaking to her but could not take his eyes off the watch. Although he wore civilian clothes, he proceeded to connect the chain to his waistcoat and then dropped the watch into the pocket made especially for such a timepiece. He patted it contentedly. "Now I have something for you. It is also not exactly from me."

He sat down again and retrieved a small box. On it was a label that said *For Eleanor*. He put the box in her hand. Despite clearing his throat, his voice broke slightly when he spoke again. "A gift from my mother."

Eleanor opened the box, and inside was a ring. It had a large diamond in the centre of the setting with smaller diamonds set all around. The ring itself was gold. She said nothing, so he removed the ring from the box and placed it on her finger. It was nearly an exact fit.

"This is my mother's engagement ring. She wanted you to have it…."

Now it was she who was completely captivated by the object in her possession. She said nothing, for she could not find the words.

He broke the silence. "If it is not to your taste or you would like a new ring, I can certainly get one for you, or have this one reset or…."

She clasped the ring upon her finger with her other hand and held it to her breast. “You will do no such thing. It is lovely and I will wear it always to honour you and your mother.” A tear escaped her.

It caused him to smile and wipe it away with his handkerchief. He then dabbed his own eye. “We have to stop this at once, Eleanor.” She nodded mutely and pressed her cheek to his. “Go and call your mother… It is time you two set to work on our wedding.”

***

Cordelia was flinging material behind Eleanor in the vestibule of the church. “Really, Eleanor, stop moving. Soon you will be wrapped like a mummy in this train.” Eleanor looked down at poor Cordelia and did as she was told. The bridesmaid’s dress worn only a few weeks ago was enhanced to be a bridal gown with a longer veil and a train that Cordelia was managing. Their bridal party was small, only Cordelia and Millie as bridesmaids and Geoffrey as groomsman with William Mosley as best man. The last thing on earth that Eleanor wanted was an elaborate wedding, and Wentworth was in full agreement. Julia and George were still abroad on an extended honeymoon and were conspicuously and mercifully absent. Nothing would spoil this day.

From the side of the vestibule, Lieutenant Wentworth appeared in his dress uniform with William at his side. Eleanor turned to look at him, followed by an audible sigh from Cordelia. “Eleanor, is it not possible to move your head without your entire body following?”

“I’m sorry, Cordelia.”

“You don’t look the least bit sorry, Eleanor,” Millie chirped.

Lieutenant Wentworth pulled his watch from its pocket and took charge. “All right everyone. It is time. Cordelia, you and your brother are leading this parade.”

Cordelia admonished Eleanor one more time then kissed her on the cheek. “I will see you presently.” The organ had started up, and Cordelia took her brother’s arm and they stepped together onto the centre aisle. Millie followed.

Lieutenant Wentworth offered his arm to Mrs Sherbrooke. “Madam, if you please.” She smiled and put her arm through his.

Lastly, Eleanor began her walk up the aisle on the arm of her father. Just as they crossed the threshold into the sanctuary, he leaned in and whispered, "He is a good man, Eleanor. I am happy for you." She gave her father's arm a squeeze.

***

Wentworth tipped the porter as he left the baggage in room 625 of the Great Northern Hotel. He turned to Eleanor, who was just removing her bonnet.

Eleanor said nothing. She was a bit nervous and wondered if he was as well. Men, though, especially soldiers, had more carnal knowledge than women. In a way, she was grateful for her experience as a nurse. At least she knew what the male body looked like unclothed. Most women of her social class went to their bridal chambers completely unprepared.

Small talk was never her strong point, and it failed her now. She fussed about unpacking a few things. They were only staying one night here close to the station so they could leave tomorrow for their honeymoon in Scotland. There was another door to open, and behind it, she found a water closet and a bath with a small furnace to heat water.

"My, this is a modern hotel," she finally managed to say. She did not turn to look at him. Taking some of her toiletries, she deposited them in the bathroom. Above the sink was a mirror, and as she busily arranged things, she chanced to look up at her face. The mark upon it was redder than ever, no doubt due to her excited state. She ran her fingers across it. In the reflection, she saw Joshua move in behind her. Eleanor quickly took away her hand. Her husband laid his hands on her shoulders.

"All right?" She nodded mutely. He kissed the back of her neck. He turned her around to him, kissing her forehead and then her lips. Eleanor's mind immediately went to the marriage manuals her mother surreptitiously left on her night table. The authors wrote at great length about what was proper for a woman to do and feel on her wedding night: shame, shyness, horror even. Eleanor felt none of those things. She knew that women were not supposed to feel the strong desire that men do, but at that moment, her body, especially that place between her legs, was throbbing with desire.

Joshua took her by the hand and sat on the bed, indicating that she should sit beside him. He did not look at her, but stared at the floor, breathing in and out in audible sighs. Finally, he raised his head to look into her eyes. “There is no one in the world who I love as much as I love you, Eleanor. No one.” He ran his finger along her face, along the mark that seemed to define her so much before this moment.

“Take the patch off your eye,” she said.

He looked alarmed. “No, Eleanor. You have seen it. It is too horrible.”

She did not reply but reached up and undid the knots that held the mask in place. He did not resist her. Throwing it to the floor, she laid a hand on one side of his face and then the other and kissed him. His arms enfolded her body immediately, and they fell together on the bed.

Neither of them spoke. Instead, she followed her instincts and could not divest herself of her clothing fast enough. Joshua had to help her with fasteners that went up the back of her bodice. His breath came in short gasps as he untied the strings of her corset.

When she turned to him, his shirt and trousers were gone, and he was pulling off an undervest to reveal his broad chest covered with black hair. She gave way to her impulse and ran her hands up from his taut belly, across his chest, and there kissed him from one side to the other. He moaned, then he aided her in the removal of her corset, which he flung to the floor. Now both of them sat upright and breathless in their marriage bed, in only their drawers.

For a moment, all movement ceased, and they looked at one another. She had an impulse to cover her bare breasts, but instead, took his hands and placed them upon her. He touched her there in a most exquisite way, and then pulled her on top of him. She could feel her skin against his, and he kissed her so that his tongue penetrated her mouth. Passion washed over her in waves. She could feel his manhood stiffen. No longer did she want any garment between them.

She undid the ties of his underclothes, and he impatiently pulled them off. Eleanor could not take her eyes off him. It was he, then, who, running his fingers along the waist of her laced drawers, pulled them down around her ankles, where she kicked herself free of them.

They lay beneath the blankets, and the sun, though waning, had not yet set. Leaning on his left elbow, he held the sheet up with his right arm and let his gaze run the length of her body. Although he was not touching her, a sensation like a chill run through her. Then, letting the sheet fall gently on her skin, he ran his hand along her breasts and down to her most secret place. Parting her legs, he touched her, explored her with his fingers, all the time tenderly scattering gentle kisses over her face, neck, and breasts.

He placed her hand upon his member, and teaching her, she touched him, caressed him, ran her fingers over all the places he longed to be touched. His breath was short now and she felt a wanting so intense she could barely contain herself. She suddenly brought her mouth to his and kissed him deeply, passionately. "I am ready, Joshua." He let her lead him and then slowly slipped into her warmth. She did not hesitate, but opened herself to him, winding her legs around his. She moved with him, and when he could no longer restrain his fervour, he plunged into her again and again. Little cries of passion escaped her, and her back arched as he drove himself into her once more. He collapsed on her, spent. Her arms encircled his neck and her hands travelled down his back.

Pushing himself onto his elbows, he scrutinised her in the fading light. "Are you all right, Eleanor? I did not hurt you…?" he whispered softly, a look of concern crossing his face.

"It was splendid, Joshua. Splendid." And she drew him to her once again.

***

By the time the newly married couple travelled home from their honeymoon in Scotland, Julia and George were already off to his family's estate in Hampshire. Eleanor was quite pleased they were gone, as she dreaded the first "family" dinner in which all of them were present. Joshua rented a rather nice house near Russell Square upon their return, and for a time, she was occupied with setting up a household. They did not want for money, but also could not be extravagant. Still, they had more than met their needs. The whirlwind nature of their hasty wedding plans left Eleanor little time to think of what her life would be like once they returned home.

The London Season was just beginning, but the newly married Wentworths were eschewing large gatherings. Eleanor was not particularly fond of balls and large dinner parties, and her new husband, with his war injury, found them a trial now. Upon entering a gathering, all turned to look at him, but not for the same reason as of old. Conversely, there were times when he and she were treated with a certain celebrity, having the combined pedigree of both the Light Brigade, and having worked closely with Miss Nightingale. Either way, neither of them found their position particularly pleasing.

Eleanor then settled into receiving callers and Wentworth into spending time at his club or at home. Now, in her own sitting room, she found herself exactly where she never wanted to be. Her husband, whom she adored, sat near the fire, reading the paper. According to popular lore, she should be happy. Yet, here she sat, needlework in her lap, staring at the hands moving on the grandfather clock. How had she come to this?

A voice floated out from behind the newspaper. "You are unhappy, are you not?" Wentworth curled the newspaper down to reveal the upper half of his face and peered at Eleanor.

Since her thoughts were already running in that direction, she drew back a bit, startled. "What?"

"I said, you are unhappy. I can see it in your aspect. I swear, Eleanor, I believe sometimes that you will sigh yourself to pieces."

"I don't know why you say that, dearest." Her voice sounded hollow and strained even to her.

Wentworth dropped the paper and joined her on the settee. Taking both her hands in his, he brought his face close to hers so that she could not look away from him. "Please, Eleanor, this is not the time to suddenly stop being frank. You are unhappy with this domestic life. To be perfectly honest, I am at a loss myself."

"Are you really?" She felt relief flooding through her.

"Indeed I am. I was thinking of it the other day. I thought to myself *you no longer have anything to prove.* It is freeing in one respect and intimidating in another."

Eleanor was not really following his train of thought. Was he trying to prove something to her? To himself? Before she could ask, he continued. "I was thinking of what you told me while we were still in Crimea. Perhaps you might be thinking of it as well."

Now she was completely at a loss. Her face must have shown him so, for he continued. "I thought you might be again thinking of India. I am sure the army could find something for me to do there and you can continue your nursing."

"India?" She thought for a moment. It was then she remembered. On that hillside, on their picnic near The British Hotel. She was so angry with him that day for bringing up Julia that she said the first thing that came into her head. "Oh, that," she said finally. "Do you yearn to be back in the cavalry?"

He shook his head. "I confess, I do not."

"Oh, I am relieved. I do not want to go to India." They sat in silence for a few moments, then she got up suddenly and flew to the desk, rolling up the top. From there, she produced a letter, and after rushing back to his side, handed it to him.

"What is this?"

"Read it and tell me what you think."

He took the envelope. "From Geneva Medical College?" He removed the letter and began reading aloud.

December 29, 1855
Dear Miss Sherbrooke,

The board of the Geneva School of Medicine has reviewed your application. Due to your excellent references and vast experience, we are pleased to tell you that the board unanimously approved your admittance to the School of Medicine beginning September 1, 1856. Your application for a specialty in surgery is still being considered by the board. We can discuss matters further once you have matriculated.

I hope that this letter finds you well. We have housing for students, or you may find your own depending on your financial circumstances. A list of fees is enclosed, payable in advance of study. You are following in the footsteps of one of our own alumni, Miss Elizabeth Blackwell, the first female student to study medicine at our school.

I look forward to hearing from you in the near future. It is advisable that you arrive well ahead of the school year to settle your housing, tour the school, and familiarize yourself with our ways of doing things. Do write and let us know when to expect you.

Sincerely,
John Towler
Dean, Geneva Medical College

His face was working with emotion as he put the letter down and looked at her. "My Lord, Eleanor. I am proud of you."

"I confess that I applied there when you were—"

"Indisposed?" he offered.

She kissed him on the cheek. "Yes. Exactly. You told me to look to my future, and—"

"And studying medicine is what you always wanted. I know. I remember those first few meetings of ours. I thought you quite remarkable."

"Remarkable and prickly, I'll wager."

He laughed. "Well, I would not put it exactly that way, but—"

"Never mind. What do you think?"

He screwed up his face. "Why did you not show me this when you first received it?" He flipped the envelope over. "This must have arrived at least a month ago."

She looked away. How could she tell him she was afraid that this letter might disrupt the peace he established for himself? She could not risk it. Men of his class usually thought it an insult if their wives were better educated or, heaven forfend, employed. She would do anything rather than hurt him. Instead of telling him her real concern, she said, "I am a married woman now and my place is with my husband."

He sighed and took her by the hand. "And as your husband, you should share all your momentous news with me, don't you think… Eleanor? Eleanor, look at me."

She turned to meet his gaze. "Yes, of course."

He gave her a knowing look. "You are afraid for me still. That's it, isn't it? Well, I am not so fragile now. I do not have to spend the rest of my life hiding at home… and you are quite brilliant. Why should you hide your light under a bushel just because you are a married woman?"

She threw her arms around his neck, and he held her tight. For a long moment, they did not speak. Finally, he let loose his hold and kissed her softly on the mouth. Then, nodding and biting his lower lip, he released her and stepped away. For a time, he seemed lost in thought. Suddenly, he turned to face her.

"What holds either of us here?" Without waiting for a reply, he continued. "Nothing. Absolutely nothing. You will write to the college forthwith and let them know you are coming. We will find a place to live in this Geneva town and you will go to medical college. It is what you always wanted, is it not?"

"But what of money for fees and books and…?"

"Eleanor, you came into this marriage with money. It is your money. Use it."

"It is no longer my money. Once I married, it is your money."

He sighed, exasperated. "All right. It is my money now. I want to spend it on medical college for you."

She threw her arms around him, kissing his face over and over. She stopped suddenly and gave him a pensive look. "But what will you do?"

He cocked his head and thought for a moment. "Oh, I don't know. Perhaps I will become a gentleman farmer." He laughed. "Or perhaps they have need of a military advisor who is an expert on cavalry…. or I will just sit at home and read the newspaper. I hear that Americans speak a sort of English there. I believe I could be made to understand." That mischievous look that she found so endearing was playing across his countenance. He took both her hands in his and kissed her fingers. "We will have a grand adventure." His enthusiasm was infectious. "All right now. Write to this Towler fellow and tell him we will be there by May. Go, go on now."

She ran to the writing desk and pulled out paper, pen, and ink. She glanced over at her husband. He did not go back to his paper but stood there smiling at her.

***

Spring, 1857…

"I am so glad you sent William off to find Joshua. I am bursting to hear all your news." Cordelia followed Eleanor into the garden of their modest brick home. "Oh, Eleanor. It is beautiful here."

"I do like it. You can see Seneca Lake from that hilltop. Joshua often rides there." Eleanor caught her friend's eye. "Before I go on and on, you must tell me news of Julia. She does not write often, and Mother hardly mentions her."

Cordelia did nothing to disguise her distaste for the subject. She rolled her eyes. “It is just as well you hear nothing of her. I am afraid that she and George are already squabbling.”

“Really? And I thought them such a good match.” Eleanor had to laugh at her friend’s shocked expression.

“Oh, you are joking. Of course, you are. I hate to be unkind, but they deserve each other.”

Eleanor had to laugh. “I suppose they do, but I hate to see anyone unhappy.”

Cordelia smirked. “It is a good thing, then, that you are here and do not have to witness it.”

Eleanor drew back and positively grinned at her friend. “Oh, Cordelia. You are wicked.” She took her friend’s arm, and they began their stroll through the large flower garden in front of the house. After walking along in silence for a time, Cordelia spoke.

“And how is Joshua faring… is he all right, then? His state of mind that is…. Oh, I am being impertinent. I don’t know what came over me.”

“You are not impertinent, and I will tell you. He is a changed man here. I am not saying that there are no more nightmares or sudden fits of temper, but they are fewer and farther between now.”

“And you?”

“Ah, yes. Me. I have not had one of those shaking spells since last autumn, and never one at the college, thank goodness. It is difficult enough being the only woman among so many men, but to show any sign of weakness….”

“You are still determined to be a surgeon, then.”

Eleanor stopped and the two of them sat on a small bench amid the tulip blooms. The garden was awash in spring flowers. “Since I have recovered my health and well-being, I see no reason not to pursue my goal. Believe me, Cordelia, if I feel that I do not have a steady enough hand for surgery, I will find another avenue. To tell you the truth, I will be happy as long as I am able to work as a physician. If the Crimea has taught me nothing else, it is that I take what comes.”

Cordelia gazed at her friend in wonder. “I do so admire you, Eleanor.”

“Oh goodness, Cordelia. You will cause me to blush. Come, I will show you my roses. I do not have a great deal of time to tend them, but I am rather proud." The two women rose and made their way to the low fence near the front gate where roses climbed and showed their pink and red faces to the sun.

***

"Hello.... *Halloo*." Wentworth could see someone waving at him in the distance. He kicked his bay stallion in the flanks and galloped across the pasture towards the figure. As he approached, his face broke into a broad grin.

"Mosley. So, you have arrived at last." He spoke as he dismounted and grasped his friend by the arm, shaking his hand. "So good to see you, old man."

"And you, my friend. You are looking well." He looked about. "This is quite a place you have here."

Wentworth squared his shoulders, arms akimbo, and perused the land in all directions: the fenced corral for the horses, the pastureland, stables, barn, and the farmhouse. "I have to admit, I am quite proud of it." He laid his arm across his friend's shoulders and gave him a friendly squeeze. "Come along. Let me show you our newest addition."

As they entered the darkness of the barn, the sweet scent of hay and the familiar smell of horses assailed their nostrils. He led William Mosley to the stall at the far corner. There, his mare stood, and beneath her, a suckling colt.

"May I introduce the fair Guinevere and her newest offspring, Merlin."

Mosley looked at his friend and nodded. "He looks as if he will do honour to his namesake. Good old Merlin."

A lump rose in Wentworth's throat at the mention of his faithful warhorse, but he swallowed it down again.

"Guinevere, Merlin, so is the horse you rode up on called Arthur?" Mosley laughed at his own jest.

"Excalibur, actually. A bit silly, I suppose?" Wentworth finally met his friend's eyes.

"No, not at all. I think it is fine."

Wentworth clapped him on the shoulder again and they began to walk towards the house. "You know, old boy, I would love to have seen your father's face when you told him you had begun your own horse farm." Mosley was grinning.

"As I. Alas, I sent him the news in a letter. Oddly enough, I am surprisingly good at business. And horses, well...."

"A cavalry man and his horses. What better match could there be?"

They walked slowly back to the house, Wentworth pointing out the borders of his property and his newest project of refurbishing the house. Cordelia and Eleanor were in the front garden. Eleanor caught sight of them and waved. "There is the better match for me, my friend." Mosley nodded and Wentworth broke into a run. When he reached Eleanor, he embraced her and kissed her on the cheek.

"I see the honeymoon is not over yet." Cordelia had an impish expression.

Wentworth laughed. "So good to see you, Cordelia. Thank you for coming." Then, indicating Eleanor with his head, he continued, "Your friend here missed you terribly." By this time, William had caught up with them. "Come along into the house and let us see what cook has prepared for us. I am famished."

***

They sat together convivially over coffee and brandy as the sweet spring breeze wafted through the curtains of the whitewashed sitting room. The previous summer, Eleanor and Joshua had come to Geneva, New York, ostensibly for Eleanor's medical training. She worried that her husband would languish here, but he astonished her by buying a neglected farm on the outskirts of town, using his inheritance, and commenced to breed horses. Now, nearly a year later, the business was beginning to bear fruit. He suggested once in jest that he might become a "gentleman farmer" and he now fulfilled his own prophecy. She could not be prouder of him.

"I had some difficulty finding this place, you know," Mosley said casually, swirling the brandy it its glass.

"Really? I can't imagine why." Wentworth stole a glance at his wife.

Mosley continued. "I asked for the Wentworth farm as you told me to in your letter, but at least three of the townsfolk I asked had no idea what I was talking about. Then one of them said, 'Oh, you mean the Light Brigade Farm.' What is all that about?"

Wentworth made a slight grimace. "It is none of my doing, I assure you. These Americans know that blasted Tennyson poem, and once they learned of my history, have given to calling this place The Light Brigade Farm despite all my efforts to the contrary."

Eleanor began to laugh. "Do not let him fool you. He acts as if he is annoyed but really is as pleased as punch about it. I am going to get a new sign made for the gate at the end of the drive."

"You will not," Wentworth said in mock seriousness.

"And why not? Everyone should know what a hero you are."

With that, William Mosley got to his feet, holding his brandy before him, his face now taking on a solemn air. "Let us raise our glasses to the hero of the Crimea."

They raised their glasses, extending them towards Joshua.

Wentworth, then, did something unexpected. He stood and, raising his glass, turned to his wife.

"Yes indeed. To the *hero* of the Crimea. To Eleanor."

"To Eleanor," they all said.

At that moment, she could not have loved him more.

ABOUT THE AUTHOR

Maggie has always been a romantic at heart. She has spent most of her life teaching music in public schools. Her travels have taken her all over Europe, and she has lived in Africa and Asia. She refined her writing penning screenplays. She's now working on her fourth novel.

Get in touch with Maggie:
Website: moohabooks.com
FB: Maggie Mooha's Book Group
IG: @mmooha5817
Twitter: @mmooha

www.BOROUGHSPUBLISHINGGROUP.com

If you enjoyed this book, please write a review. Our authors appreciate the feedback, and it helps future readers find books they love. We welcome your comments and invite you to send them to info@boroughspublishinggroup.com. Follow us on Facebook, Twitter and Instagram, and be sure to sign up for our newsletter for surprises and new releases from your favorite authors.

Are you an aspiring writer? Check out www.boroughspublishinggroup.com/submit and see if we can help you make your dreams come true.

www.ingramcontent.com/pod-product-compliance
Lightning Source LLC
LaVergne TN
LVHW091035080826
845145LV00002B/497

* 9 7 8 1 9 5 3 8 1 0 6 1 8 *